Publisher

POOLBEG PRESS

giving *you* or your *book club*

the chance to win

€1,000

orth of Poolbeg books

...ntastic prize all you have to do is answer this question:

Name two other novels by Kate McCabe:

_____

_____

: / _____

_____

_____

in an envelope to: *The Book Club* competition, Poolbeg Press,
123 Grange Hill, Baldoyle, Dublin 13.

...out all our books on poolbeg.com

THE Book CLUB

KATE McCABE

POOLBEG

This novel is entirely a work of fiction. The names, characters and incidents portrayed in it are the work of the author's imagination. Any resemblance to actual persons, living or dead, events or localities is entirely coincidental.

Published 2007
by Poolbeg Press Ltd
123 Grange Hill, Baldoyle
Dublin 13, Ireland
E-mail: poolbeg@poolbeg.com
www.poolbeg.com

13 5 7 9 10 8 6 4 2

A catalogue record for this book is available from the British Library.

ISBN 978-1-84223-281-1

Typeset by Patricia Hope in Bembo 11.75/15.2

Printed by Litografia Rosés, S.A., Spain

About the Author

Kate McCabe lives in Howth, County Dublin where she enjoys walking along the beach. Her hobbies include travel, cooking, reading and dreaming up plots for her stories. This is her third novel.

Acknowledgements

I am indebted to many people for bringing *The Book Club* to the reading public.

My heartfelt thanks to my family; Gavin, Caroline and Maura for their enduring encouragement and support; to all at Poolbeg Press, particularly Paula Campbell, Lynda Laffan and Niamh Fitzgerald; to my superb editor, Gaye Shortland; to my computer doctor, Marc Patton; to Deirdre McQuillan, Fashion Editor of *The Irish Times* who kindly agreed to cast a professional eye over my characters' clothes; to the media for their consistent support and to my new best friends, the booksellers.

Finally, I would like to thank you, dear reader, for having the good sense to buy *The Book Club*. I hope it gives you as much enjoyment to read as it gave me to write.

For Maeve Binchy and
Gordon Snell

Chapter One

Whenever people asked Marion Hunt why she started the book club in the first place, she would always say it was because of the weather. It was the first week in January, the worst time of the year as far as she was concerned with cold, wet, miserable days and long dark nights and nothing to look forward to till Easter which seemed so far away that she couldn't even summon the energy to think about it.

Every year she swore that she was not going to spend another January in Dublin if she could possibly help it. Come hell or high water, she was getting out. She would save up her annual leave and take herself off to somewhere nice and warm where she would spend the entire month lazing on a sandy beach, sipping ice-cold Pina Coladas and watching the handsome lifeguards playing volleyball. And she would text her friends back at home about the clear blue skies and the golden sun and drive them mad with envy while they shivered in the cold.

But each year, January came around again and Marion was still stuck in Ireland. With all the crazy spending at Christmas and her credit-card limit just a distant memory and bills arriving with every post so that she began to suspect that the postman was conducting a personal vendetta against her, she just didn't have the money to spend a whole month in the sun. She didn't even have the money for a weekend break. So each January she gritted her teeth and solemnly promised herself that the following year she would definitely manage things differently. But of course, she never did.

And that was how she came to be sitting at the window of her apartment in Smithfield in Dublin on a grey Saturday afternoon staring out at the rain instead of sipping a *cerveza* at a sidewalk café in Los Cristianos – which was what she had promised herself twelve months before. The rain had been falling like a grey sheet since early morning and one glance at the menacing sky told Marion that it was likely to continue for the remainder of the day and probably tomorrow as well.

Oh well, she thought, trying to make the best of things, at least I'm nice and cosy in here and I don't have to venture out for anything. She had done her weekly shop the evening before after returning from her job at the Department of Education where she worked as an Executive Officer in the School Buildings division. So she had all the provisions she required to feed and sustain herself even if the rain didn't stop till Monday.

Marion's apartment was her pride and joy. It was a smart two-bed in a bright new building called The Cloisters which was just a stone's throw from the river and ten minutes' walk from the centre of town. She felt so proud of her new home and the fact that she owned a piece of Dublin property, particularly since prices kept spiralling upwards as if there was no tomorrow. She had bought it the previous September after months of heart-searching and further months traipsing all over the city to view properties till she felt she had become an expert on the apartment scene and could probably write a book about it.

But once she saw the plans for The Cloisters, she knew her searching was over. The apartment had everything she was looking for. It had two large bedrooms – the main one with a smart en-suite bathroom and a smaller one which she sometimes considered turning into a study. In addition, it had a second bathroom, a large sitting room with an adjoining kitchen and the pièce de résistance – a beautiful timber-decked terrace from where you could see the whole city skyline on a fine day.

This was the place for her and she just had to have it even though the asking price was a staggering €350,000. It was at the very outer limit of what she could afford. To buy it, she had to take out a hefty mortgage that gobbled up a large chunk of her salary every month and was another reason why she couldn't spend January in the Canaries. Purchasing in The Cloisters left Marion broke but at least she owned something and she kept telling herself that the repayments were chipping away at her loan – which was much better than paying rent that went straight into the pocket of some greedy landlord.

And by buying off the plans, she was able to save some money and managed to secure one of the best units in the development which pleased her no end. She also congratulated herself that she had the foresight to fix her loan at 3 per cent before the interest rates had started to go up. Some of her colleagues had advised her to go for a variable rate so that she would benefit if interest rates fell. Where would she be now if she had taken their advice? Probably in the Debtors Court, she thought, ruefully.

To help pay the mortgage she had briefly considered taking a lodger for the spare bedroom instead of converting it to a study. But she didn't think about it for long. What held her back was the thought of sharing her home with a stranger, maybe someone she might not like who would leave wine stains on the carpet or block the sink with tea leaves or horror of horrors, leave underwear drying on the radiators. Besides, she had already had one bad experience with a flatmate years before and she had never forgotten it.

So, despite the crippling mortgage, she took comfort from the thought that in ten years' time, her salary would have risen and the monthly repayments might not seem so much. And if she ever decided to sell, she was sure to make a profit. Not that she had any intention of selling. As far as Marion was concerned, she was here to stay. The Cloisters was her home. She was happy here. She often joked with friends that the only way she would ever leave was if she won the lottery when she might consider buying a mansion in

Wicklow – and the chances of that happening were about the same as the odds on Brad Pitt asking her to marry him.

Marion was twenty-nine, although she kept reassuring herself that she was a *youthful* twenty-nine with all the vigour and energy of someone five years younger. The Big Three O might be drawing closer but it held no terrors for her. Marion was a firm believer in positive attitude and in her mind she was still twenty-four with the idealism and enthusiasm of youth but tempered with the life experience of someone older. She told herself it was a good combination and she was lucky to have it.

Her family were hard-working farming folk from County Offaly so owning property was in her blood. Her father, who had a good eye for a bargain, had succeeded over the years in buying up small parcels of land and adding them to the family farm so that it now stood at a respectable 200 acres. He was fond of saying that land was one thing that God was making no more of. And he impressed on all his children that once you had the title deeds to a property in your fist no one could ever put you out on the street. Provided you kept up the mortgage repayments, Marion thought ruefully.

She had come up to Dublin ten years earlier filled with wild excitement after successfully completing the Executive Officer exams for the Civil Service. Marion was too laid-back to be an academic high-flyer so she was never destined to become a vet or a barrister or a heart surgeon. But she was bright and she always managed to study just hard enough to pass her various exams. So her family were proud of her success in securing a good well-paid Government job with a pension. Her father was particularly pleased. He said a pension would provide her with a guaranteed income when she came to retire and went about telling all the neighbours about her great achievement and the fancy job she had landed in Dublin.

For a while, Marion was proud too until the reality began to sink in. She quickly discovered that the work was routine and repetitive and she soon got bored with it. She was just a small cog in a vast administrative machine. And worst of all, she never got out of the office to meet people. As for the pension, it seemed so far away that she couldn't even contemplate it. For all she knew she could be dead by the time retirement came around – probably found suffocated under the weight of paper that descended on her head every day.

She watched with envy as some of her friends secured glamorous jobs in advertising and journalism and publishing. They seemed to spend most of their time at drinks parties and receptions and product launches meeting exciting people and attractive men. They were out and about having a gay old time while she was stuck at her desk reading letters from school principals complaining about leaking toilets and broken windows which she duly initialled and stamped before passing them on to her supervisor, Mr McDonald.

But despite the drawbacks, she never once thought of giving up her job. She knew she had found a good safe berth even if the work had become so mechanical that she could do it in her sleep and with one hand tied behind her back. The world outside the Civil Service might appear more exciting but it had its price. There were frequent casualties. Some of the companies her friends worked for eventually went bust and they were let go. Marion knew that would never happen to her. The Department of Education would never go bust. She had a job for life.

In those early days in Dublin, she shared a large flat with three other girls in Ranelagh. It was the top floor of an old Edwardian building with big bay windows that looked out onto a quiet tree-lined street. There was a large kitchen and one bathroom, which meant there was always a clamour in the morning to use the loo as people tried to get ready for work. And in the evening, somebody was always fussing over the stove in the kitchen cooking up a meal. But she loved it there.

After her sheltered life on a farm, she found the experience exhilarating. It was like living in a hippy commune. People were always coming and going and it was never dull. Her flatmates were forever bringing home friends so very quickly she got to know a wide network of people. And most weekends there was a party. People would arrive from the pub with bundles of tapes and bottles of wine and they would dance and sing and have a wild time till the old lady in the flat above banged on the ceiling with a broom to get them to quieten down.

Marion had grown up to be a very attractive young woman. She was five feet eight inches tall, slim but with a good figure. She had dark skin and ebony hair which she wore to her shoulders. But it was her eyes that most people remarked upon. They were a delicate shade of green and for some reason men seemed to find them fascinating. As a result, she was never short of boyfriends.

It was at one of these parties that she first met Alan McMillan. Later, she was often to ask herself what she ever saw in him for Alan McMillan was not her type at all. He was from Belfast and was training to be a solicitor. He was pale and slightly built and of average height. He had the type of undistinguished features that would never cause anyone to give him a second glance. But he had excellent manners and was very attentive. He seemed to fasten onto Marion. He asked her to dance and then stayed by her side for the remainder of the evening. When the party was over, he wrote down her telephone number in a little notebook he kept in his breast pocket and asked if she would like to go out with him some evening. Marion, who didn't have a regular boyfriend at the time, felt sorry for him so she agreed.

For their first date, he took her to the Savoy cinema to see Nicholas Cage in *Leaving Las Vegas* and afterwards they went to an Indian restaurant on O'Connell St where Alan treated them to a bottle of house wine to accompany their chicken korma. It was a very pleasant evening and Marion enjoyed it. At least it was better than sitting at home in the flat watching soaps on television. After the meal, they shared a taxi to her flat and Alan deposited her safely on the doorstep where he kissed her goodnight and asked if he could see her again. Marion agreed and a few days later he rang her at work and took her to see a play at the Peacock Theatre.

Before long, she was seeing quite a lot of Alan. She found him interesting company and a change from the wild young men who usually frequented the Ranelagh flat. And she enjoyed the attention he lavished on her. In those days, neither of them had very much money but Alan always managed to buy her little presents. As the weather turned warmer, they sometimes went for walks in Stephen's Green or took the train out to Dalkey and strolled over Killiney Hill. Since they were both from outside Dublin, there was a sense of adventure in discovering the delights of the city. Occasionally, instead of going to the cinema, they went to a pub and spent the evening chatting over half pints of beer which was all they could afford.

As time passed, she got to learn all about Alan. She discovered that he was an only child whose father had died when he was young leaving him and his mother in very poor circumstances. But he was a clever student and did well at school. He proceeded to study Law at Queen's University and was now in his final year of apprenticeship with a firm of solicitors in Drury St.

But perhaps his most outstanding characteristic was his obsessive personality. Once he got his teeth into something, Alan refused to let go. This was something she would regret later. But when she first met him, she found it attractive. Alan was *driven* and the thing that most obsessed him was his career. His early experiences had left their mark on him and he was determined to get on in the world.

"I'm going to be rich some day," he would boast. "Money gives you the freedom to do what you want."

"Oh, and how are you going to do that?"

"By specialising in employment law," he told her. "That's a growing area. There's a whole raft of EU legislation coming down the tracks and there aren't too many lawyers who know anything about it. I'll become an expert and make lots of money. You just wait and see."

Marion would listen attentively while he outlined his plans till suddenly he would stop and sit up straight.

"I'm boring you," he would say. "You don't want to listen to all this stuff."

But Marion would gently press his hand and urge him to continue. She found a strange fascination listening to Alan confide his dreams and ambitions. And he seemed so dogged and convincing that she believed him.

"Please go on. I find it interesting."

"Are you sure?"

"Yes. I always thought the Law was stuffy, you know, old dusty books and things like that. I didn't know it could be so fascinating."

His eyes would light up. "Oh, it's far from stuffy, Marion. It's certainly a lot more exciting than most people realise. And when I'm rich, maybe you will share it with me. That would make me very happy."

But Marion wasn't so sure. Sometimes, she would ask herself where this situation with Alan was going. She liked his company but that was all it was – company. She was forced to admit that there was something cold and calculating about him. Underneath his dull exterior she could sense a streak of ruthlessness. And he lacked romantic passion. He wasn't the kind of man she read about in novels who would sweep her off her feet and take her breath away. Their relationship was more like a friendship than a romance. Never in a million years could she imagine herself falling in love with Alan McMillan.

One by one, her original flatmates left and the Ranelagh flat became much too big and the rent too costly for just one person. Marion moved into a smaller apartment in Harold's Cross with a girl called Julie who she met through an ad in the *Evening Herald*. Julie was from Arklow and worked in a restaurant in South George's St. She wasn't exactly Marion's ideal flatmate. By now, she was beginning to outgrow her earlier bohemian phase and was starting to prize stability and order in her life. So she found Julie a bit on the wild side with her tendency to stay out all night at parties and bring strange men home in the wee small hours of the morning. But she was clean and tidy and paid her share of the household expenses on time, so Marion put up with her. It was easier than trying to find another flat.

Then came her sister's twenty-first birthday and a big party was organised to celebrate the event. Marion planned to go down to Offaly on Friday evening after work and return on Sunday night. So when Alan rang on Thursday afternoon to inquire about her plans for the weekend, she explained that she had to go home for the party and wouldn't be able to see him again till Monday. She thought he sounded disappointed that she hadn't invited him to join her but there was no way she was bringing him down to Offaly. It might give him ideas that this relationship was heading somewhere that it wasn't.

The party was held on Saturday night in the local hotel and was a mad success. Marion dressed up in her best gear and met lots of her old school friends who were dying to hear stories about her exciting life up in Dublin which she happily provided. What with all the chatting and the dancing and the flirting, it was after four when she finally fell into bed and the following day she was exhausted. The return train left at six and got into Dublin around eight-thirty. But on this particular Sunday there was an accident on the line outside Tullamore and the train was cancelled. Marion's mother heard about it on the radio after lunch and immediately flew into a panic.

"You'll have to take the bus," she said, fussing round her daughter. "Otherwise you'll be stranded here till Monday. C'mon, you'd better get moving. The bus leaves the depot at three o'clock."

Marion hated the bus. It was usually packed and the passengers were stuck in their seats like sardines without the freedom to move around that you enjoyed on a train. But this was an emergency and she had no choice. Reluctantly, she packed her bag and her father drove her to the depot, kissed her goodbye and instructed her to ring her mother as soon as she got home to say she had arrived safely.

The bus was even more cramped than usual because of the cancelled train and she had to endure three hours of misery till they finally pulled into their destination. She was so worn out by the journey that she just collapsed into the first available taxi and asked to be driven directly to her flat.

It was half past six when she arrived. As she turned the key in the lock, she thought she heard laughter coming out of Julie's room. She gave a weary sigh. She was in no mood to meet another of Julie's stray men. She just wanted to take a hot bath and settle down in front of the television with a nice glass of wine while she recovered from her bus ordeal.

But just as she put her bag down, the door of Julie's bedroom opened and a figure came out.

Marion couldn't believe her eyes.

Alan McMillan emerged, dressed only in his underpants. It was the first time she had seen him in this state and her stomach immediately threatened to disgorge her mother's Sunday lunch. His pale skin and scrawny legs made him look like a freshly plucked chicken while his bulging eyes reminded her of a rabbit caught in the headlights of a car.

For a moment, they stared at each other in shocked silence. Then, Marion quickly averted her gaze.

"Excuse me," Alan said remembering his good manners, as he hurried past her into the sitting room where she could see his shirt and trousers draped over the back of the settee.

The incident shattered her faith in Alan McMillan. He rang the following day to explain.

"Nothing happened," he began, nervously. "It's not what you think."

"What do I think?" she asked, coldly.

"That we were up to hanky-panky. All we were doing was discussing music."

"Oh?" Marion said, with such ice in her voice that she could feel the handset freeze. "And you normally discuss music in your underwear, do you?"

"Of course not. I got wine on my trousers. I was drying them, that's all."

"Why is it that I don't believe you?" she said with as much sarcasm as she could muster. "Why is it that I think you are lying through your teeth?"

"At least let me explain," he pleaded.

"No," Marion said, flatly. "I don't want to hear any more lies."

"You're emotional," he said. "I can understand that. But you'll think differently when you calm down. You should never do anything when you're angry, Marion. You might regret it."

She gasped at his bloated arrogance. Regret packing in Alan McMillan? Her real regret was that she hadn't done it sooner.

"Listen carefully, Alan. I don't want to see you ever again. I don't want you trying to contact me. You and I are finished. Goodbye."

She put the phone down as firmly as she could without smashing it to pieces. She *was* emotional, that much was true. But who wouldn't be under the circumstances? What a selfish prick Alan McMillan had turned out to be. But what really hurt her was the betrayal, the fact that someone she had trusted could behave so callously. And in *her* home! Marion's pride was hurt but in a strange way she was glad because the incident had brought matters to a head and gave her a good excuse to get rid of him.

Of course, Julie had to go. There was no possible way the two of them could share the same small living space after what had happened. She didn't argue, just packed her bags and left the following day. Marion cancelled the lease and moved out of the apartment and stayed with a colleague from work till she decided what to do next.

By now, she'd had enough of flat sharing. It was time to settle down. Her career lay in Dublin so it made sense to have a permanent home in the city. She decided to buy an apartment and began to save, setting herself a target each month and lodging the money in a deposit account with her bank. She knew the account would stand her in good stead when the time came to look for a mortgage.

But trying to save had a severe impact on her social life. She was forced to cut back on clothes, she stopped eating in restaurants and limited her outings to pubs and clubs to Friday nights. She told herself that the deprivation was worth it. In no time at all – two years at the most – she would have the money saved for a deposit and then she would get her own place. But something else was beginning to happen too. Her circle of acquaintances was starting to shrink as people settled into relationships or got married. In the end, she was left with only two or three people she could call real friends. Of these, Trish Moran was by far the closest.

She had known Trish since her schooldays. She had started off as a clerk in a bank in Dame Street and now she had risen to be a personnel officer in the Human Resources department. She was a large, chubby woman who seemed to have a permanent sunny disposition. In any situation, she could always be relied upon to see the positive side. It was Trish who had counselled her after the incident with Alan.

"The first thing to bear in mind is that this is not the end of the world."

"Are you kidding? I feel like I've just got out of jail," Marion replied.

"Good. But you realise you can't possibly take him back," Trish said, firmly. "If you do, he'll know he can get away with this sort of thing again. And then you'll really have a problem on your hands."

"I've no intention of taking him back."

"Excellent. You weren't in love with him, were you?"

"Are you mad?" Marion exploded. "I'm surprised I went out with him for so long. He's not even my type."

"Well then, nothing is lost. Just forget about him. It won't take you long to meet some other nice man. You're an attractive woman and you'll find lots of admirers. Now what are you drinking?"

On Friday nights after work, Marion and Trish would meet in a city-centre pub and have a few drinks and then go for a meal and end up in a club. But Marion was beginning to find the clubs too noisy and a lot of the men were either drunk or so high on drugs that you couldn't hold a sensible conversation with them.

And then, Trish met a young policeman from Cork called Seán and before long she was seeing him all the time. Marion contacted some of her other friends and discovered that they too had steady boyfriends. Suddenly, she woke up to the fact that all her friends had settled down and she was now more or less on her own.

But Trish was right about one thing. Marion had no trouble attracting men. It was the men who were the trouble. After dumping Alan, she went out with a handsome young administrative officer called Brendan who worked in her department. He was six foot tall, dark, thirty-one years old and played rugby for Old Belvedere. Marion had spotted him one day talking to her supervisor Mr McDonald and thought he looked quite dishy.

For their first date, he took her to a nice restaurant on the quays where they held hands and looked into each other's eyes while Brendan told her funny stories about his flatmates and his family and the people he worked with. He seemed to have a laid-back, relaxed attitude to life which made a nice change after Alan McMillan's intense obsession with his career. It was on the second date that Marion sensed something was going wrong.

This time, Brendan was morose and depressed.

"What's the matter?" she asked, gently stroking his hand and looking into his intense brown eyes which seemed like deep wells of sorrow.

"Nothing," he said with a shrug and tried to look away. "It's just, well, my girlfriend rang this afternoon. Sorry," he said, correcting himself, "I should have said my ex-girlfriend."

For the remainder of the meal, Marion had to endure a lengthy tale about some woman called Sinéad who Brendan had been seeing for the past eighteen months and who had recently left him for another man and how his heart was broken as a result. By the time the desserts were served, she was ready to scream for help. It was obvious that Brendan was still in love with this Sinéad person. Marion made up her mind. There was no way she was going to nurse this guy through his broken romance. Life was just too short. When the bill came, she suddenly remembered an urgent phone call she was expecting, ordered a taxi and beat a hasty retreat.

Next, she took up with a young rock journalist called Phil who she met one Friday night at a club in Temple Bar. Phil was like a breath of fresh air. He was an inveterate partygoer and seemed to know all the movers and shakers in the music business. And he got free tickets to all the big concerts. For a while, Marion's life was an exciting round of gigs and promotions and champagne-swilling sessions in Lillie's Bordello. All her colleagues envied her glamorous lifestyle till one evening she found Phil snorting a line of cocaine in the bathroom of her flat. That was it. She quickly got rid of him. She didn't see her future tied up with a man who had to face the rigours of life with the help of Colombian marching powder.

After that she had a string of relationships but none of them worked out. The men were all too weak or clingy or pompous and arrogant and immature. She longed for a sensible, handsome reliable man. Someone she could put her faith in, someone she could look up to, someone she could share her life with. But she was finding that men like that were thin on the ground in Dublin.

Meanwhile, Trish kept telling her she had to find a boyfriend.

"You're not a youngster any more," she said, "and if you leave it too late all the best men will be gone."

"Don't say it," Marion warned. "Don't tell me I'll end up on the shelf like a special offer in Tesco's."

"I didn't mention Tesco's," Trish said, looking offended. "But just bear in mind that while you're getting older, the competition is getting younger every day."

But after her recent experiences, Marion had become quite choosy and she wasn't going to throw herself away on just anyone. She knew she was attractive because people kept telling her. But she was also a romantic. The man she would settle for didn't have to be rich like Alan McMillan planned to be. And he didn't have to so breathtakingly good-looking that women would fall at his feet. But there was one vital qualification and she wasn't going to compromise on it. He had to be a man she could fall in love with.

However, all this debate about men was quickly forgotten with the purchase of the apartment and the attendant excitement of decorating it and buying furniture and choosing floor coverings and drapes and decking out the kitchen. Trish, who had a good eye for décor offered to help and together they had a dizzy time visiting department stores and warehouses and looking at settees and kitchen appliances and fabrics.

In the end, they opted for light pastel shades for the walls and Scandinavian minimalist furniture for the sitting room and some smart pictures and cosy rugs for the pine floors. When they were finished the apartment looked absolutely stunning and Marion was bursting to show it off so she gave a housewarming party and invited all the people she knew.

About sixty guests turned up and it was just like the old days when she lived in the flat in Ranelagh. People brought little presents of tea-towels and toast-racks and egg-timers and someone even gave her a fancy juicer. She served wine and canapés while her guests admired the apartment and made wowing sounds and complimented her exquisite taste and told her how much they envied her good fortune to have such a lovely home of her own like this and her not even thirty yet. It made her feel warm and grateful and smart.

When they had all finally left, she took her glass of wine and sat on her terrace in the warm night air and admired the lights of the city twinkling before her like a canopy of stars. She had been in Dublin for almost ten years. She had a good steady job and she was independent and now she had her own place. She *was* a lucky woman. She told herself she was happy.

Now she sat at her window and looked out at the rain. It fell in a steady downpour, gusting against the pane in a familiar dreary rhythm. She sadly shook her head. Come next January, she *would* go to the Canaries no matter what happened. But now, there was nothing for it but to make a nice cup of tea and finish the book she had been reading. It had been a Christmas present from Trish, a wonderful tale of love and intrigue that had Marion totally absorbed. She had about two chapters left to read and couldn't wait to get to the end.

Twenty minutes later, she put the book down and gave a contented sigh. The novel had finished beautifully with an ingenious twist that had taken her completely by surprise and left her feeling good. She would have to ring Trish at once to tell her and offer to lend her the book so that she could read it for herself.

But when she rang her number, there was no response. She was probably out somewhere with her boyfriend, Seán. Who else could she call? She was so excited that she had to talk to someone. But the next half dozen numbers she rang were either engaged or didn't answer. Marion put down the phone with a feeling of disappointment. Part of the joy of reading a good book was being able to talk about it with other people. But what did you do when there was no one available? She could hardly run out onto the street and stop the first passer-by.

Maybe Trish is right, she thought. Maybe I should make more

effort to find myself a man. At least if I had a steady boyfriend, I wouldn't be sitting all on my own like this on a wet miserable Saturday afternoon with no one to talk to. And then a thought struck her. There was one sure way she could discuss books with people. She would join a book club!

She had heard about the idea on a radio chat show recently. The plan was that everyone in the club would read a selected book and then they would meet a few weeks later and discuss it. It was a brilliant concept. It would provide an opportunity to meet new friends and would help to while away these long, dreary winter nights. And she would also be doing something that she thoroughly enjoyed.

But Marion didn't have any luck. After spending another half hour on the phone, she came away with the information that the nearest book club was in Sandymount, several miles away across the river and it had a waiting list to join.

"Dammit!" she said to herself. "I'm not giving up. There's only one thing for it. I'll start my own club."

She reached for a notepad.

Now, she thought. The first thing to do is put up some notices.

Chapter Two

Christy Grimes paused as he pushed open the glass doors of the library and found himself standing beside the notice board in the hall. He always made a point of studying the notice board. It was amazing the amount of information you could pick up by spending five minutes reading the notices stuck up by the librarian with shiny red drawing pins. It was better than reading a newspaper because the information on the board nearly always related to events that were happening right here in Phibsboro on his own doorstep.

He had been studying the board for the past eighteen months now, ever since his wife, Ellie, got the stroke that had left her partly paralysed and relying on a walking frame to get around. But the physiotherapy classes she was attending twice a week at the Health Centre had helped her make impressive strides back to full mobility. Dr Hynes, who was looking after her, had said only last week that he was amazed at the progress she was making. When he said that, Ellie had smiled proudly and Christy had gently massaged her shoulder before planting a big wet kiss on her cheek. But if Dr Hynes was amazed, Christie wasn't. He had always known that Ellie was a fighter – ever since that day, forty years ago when he had first set eyes on her.

It was at the Saturday night dance in the Gardiner St Hall. Ellie was seventeen at the time, although she always claimed she was eighteen. But Christy distinctly remembered buying her a lovely charm bracelet for her 18th birthday and that was *after* they had met. But whenever the subject came up, he always made a point of agreeing with his wife. It was only a minor detail and he couldn't see any reason to have an argument about it. But he knew he was right.

When he met her, she was working in a factory in East Wall that made ladies' jeans and he was in his third year as an apprentice butcher with Madigan's of Moore St. Being a trainee butcher gave Christy a certain degree of social standing in the local community around Ballybough where he lived. He was going to be a tradesman, which was something to be proud about and being a butcher meant there would always be meat for the dinner table. So it was with an air of confidence that he approached Ellie and asked her up for a dance.

She was small and thin and had her hair cut short in a dark fringe that was the fashion at the time. She wore a black skirt and a white blouse that showed off her trim little figure to very good effect. And boy, could she dance! When the DJ put on the latest *Beatles* record, Ellie just took off, twisting and shaking and kicking her legs till Christy was out of breath and was glad to take a break when the record finally came to an end.

"Can I buy you a Coke?" he managed to croak when the music stopped and they stood looking awkwardly at each other.

There was a strict No Alcohol policy in the hall and the bouncers on the door checked everybody coming in to make sure they weren't trying to smuggle in cans of lager. But there was a bar that sold soft drinks.

"Well?" Christy urged. "You must be thirsty after all that dancing."

He was expecting her to say yes but Ellie surprised him.

"Thanks very much," she said. "I think I'll go back to my friends."

She turned on her heel and began to walk off the floor.

Christy felt his heart sink. Even though he had only danced with her for five minutes and could only mumble a few snatches of conversation above the noise from the amplifier system, he was already smitten. As far as he was concerned, Ellie was the most beautiful creature he had ever seen. He thought she looked terribly sophisticated with her dark stockings and that haughty look in her flashing eyes.

But as she walked away something caused her to stop and turn around.

"I've changed my mind," she said. "I think I'll have that Coke after all."

Christy was delighted. He eagerly led her upstairs to the bar where they could look down on the dancers below. He found her a seat and went off to get the drinks. When he returned, he found Ellie carefully applying bright red varnish to her fingernails.

"What's your name?" he asked, handing her a plastic cup. Christy hated this chatting-up business. He wasn't very good at it. Not like some fellas who were full of smart remarks that the girls always thought were hilarious.

Ellie sniffed and gave him a disdainful look.

"Eleanor Doyle. What's yours?"

"Christopher Grimes. I don't think I've seen you here before."

"How would you know?" she said tartly, continuing to work on her nails.

"Oh, I'd know all right. Sure you're easily the best-looking girl in the hall."

She looked up quickly and a smile crept into her face.

"You're only saying that."

"No, I'm not. I mean it."

"Well if you must know, I was here last week."

"That explains it. I wasn't able to make it."

"Why not?"

"Working," Christy said.

"And what sort of job do you do?"

"I'm a butcher."

"Oh!"

"Yes," Christy said, straightening his tie and sticking out his chin. "Madigan's of Moore St. Every second Saturday night I have to work late because it's the weekend."

After that, the conversation quickly warmed up. They talked for

19

another half hour and then they danced some more. At the end of the evening, Christy asked if he could leave her home and Ellie agreed. While she went off to get her coat, Christy stood at the door whistling softly and feeling very pleased with himself.

The following night, they met under Clery's clock in O'Connell St and he took her to the cinema and then to Cafolla's for ice-cream sundaes. He got to know more about her. Her mother was a housewife and her father was a docker. She had five brothers and sisters and Ellie was the eldest.

"What about you?" she asked.

Christy told her about his mother and father who worked for CIE and his eldest brother, Lar, who was working in England and his three sisters and his uncle Vinnie who was also a butcher and had got him the apprenticeship with Madigan's.

"You'll have to meet them," Christy said. "You could come some Sunday for your tea."

"That would be nice," Ellie said. "I'd like that."

Two weeks later, he brought her home to their house in Ballybough and Mrs Grimes made a big fuss, laying out the table with ham and tomatoes and a freshly baked apple tart. Christy sat smiling and looking adoringly at Ellie who wore a nice mini-dress that came slightly above her knee but wasn't too short that it might draw remarks. Already he believed he was falling in love.

A few weeks later, Ellie brought Christy to meet *her* family. Her father, Dando Doyle, was a big strapping man who wore an open-necked shirt and braces. He had hands like shovels. He offered Christy a bottle of Guinness and asked if he followed the dogs at Shelbourne Park. When Christy said no, he didn't gamble, Dando said he was a wise man for he personally had lost enough money in Shelbourne Park to pay for a new stand for the stadium. While they talked, Ellie's younger sisters sat on the settee and stared at Christy and when he winked at them they dissolved into fits of the giggles.

By now, Christy was seeing Ellie most nights with the exception of Tuesdays when she stayed at home to wash her hair and Thursdays when she went out with her girlfriends. They went to the cinema and to dances and on Sunday afternoons they went walking in the Phoenix Park or took the bus out to Dollymount strand.

Christy was the proudest man in Dublin when he walked out with Ellie on his arm. He could see the way other young fellas glanced at her and occasionally turned their heads to stare. He was planning to propose to her at Easter and was already saving hard to buy the engagement ring. So it was a big shock when she told him one evening that her period was two months late.

He felt a chill run up his spine. If she was pregnant it would spoil everything. Some people would say that they only got married because they had to, whereas nothing could be further from the truth. And it would mean that the wedding would be a rushed job and not the grand affair that Christy was secretly planning.

But she *was* pregnant. Her doctor confirmed it two weeks later. Ellie was frightened of the prospect of telling her parents but Christy said not to worry, he would go with her and take full responsibility and of course he would marry her.

"Are you sure?" Ellie said. "I wouldn't want you to marry me just because I'm in the pudding club."

"Don't be stupid," Christy replied. "I want to marry you because I love you. I was going to ask you anyway at Easter."

They were married six weeks later at the side altar of Sean McDermott Street church. Ellie insisted on carrying on as if everything was normal.

"What's it matter if I'm up the pole? I'm sure I'm not the first one. And I'll hardly be the last."

She wore a white dress and had two bridesmaids and for the reception everyone went off to a hotel in Amiens Street where they had drinks and a sit-down meal and afterwards a singsong that went on till the early hours of the morning.

The only thing they didn't have was a honeymoon. Here, Ellie revealed a practical side that he hadn't seen before. She said they were going to need all their money as a deposit for a house and later on when the baby was born they could go on a nice holiday somewhere. Money spent on a honeymoon would only be wasted.

In the meantime, they rented a cramped little two-room flat in Talbot Street. When Christy told Mr Madigan he was now a married man, his employer agreed to advance his apprenticeship and put him on the full rate straight away. Ellie continued to work in the jeans factory till a fortnight before the baby was due and Christy worked overtime on Friday and Saturday nights. The money went straight into an account in the local credit union.

The baby was born in October, a beautiful little girl with a head of jet-black hair who was the spitting image of her mother. They decided to call her Jackie. Everybody cooed and made a fuss of her and said what a fine healthy child she was and that Ellie must be delighted, which of course she was. Dando held a christening party in their house in Dixon Street with a keg of porter and another keg of beer and bottles of sherry for the women. He gave Christy a cigar and clapped him on the back.

"I'm proud of you, son," he said. "Being a father is a big responsibility. But try and keep your pants on from here on. Chisellers are fierce expensive items."

Christy looked at Ellie as she sat amongst a crowd of adoring women holding the baby in its white christening robes. She looked angelic; more beautiful even than when he first met her at the Gardiner St Hall. He thought his breast would burst. He took a puff at his cigar and beamed from ear to ear even though the smoke was choking him.

By the following summer, they had enough money saved for a deposit. While Christy worked hard in the butcher's shop, Ellie spent her days pushing Jackie in her buggy while she did the round of estate-agents' offices. He came home from work one evening to find her in a state of high excitement.

"I've found the very place," she said. "It's perfect. A lovely house with four bedrooms and a big garden for Jackie to play in when she gets older. It's up in Phibsboro."

Christy's jaw dropped in alarm. "*Four* bedrooms? What do we want four bedrooms for?"

"For the children, of course. You don't think we're going to stop at one?"

"How much?" he asked, nervously.

"Three thousand pounds."

Christy could feel his heart give a leap. He had no idea that a house could cost £3,000. It sounded like an awful lot of money.

"It better be good," he said.

They went to see it the following Sunday afternoon. It was about fifty years old and stood in a terrace of red bricks in a quiet road near the church. But it needed repairs.

"Don't you think it's a bit big?" he said afterwards when he was alone with Ellie.

"You have to think of the future," she said.

"It will cost a fortune to heat. Maybe we should look for something smaller."

"Oh, c'mon, Christy! It's lovely. Me da knows a builder can do it up for us."

"And the cost of it. Three thousand bleedin pounds!"

"It's a bargain," Ellie said, firmly. "I've been round all the auctioneers in the district and I know what houses cost."

"Do you really want it?" he asked at last.

She looked into his eyes and slowly nodded her head.

"Okay. Then you're going to have it."

He rang the estate agent on Monday and after some haggling, managed to get the price down to £2,750. Now he had to raise the cash to pay for it. He made an appointment to see the manager of the local credit union where their savings were invested and came away an hour later with a loan of £3,500 to be repaid over a term of 25 years.

But that was only the beginning. Next, they had to hire a solicitor to arrange the conveyance and engage Dando's builder friend to install new wiring and plumbing and put in a modern bathroom. And then, when all the work was completed, they had to furnish the house and have it decorated.

When it was all over, they were broke. Christy sat down one evening with a pencil and paper and worked out their income and expenditure. With the repayments on the mortgage and their food and gas and electricity bills, not to mention clothes for the baby and themselves, they had barely anything left to live on. It suddenly dawned on him what enormous responsibilities he had taken on. Here he was at twenty-two with a wife and child and a mortgage that seemed to hang like a ball and chain around his neck for as far as he could see. It gave him nightmares.

But they were deliriously happy. Ellie was an excellent homemaker and worked wonders with their meagre budget. She seemed to take a delight in keeping the house looking spick and span. Everything glistened and shone. Little Jackie was always dressed in fresh clean baby clothes. And being a butcher, Christy regularly brought home parcels of meat. There was always food in the fridge and nice tasty meals on the table when he came home from work. When the spring came, Ellie decided it was time to tackle the garden.

The problem was, she knew absolutely nothing about plants. Her family home in Dixon St was a terraced house with a backyard and the nearest green space was a mile away in Fairview Park. But one afternoon when she was out for a walk with Jackie, she called into the library and the kind lady in charge helped her choose a couple of gardening books to get her started. With the aid of the books and a spade she borrowed from Dando, she began to tackle the wilderness that had sprouted up from years of neglect at the back of the house.

Slowly, the garden began to take shape. One of the neighbours, an elderly man who had retired from his job in the ESB, lent Ellie clippers and shears and helped her cut back the weeds and briars that had been allowed to run amok. On Sundays, Christy went out with the spade and spent hours digging and turning the soil to make a lawn. Another neighbour gave her clippings and surplus plants from her own garden. By the time June arrived, they had licked the wilderness into shape. Ellie would gaze with satisfaction at the clumps of lupins and irises and roses that sent a blaze of colour shimmering along the borders of the green baize that had miraculously become a lawn.

And she was proved right about something else. They didn't stop at one child. The advice that Dando had given his son-in-law at the christening seemed to have fallen on deaf ears. Every year or eighteen months, Ellie became pregnant again. Within six years, they had four children, two more girls and a little boy. It seemed to Christy that the kitchen was permanently filled with the smell of drying nappies and babies' bottles. But strangely, the extra mouths to feed and the little bodies to clothe appeared to make no difference to the household finances. They always seemed to manage, even if they had little cash to spare for luxuries.

One by one, the children grew up. Tina, their second child, was the first to go. At twenty-one, she got married to a young man from Swords who had a good job in a bank. They bought a spanking new house in Balbriggan and set up their own home. Jackie was next. She was working for an electrical company in Artane and it was here that she met her husband. Within a year, she too was married and living in Coolock.

Fiona, who was the bright one of the family, had finished a university course in Marketing and moved into an apartment in Blackrock with her boyfriend. And Christopher, who was the youngest and had followed his father into the butchering trade, decided to rent a flat in town with some of his pals. Christy woke up one morning to a strange silence in the house and realised that the family was reared!

They came back of course, particularly at weekends when Ellie would cook a big Sunday joint and they would all gather round the kitchen table that looked out on the garden and admire her handiwork. Only now it was bottles of wine they drank with their Sunday lunch instead of the bottles of Guinness that Dando had favoured. Christy would sit at the head of the table and look with affection on his offspring and their partners and wonder where the time had gone.

But there were compensations. By now, he had taken early retirement from his job so they had time to themselves and a bit of spare cash to spend. Christy wanted to buy a big new television and a DVD player to replace the tiny little set they had bought on hire purchase years ago when things were tight.

"We can get a package that will give us thirty channels. You'll be able to watch all your soaps on a big screen," he announced.

But Ellie wasn't convinced. Ever since the time when she had called to the library for the gardening books, she had become an avid reader. Once a week she made the trip down to the library and came home with an armful of books. Nothing gave her greater pleasure than to sit in the shade of the garden with a good novel in her hands while she listened to the birds quarrelling in the trees.

"If we got a big TV, I'd feel obliged to watch it and it would only interfere with my reading. But don't let me stop you. You might want to see the Sports," she said.

"Ah, no, no," Christy said. "I was thinking of you."

She sat watching him intently for a moment as if something was going through her mind. Then she said: "I'll tell you what. Why don't we treat ourselves to a good holiday? Remember when we got married and we hadn't got the money for a honeymoon? We said we'd have a holiday and we never did."

"You're right," Christy said, sitting up straight in his armchair by the fire. "Where will we go?"

"Why don't I drop into the travel agent's when I'm out and get some brochures? Then we'll be able to decide."

"Game ball," Christy said.

That afternoon, Ellie came home with a bag full of glossy new brochures. After the dinner dishes had been cleared away, they sat down at the kitchen table and started to read through them. Apart from the obvious destinations like Spain and France and Greece, there were brochures offering trips to out-of-the-way places like Mexico and Thailand and Vietnam. There were skiing holidays and adventure holidays and camping holidays. There was even a brochure offering holidays in a chateau that had its own extensive vineyards.

"I didn't realise there were so many places to go," Christy said in amazement.

"People have more money nowadays," Ellie replied.

"Who are you telling?" Christy said, thinking of the brand new kitchen Tina had got installed in her house in Balbriggan with dishwashers and walk-in fridges and even a yoke for making coffee.

"Let's see if we can narrow it down. You don't want a long plane journey, do you?"

Christy, who had never been on a plane in his life, said, "Oh, no."

"And you want good weather, a nice bit of sunshine?"

"I thought this holiday was for you?"

"It's for both of us."

"Okay, then," Christy said.

"And you want somewhere that's not expensive?"

"Well, not *too* expensive."

"In that case, I've found the very place." She pushed the brochure across the table and pointed with her finger.

"Sorrento?"

"That's right. It's in Italy."

"I knew that," Christy said.

"Well, then," Ellie said. "That's where we'll go. It's got a lovely climate and the scenery's beautiful and we'll be right beside the Isle of Capri. Remember that old Frank Sinatra song?"

Christy smiled. "Would you like me to sing it for you?"

Ellie gave him one of her looks. "Sorrento's the place. And I love Italian cooking. If you're happy with that, I'll go first thing in the morning and book it for us."

"Okay," Christy said. "Why don't you do that?"

The holiday was booked. On her next trip to the library, Ellie came back with several books about Sorrento. Even Christie, who never read anything except the sports pages of the *Evening Herald*, was excited enough to open them and look at the pictures.

"Did you know it's near Pompeii," he said.

"Where?"

"Pompeii. Where the volcano erupted. We'll be able to go and look at it."

"I'm not so sure about that," Ellie said. "But the hotel has a swimming pool. You'll be able to do a bit of sunbathing."

"I don't know," Christy said cautiously, thinking of his skinny frame in a pair of swimming pants and everybody staring at him.

"Oh come on, Christy," Ellie remonstrated. "You'll have to get a tan. Otherwise people won't even know you've been away."

As the time for the holiday approached, Ellie took her husband to the ILAC centre and bought some light summer clothes: casual shirts and slacks for Christy and a couple of dresses for herself.

At last, they were ready to go. The cases were packed and tagged and the taxi booked to take them to the airport in the morning. After dinner, Christy said: "Why don't we go and have a little drink in Mohan's? It'll get us in the holiday mood?"

Ellie, who would have preferred to sit at home and finish the book she was reading, reluctantly agreed. She put on some make-up and at nine o'clock they set off for the pub. It was beginning to fill up but they found a quiet spot in the corner and Christy went up to the bar to order the drinks.

When he returned, he thought Ellie was looking a bit pale.

"Are you all right?" he enquired nervously as he put the glasses down on the table.

"I'm feeling a wee bit queasy," she admitted, "but I'm sure it'll pass. It's all the excitement of the holiday."

She reached out to lift her glass and next moment, her arm seemed to give way under her and she fell crashing across the table.

Christy stared in horror. He tried to lift her up. Her face had now gone the colour of putty. Her eyes were closed and a thin dribble of saliva was beginning to slide from the corner of her mouth.

All around the pub, people were standing up to see what had happened.

"Oh my God!" Christy shouted. "Somebody call an ambulance. My wife's after having a turn."

It took ten minutes for the ambulance to arrive but it seemed forever. Two paramedics lifted Ellie onto a stretcher and put a blanket around her. Then they went racing through the crowded streets to the Mater hospital. Christy went with her, holding her hand and whispering in her ear. When they arrived at A and E, an oxygen mask was placed across her face and she was whipped off down a corridor. Christy was taken to a room and asked to wait.

He paced the little room, his mind in turmoil, his lips moving in silent prayer: *Please, God, don't let her die. Please, God, don't let her die.* He willed himself not to think, to let his mind go blank. But he couldn't stop the wild thoughts that kept tumbling into his head. After an eternity, the door opened again. A white-gowned doctor was framed in the doorway.

"Mr Grimes, I've got bad news," he said. "Your wife has had a stroke."

Christy felt his heart jump into his mouth. He stared at the doctor as if he couldn't believe what he was hearing.

"Is she going to live?"

"Yes, she'll live. But I'm afraid there's been some damage."

Ellie was in intensive care and couldn't be disturbed. A nurse gave Christy a cup of tea and helped him ring the children and Fiona arrived twenty minutes later with her car to take him home. She bombarded him with questions, wanting to know what had happened and what condition her mother was in.

"I don't know," Christy confessed. He was still in a state of shock. "The doctor said there'd been some damage, whatever that means."

Fiona bit her lip. "Look, Dad, why don't you stay with us tonight?"

"Ah, no, thanks," Christy said. "I'd rather go home."

He couldn't sleep. The following morning as soon as it was light, he rang the hospital to ask how Ellie was.

"She's resting," the duty nurse told him.

"When can I see her?"

"You could visit this afternoon for a while. But you can't stay too long. And only three of you. She mustn't be excited."

Tina and Jackie came with him. He brought a big bouquet of roses and gripped Jackie's hand tightly as they followed the directions to the intensive care ward. He was so nervous he didn't know what to expect. All he knew was that he desperately wanted to see his wife again, to hold her tight and kiss her and thank God that she was still alive.

He held his breath as the nurse drew the curtains around Ellie's bed. Her head was resting on a bank of pillows. A drip fed into her right arm and her left arm was strapped to her side. But it was her appearance that shocked him most. She seemed to have aged overnight. The beautiful face was now stretched and taut. Her soft skin seemed brittle as tissue paper. Her hair had turned grey. She looked at them and tried to smile and Christy felt the hot tears well up in his eyes.

They stayed for ten minutes. As they were leaving, a doctor drew him aside and explained the extent of Ellie's injuries. The stroke had left her paralysed along her left side.

"Does that mean she won't be able to walk?"

The doctor wouldn't say.

"It's too early. When she's well enough, we'll arrange a course of physiotherapy sessions. Some patients make a very good recovery."

"I don't think she could take it if she couldn't walk," Christy said. "You don't know her. She's so full of life."

"We have to look on the bright side, Mr Grimes. We must never give up hope."

Ellie remained in hospital for six weeks. Christy visited every day and usually one of the children came with him. Before she came home, Christopher helped him to move a bed into the living room so that she wouldn't have to climb the stairs. They installed an easy chair and made the room as comfortable as possible.

The day Ellie came back, all the family gathered in the house. They had a cake and flowers and a bottle of champagne. When she came through the door, supported by Christy and Jackie, they all gathered round to welcome her.

Her eyes misted over as she surveyed the crowded room. Then she gripped Christy's arm. In a trembling voice she said: "I've only got one thing to say and it's this. I don't want you worrying about me. I'm going to beat this, if it's the last thing I do."

She kept her word. The hospital had given her a diet sheet that listed all the foods to be avoided because of their high-fat content. She was put on a range of medication to thin her blood and lower her cholesterol level. Twice a week, she went for physiotherapy sessions. She found it hard at first but she was determined. Gradually she began to improve. She regained the use of her arm and then her hand. With the aid of the walker, she made a round of the garden twice a day, gradually building up the strength in her legs. Christy watched her slowly get better. He was so proud of Ellie and the way she refused to give in.

Her one big pleasure was reading. She would devour books, sometimes finishing one in a single day. Several times a week, Christy made the journey to the library to get books for her. The librarian knew him well by now and also knew the kind of books that Ellie enjoyed and made a point of setting them aside. Christy collected the books and brought them back home and Ellie would sit by the window with her knees covered in a rug and read for hours. But she was making good progress. Dr Hynes had said he was amazed. That seemed to make her happy. And if she was happy, then so was he.

Now he stood in front of the notice board in the library and scanned it for fresh information. It was mostly the same stuff. Yoga classes, Tai Chi, French for beginners, a Classical music recital in the church hall. But his eye was drawn to a new notice that had gone up in the last few days. It was written out in block capitals: MEMBERS REQUIRED FOR A BOOK CLUB BEING SET UP SOON.

Christy thought for a moment. A book club sounded like a good idea. It would give Ellie an interest and she'd be able to meet new people. He would mention it to her when he got home. In the meantime, he would write down the telephone number from the board.

He searched in his pocket for a pen.

Chapter Three

Nick Barry was 32, extremely handsome in a smouldering, bohemian sort of way that women found irresistible, held down a well-paid job as a journalist on a national newspaper and owned his own small house on the North Circular Road in Dublin. Many men would have been happy that life had been so kind. But not Nick. He had tasted fame and adulation, been hailed as a genius and then Fate had turned on him and brought him tumbling down to earth. And the bitter experience had left a mark on him.

Ever since he was a small boy, Nick had cherished one ambition – to be a successful writer whose work would be acclaimed. This ambition dated from the time he had won first prize in the school essay competition when he was ten years old. The prize was twenty-five pounds which was a lot of money for a boy of Nick's age back in the 1980s. But it wasn't the money that excited him so much. It was the fact that the headmaster, Mr Dunne, invited him to read the winning essay to the entire senior school from the stage of the assembly hall.

What would have been a scary ordeal for most students turned into a triumph for Nick. He always remembered that experience; the thrill of being at the centre of attention, standing there with all those faces listening closely to every word he spoke. He wasn't the biggest boy in the school or the most popular or the best at sports but that day he learned something that was to stay with him forever. He discovered the power of words.

He had always liked reading. From the time he was six years old, his mother had enrolled him at the local library and every Friday afternoon after school, Nick visited the library and came home with two books which was the most he was allowed as a junior member. In those early days, he read everything. At first, it was books about trains. For some reason that he never fully understood, he had a fascination for locomotives. Before long, he had devoured every book about trains that the library possessed and the librarian was forced to scour outlying branches to satisfy his demand.

Then he moved on to books about battles; then ships and birds and prehistoric animals. He rapidly picked up a wide range of knowledge about a bewildering array of subjects. But interestingly, it wasn't till he was eight years old that he read his first storybook. It was a battered copy of children's fairy tales and it made an immediate impression on him. Reading those stories unlocked his imagination. They opened a mysterious world where he could roam with goblins and elves and wizards and where strange and wonderful things could come true.

Nick quickly became an avid reader of fiction. While other boys of his age were happy to settle down in front of the television on a cold winter's evening to watch *Wanderly Wagon,* Nick would have his head stuck in a copy of *Kidnapped* or *Treasure Island* or *Huckleberry Finn.* This exposure to books had the effect of expanding his vocabulary and moulding his composition style. English became his best subject at school. But it wasn't till he won the essay prize that he decided that he wanted to become a writer.

And here he ran into a problem. How *did* you become a writer? What exactly did you do? He knew there were clearly established paths to other professions. If you wanted to become a doctor or a lawyer, you studied medicine or law at university. If you wanted to be a plumber you served an apprenticeship. But what did you do if you wanted to be a writer? It took Nick some time to figure out that the only way to do it was to sit down and actually write something.

But first, he had to get through school. He was a bright student and had no difficulty passing the various examinations that popped up at regular intervals. And that was how he found himself at the age of eighteen studying English Literature at Trinity College. By now, his father had bought him a word processor as a birthday present and so he took his first tentative steps at creative writing.

At weekends and evenings, Nick sat for hours in the privacy of his bedroom and struggled to produce short stories. But the results were disappointing. Even though he had a vivid imagination, he found the craft of writing painfully difficult. He soon discovered that the techniques he had used to write prize-winning essays at school were not much use to him now. His plots progressed with dreary slowness. His descriptions seemed flowery and overblown. When he read back the dialogue he had written, he was forced to admit it was wooden and uninspired and nothing like how real people spoke.

Nick was excited to be at Trinity. He loved the relaxed atmosphere of the place, the quiet little corners, the green playing fields, the squares where he could sit and read when the weather was good, the sense of history and learning that seemed to seep out of the very cobblestones in the quad. He enjoyed the company of other students and the sense of freedom that the university provided.

One of the very first things he did was to join the staff of a college literary magazine called *Horizons* and it was here that he came across Arminta O'Shea. Arminta was a third-year student and older than Nick and had an air of bored weariness with life. She had long blonde hair and lots of bracelets and beads and smoked marijuana. He had met people like her before and was instinctively wary of them. In Nick's experience, they were frivolous people who weren't living in the real world. But Arminta appeared to be different and she also had something that Nick needed. She possessed an intimate knowledge of the college literary scene.

They soon became friends and one afternoon over coffee and scones in the Buttery restaurant he unburdened himself to her about his writing ambitions.

"I'm hoping to publish a novel some day," he confessed after they had chatted for a while about mundane topics like the college rugby team's chances in the university league.

"Really?" Arminta said, stifling a yawn.

"Yes. It's my life's ambition. That's why I'm here."

"Bully for you," she said.

"You don't sound very excited," Nick said, beginning to get aggrieved. He had expected Arminta to show a bit more interest in his announcement.

"Well, if you must know," she replied, "half the students in the English department are planning to publish a novel. They all fancy themselves as budding literary superstars. And most of them haven't even progressed beyond selecting a title."

"But I've actually made a start," Nick said eagerly. "I've been trying my hand at short stories."

"Well, that certainly puts you ahead of the game," she admitted. "But you do realise that getting published isn't as easy as you might think? There are an awful lot of hoops to jump through."

"I'm very determined," Nick said. "The trouble is, I'm finding it rather tough. I was wondering if you might give me some tips."

"It *is* tough. But the short story provides a good vehicle for practice. Mind you, it does have its drawbacks. And of course, there's a very limited market for short stories. Have you ever thought of poetry?"

"No," Nick admitted. Writing poetry had never crossed his mind.

"Why don't you give it a lash? Poetry has one big advantage over prose. It takes less time to write."

He decided to take her advice. But first he had to choose a theme. All the obvious subjects for poetry such as Nature and Love and Beauty appeared to have been staked out already by other poets who guarded their territory jealously and didn't welcome intruders. After some consideration, Nick decided to write about life in the depressed inner city. There didn't seem to be anybody writing about that.

Next he had to choose a form. In recent times, there seemed to have been a trend towards free verse. It seemed to Nick that this gave the poet much greater licence. The verses didn't even have to rhyme. In no time at all he had produced several short poems. The one that most satisfied him was titled: "Spar Grocery: Winter 2000".

I see them at nightfall, coming from grey, dilapidated flats,
Shuffling in trainers and tracksuits, their crumpled lives in a carrier bag,
Drawn like moths to the bright lights of the store,
To top up on provisions: a carton of milk, a tin of beans, a sliced loaf and
twenty Silk Cut tipped.

He spent another week revising the poem before showing it to Arminta. She was very impressed.

"It's so gritty," she said, "and so profoundly realistic. You know, I think I'll ask Trevor to publish it in the next issue of the magazine."

"Are you sure it's good enough?" Nick asked, uncertainly. "It's only my first attempt."

"I think it's brilliant. It's a new departure. Nobody's writing this kind of stuff."

He allowed Arminta to approach Trevor Arbuthnot who was the tall, effete, editor of *Horizons* and an MA student. Trevor quickly read the poem and since he had a hole to fill at the bottom of Page 22 where a promised advert had been dropped at the last minute, he decided to stick it in. Nick was delighted. This was his first published work, the first time his name had appeared in print. He gazed at the poem till his eyes began to gloss over then went out and bought another dozen copies of the magazine to give to friends and relations and to keep as mementoes.

But nobody could have foreseen the reaction it would bring. Within a few days, the Arts Editor of *The Irish Times* rang looking for an interview. Nick, who was totally unprepared for this development, once more sought Arminta's advice.

"What do you think I should do?" he inquired.

"See her, of course. Established poets would kill each other for an interview in *The Irish Times*. Think of the publicity it will bring."

The Arts Editor turned out to be a middle-aged woman with glasses, a large Labrador dog which kept trying to bite Nick's leg, and a rather distracted manner. Nick was intimidated by her. She talked to him for an hour and a half and asked a lot of probing questions about his favourite poets and the influences on his work. Nick answered as best he could and when the interview was completed, a photographer took his picture standing against a statue in Trinity quad.

Three days later, a half-page article appeared in the paper under the heading: *RARE DIAMOND SHINES IN THE DARKNESS OF THE INNER CITY.*

A photograph of Nick looking like a sulking Colin Farrell accompanied the text that proceeded to hail him as a "working-class poetic genius who champions the downtrodden in his raw and invigorating verse." The rest of the article went on to compare him to Brendan Behan, Seán O'Casey and George Orwell.

After that, all Hell broke loose. The magazine's phone didn't stop ringing with reporters scrambling for interviews. Nick appeared on national television. The BBC flew a team from London to interview him for a culture programme. He couldn't believe what was happening to him. Almost overnight, he had become a literary celebrity and all on the strength of one poem that had taken him half an hour to write.

Arminta very quickly claimed the credit for discovering him, which was fair enough since it was her suggestion that led him to write poetry in the first place. But Trevor Arbuthnot wasn't to be so easily edged off the stage. He claimed his share of the glory as the editor who had first published him and promptly put up the price of the magazine.

Nick was transported back to his childhood days, standing on the stage of the assembly hall and reading his prize-winning essay. This was the adulation he had craved. This was what had propelled him to become a writer in the first place. He was the centre of attention again and enjoying every glorious moment.

But while the storm of publicity raged about him, a small termite of doubt was beginning to gnaw at his peace of mind. Something was bothering him. He confided in Arminta one evening after several pints in Mulligan's pub in Poolbeg St. By now, they were seeing quite a lot of each other and she had become his confidante and unofficial literary agent as well as his occasional lover.

"I'm not actually from the inner city," he confessed. "I'm from Sandycove and I went to Blackrock College."

This information didn't seem to faze her. "It doesn't matter. Who's to know?"

"But *I* know. And my friends know. To tell you the truth, I feel like a bit of a fraud."

"Look," Arminta said. "You didn't actually tell that *Irish Times* woman you were from the inner city, did you?"

"No," Nick admitted.

"Then you're in the clear. If the silly cow wants to write you up as a working-class hero, that's none of your business. Besides, all those British radical poets of the sixties came from solid middle-class homes and many of them went to Oxbridge. Take my advice and forget all about it."

"There's one other thing. What about my novel? That's what I really want to write."

"Forget about your novel. Go with the flow. You're a poet now."

"Are you sure?"

"I'm positive," Arminta said. "Now, will we have another pint for the road?"

One day, several weeks later, Nick received a phone call from a man with a very silky voice.

"Am I speaking to Mr Barry?"

"Yes," Nick replied.

"Pardon me for disturbing you like this. My name is Partridge. I'm a publisher. Wounded Knee Press. Perhaps you've heard of us?"

"Yes," Nick said and sat up straight. Wounded Knee was a well-known publisher of poetry.

"I've been reading about you and I'd like to discuss the possibility of bringing out a collection of your poems. Would it be possible for us to meet?"

"Sure," Nick said, suddenly becoming fully alert.

"When would be most convenient?"

"Tomorrow?" Nick suggested.

"Tomorrow is fine, Mr Barry. I look forward to making your acquaintance."

They met in a quiet restaurant in Donnybrook. Mr Partridge turned out to be a well-preserved little man with grey hair who wore a pinstriped suit with wide lapels and a silk handkerchief in his breast pocket. Nick brought Arminta with him for support. She proved to be a tough negotiator. Mr Partridge offered to publish a collection of Nick's work for £1000 but before the lunch was over, Arminta had successfully revised this figure up to £5000 which was more money than Nick had ever possessed in his life. They shook hands on the deal and Mr Partridge promised to have a contract sent to him in the next few days.

"How many poems are in a collection?" Nick asked Arminta after Mr Partridge had paid the bill and departed.

"Depends. Twenty-five? Thirty? How many have you written?"

"About a dozen."

"Well, you'll have to get your skates on," Arminta said. "He wants all the material in four weeks. Do you think that's enough time?"

"I don't know," Nick conceded. "I've never done this sort of thing before."

He retreated to his bedroom and set to work. He was amazed how quickly the poems seem to flow from his brain. He would get an idea and half an hour later, he would have the finished work on his word processor. Sometimes, he would be walking along the street and a line of poetry would pop unbidden into his head. After the tedium of writing short stories, he found poetry a very easy proposition. Within a fortnight, he had produced another twenty poems and now had his collection.

Arminta read them eagerly. She was exultant.

"You really do have a wonderful gift," she said. "You make it all

appear so simple. This one for instance – 'Lower Basin Street Blues'."
And she read it aloud.

"Night falls like a soldier, dead upon the battlefield of life,
The bright dawn explodes like a landmine fresh from the carnage,
Scattering the illusions of normality with the debris of the day,
The bright stars fading like shrapnel over the waking city."

"It's got so much energy," Arminta went on. "And anger. The imagery is perfect. You know, I think we're onto something here."

Mr Partridge was equally enthusiastic. He read Nick's collection and pronounced himself very satisfied. Six weeks later, the book was ready. Nick had decided to call it "View from Matt Talbot Bridge".

It was launched at a party in the Writers Club attended by critics and people from the book trade. Nick made a little speech thanking everyone for their support and then read several of the poems to thunderous applause. When he was finished, he found himself besieged by people wanting to interview him and get his autograph.

The reception for the book was overwhelming. Reviewers grappled with superlatives in their rush to welcome the collection. One critic said that Nick's poetry "grabs you by the throat before head-butting you in the face".

Another said: "in Nick Barry, the marginalized have at last found a defiant voice. His poetry has all the threatening energy of broken glass."

The book was in all the shop windows accompanied by a brooding photograph of Nick in a heavy overcoat standing on waste ground beside a burnt-out car. In no time, it had shot to the top slot in the bestsellers lists, something unheard of for a poetry collection. It quickly sold out and another print run was ordered. A punk rock band approached him with a suggestion for putting his poems to music and releasing an album. They even invited him to tour with them. Meanwhile, Mr Partridge was pursuing him with his chequebook to write another collection.

Nick was completely bowled over by the reaction. He had found the process of writing the poems relatively simple. There had been very little effort on his part; indeed the poems had practically written themselves. And his success had been so sudden and so fast that he was left wondering if it wasn't all just a wonderful dream and he was going to wake up to cold reality.

In the meantime, he had some practical matters to attend to. He had an important examination coming up and in the past few months with all the excitement, his studies had fallen behind. He left Arminta to handle media requests for interviews while he withdrew from the public gaze and concentrated on catching up with his exam work.

But even this event was seized on by the media. Reports began appearing in the press that he had gone off to live in a mud hut in a remote bog in Connemara or even that he had fled to a bleak island in the Outer Hebrides to escape the publicity.

RECLUSIVE POET FLEES INNER CITY TO COMMUNE WITH NATURE was a typical headline. Nick woke up one morning to the realisation that his life had been taken over. He had become public property. No matter where he turned, he couldn't escape.

Arminta thought it was wonderful.

"Do you realise how fortunate you are? There are poets out there who count themselves lucky to get a single poem published in a magazine once a year. Ask Trevor if you don't believe me. He has a sack full of stuff from people begging him to print it in *Horizons*. "

"But I didn't realise the cost to my privacy. I had six people come up to me on the DART this morning asking for my autograph."

"It's a small price to pay," Arminta replied. "You should be grateful. You're building a reputation and what's more, you're getting paid. What are you complaining about?"

He *was* getting paid and handsomely. He had quickly earned out the advance for the first collection and was now receiving royalties from Mr Partridge. In addition, Arminta had negotiated an advance of £30,000 for his next book, tentatively called *Wasted Lives*. He had agreed to pay her an agent's fee of 20 per cent, which he considered fair given that she was doing most of the donkey work.

As soon as his exams were over, he concentrated on this second collection. It took him a week. He produced another thirty poems and gave them to Mr Partridge who was delighted. The second book was published to even greater acclaim than the first. One critic said that Nick's voice had matured. Another said that he now had a confidence and authority that belied his tender years. A third said he was the angry voice of a lost generation and compared him to WB Yeats.

The book sold in massive quantities. Mr Partridge sold the rights to an American publishing house and Nick received another wad of money. He was awarded the Archibald Moriarty prize for literature, an award given to honour an obscure poet who had died from starvation in a garret in the Dublin Liberties in 1782. He was invited to give talks to schools and asked to open a supermarket. He was even given a civic reception by the Lord Mayor at the Mansion House.

At college, Nick was the subject of intense awe and admiration. All his professors and lecturers were pleased at his success and basked in the reflected glory of his new-found fame. The other students looked up to him as a hero and a role model. Women who had always found him attractive now began throwing themselves at him so that Arminta took to clinging tightly to his arm whenever they were in public and scowling threateningly at any female who approached.

But there were some discordant voices. Not everyone was pleased. A carping review of *Wasted Lives* appeared in the next issue of *Petals,* a fringe literary magazine with a minute circulation. It was written by an unsuccessful scribbler called Hugo de Lacy who blasted Nick's poetry as shallow, derivative and lacking in depth. Nick, who happened to see the review by chance, was hurt by the comments. It was the first negative publicity he had received. But Arminta brushed it aside with contempt.

"Nobody reads that rag. It sells about a hundred copies if they're lucky."

"He said my poetry was shallow."

"He's jealous, that's all. He can't get published himself. He's been tormenting Trevor for months to print his stuff."

"Nevertheless…"

"For God's sake, Nick. This is Ireland. You've got to expect this sort of thing. Whenever you're successful, there is always some little bastard who wants to pull you down. And the poets are the worst. They watch each other like sharks in a fishpond. Put it out of your mind."

But the review had the result of resurrecting the doubts that had plagued Nick from the very beginning. It had all been too easy. He had expected writing to be hard work and instead, it turned out to be like falling off a log. His poems had practically flown off the word processor. Besides, he was beginning to grow tired of poetry. He longed for his true vocation, writing a full-length novel. Poetry seemed to him to be just playing around with words, whereas fiction, now that was a real challenge!

But he was totally unprepared for the next development. He was in the college bar one afternoon, having a drink with some admirers when a breathless Arminta appeared by his side. Her face was flushed and there was a concerned look in her eyes.

"I've got to talk to you," she said in a loud whisper. "At once."

Nick got up and followed her outside.

"Look at this," she said, dramatically pulling an evening paper from her bag. She spread it out for Nick to read.

Immediately he felt his heart jump.

WORKING CLASS POET REVEALED AS FAKE, the bold headline read. Most of the page was taken up with the large photograph of Nick standing beside the ruined car. But the report was damning. Nick felt the blood drain from his face as he read.

"Nick Barry, the award-winning poet and self-proclaimed champion of the working class is today unmasked as an impostor. We can reveal that Mr Barry was brought up in a lavish semi-detached house in the posh Dublin suburb of Sandycove. And he was educated at the upper-crust Blackrock College. The poet, who has become wealthy writing about life in the ravaged inner-city, gazes each morning across Dublin Bay to the plush slopes of Howth Head instead of looking at the run-down flats he celebrates in his poems."

When he had finished reading, Nick's face was ashen.

"*Lavish* semi-detached? It was just an ordinary house," he said, lamely. "And I never claimed to be the champion of anything. I never once said I was from the inner city. That all started with that woman from *The Irish Times*. Do you think we can sue?"

Arminta shook her head.

"Not a good idea. It will only bring further attention."

"So what do you think we should do?"

"Nothing," she said with a grim face. "We just sit tight and wait for it to blow over. You keep a low-profile and let me handle this."

For a couple of days, nothing happened and Nick began to hope that Arminta was right and the matter had died away. But the following day, a radio phone-in programme returned to the article. They had lined up Hugo de Lacy who proceeded to denounce Nick as a sham and a parasite on the underprivileged people of the inner city. De Lacy didn't pull any punches as he launched a bitter attack on Nick and his poetry.

"But what does it matter if he's not from the inner city?" the presenter argued. "Where the poet comes from should be irrelevant. Surely the work should speak for itself?"

De Lacy gave a loud snort that almost blew the microphone away.

"But that's the very point. Mr Barry's poetry is the kind of juvenile rubbish that wouldn't get published in a school magazine," he said, contemptuously. "It's the sort of stuff you could scribble in ten minutes on the back of a cigarette packet. How he ever managed to be regarded as a serious poet belongs up there with the third secret of Fatima."

Nick winced at these words as if he had been struck a blow and turned off the radio.

It was a slow week and the media was hungry for news. Within twenty-four hours, the story had been taken up by the main newspapers and the television stations. Arminta rang Nick to tell him that a bunch of journalists were camped outside her flat and warning him to keep out of sight.

For the next few days he holed up in his house, afraid to go out for fear of having a microphone stuck in his face. But by the third day, he had run out of food and decided to venture as far as the local shops to stack up on provisions. Having first checked to make sure that the coast was clear, he stepped carefully out onto the street. Immediately, he was accosted by a reporter and photographer from the *Daily Bugle* who seemed to appear out of nowhere.

"Mr Barry, have you anything to say to the accusations that you're a phoney?" the excited reporter asked.

"No comment," Nick muttered and attempted to walk past while the photographer proceeded to snap away furiously.

"Mr Barry. Is it true that you're not from the inner city?"

Nick kept his head down and tried to press on while they pursued him along the street.

"Mr Barry. Do you accept that your poems are rubbish?"

Suddenly Nick's temper snapped. He felt like a hare being tormented by baying hounds. He turned round to confront his accuser.

"First, I never said I was from the inner city. Second, I never made any claims for my poetry. Third, I just want to be left alone to get on with my business."

The reporter frantically jotted down his replies while a shaken Nick brushed past him and hurried into the store.

It was a mistake, as he was soon to learn. The following morning, the television review of the papers showed a front page with a picture of a frightened-looking Nick beside a headline that read: POSH POET ADMITS INNER-CITY CLAIMS ARE BOGUS. AGREES POEMS ARE RUBBISH.

He tentatively pulled back his bedroom curtains to reveal television vans, camera crews and a posse of reporters lined up across the street. He let the curtains fall back as his heart sank into his boots.

Ten minutes later, Arminta rang.

"Have you seen this morning's paper?"

"Yes," Nick groaned.

"Where on earth did they get this stuff?"

"They twisted my words."

He could hear her loud gasp on the other end of the line.

"You mean you actually talked to them?"

"I'd no option. They ambushed me on my way to the shops."

"My God!" Arminta screamed. "Have you no sense? I thought I told you to keep out of their way? You've no idea what these bastards are like once they get their teeth into you."

The barrage continued for a further week and then it died down as quickly as it had begun. But by then, the damage had been done. A group of inner-city residents with placards held a demonstration outside his publisher's office seeking compensation for emotional distress and humiliation caused by Nick's poetry. Sales of his latest volume sank like a stone and thousands of copies had to be remaindered. Mr Partridge wrote to say that he was postponing publication of Nick's third collection till the dust had settled. He was asked to return the Archibald Moriarty prize and fired from the staff of *Horizons*.

When he eventually emerged from his flat, blinking in the clear light of day, his reputation was in ruins. Even Arminta had deserted him, claiming that she could no longer afford to be associated with a man who was such an obvious drawback to her career. Nick was devastated by the cruel way the media had turned on him and the callous manner in which Arminta had dumped him when the going got rough.

But curiously, he was glad it was all over. He had never set out to be a poet and he had been uncomfortable at his success. In an odd way, he thought the newspapers were right. He *did* feel like a fraud. And there were compensations in being able to go about his daily business without being stared at in the street or asked for autographs on the DART. Eventually, he got his degree and graduated from Trinity College. He secured a job as a sub-editor on *The Daily Trumpet* and with the money he had earned from his poetry books, he bought his little house on the North Circular Road.

Here he began to put his past behind him and pick up the threads of his life. His broody good looks and dark dreamy eyes meant he had no trouble finding girlfriends and a string of young women trooped in and out of his bedroom at regular intervals. But from time to time, he still thought about Arminta. She had been special. She hadn't been beautiful or particularly attractive but she had been worldly-wise and she had taught him a lot. He was hurt by her callous desertion. It took him a long while to get over her.

But he hadn't forgotten his earlier dream. As time passed, his desire to write began to grow again. Despite what he had gone through, he still wanted to be accepted as a writer. But now his ambition was tempered by the mistakes of the past and spurred on by the memory of the humiliations he had suffered. This time, he was determined to write his novel and make it a resounding success. He had a burning desire to disprove all those critics who had dismissed him as a fake. He wanted to be acclaimed as a bestselling author and hold his head up high again.

He was older now and less naïve. He had learned some lessons. This time, he would do his research. He would plan his book carefully. He would find out what ordinary people thought and what sort of material they liked to read. And when he was ready, he would begin. For months he sought a way of tapping into the popular mood and finding what people liked. And then one day, an idea came to him. He would join a book club!

What better way to gauge the views of ordinary readers than to join a club where people met regularly to discuss books and talk about what they liked? A book club would be the perfect place to take the pulse of the common reader. And he would enjoy it. Books were his main hobby. He was constantly reading and had developed a well-tuned critical sense. And he would be among readers – the final judges who went out and spent their hard-earned cash to buy the books. Their views would be much more valuable than the bitter, carping words of the professional critics.

Fired up by his decision, Nick set about finding a book club to join. He wondered if there was one in the neighbourhood. He searched the phone directory and the *Golden Pages* but could find nothing. And then another thought came to him. He would go down to the library this very afternoon and ask them. The library was the obvious place to start. Librarians were the kind of people who knew these things.

Chapter Four

Liz Broderick saw Marion's advert as she was coming out of the delicatessen after picking up a tub of hummus for her supper. A year ago, she had never heard of hummus and wouldn't have recognised it if it had sneaked up and bitten her on the leg. But a lot of things had happened in the past twelve months to change her views on life. Chief among them was the death of her husband, Tim.

He was only thirty-five when he died and Liz had still not recovered from the shock. It had all happened so suddenly. There he was, a fit, healthy man setting off to the pub for his lunchtime pint and fifteen minutes later the police were ringing to tell her there had been a serious accident and they were sending a car to pick her up. She still hadn't come to terms with it.

She kept telling herself if he had been older or suffering from some terminal illness, his death might have been easier to accept. But Tim was young and full of the joys of living. It was as if the whole thing was a ghastly nightmare and she would wake to find him in the kitchen with his briefcase in his hands, asking what they were going to do about dinner.

The event had made Liz extremely conscious of her own mortality. She had seen how easily the candle of life could be snuffed out. Now she paid close attention to her health. She watched her diet and was careful what she ate. She took regular exercise. She tried to avoid stressful situations. She had stared sudden death in the face once and was anxious that it wouldn't happen to her a second time.

The one good thing to come out of the whole tragic episode was that she had happy memories. She had been married to Tim for nine years and in all that time they had never had an argument. She knew of couples who seemed to spend their whole lives fighting with each other. But Tim was the most easy-going man she had ever met. Nothing excited him or made him angry, nothing got him upset. He seemed to have been born with the golden gifts of patience and even temper. As a result, he was a joy to live with, a dream to work with and everybody loved him.

Unlike her own father, she thought ruefully. He had an extremely bad temper and was forever banging down the telephone or kicking the furniture when he was annoyed. And *he* was still alive and thriving at the ripe old age of seventy-eight.

A few weeks after Tim's funeral, Liz read an article about food and was shocked to discover just how much salt and sugar and preservatives so many processed foods contained. Food was a ticking time bomb the article stated in its snappy overblown prose. She went immediately and cleared out the cupboards and the fridge, dumping anything she felt might be bad for her into a large black bin bag which she left in the rubbish disposal.

She bought a book on diet and read it from cover to cover. When she was finished she had been converted to the low-fat cause. She stocked up on fresh fruit and vegetables, used hummus instead of butter, cooked with extra virgin olive oil and switched from meat to fish. And on her doctor's advice, she limited herself to three eggs a week. Having witnessed an untimely death at first hand, Liz was determined to take no chances as far as her own health was concerned.

But it wasn't just her diet that changed as a result of Tim's death. It caused an upheaval in every aspect of her life but most particularly in her social activities. When her husband was alive, they had been familiar figures on the social scene. They were young and popular and well off and could afford to spend money enjoying themselves.

They were regular visitors to the races and the theatre and there was scarcely a weekend when they weren't invited to a dinner party in somebody's house. Liz revelled in this life. She loved the chat and the gossip and the laughter and the wonderful meals that you would pay a fortune for in some of the better restaurants in town. It often caused her great amusement to observe the way various hostesses competed to provide the best menus, each one trying to outdo the other with lavish dinners – until her turn came around, when she would dissolve in a crisis of confidence trying to decide what to feed her guests.

But that lively social life quickly vanished when Tim died. At first people had been very sympathetic. Her phone had rung constantly with friends wanting to take her out or offer advice or just help her get through her tragic loss. People were very kind. They knew she needed comforting. They knew she needed solace and distraction and the warm company of others. And they were anxious to provide it.

But gradually the invitations dried up till they practically disappeared. Liz wasn't offended. She understood perfectly. Dinner parties were for couples. A single woman caused problems for the hostess. Where did they seat her? And what if the men paid her too much attention? Would the wives get jealous? It was worse, of course, in the case of a widow for while everyone naturally felt sorry for her, it did cast a mournful pall over the gaiety of the proceedings.

It might not have been so bad if she had a partner to accompany her. But a single woman as young and good-looking as Liz could be a threat. She was still extremely attractive. She could still cause heads to turn when she entered a room. So gradually, the phone stopped ringing and the invitations stopped coming and she was left alone with her grief.

It was a difficult time and she was often lonely. When the people she used to know were off enjoying themselves, Liz would be sitting at home watching old movies on television or tucked up in bed with a mug of cocoa and a good book. The days that used to be filled with excitement and fun now seemed to stretch endlessly. She began to wonder if Tim's death meant that her life too had suddenly come to an end. She began to ask herself if the future held anything for her but sadness and if she would ever be happy again.

But she wasn't entirely alone. She had one friend who stuck by her – Cathy Burke who she had known since her college days. Cathy was married to a dentist with a busy practice and had three young children but she still found time to keep in constant touch with Liz and made sure that they had lunch together at least once a week. Liz trusted Cathy and she listened to her because she knew that her friend had her best interests at heart. So she wasn't shocked or surprised when Cathy suggested diplomatically one afternoon that Liz shouldn't entirely close her mind to the possibility of a new relationship.

"You're only thirty-three," she said. "And you can't mourn forever. Life still has a lot to offer."

Liz smiled knowingly. "Are you trying to fix me up with someone?"

"Oh God, no! Heaven forbid."

"Some nice man you have in mind?" Liz teased.

"Not specifically. But you shouldn't dismiss it entirely. I know if Max died, God forbid, I would certainly think about it. You're a very attractive woman and you have no children. It's almost as if you have always been single."

Liz allowed the thought to play around in her head. Privately, she admitted it might be pleasant to be involved in a relationship again. "I'm not sure if I'd be able for it just yet."

"Oh don't be silly! You'd enjoy it. And you'd have no difficulty finding a man. A lot of them prefer women of your age. You're more mature and you're not as giddy as some of these younger girls with their heads filled with nonsense."

"Let me think about it," Liz said.

"You should, definitely. I'm sure Tim wouldn't mind. He'd want you to be happy, wouldn't he?"

"Oh, sure he would. That's not the problem. But would I ever be content with someone else after living with him?"

That was the real question. Liz had been in love with her husband almost from the first day she saw him. Really in love, not the teenage flirtations and infatuations that had passed for love before they met. She was twenty-one and Tim was twenty-three and they were both students at UCD. She had never regarded herself as particularly good-looking. She was tall and slim with blue eyes and a head of fine blonde hair but until she met Tim she had never thought she was anything special. He was responsible for that.

She never forgot that important day. It was a fine March afternoon and she was studying in the college library when a young man sitting across from her asked if he could borrow her pen for a moment. She hadn't given him a second glance. In fact, she had forgotten all about him till she had left the library and was in the corridor outside when she heard a voice calling after her.

"Hey! Hey! Your pen!"

She stopped and he caught up with her, slightly out of breath.

"You forgot your pen," he said.

She looked into his face. It was a handsome face with sensuous brown eyes and high cheekbones and clear skin beneath the untidy mop of dark hair.

"So I did," she said, taking the pen from his outstretched hand.

"I didn't even get a chance to thank you properly," he went on, his loud voice echoing all over the corridor.

"Sssh!" She put a finger to her lips and pointed to the sign on the wall that read: SILENCE.

"I'm Tim Broderick," he said, ignoring the sign and continuing to talk in his booming tones. "And who are you, might I ask?"

Liz quickly grabbed him by the arm and marched him to the exit. Once outside, she rounded on him.

"What are you trying to do?" she demanded. "Get me banned from the library? I've got a very important examination coming up and I have to prepare."

But he was grinning at her now, a big warm smile spreading all over his handsome face.

"I like that," he said.

"Like what?"

"The way you get all excited."

Liz glared at him. "You do, do you?"

"Yes. It shows you've got spirit and I admire that."

They went for coffee in the dining hall and Tim insisted on paying.

"You still haven't told me who you are," he said, placing the mug of coffee on the table in front of her.

"Why do you want to know?"

"No reason. We're sitting here enjoying a friendly chat. It's not a state secret, is it?"

"My name is Elizabeth McCarthy. I'm a final year Arts student. Anything else I can tell you?"

"Elizabeth?" he replied. "That's a bit of a mouthful. I think I'll call you Liz."

She bristled. The cheek of him!

"And what is this important exam you're studying for?" he wanted to know.

"History, if you must know. And there's an awful lot of reading to be done."

"I *do* know. And I also know something else. You'll stroll through it."

Liz sat back in her chair and stared at him. This guy was like no man she had ever met. So confident and cock-sure of himself. What made him think he possessed all the answers?

"Really?" she said. "That's nice to know."

"Yes. I don't think the examiners even bother to read all those boring scripts," he continued. "As long as you write plenty and sound intelligent, you'll get your grade."

She opened her eyes in wide surprise. "And you're some kind of expert, are you?"

"Not really. But I studied History too. Three years ago. So I've been over the course."

"And what are you studying now?"

"Computer Science. I switched. I think computers are the coming thing. That's where all the action's going to be."

"Okay," Liz said. "So all I have to do is write reams and the examiners will pass me?"

"That's what I did."

"And what did you get?"

"A First Class Honours," he said with a smile.

"Right," Liz said, running out of smart replies. "Maybe I will take your advice after all."

When they had finished their coffees, he offered her a lift into town in his car. He dropped her home and as she was getting out of the vehicle, he asked, playfully:

"What would you say if I invited you for a drink some night?"

Liz looked once more into those intriguing brown eyes. "I'd probably say yes."

For their first date, he took her to a pub in Baggot Street where a live rock band was playing. But the music was so loud they could barely hear themselves talk so they left and went to a quiet little wine bar. In the course of their conversation, Liz discovered that Tim's family was in the electronics business and owned several retail shops where he worked at weekends. It was this that had fuelled his interest in computers.

"My father wants me to work full-time for him when I graduate but I'm not so sure. I think I'd like to strike out on my own."

"How do you mean?"

"Start my own company."

"But wouldn't you need finance?" Liz asked.

He waved a hand as if he was swatting away a fly. "That won't be a problem."

"No?"

"I've got some cash that an old aunt left me in her will and I could probably borrow the rest. I'm sure I could convince my bank manager if I came up with a sound business plan."

"And when is all this likely to happen?"

Tim swallowed a mouthful of wine. "When I finish college in a couple of months' time."

"You sound very sure of yourself," she said.

"You have to be. No point being beaten before you even start."

Tim was the first man she had met who seemed to know exactly what he wanted and how he was going to achieve it. He sounded so convincing that she found herself believing him. Now that he had captured her imagination, she was eager to know more about him. So when he suggested meeting her again, she readily agreed.

This time, he turned up wearing a smart business suit and tie and with his unruly locks neatly trimmed after a visit to the hairdresser. He was also carrying a spray of roses.

"For me?" she asked, in surprise.

"Well, you don't think I normally walk around carrying flowers. Of course they're for you."

Liz was impressed. She couldn't remember a man ever giving her roses before. But she was even more impressed when he took her to a trendy bistro in Dawson St where he insisted on starting the meal with glasses of champagne and ordering a bottle of fine Burgundy wine to accompany their food.

"You're looking very smart tonight," she told him.

"Do you think so?"

"Yes. I like your suit."

"Well, that's good to know," he said with a grin. "I bought it for my visit to the bank manager. I just thought I'd run it past you."

"You mean you didn't get dressed up for me?" she said flinging her napkin at him.

"Only kidding," he said, grinning and ducking as the cloth went sailing past his head onto the empty table behind.

Soon, they were meeting several times a week. Her father wasn't exactly happy with the arrangement. He thought she should be studying hard for her exams.

"Oh, leave her alone, James," her mother would say. "She deserves a break from time to time. It will do her good."

"She'll have plenty of time for gallivanting when she gets her degree," her father grumbled. "She should be paying more attention to her books."

But Liz had learned how to deal with her father. She smiled at her mother while she gently stroked his greying hair.

"I need to relax, Dad. My tutor says it's important that I take time off. She says too many students burn themselves out by overwork."

It wasn't entirely true but it sounded convincing.

Her father glanced from his wife to his daughter. He knew when he was outgunned and it was time to shut up.

"Hmphhh!" he said and quickly turned the pages of his newspaper.

By now, Tim had come up with an idea to manufacture security software for the computer industry. And as soon as he graduated, he set about establishing his own company as he had promised. Now, his time was largely taken up with meetings and planning sessions as he struggled to develop a marketing strategy and raise the necessary finance.

Meanwhile, Liz's exams were drawing closer. It meant long days in the college library, for despite what Tim had said she was determined to prepare. She didn't want to face the ire of her father if she should fail. As a result, they saw much less of each other. But the break also provided her with a breathing space to assess the relationship and where it might be going. Until now, it had been conducted at break-neck speed and she couldn't escape the feeling that she had been swept off her feet by Tim without knowing what was happening to her. Maybe, she should allow things to settle down a little. She was only twenty-one. What was the rush?

But now that they were apart, she found herself missing him and looking forward eagerly to the next time they could meet. As one week rolled into another and she didn't hear from him, she began to wonder if he had grown tired of her. Maybe the romance had lost its bloom. Maybe it had only been a flash in the pan. Maybe he had even met some other girl. She rang him several times but he always sounded busy and their conversations were brief and hurried. And then before she knew, the exams were upon her and all thoughts of Tim were pushed to the back of her mind.

For the next two weeks she had papers almost every day. It meant a rigid regime of study, sleep, exams and then more study. It was like swimming in the sea. No sooner had she surmounted one wave than another came along immediately to challenge her. And then one evening in June as she stepped out of the exam hall after finishing the final paper, she heard someone call her name.

It was a beautiful evening. The sun was casting long shadows on the lawns. There was a scent of new-cut grass in the air which heralded the advent of summer. At the sound of her name, she stopped to look around. The hall was closing and a crowd of students was streaming out, excitedly chatting and comparing notes. She began to walk on when she felt a hand touch her shoulder.

"Liz!" a voice exclaimed.

She turned to see Tim smiling down at her. So he hadn't forgotten her after all! She felt her heart warm at the sight of him.

"How did you get on?" he asked, excitedly sweeping her into his arms and kissing her.

"All right, I think. I took your advice and wrote reams. And I tried to sound intelligent."

He smiled. "You'll be grand. Believe me. How have you been keeping?"

"Fine, thanks."

"I'm sorry I haven't been in touch. I've just been so damned busy."

"I understand," she said. "I've been busy too."

"I came specially to see you. Now that your exams are finished, let's go and celebrate. I've got something to tell you."

He took her to a little Italian restaurant behind Grafton Street where he immediately ordered a bottle of Chianti.

"You must be glad it's all over," he said as the waiter poured the glasses. "I'm sure you're exhausted."

"Never mind about me," she said. "What is it you want to tell me?"

"I've got very good news," he said, beaming at her from across the table.

"For God's sake, put me out of my misery. What is it?"

"The bank has agreed to advance me a loan. I wanted you to be the first to know."

"Oh Tim, that's wonderful."

She stood up and hugged him. This was marvellous news. It meant he could start his company. It meant the bank had faith in him.

While they ate, he told her how he had persuaded the manager to advance him £100,000 on the strength of his business plan. And he had even secured his first customer, an online travel company which had promised to buy his product provided he could convince them that it worked.

She found herself caught up in his wild enthusiasm. She knew nothing about business matters and was even a little frightened by the enormous risks he appeared to be taking. A hundred thousand pounds was an awful lot of money. But his sheer confidence carried her along.

"How do you propose to pay them back?" she asked.

"From the profits."

"And you're quite sure there will be profits?"

He laughed, heartily. "Of course there'll be profits. Banks aren't charities. They wouldn't have loaned me the money if they didn't think I was going to succeed."

"I'm so excited for you," she said, bubbling with excitement. "You've worked so hard. You deserve to succeed."

He refilled their glasses and proposed a toast.

"To Broderick Security Systems!"

"What's that?"

"My new company. I registered the name today."

Liz graduated in August with a good Honours degree. Everybody was pleased, especially her father who tried to claim some of the credit by saying it was all as a result of the close eye he had kept on her. She was relieved that her studies had finally come to an end. She'd had enough of university life. Now, all she had to do was find a job.

But this wasn't as easy as it sounded. During her four years at college she had barely given a thought to what she might do when she was finished. Unlike Tim, who knew exactly what he wanted, she had barely considered what sort of career she would pursue. She had been preoccupied with passing her exams and had foolishly assumed that once she had her degree, a job would miraculously materialise in some vague way. It was a foolish misapprehension.

Her first port of call was a recruitment agency where an efficient young woman sat her down and helped her fill out an application form.

"What sort of career are you looking for?" she asked.

"I'm not sure," Liz replied.

The woman gave her a strange look as if she had just stepped off a space ship.

"You must have some idea. What qualifications do you have?"

Liz told her proudly about her Honours History degree. But the woman didn't seem particularly impressed.

"Are you planning to be a teacher?"

"Oh, no," Liz replied. She knew she didn't have the stamina to stand in front of a class of students while she tried to get them worked up about the Cromwellian plantation.

"What about sales?"

"I wouldn't be able for the pressure," she said, hurriedly.

"Clerical? We have a number of positions in that field if you are interested."

Liz shook her head. She hadn't spent four years at university to sit behind a desk and push pieces of paper around all day. But she was rapidly coming to realise that her degree really didn't fit her for anything except perhaps teaching and that would mean further study.

"I thought you might be able to help me," she said, appealing to the efficient young woman. "What about a job in management?"

"You have no management training or experience. And those jobs are usually filled from within the existing staff."

They stared at each other for a few minutes while Liz's heart began to sink.

"You have a good general degree," the woman said at last. "But the reality is that you need to specialise with another qualification."

Liz tried to hide her disappointment. In the end, she left with a printed list of vacancies and spent the afternoon ringing them one by one till she finally got an interview for a position with a furniture store in Blanchardstown. It wasn't exactly the career she had envisaged and she was sure her father wouldn't be pleased. But even this small opening proved disappointing. Having spent ninety minutes getting there by bus she was interviewed by a plump man in a loud suit whose forehead dropped sweat throughout the entire meeting.

The job on offer involved selling dining tables. It would mean leaving her home at half six in the morning and getting back at eight o'clock at night. The wages would barely cover her bus fares and lunch. And to put the tin hat on it, the position was temporary and subject to a six-week probation period. Liz quickly thanked the man, said she would have to think carefully about it and beat a hasty retreat.

Meanwhile, Tim's business was going from strength to strength. He worked long and hard but he appeared to thrive on it and never seemed to get tired even when he managed only a few hours' sleep. By now, he had secured his first sale to the travel company and the success of the system he installed had roused the interest of other prospective customers. Before long, he had hired another young computer engineer and had managed to repay some of the bank loan.

When Liz told him of the difficulties she was experiencing in finding employment, he thought for a moment and then said: "I know what you'll do. Why don't you come and work with me?"

"Work with you?" she said in surprise.

"Why not? If you can stick being with me all day."

"But what would I do? I know absolutely nothing about computers."

"I'll find plenty for you to do," he said. "The company is expanding at such a rate I can hardly keep abreast. I need someone to take care of the business side of things while I concentrate on developing the software programmes."

"But – but," she stammered, "I have no experience of business."

"Look," he said. "You're a smart woman. You'll learn on your feet. You'll soon pick it up."

The proposal sounded marvellous. But she had one other doubt. "Are you sure you're not just doing me a favour?"

"Not at all. There's a real job to be done. And because I already know you so well, I won't waste time with a job interview." He smiled. "However, you can't claim special privileges just because we're romantically involved. I'll have to treat you exactly the same as Jeff."

"Who's Jeff?" she asked.

"My other employee."

He was right. There *was* a real job to be done and Liz was amazed how quickly she got to grips with it. With a little guidance from Tim, she was soon negotiating with customers, placing adverts, dealing with inquiries, wooing the media and managing the general day-to-day running of the business. She had never worked so hard in her life but she enjoyed every hectic minute. Working for Broderick Security Systems was a completely new learning experience. At the end of six months, she felt she would have no problem taking the helm at Ryanair. And being in the presence of Tim all day long was a wonderful bonus.

As the business expanded, Tim was forced to hire more staff just to keep up with the increasing demand. Within a short time, there were seven people crammed into the little office he rented above a newsagent's shop in Camden Street and Liz was asked to look for larger premises.

She spent a few days talking to estate agents and viewing office space until eventually she found the perfect place – a suite of offices in a new business park which was just being completed at the Financial Services Centre. It was large enough to accommodate the growing staff, it had all the most up-to-date equipment and it was smack in the centre of town. And if they were willing to take a two-year lease, the developers were prepared to let them have it at a reduced rent. Tim took time off from his busy schedule, had one look at the place and agreed. A few weeks later, Broderick Security Systems moved to their new swanky premises besides some of the biggest commercial names in the world. Tim said they had finally arrived.

One evening about eighteen months after she had gone to work for Broderick Security Systems, Tim took her to dinner. By now, he had succeeded in repaying the bank loan and the company was beginning to show healthy profits.

"I want to thank you for your support," he said when the desserts had been cleared away and they were sipping Tia Marias. "You've been absolutely bloody marvellous."

She found herself blushing. "That's very nice, Tim. But you did all the work. I only followed your instructions."

"You're too modest. I couldn't have done it without your encouragement. You had faith in me. When other people had doubts, you stood by me. And now that the company is established and doing well, I want to reward you. I'd like to make you a partner."

"A partner? Would that mean I'd have to invest some capital?"

An impish gleam had now entered his eyes. "Of course."

"But I've no money, Tim."

"I'm not talking about money," he said. "I'm talking about love and devotion. I want to make you a life partner. I'm asking you to marry me."

Liz's mouth fell open. His announcement had taken her completely by surprise. She had known for a long time that she was in love with Tim but they had never before discussed marriage. And with him working so hard, she wondered that he even had time to think about it.

"Well?" he asked, playfully. "Are you going to keep me waiting? What do you say to becoming the new Mrs Broderick?"

"Oh Tim, what do you think? There's no one else in the world I could possibly marry."

"You sound hesitant," he said.

"Not hesitant. But maybe we should wait a while. You're so busy right now. And when we are married I would want to spend more quality time with you."

"I've already thought about that," he said. "It may be under control."

"How do you mean?"

He lowered his voice and glanced around at the nearby tables.

"Just between you and me, I've had an approach from Bucon."

She put down her glass. Bucon was a giant American internet company, one of the biggest players in the industry. It was reputed to be worth billions of dollars.

"They want to take a share in the company. We would remain in place of course but much of the day-to-day running of the business would be taken out of our hands. It would allow me to concentrate fulltime on research."

"Are you going to accept?"

"It's a good offer. I'm certainly going to think about it very carefully."

"Oh Tim, that's wonderful news. No one deserves it more than you."

"Well, let's take one thing at a time, in order of importance. Now, are you going to marry me or not?"

The wedding was a small intimate affair attended by both families, some close friends and the staff of the company. Liz's father dropped any doubts he harboured once she assured him that Broderick Security Systems was doing well and she wasn't going to end up living in a tent in the Phoenix Park.

She had always dreamed of a grand wedding with three or four bridesmaids and yards of silks and satins but now that the occasion had arrived, she baulked at all the fuss and organisation involved. Her sister Anne acted as bridesmaid and an old school friend of Tim's was best man. They had a small reception at a local hotel and then it was off to Paris for a two-week honeymoon.

They had a wonderful time. The weather was glorious – blue skies and sunny days and a gentle breeze blowing up from the Seine to cool them as they wandered the streets of Paris locked in each other's arms. They slept late, breakfasted on chocolate croissants and spent their days visiting museums and galleries and taking trips to places like Versailles and Fontainebleau. When they got hungry they stopped at a little restaurant somewhere and ate from the menu du jour.

But in the evenings they really let their hair down. Tim insisted on booking a table at some elegant restaurant where they dined on oysters and lobster and tender, juicy steaks washed down with champagne and fine wines. When she complained about the expense, he brushed her objections aside.

"We've worked our backs off to make the company a success. Now let's spend a little bit of the profits."

After dinner, it was off to a jazz club in Montmartre where they danced to the early hours only to fall into bed for some passionate lovemaking before drifting off to sleep. Liz came to see a different Tim now that he was removed from the relentless pressure of work – someone carefree and relaxed. Since she had first met him, he had always been busy. But on the honeymoon he seemed to unwind far away from pressing deadlines and ringing phones and the hectic scramble of the office.

By now, they had decided to accept the offer from Bucon. It would mean a cash payment of over a million pounds and an annual salary of £150,000. They would be wealthy. While they strolled along the grand boulevards of Paris in the bright evening sunshine or sat over dinner on a quiet terrace under the shadow of the Eiffel Tower, Liz kept thinking how lucky they were. They were young, healthy, financially secure and they had each other. She couldn't help dreaming of the wonderful life that lay ahead.

Tim would be working at something he loved and she would see to it that he slowed down and spent more time with her. They would take up golf. Perhaps they would buy a boat and go sailing. They would go on foreign holidays just like this one, but to more exotic places. They would be able to travel first-class and stay in the best hotels. And when they had finished travelling they would start a family. They both wanted children and Liz was looking forward to motherhood. Sometimes she had to pinch herself just to make sure that all this good fortune was really happening to her.

As soon as they returned to Dublin, they set about finding

somewhere to live. Because of the Bucon offer, Tim was constantly tied up with accountants and lawyers while he negotiated the finer details of the deal. So he left the house-hunting to her. She recruited Cathy Burke who had already been through this with the purchase of her own house and knew the pitfalls to look out for. Together they began an exciting inspection of properties that led them from Malahide to Glasnevin and out to Sutton.

But within a matter of weeks, she had found exactly what she was looking for; a large detached house with extensive gardens in Clontarf. It had four bedrooms, two bathrooms and a wonderful living room with sliding doors leading out to a beautiful sunlit patio. It was perfect. The house was in a mature residential area close to her family home in Raheny and also within easy access of the city. And at £200,000, the asking price was exactly right.

Tim came to view it and was immediately convinced. The house was large enough to provide him with a study and office where he could work from home if necessary. And there were enough bedrooms for the family they planned to start. They put in their offer and it was quickly accepted. Then it took several more weeks for the legal work to be completed and the contracts signed. By the end of July, they had received the keys.

The house had recently been restored but now Liz had to furnish and decorate it. She decided to engage a firm of interior designers who spent another couple of weeks advising on colour schemes and furnishings. By the first week in August, the painters had moved out and the furniture had been installed. The following day, Tim drove them out to Clontarf, produced a bottle of champagne and two glasses from his briefcase and popped the cork.

"To our new home and our new life!" he said as he filled Liz's glass and kissed her gently on the cheek.

Now began the happiest period of her life. Every day seemed golden, every morning a bright new dawn of promise. She continued working for Broderick Security Systems for a few more months but once the Americans were in place they installed their own management team and she was content to leave. As part of the agreement, Tim continued to work on research and development. Liz had already mapped out an alternative lifestyle to occupy her free time. She held coffee mornings for her friends and gave dinner parties where the guests admired the décor of the house and complimented her on her recently acquired cooking skills.

She quickly found that she had plenty of things to keep herself occupied. She tended the garden, she ran the house, she organised their increasingly crowded social calendar. She was able to resume her interest in reading and joined the local library. And she also made sure that Tim didn't slip back into his bad old ways by arranging regular holiday breaks to the Algarve and Marbella and the south of France.

As part of her plan to get him to relax, she persuaded him to take up golf and they both enrolled for lessons. But he turned out to be a better player than she was so she dropped out while he began to spend his Sunday afternoons on the golf course with some old friends from college. But she had less success with sailing. A friend offered to take them out on his yacht from Howth but he picked a very bad day. They had barely proceeded beyond the harbour when a storm blew up and they all got drenched. Liz spent the rest of the trip being seasick as the boat bucked and heaved in the waves and she prayed that they wouldn't capsize. Once back in the warmth and comfort of the yacht club with a glass of brandy in his hand, Tim swore he would never leave dry land again unless it was on board an ocean liner.

By now, he had adopted a nine to five working schedule and took the weekends off. He left the house each morning at half past eight and returned punctually at six o'clock. Sometimes they had dinner out but often she prepared something light that they could eat together at the coffee table in front of the television. There were trips to the theatre and the cinema, visits to their families and the round of parties at the homes of their friends and colleagues. On other occasions, Liz would curl up on the settee with a good book while Tim wrestled with some research problem in the quiet of his study.

She confided to Cathy Burke that she couldn't imagine her life being any happier.

And then disaster struck.

It happened one bright Saturday morning. Tim left the house at eleven o'clock and set off with the dog for a walk along the seafront at Clontarf. It had become part of his regular Saturday ritual, something he looked forward to all week. It gave him an opportunity to get some exercise and always ended in a visit to the local pub where he studied *The Irish Times* over a quiet pint while Liz prepared lunch. She kissed him goodbye and waved him off. Later, she would thank God for that kiss.

Shortly after noon, she was chopping vegetables in the kitchen when she heard the phone ring. She wiped her hands on her apron and picked it up.

"Mrs Broderick?" she heard a sombre voice inquire.

"Yes," she said.

"This is the police," the voice continued. "There's been an accident."

Her first reaction was to wonder why the police were ringing her. Was it a neighbour? Did they want her to go and break the news?

"What kind of accident? Where?"

"It's your husband, Mrs Broderick. I'm afraid it isn't good."

She felt a cold tremor go shivering along her spine as the realisation sank in. She began to take off her apron.

"I'll come at once."

"No, just stay where you are. A car is on its way to pick you up."

When they got there, she found Tim lying on the side of the road where a small crowd had gathered. A car with its hazard lights flashing was parked several yards away on the footpath. Beside Tim, the dog was whimpering in distress.

A woman police officer cleared a path for her through the knot of onlookers. With her heart thumping in her breast, she approached the prone form of her husband. He looked as if he was sleeping, as if he had just stretched out to take a rest. But as she drew close she could see the blood coming from a wound on his forehead.

A doctor was examining him, feeling for his pulse, his head bent on Tim's chest listening for a heartbeat. He stood up as she drew near.

"Are you his wife?" he asked.

She looked into the doctor's face seeking for a sign of hope. She nodded. "Yes."

"I'm terribly sorry," the doctor said. "There's nothing I could do. I'm afraid he's gone."

After that, everything seemed to pass in a blur. She remembered an ambulance coming, its siren wailing to scatter the traffic in its path. The doors were opened and Tim was lifted inside. She got in beside him along with an attendant and a nurse who gently held her hand. At the hospital, she was asked if she wanted to contact a friend and she gave them Cathy's number and before she knew Cathy and Max had arrived and were leading her outside to their car and taking her home.

The next few days were a blank. She was pumped full of tranquillisers so that nothing was real. But bit by bit, she learnt what had happened. As Tim approached the pub, the dog managed to slip its leash and run into the road in front of an oncoming car. The driver had swerved to avoid the animal, mounted the pavement and struck Tim. Another few yards and he would have reached the safety of the pub. It was one of those utterly senseless accidents that should never have happened.

Then came the funeral. Liz was so traumatised by the suddenness of events that Tim's father and brother had to step in and make the arrangements. She stood by the grave and saw his coffin being lowered into the ground. She heard the hollow sound of the earth being shovelled on top. It was like watching a movie. Throughout the grim ordeal one question kept hammering in her brain: *Why did this have to happen to us when everything was going so well?*

After he was buried, she decided to go away. She needed to be on her own for a while so that she could think about her life and where it was taking her and what she was going to do. She booked into a small hotel in west Cork. It was crowded with people on holidays. Each day she walked the beach, speaking to no one, a lonely figure battling her grief among the jolly groups of laughing tourists.

But slowly she began to emerge from the nightmare that had overtaken her. She forced herself to think about the future. Tim's death was going to mean big changes to her life. She would have to sell the house. It was too big for a single person and besides, it would remind her too much of the happy times that were now gone forever. She would have to find something to do with her time. Maybe she would take a job. It would keep her busy. The discipline would be good for her.

Eventually, she returned to Dublin and began to put her plan into action. There was no difficulty selling the house. Property prices had soared since they bought it and she sold it easily for a handsome profit. She gave the dog to her sister and bought a smaller townhouse in the same area so she would be close to everyone.

She started looking for employment. Because of her experience with Broderick Security Systems she was able to find a position as office manager with a small printing company in town called Quick Print. It was a job she enjoyed and it introduced her to new people. And it kept her mind occupied while she struggled to come to terms with the terrible events that had wrecked her life.

She kept in touch with her friends, particularly Cathy Burke. Everyone was kind and sympathetic but it was amazing how quickly some people fell away. Death embarrassed them. She knew it carried an uncomfortable presence. People just didn't know how to deal with it. Beyond the stock responses, they were unsure what to say. And they had their own lives to live and their own day-to-day problems to battle with.

Now that she was busy she found that time passed quickly again. The days rolled into weeks and suddenly it was Christmas. It was a very painful period; the first Christmas she had spent without Tim for almost twelve years. She accepted her parents' invitation to spend the holiday with them but when it was over she was glad to return to her own home. The weather turned bad and the days grew cold and damp. Liz longed for some diversion, something to take her mind off the relentless cloud and rain and the terrible pain of loss that still tore at her heart.

It was Cathy's idea that she should join a club.

"It will be something to look forward to," she said, trying to sound positive. "And I'll come with you, if you like. We could join together."

But what sort of club? Liz had no interest in bridge or ballroom dancing or amateur dramatics. She was too young for bowls. She couldn't sing, so music was out. In fact the only thing that really interested her was reading. She had been reading all her life. It was one of the few things that continued to give her comfort. And then she happened to see the small neatly written notice announcing the formation of a book club as she made her way out of the delicatessen after buying her tub of hummus.

She hesitated and read it again. *New members required. Ring Marion*, it said. I wonder if I should apply, she thought. Maybe this is the thing I've been looking for? At least there would be no harm in taking down the details. She searched for a pen and a piece of paper and carefully wrote out the phone number. Satisfied, she put it away in her bag.

Then she set off into the dark night, back to her cold house and the quiet rooms and the inevitable grief and loneliness that waited her like a black pit.

Chapter Five

Matt Bollinger wasn't the type of person who was easily surprised. He was a man of the world and had seen a lot of things in his time so he always prided himself on his ability to take life in his stride. Once he won €20,000 on the lottery and didn't get round to claiming his prize till two days before the ticket expired. When people afterwards expressed amazement, Matt said he didn't understand what all the fuss was about. He'd got his money, hadn't he? And besides, he'd been busy with an important project at work. But all that changed when his wife of seventeen years told him one evening that she was leaving him for another man.

That really floored him. Mind you, the circumstances of the announcement had a lot to do with it. His wife, Anna, chose the occasion of their wedding anniversary to break the news. Long afterwards, he often wondered if she had done that deliberately to hurt him although she swore it was just coincidence. Matt never knew whether to believe her.

They had just finished a celebratory meal in the Pergola restaurant in Dawson Street and the waiter had served them two Irish coffees when she told him.

"I'm leaving you," she said. "I don't love you any more."

Matt blinked. Was he hearing things? "You're what?"

"Leaving you. I've made up my mind."

His first reaction was that this was Anna's idea of a joke although his wife had never been known for her sense of humour. There was absolutely no warning. They hadn't had an argument. There was no stress in the marriage that Matt was aware of. There were no debts, no excessive drinking, none of the problems that he had heard about in other people's marriages.

Everything was going along smoothly and then suddenly she made her announcement and practically the next minute she wanted to discuss the separation arrangements and how they were going to tell the kids. Matt felt like a man who is walking along quietly minding his own business when suddenly a building falls on top of him.

"Please tell me you're joking," he said, struggling to come to terms with the enormity of what he had just been told.

"No, Matt, I'm not. I'm deadly serious."

He stared at her across the table, his mind numb with shock. Was this really happening to him – Matt Bollinger – who had always been a good husband and father, who had never been unfaithful, who hadn't once since they were married, cast a flirtatious eye at another woman? Surely this couldn't be real?

"You don't really mean this, Anna," he managed to say.

"I do, Matt. I do mean it."

He sank his head in his hands. Matt always believed he had a perfect marriage. They both had good jobs. He was a marketing consultant and she was an advertising executive in a big Dublin agency, so money was never a problem. They lived in a nice four-bed detached house in Monkstown and had two lovely children – a boy and a girl called Peter and Rachel. They never fought, they shared the same friends and their sex life had always been satisfying. At least Matt thought so. So what on earth could have brought this on?

It occurred to him that it could be a phase Anna was going through, maybe the early onset of menopause. He knew it could do strange things to women, drive them half-crazy sometimes. But

Anna wasn't even forty and that was surely a bit early for a mid-life crisis.

"Look," he said, "let's not do anything hasty. We've got the children to think about."

"I know. We've got a lot of things to discuss. I thought it might be best if we went straight home and told them. They're old enough now."

"No," he said, quickly. "We have to be careful. We don't want to distress them."

He was trying desperately to remain calm even though he felt like a bomb had just exploded in his face. What was the best way to handle this catastrophe that had just landed in his lap?

"Let's take our time," he said. "Let's not rush things."

"I'm not rushing," she replied. "I've been thinking about this for months. Now, I just want to get it all sorted out."

"Well, it's too fast for me. You've shocked me. I had no idea you were unhappy."

"I'm sorry," his wife continued. "I don't want to hurt you. But I can't go on."

"Can't you give me a clue, for God's sake? Just tell me what I've been doing wrong."

"You haven't been doing anything wrong," she said, tears welling in her eyes.

Oh God, he thought, now the waterworks are going to start on top of everything else. I'm just not able for this.

"It's got nothing to do with you at all," she went on. "It's entirely my fault. I accept all the blame."

He quickly looked around the restaurant to see if anyone was listening. If she caused a scene he would just have to get up and leave.

"Look," he said, keeping his voice low, "let's not apportion blame. Have I been neglecting you?"

She vigorously shook her head. "You don't understand. I've met another man and I've fallen in love with him."

Matt gasped in amazement. Anna and another man! He felt like he had just been kicked in the face. He listened with mounting disbelief as she explained what had happened. The man she was in love with was an old boyfriend, someone she hadn't seen for years. But he had recently returned from London and accidentally bumped into her on the street one day. They had agreed to meet for a drink and matters had progressed from there.

"What's his name?" Matt demanded.

"Jack Arnold."

"How long have you been seeing him?"

"Ten months."

He felt like he was going to be sick. So this wasn't a sudden affair. It had been going on behind his back for almost a year. He tried to catch her eye but she avoided his gaze and he knew without being told that she had been sleeping with him. She lowered her head and he could suddenly see how beautiful she was and what he was going to lose.

"Give him up and stay with me. We'll forget this ever happened."

"I can't," she said. "I'm head over heels in love with him."

"I'll give you one thing," he said as the waiter approached with the bill. "You have an impeccable sense of occasion."

That night Matt stayed in the guest bedroom. It was first time he had slept apart from his wife in the seventeen years of their marriage. He barely slept as he lay in the darkened room turning things over in his head. It was incredible, Anna leaving him for another man. His one hope was that she would have changed her mind by the morning and they could get things back under control. Although he was sure they would never be the same again, not after what she had said.

But the following day brought no change of heart and no respite. He waited till the children had left the house and confronted his wife again.

"I was hoping you might have changed your mind," he said when they were alone together in the kitchen. "This is a very serious thing you're contemplating."

"Don't you think I've considered that?" she said, angrily. "Please don't make it harder for me than it already is."

Matt recoiled, feeling wounded. Now she was making him feel guilty for trying to save their marriage. He thought he knew Anna but now he couldn't figure her out at all.

"Just don't do anything for a week," he asked, finally. "Give things a chance to settle down. Can't you do that, at least?"

"All right," she said reluctantly. "One week and then I'm going."

Matt spent the next seven days trying to convince his wife that Jack Arnold was just an infatuation and in a few months' time she would be wondering what had come over her. It had happened to a colleague in work. Why cause all this pain and disruption for something that was just a nine-day wonder? Why put the children through the trauma of a parental break-up simply because she had met an old boyfriend at a time when she was feeling vulnerable?

But it was no use. Anna's mind was made up. He could see that pleading with her was not going to change her mind. In fact, it only seemed to strengthen her resolve to get out of the family home as quickly as possible. In the end, the best he could achieve was a commitment to stay for another few weeks while they sought marriage counselling.

The counselling sessions were held in a room at the social services centre. They trooped in and sat down at a table feeling very self-conscious. The sessions were conducted by a sympathetic middle-aged woman who began by asking them to discuss the problems they were experiencing in their marriage. She urged them to speak frankly, stressing that this was an entirely confidential service and everything that was said would remain in the room.

Matt and Anna stared at each other.

"Well?" the counsellor urged. "Who would like to go first?"

No one spoke.

"Who is looking for the separation?"

"I am," Anna said.

The counsellor smiled. At least she had got them to talk.

"Would you like to explain? Would you like to tell us what is causing your problems?"

Matt looked at Anna and she shook her head.

"What about you, Mr Bollinger? Would you like to tell us your side of the story?"

But suddenly Matt found that he couldn't speak either. Despite the counsellor's best efforts, neither of them could come up with anything that might explain what was happening. The counsellor talked about the need for understanding and tolerance. She urged them to think of the other person's requirements and not to be selfish. She said it was important always to be open and honest with each other and not to keep grievances bottled up. The woman was well intentioned but Matt found the whole experience embarrassing.

After attending several sessions together, they agreed that the counselling wasn't working. It wasn't the counsellor's fault. She was well meaning and she tried her best but something was missing. Perhaps it was that, deep down, Anna didn't want to be reconciled. In the end, Matt was forced to accept that it was just as his wife had said; she had drifted out of love with him and into love with Jack Arnold. She was going to leave and it was unlikely she would ever come back. And there was absolutely nothing he could do.

That's when he began to get angry. He couldn't help the wave of self-pity that engulfed him and the urge for revenge. What right had this Arnold guy to walk into his life and destroy it? If he wanted a woman why couldn't he find someone else? There had to be thousands of single women out there. Why did he have to pick Anna? Matt felt his anger mounting the more he thought about his situation. He had never done anything to harm Jack Arnold. He didn't even know the man. Yet Arnold thought nothing about stealing his wife and wrecking his home. Seventeen years of happy marriage and all the work that had gone into it were about to be flushed away to satisfy this man's capricious whim.

Thoughts of violence crossed his mind. Maybe Jack Arnold needed to be taught a sharp lesson. Matt knew about certain pubs in Dublin where you could arrange for someone to be given a serious beating for as little as €500, but he wouldn't delegate this work to some anonymous thug. This was something he would do himself. He would take care of Arnold on his own. He would enjoy the satisfaction he would get from watching the bastard suffer.

But eventually, he calmed down and reason prevailed. What good would come from beating up Jack Arnold? It wouldn't make Anna change her mind. It would probably just alienate her further. And there was the added danger of police involvement and court charges and all the attendant publicity. His thoughts of revenge began to cool. Matt realised that despite his anger, there was little he could do but accept the inevitable. If Anna wanted to leave, he couldn't stop her.

All this time, he had been desperate to keep the break-up from the children. But somehow they picked up that there was something wrong. They could sense the tension in the air. They could feel that the normal rhythm of the household had been disturbed. Peter was now seventeen and about to go to college to study communications and Rachel was fifteen and still at secondary school. Matt and Anna decided it was time to tell them what was happening.

It was a very painful experience. One Sunday afternoon, they sat awkwardly at the kitchen table after the lunch had been cleared away and he began to explain.

"Mum and I have decided to split up," he said, trying to be as light-hearted as possible. He wanted it to sound as if it was no big deal. "But we're still going to remain good friends. We've just kind of become incompatible."

He shrugged and glanced at the kids to see how they were taking it. They stared back at him with horror on their faces.

"Nobody is to blame," he said. "It's just one of those things that happen."

He glanced at Anna for support and she nodded her agreement. He was making it sound as if it was a simple disagreement over which television channel to watch.

"We don't want you guys worrying about it. Everything is going to work out all right."

He was interrupted by loud sobbing from Rachel who got up

quickly from the table and ran to her bedroom in tears. Peter stared sullenly at his mother. The meeting broke up without any real decisions being made.

Next came the settlement terms. Matt had been hoping they could come to an amicable arrangement and keep the matter out of the hands of lawyers. But unfortunately that was where it ended up because Jack Arnold popped up once more and insisted that everything should be put on a sound legal basis. He told Anna she had her entitlements and it was best if it was all above board. By this stage, Matt would have cheerfully murdered Jack Arnold. His resentment against him was hardening into bitterness. He had taken his wife and destroyed their happy family and now he was interfering in the separation. Who the hell did this guy think he was?

By now, Anna had moved her belongings out of the family home and was living full-time with Arnold. Rachel, who was torn between both parents, finally agreed to go with her mother and visit her father at weekends. Peter decided to stay with Matt. There began a lengthy series of meetings in solicitors' offices where sharp-suited lawyers dissected the marriage and haggled over terms. It was a nightmare. The dreadful business seemed to drag on forever and Matt found it harrowing and very costly. The legal bill alone came to almost €30,000.

The final settlement left him in possession of the family home. But he had to give his wife a sum equal to half its value and also pay the legal costs. And he assumed responsibility for the children's maintenance and education. To pay for it all, he had to remortgage the house and take out a loan from the bank. When it was all over, he found himself alone and practically penniless. Jack Arnold had waltzed into his life, taken his wife, broken up his family and left him almost bankrupt. And he was the innocent party. He felt like he had just been mugged.

But once Anna was gone and he was left alone with Peter, Matt began to pull himself together. He might feel hard done by but there was no advantage to be gained from basking in self-pity. Even though he had come through a bruising experience, he was determined to get his life together again. He was thirty-nine, he was still a young man and there was a great big world out there and a life still to be lived. But before he could do that, there were several bridges to be crossed.

After a few months, it became evident that the break-up was having a bad effect on the children. Peter barely spoke to his mother and refused even to meet Jack Arnold. Outwardly, Rachel appeared to take it all in her stride but soon they began to get reports from school that she was being unruly and disruptive in class. She fell behind in her studies. After six months, she had a blazing row with Arnold, told him she hated him and announced that she wanted to return to live with her father.

Contact between the parents was now confined to telephone discussions about Rachel and what to do about her. She was getting into deeper trouble at school and threatening to leave altogether. It was agreed that they should meet to discuss what to do. Jack Arnold insisted on accompanying Anna to the meeting. It was the first time the two men had met and Matt was amazed to discover that he wasn't the handsome man-about-town he had imagined; just a thin middle-aged stockbroker with a rather shifty look and an irritatingly arrogant manner. He couldn't help feeling disgusted that his wife could fall for such a creature.

The meeting was held in a local hotel. It was strictly formal and businesslike. After seventeen years of marriage, Matt and Anna could no longer talk to each other like ordinary human beings. Matt sensed that he was being blamed for Rachel's behaviour. They obviously thought he had influenced her against her mother. But he had no doubt where the fault lay. He was certain that Rachel's problems would vanish overnight if they were all living together again as a happy family.

Meanwhile, he was finding it difficult to keep his head above water. Money was always tight. He took on extra projects to earn commissions and did some independent consultancy work in his spare time. He sold the car and bought a cheaper model. He tried to economise on household bills but it wasn't easy with two young adults to feed and clothe and educate. But slowly, the financial pressures began to ease and Matt was able to breathe again.

Gradually, the children grew up and one by one they left home. Peter graduated and got a job as an information officer with a welfare charity. He met a young woman at work and they decided to rent a flat and move in together. Then Rachel, who was working as a children's nanny, announced that she was moving to London where there were more opportunities and a chance to gain greater experience. Matt was now on his own. But little did he know that big changes were about to occur in his life.

The first happened a few weeks later. He came into the office one morning to find a note from his boss, Jim Carville, inviting him to lunch. Carville's lunches were usually brainstorming sessions with the senior management team where they kicked about ideas over some rarely done steaks and few bottles of wine. But when Matt arrived at the restaurant, he was surprised to find he was the only one there.

"No one else coming?" he asked as he slipped into the seat beside his boss and shook out his napkin.

"Just you and me," Carville replied. "I wanted to speak to you alone."

"Oh?" Matt said, not sure whether this was good or bad.

"I've got a proposal to put to you," his boss continued. "But first, let me get you a drink."

He collared a waiter and briskly ordered two gin and tonics.

When the man had delivered the drinks and left, Carville leaned closer to Matt.

"What I'm about to say to you must go no further. Understood?"

"Of course," Matt replied, his interest aroused now.

"I've been approached by a large US multinational. A company called Atlanta Technologies. Ever heard of them?"

"Vaguely," Matt replied.

"They manufacture mobile phones. They're planning to start up here in Dublin. They are going to be big, Matt."

"Go on."

"They want to put in an Irish management team and they've invited me to come on board. They've told me I can pick my own people. I'm going to need a marketing manager and I immediately thought of you. Are you interested?"

"Tell me more," Matt said, pushing his gin and tonic aside.

Over the next half hour, Carville outlined the terms. It was a very generous offer. Matt would practically double his salary. In addition, there were share options, a productivity bonus, expense account, pension and health provision and a company car.

"This will mean a fresh challenge for you. New opportunities. You've been in a bit of a rut recently. This will lift you out of it. And you'd be perfect for the job. What do you say?"

"I'm certainly interested but I would like some time to think it over."

"Take a while. And remember, Matt. Whatever you decide to do, this is strictly between us. Nobody else must know."

"Sure," Matt replied. "That goes without saying."

Over the next few days, he thought hard about the offer. It was very tempting. Apart from the salary and the other benefits there was the challenge that Carville had mentioned. For some time, Matt had felt he was at a crossroads in his career. He had been with his present employers for nearly fifteen years. Maybe it was time to move on. And there was the fact that he had always got on well with Jim Carville. Together, they would be a good team. He decided to accept.

Six weeks later, he started with Atlanta Technologies as the newly installed Head of Marketing. From the beginning, he settled in comfortably. He continued to work closely with Jim Carville. He was given a large budget and allowed to develop his own strategies. There was a lot of work to be done in setting up the new division but it was exciting, creative work and Matt felt great satisfaction. Suddenly, there was a fresh spring in his step as he set off for work each morning.

But now that he was in the mood for change, there was something else that needed to be addressed. For some time, he had been thinking about the house in Monkstown. It was too big. With the children gone, the place felt cold and empty. There were far too many rooms for one person. It would make financial sense to sell it and find a smaller place. And the balance would enable him to pay off the outstanding bank loan. But where would he go?

He spent the next few weeks scouring the property supplements looking for something suitable. And then one day he saw an advert for new apartments that were being built in Smithfield. They sounded interesting. They were right in the centre of town so he would be close to work. Matt rang the developer and made an appointment to view.

The following Saturday afternoon, he drove into Smithfield and looked over the development. He liked what he saw. It was a gated complex and secure. It had nice gardens around a central square. The apartments were bright and airy and stocked with modern appliances. And the price was right. After studying the plans, he saw a smart two-bed unit that he liked. It would be ideal and the spare bedroom would come in handy if any of the children wanted to stay over. He decided to buy. He gave the keys of his house to an auctioneer and placed it on the market. It took six weeks to sell and Matt was more than happy with the price. In September, he moved into his new home.

At first, he found apartment living a big change and it took him a while to adjust. For one thing, he didn't know anybody and opportunities to meet his new neighbours were severely limited. Most of them seemed to keep strictly to themselves. But that didn't bother him too much. Matt valued his privacy and besides he had plenty of friends and colleagues from work. And there were advantages too. There were no gardening or maintenance jobs to do. The apartment was cosy and easy to keep clean. There were plenty of restaurants and bars nearby and a lively buzz of activity around the neighbourhood. He was right in the heart of the city and could walk to the office each day when the weather was fine.

And the children kept close. Most weekends, Peter and his girlfriend dropped by to see him and they would all go out for a meal together. Every couple of months, Rachel came over to stay for the weekend. The transfer to London appeared to have worked well for her. It seemed to Matt that she had shed much of her rebelliousness and was becoming more mature. And she had found a good job; something she enjoyed and which gave her responsibility.

Gradually, Matt discovered that he was settling into his new environment.

But there was one department of his life that still needed attention. After Anna had left, several friends suggested he should follow her example and get some romance back into his life. What was sauce for the goose was sauce for the gander. She had left him, why should he feel guilty about finding another partner?

But something held him back. He had just been badly burned and some instinct made him wary of getting involved again with another woman. How could he trust her? How could he be sure that the same thing wouldn't happen all over again? Besides, he felt the children had suffered enough trauma over Anna without him adding further disruption to their lives.

But with the children grown up and his new job and new apartment and money to jingle in his pocket, what was stopping him now? Every time he looked in the bathroom mirror, he told himself he saw a handsome man staring out. He was almost six feet tall. His dark hair had kept its sheen. He was forty-three years old but he looked young and he felt young and he was sure his rugged good looks would not let him down. After giving the matter some more consideration, he decided to take the plunge and hit the nightclubs.

He wasn't disappointed. Before long, he had a string of girlfriends, most of them younger than himself. Age didn't seem to matter. He had an easygoing charm which women seemed to find attractive. He felt like a youngster again going out to pubs and being invited to parties. He found himself in great demand as a dinner guest when a spare man was required. He began to realise that he had finally put the sad business of Anna behind him and was enjoying life to the full.

But none of these romances ever came to anything. Matt was still wary of commitment and now his standards had become quite rigorous. He knew exactly the sort of woman he wanted – someone good-looking of course but someone with a personality to go with it, someone intelligent, someone witty and compassionate, someone loving and caring, someone he could trust and rely on. He knew it was a tall order but he wasn't prepared to settle for second best. Matt enjoyed the company of women but none of the girlfriends he managed to acquire seemed to measure up - even though they were all nice women.

And then he began to notice a tall, willowy dark-haired woman around the apartment complex. He reckoned she was in her late twenties. She intrigued him. He would see her sometimes parking her car in the bay or waiting for the lift. He watched the way she walked, the swing of her hips, the tantalising green eyes and pleasant smile. The more he saw her, the more attractive she appeared. He made a mental note to find some excuse to speak to her, maybe invite her for a drink some evening.

But the opportunity never came and Matt began to wonder if it ever would. Until one dreary morning in January as he was trying to decide whether to walk to work or take the car, he ran into her on the stairway. He opened his mouth to say hello but before he could speak, she had already silenced him. She advanced towards him with a charming smile and a determined look in her sexy green eyes.

"Excuse me," she began. "My name is Marion Hunt. I live in number 65."

Matt hesitated for a split second. The suddenness of her approach had taken him completely by surprise. After weeks of seeking an opportunity to speak to her, she had taken the initiative and now she had thrown him off balance. But he quickly recovered.

"Matt Bollinger," he said and held out his hand. "I'm pleased to meet you."

"Bollinger?" she said, raising an eyebrow slightly. "As in . . ."

"The champagne. It's spelled exactly the same."

She clasped his hand and gave it a polite little shake. "How odd," she said with a smile.

"Odd? Why do you say that?"

"I've never met anyone called Bollinger before. I always assumed it was a trade name."

"Well there aren't very many of us around," Matt admitted. "But my family have been living in Dublin for generations. I believe there's a French connection somewhere in the family tree."

"Ah, that would explain it. Do you mind if I ask, Matt? Are you a reader by any chance?"

Matt hesitated. Had he completely misunderstood her? Was she really trying to sell him an encyclopaedia?

"Occasionally," he managed to say.

"That's good," Marion continued. "You see, I'm starting a book club. Would you be interested in joining? And maybe your wife?" she added.

"I don't have a wife," Matt said, quickly.

"Well, that doesn't matter. You can come along on your own. Look, I've got a little notice here that explains it all. Can I give you one?"

"Sure," he said and took the piece of paper she thrust into his hand.

"It's a way of passing these boring winter nights and hopefully having some lively discussion," she went on. "Have a think about it and if you're interested, give me a call. My number's right there on the notice. We'd be delighted to have you."

She smiled again and Matt could see close up that his first impressions hadn't been mistaken. She really was a very attractive woman with her rich dark hair and those fascinating green eyes. And here she was, presenting him with the chance he had long been hoping for.

"Thank you very much," he said, folding the paper away in his pocket. "A book club sounds like an interesting idea. I'll be in touch, Marion."

"Great! Have a nice day."

He proceeded down the stairs and into the hall. Outside, it had started to rain but this morning, Matt didn't mind. After his encounter with Marion Hunt he was in sparkling form. Instead of driving, he shook out his umbrella and decided to walk. He could do with the exercise.

Marion watched him go. What a fascinating man, she thought and quite handsome too. And what a very odd name but an exciting name nevertheless, an exotic name – one you weren't likely to forget, the same as the champagne. She should have known there'd be some French connection. The name carried a whiff of glamour and allure unlike her own surname – plain old boring Hunt. And he had definitely sounded interested in the book club. She was glad she had taken her courage in her hands and approached him.

But her reverie was interrupted when she reached the hall and saw the rain. It was coming down in sheets. She felt disgusted. She had seen enough rain recently to last her for a lifetime. It reinforced her determination to spend next January in the Canaries – even if it killed her. She stood for a moment trying to decide whether to take her car with all the attendant hassle of driving through the wet streets and then trying to find somewhere to park when she got to work.

There was a bus which passed the bottom of the road that would get her into work safe and dry in about twenty minutes. Provided it came on time. She had noticed recently that the buses were always late whenever the weather was bad. No doubt it was all these drivers deciding to bring the cars into town and tying up the traffic. She pitied anyone who lived in the far-flung suburbs like Clondalkin. They could be waiting for ages and getting soaked into the bargain.

She opened her umbrella and began to walk. Yes, she was glad she had approached Matt Bollinger. She had first noticed him one day just before Christmas, when he was bringing a load of groceries up in the lift. He had been on his own, just like this morning, and he had always been on his own and usually laden with groceries whenever she had seen him since. So she wasn't surprised to hear that there was no wife. A man who went shopping on his own was a dead giveaway and besides, she had never seen any sign of a female presence around the second floor where he got out. Marion noticed these things.

She wondered why there was no wife. Perhaps he was widowed or divorced. Or maybe he had never married, although he was attractive enough to find a partner without any difficulty if he wanted to. She thought of the firm set of his jaw and his strong manly face. It was the sort of face that inspired confidence, Marion thought as something else occurred to her. Maybe he was gay! You could never tell these days although she didn't think so. Maybe he was just another single man who had never settled down.

There were a lot of single people in The Cloisters which was one of the reasons she liked living there. She wasn't sure she'd be happy if the place was full of noisy families with screaming kids. But apartments didn't really suit families. They needed gardens and space. Mind you, single people could be noisy too. There was a guy on the eighth floor who held a party last weekend which went on till five o'clock in the morning and must have kept the whole block awake. And it was the third party in the past fortnight. That sort of behaviour really wasn't on. No doubt the residents' committee would be paying him a visit pretty soon.

Her mind drifted back to Matt Bollinger. So should she put him down as a possible for the book club? She desperately needed members if she was to get it off the ground. So far the response had been very disappointing. In fact it had been worse than disappointing. It had been dire. She had only managed to recruit one other person – her best friend Trish Moran who had only come on board to do Marion a favour and had warned that she wouldn't stay unless she managed to attract some interesting men.

Marion was at a loss to know what to do. She had stuck up her little hand-written notices all over the place in shops and supermarkets and libraries. She had even put one in the foyer of the church beside a notice for the Legion of Mary but someone had taken it down again. She must have put up more than thirty but so far she had not had a single response.

She consoled herself with the thought that it was so soon after the Christmas holiday. People were only getting back into their normal routines. Maybe in a week or two the phone would start ringing. She regretted that she hadn't asked the local free-sheet to give her a write-up. That would have got her a lot of publicity. If the notices didn't draw in members she might have to give the editor a ring. Otherwise, she'd be forced to drop the whole idea and join the waiting list for the book club over in Sandymount.

She made up her mind. If Matt Bollinger hadn't responded by

tomorrow, she'd go after him again. She'd wait for him on the stairs and pretend to bump into him, just like this morning. Sometimes you had to be ruthless in these matters. Matt Bollinger was too good a prospect to let him slip through her fingers.

Her thoughts turned to work. She had a busy morning ahead. Yesterday afternoon, her supervisor, Mr McDonald, had dumped about half a ton of files on her desk and asked her to check them. They would still be there waiting for her as soon as she got in, including one complaint from a principal in County Leitrim about a wild animal that was loose in the school grounds variously described as a mad dog or possibly a werewolf. As if! Although you never knew what went on in some of those remote parts of the country. But why was *she* being asked to deal with it? In Marion's opinion this was either a hoax or a clear case for the Department of Agriculture to handle.

She uttered a loud sigh. She was dying a painful death from boredom by a thousand cuts. Why hadn't she joined something interesting like the Department of Justice which never seemed to be out of the news? Or the Office of the Taoiseach. There was always plenty of excitement going on there! Why did it have to be slow suffocation the stuffy old Department of Education?

She was still wrapped in thought when she came to the bottom of the road just in time to see the bus for town pull away from the stop. She immediately checked her watch. It was only twenty-five past eight. The bloody bus was early! Damn it, she thought. It was going to be one of those days.

Chapter Six

Christy Grimes forgot all about the book club until the weekend when the family was gathered for Sunday lunch. Over the years, the lunch had become a tradition in the Grimes' household and Ellie had insisted on keeping it going despite her stroke. She hated fuss and change and wanted her life to continue as normally as possible. Maintaining the tradition of the Sunday lunch was one way of doing that. Besides, she loved to see the family gathered round the kitchen table with their smiling faces, chatting and catching up on the news. She eagerly looked forward to it. It was the highlight of her week. She often said it was better than any tonic and she seemed to draw strength and energy from the occasion.

Of course, she was no longer able to cook a big roast with all the trimmings the way she once did and nobody trusted Christy to do it without setting the kitchen on fire – a slur he bitterly resented. So it was agreed that the children would take it in turns to prepare the various dishes and bring them to Ellie's house and then they could simply be popped into the oven. On this Sunday, Jackie had cooked a vegetable lasagne from a recipe she had cut out of a magazine and Tina had prepared a salad with nice crispy lettuce and tomatoes and peppers. Fiona had brought a dessert she had picked up at the last minute in the

Centra store at the top of the street – low in sugar to comply with Ellie's diet sheet. Meanwhile Christopher had arrived with a brown-paper bag containing two litre bottles of Valpolicella wine.

"What's happened? Guinness gone on strike?" Christy demanded as his son opened the bag and placed the bottles on the table. He hadn't quite got the hang of drinking wine.

"I just thought wine was more suitable for the lunch, Da. Besides, we've got the women to think about."

"What's to stop them drinking Guinness?"

"Nothing, I suppose. But they seem to prefer wine."

Christy sniffed. "There was none of this palaver in my day. The only thing the women ever drank was a vodka and orange or a gin and tonic when they went out for a night. And I never heard any of them complaining. I suppose you'd better get the cork out of them bottles and pour me a glass before I die of thirst."

Meanwhile, Jackie's husband Anto was taking the lasagne out of its silver wrapping and fitting it into the oven.

"You can pour me some while you're at it," he said.

"Me too," Tina's husband Johnny added as he set the bowl of salad in the centre of the table.

"Would somebody make a point of bringing some cans of Guinness next week," Christy groaned as he thought of how quickly the wine was going to disappear.

Jackie was explaining the choice of lunch to her mother.

"We thought we'd go Italian for a change. This lasagne is nice and light. It's got no meat in it so you don't have to worry about your diet."

"You're very good," Ellie said. "Going to all that trouble. Sure, there was no need."

"It was no trouble," Jackie responded. "I enjoyed baking it. And it will get you into the mood for all the lovely food you're going to be eating as soon as you're well again."

"Yes," Tina joined in. "We've been talking and we've decided that the first thing you're going to do when you get better is take up that holiday in Sorrento. We're all going to chip in to pay for it."

"Oh there's no need to do that," Ellie said, quickly. "Sure we got a refund from the insurance because we couldn't go."

"You can use that as spending money," Fiona said. "It's our treat and we're insisting. So we don't want to hear another word."

Ellie looked out the window at the dark clouds scudding across the sky.

"Well, I hope the weather is better over there. The woman in the travel agent's said the sun shines all day long."

"You'll find out soon enough," Tina said. "Now tell us all how you're getting on."

"She's doing brilliant," Christy said, with a proud gleam in his eye. "Those physio sessions are working a treat. Aren't they, Ellie? And guess what? I'm thinking of entering her for next year's Dublin City marathon."

Anto forced a smile onto his face. Christy had been making the same joke for the past few weeks and it was starting to wear thin.

"You will and me foot," Ellie said, nudging him with her good elbow. But everyone could see that she was delighted by the praise.

"Maybe you will too," Christopher said, struggling with the corkscrew. "Remember that little speech you made when you came home from the hospital? You said you weren't going to let it beat you. Well, we're going to hold you to that."

"That's right," they all chorused. "We'll be watching you."

Christy smiled lovingly at his wife. "Dr Hynes said she's making great progress. Remarkable was the word he used. He said he's never seen anything like it."

"Well, let's all drink to that," Christopher said, finally extracting the cork and pouring wine into their glasses.

When the meal was ready, Jackie cut the lasagne into portions and Tina ladled the salad onto the plates and they all tucked in.

"Would you like me to cut up that food for you?" Christy asked Ellie.

"You'll do no such thing," she muttered. "I'm well able to do it for myself."

"Only asking," Christy said and turned his attention to his own plate. The others smiled. They admired their mother's independent spirit. In no time, the room was a buzz of conversation about work and gossip. Tina was telling them about the bargains she had picked up in Penneys sale. Meanwhile the men discussed football and Liverpool's chances in the Premiership.

Christy sat at his usual chair at the head of the table with Ellie beside him. He could feel the love and warmth that radiated around the room. It was a nice comfortable feeling. They were good kids. That's one sure thing he could say about Ellie: she had reared good children. And it was a very generous thing to offer to pay for another holiday. Maybe they were right and Ellie would soon be well enough to travel. If only that would happen, he would be the happiest man in Phibsboro.

By now, the conversation had shifted to finding a hobby for her.

"When the weather improves, do you think you might be able to take up the gardening again?" Fiona inquired. "Just light stuff, mind. I know how much you used to enjoy it."

"I asked Dr Hynes about that," her mother replied. "And he said I'd have to get a bit stronger before he'd allow me to do anything strenuous. Gardening is harder work than you think. There's all that bending and stretching."

"Do you not get bored?" Tina asked. "Especially now that the weather is so bad?"

"Not at all. I've got plenty to do with my physio and my exercises. And your father has promised to walk me to the shops in a few weeks time. And of course, I've got my books. Do you know, I'm reading six books a week now?"

At the mention of books, Christy, who had only been listening with half an ear, suddenly sat up.

"My God, I forgot," he said, smacking his hand against his forehead.

The others turned to stare at him.

"Forgot what?" Christopher asked.

"The book club."

"The what?"

"It was a notice I saw in the library. Some woman is starting a book club and she's looking for people to join. And I immediately thought of you," he said, turning to Ellie.

"That sounds like a brilliant idea," Jackie said.

"How does it work?" Anto wanted to know.

"I heard something on the radio about book clubs," Jackie continued. "They meet every couple of weeks and the people pick a book and then they all sit around and talk about it."

"Oh, no," Ellie said. "I'd never be able for that. Sure what would I know about books?"

"As much as anyone else and maybe more," Tina said. "Haven't you just told us you read six books a week?"

"But I only read them for my own enjoyment. I wouldn't be able to *talk* about them."

"Nonsense," Fiona put in. "Don't be putting yourself down. You're probably the best-read woman in the neighbourhood. And just think, it would be a perfect way to pass these long winter nights."

"Yes," Christy said. "And it would be a good opportunity to meet new people."

They all turned their attention on Ellie.

"Dad's right, you know," Tina said. "You should join. Sure if you don't like it, you don't have to go back."

"I don't know," Ellie said. "They could be a load of posh people and I mightn't fit in."

"Rubbish," Jackie said. "Sure you're as good as anyone. You could fit in anywhere."

"I'd have to think about it."

"What's there to think about?" Fiona said. "If you leave it too late, the club might be full up. Why don't you just ring up and tell her you'll join?"

Ellie struggled to make up her mind. In the end, she turned to Christy. "All right, I'll do it. But under one condition."

"What?" Christy asked.

"You come with me."

Christy looked like a man who had just been given electric shock treatment.

"But I know absolutely nothing about books. I haven't read a book in years."

"Well, maybe it's time you got started," Ellie said, with a twinkle in her eye.

Liz Broderick knew she was getting better when she recovered her sense of humour. She took it to be a positive sign. About eight months after Tim died she saw something on television that struck her as bizarre and she found herself breaking into a laugh. That surprised her. She couldn't remember laughing for a very long time, although when her husband was alive there was always laughter around the house. He'd had a lively sense of humour and such an easygoing personality that a smile was rarely from his lips. It was one of the many things she loved about him.

In the last week, her life had got extremely busy and Liz regarded that as another good thing. Her boss said it happened every January. People who had put printing jobs aside in the run-up to Christmas suddenly wanted them done in a hurry now the holiday was over. Yesterday, for instance, there had been a mini-crisis at work over a delivery of paper than hadn't arrived and Liz had spent hours trying to sort it out. Then this morning her car wouldn't start and she had to arrange for the garage to come and tow it away although thankfully it was only a minor job and they had it repaired in no time.

Then there was a dental appointment which she almost missed because of all the distraction. And now her house insurance was due for renewal and needed urgent attention. Her sister, Anne, had given her the name of a broker who she swore would get her a very good rate but she had lost the piece of paper where she had written it down. It was when she was searching for it in her handbag that she came upon a strange phone number that she didn't recognise.

She laid it on the kitchen table and stared at it. Where had she got it and why had she written it down? It might have been in Chinese for all the sense it made to her. The letters BC were scribbled next to it but that meant nothing to her. Who was BC? She hadn't met anyone recently with those initials. Was it the plumber she had been looking for? Or was it the man who fixed lawnmowers? Her mower was due for a service after lying in the garage all winter and she wanted to get the job done before spring arrived and everybody got the same idea.

And then she remembered. It was the scribbled letters that jogged her memory. BC! Book Club! She had taken down the information from the notice board on her way out of the delicatessen a week ago and stuck it in her handbag and then forgotten all about it.

She pushed the paper to one side and continued looking for the number she was seeking. This broker was red hot, Anne insisted and very efficient. He had managed to get her a quote that saved her €200. But now that Liz needed the information, she couldn't find it. Maybe she hadn't put it into her handbag after all.

She let out a loud groan. She would really have to get some order into her affairs. There had been a time when she was extremely well organised, when everything went into separate files marked Bills, Accounts, Tax, Bank Statements and so on. In the same way, all phone numbers and addresses went into her address book or her mobile directory. It meant that she could immediately lay her fingers on whatever she was seeking.

But since Tim's death she had become very scatterbrained, forgetting where she had left things and then having to turn the whole place upside down while she searched for them. Anne had commented on it more than once. And to think she was an office manager, for God's sake. She could keep the business of Quick Print ticking over like clockwork but she couldn't find a simple phone number for herself when she needed it. The irony of the situation wasn't lost on her.

After the funeral, she had made an appointment to speak with a bereavement counsellor. She hadn't wanted to go. She wanted to be left alone with her grief. But Cathy Burke had insisted. Cathy had a neighbour who had suffered a similar bereavement and counselling had worked for her. Reluctantly, Liz had gone to see the counsellor at her clinic in Rathmines. One of the things she told her was that sometimes the reaction to a death was delayed; particularly a sudden death. Sometimes it took months before the reality sank in. Afterwards, Liz had considered what the woman had said and wondered if it was happening to her. Maybe she still hadn't come to terms with the full meaning of Tim's loss.

She noticed it in small ways. Sometimes in the middle of a conversation she would refer to her husband in the present tense as if he was still alive. Occasionally, when she was doing a task around the house, she thought she could hear the sound of his car in the drive. There were times when she woke in the morning and turned towards him in the bed only to find that he wasn't there. And only last week, there had been that strange incident when she had found herself setting out two places at the dinner table before she realised that she was eating alone.

She knew what Cathy's reaction would be. She would tell her to pull herself together and get out and meet a nice man as if a nice man could wave a magic wand and make all her troubles disappear.

"It doesn't even have to be serious," Cathy had said. "I'm not suggesting you have to rush off and marry him. But the diversion of having a new man in your life will lift you out of yourself. I've seen it happen before. And believe me, a man on the scene works wonders for the morale."

"Why are you so sure that a man will solve anything?"

"It will perk you up. You need to move on, Liz."

"I don't think I'd have the energy for a new relationship."

"Oh c'mon, you're very attractive," Cathy coaxed. "You'd have no difficulty finding a suitable guy. You can't go around playing the grieving widow for the rest of your life."

But Liz wasn't convinced despite Cathy's persuasion. She knew she wasn't ready for this. Not yet. It didn't seem right with Tim barely cold in his grave. And how could she be certain that she wouldn't always be comparing the new man to her dead husband? No, she decided. Maybe she might consider a little romance further down the road. But definitely not now.

She poked around in her handbag but still couldn't find the broker's number. In desperation, she took the bag and emptied the entire contents on the table, then rummaged through the lipsticks and combs and compacts till at last she discovered the piece of paper she was looking for. She immediately rang him and ten minutes later had sorted out the insurance problem with a quote that was €250 cheaper than her present policy. At last, she had managed to do something right. She couldn't resist feeling a small glow of satisfaction.

She sat at the kitchen table and found a smile playing around her lips as the humour of the situation began to sink in. She really was turning into a desperate case. How did people put up with her, with her scattiness and her constant complaints? Cathy was right, she really would have to pull herself together.

She picked up the paper she had discarded earlier with the book club number. This was another of Cathy's bright ideas. She had told her to go out and join a club. She had even offered to come with her.

She stared at the paper. She *did* enjoy reading and she *would* be meeting new people. This book club might be the ideal solution. It would give her something to look forward to, especially now that the weather had turned cold and the nights were so dark. One thing was for sure, she would get more pleasure from the club that she did from pumping iron in that sweaty gym.

And there was an added bonus – it would stop Cathy nagging her about meeting an eligible man. There was little danger of bumping into any Casanovas at a book club. And who knows, she might even enjoy it. What the hell, she thought as the smile on her face turned into a laugh. I'll surprise them all.

She lifted the phone again and tapped in Marion's number.

Chapter Seven

The librarian paused to look over the top of her glasses at the young man who had just come in through the door. She had worked here for ten years and prided herself on knowing most of the regulars who used her library but this man was definitely not one of them. He was quite tall and rather handsome in a casual sort of way. Bohemian, she thought. That was the term to describe him. He was dressed in chinos and a casual shirt under a black leather jacket. But even though he wasn't a regular, there was something familiar about him. The librarian was certain she had seen his face before.

She watched him stop inside the door and glance around uncertainly. Where *had* she seen him? Was he a television presenter or maybe a minor pop-music celebrity? It bothered her that she couldn't place him. But she stopped staring and quickly lowered her head when he turned his gaze in her direction and began walking quickly towards her desk. The librarian pretended to be interested in some catalogues and didn't look up again till she heard his voice close to her ear.

"Excuse me," Nick began. "I wonder if you could help me?"

Immediately she raised her eyes and flashed her professional smile. This was the part of the job she most enjoyed, displaying her considerable knowledge of books and local affairs.

"Of course. What is it you wanted to know?"

Now that the young man was standing right before her, she could see that he really was very handsome with his dark hair and broody eyes and dreamy lashes. In fact, he looked exactly like Lord Byron. That was it, she decided. She knew where she had seen him before. On television. He must be an actor!

"I'm interested in joining a book club," Nick said. "I was wondering if you knew of one in the neighbourhood?"

A book club? No one had ever asked her about a book club before. The librarian, who never liked to admit ignorance about anything to do with reading, suddenly looked perplexed. Her face broke into an uneasy smile.

"I'm not sure," she said, slowly shaking her head.

"Is there a central register or something? Someone I could call? I've tried the Golden Pages but there's nothing there."

At that moment, the librarian's assistant, a smart young woman in tight-fitting trousers, happened to pass and overheard part of the conversation.

"Did you say you're looking for a book club?"

"That's right," Nick said, eagerly turning to her.

"Well I can't say if there's an established book club," the young woman continued. "But I do know that a lady came in recently who wanted to start one. She asked permission to put up a notice. I think it's still on the board."

Nick brightened up at once. "Where would I find it?"

"Out in the hall. You passed it on your way in."

"Thank you very much," he said. "That sounds exactly what I'm looking for."

Meanwhile, the librarian had continued to study him intently. Suddenly it dawned on her. Now she knew exactly who he was.

As he turned to go, she detained him.

"Forgive me," she said. "You're Nick Barry the poet, aren't you?"

Nick started to blush. It was a long time since anyone had recognised him. Please God, she wasn't going to start abusing him and calling him an impostor.

"Yes, I am," he said, looking her firmly in the eye.

Immediately the librarian assumed a triumphant smile. "I knew I recognised your face. The finest poet of your generation. That raw energetic style, those stark images."

She gazed at him with unrestrained admiration. "Are you still writing poetry?"

"Not really," Nick said, trying to cover his embarrassment.

"Oh you must keep it up. You have such an important gift. I read both your volumes and they were absolutely brilliant."

"Thank you," Nick said.

The librarian shyly produced a ballpoint pen. "May I ask a favour?"

"Of course."

Several people had also stopped and a small crowd was beginning to gather.

"Would you mind giving me your autograph?"

Outside in the hall, he found the notice he was looking for and quickly wrote down the name and telephone number. Now that he had obtained the information, he was anxious to get away as fast as possible. That incident with the librarian had unsettled him. He thought he had left all that poetry business behind and here it was surfacing again like a ghost from the past. Nick had too many unhappy memories of the abuse he had suffered at the hands of his critics. He knew how fickle the public was and how easily they could turn on you. With his errand completed, he hurried from the library and out to the busy street.

But at least the woman had been positive. In fact, she had been gushing in her praise for his work. It was obvious she was impressed. And librarians were cultured people who had good taste and judgment, not like the miserable vipers who had brought him down. Most of them wouldn't know a decent poem from a hole in the road. He felt a small glow of satisfaction at the thought that there were still people around who didn't regard him as a fake. There were people who saw the merit of his work. It was a nice thing to know. Maybe it was a good omen for this novel he was planning to write, he thought as he quickly headed away from the library.

Nevertheless, he would need to be careful. When he published his novel, he didn't want his old life coming back to haunt him. He didn't want all that inner city stuff being dragged up again to distract people's attention. It could be a deathblow. Nick wanted a fresh beginning. He wanted to forget the past. The last thing he needed was that old controversy to erupt all over again.

By now, he was itching to get started. If he had learnt anything from previous experience it was that a writer had to be disciplined. He had to sit down and write every day or else he would fall into a rut. And talking about your plans was the worst thing of all. He had seen what had happened to others. His old college editor, Trevor Arbuthnot was a classic example.

When he was running *Horizons* magazine, he was never done telling everyone that he was going to write the novel of the decade. He was forever boasting that his book would take the world by storm. He had even chosen the publishing house he was planning to honour with his manuscript. And where had it got him? Not very far. The last time Nick had seen him, Trevor was propping up a bar stool in McDaid's public house, half sozzled at two o'clock in the afternoon and still talking about the novel he was going to write. He had even managed to cadge €20 off Nick before he was able to escape.

There was no way Nick was going to fall into that trap. He was determined to be a success. He wanted his novel to be acclaimed. He wanted people to sit up and take notice. He wasn't doing it for the glory or the money, although that would come in handy. It was to prove he could do it. It was to shake off forever the memory of the cruel taunts he had endured from those people who had denounced him as a charlatan and a fake. Nick was determined to be vindicated and recognised as a real writer. He wanted to feel again the thrill he had enjoyed all those years ago when he stood on the stage of the school assembly hall and Mr Dunne had got him to read his prize-winning essay.

He wasn't going to waste time talking about his novel. He was going to sit down and write it. And he would keep it secret till it was finished. It might take a long time and there would probably be setbacks and disappointments along the way. So the fewer people who knew about it, the better. He didn't want people constantly asking him how he was getting on or demanding to read bits of it. He didn't want to spend his time making excuses and giving explanations. He just wanted to get on with his work in peace and quiet and when it was ready – then he would surprise them.

He still had some cash left over from the publication of his two poetry volumes, despite Mr Partridge's best efforts to claw it back after the Hugo de Lacy debacle. Mr Partridge had turned out to be something of a snake in the grass, threatening to sue Nick if he didn't return the advance he had received. But Nick had ignored all his threats and in the end Mr Partridge had gone away leaving him in possession of the money.

And thankfully, he had the good sense to invest it in his small house off the North Circular Road. It left him with only a tiny monthly mortgage to pay. Now he had a permanent roof over his head and with the income he earned from his newspaper job, there was no danger of starving to death.

The one person he missed was Arminta O'Shea. She had known exactly how to handle publishers and the media. She was an expert in navigating the rocks that could shipwreck the unwary writer. But the last time he had heard about her, she was living with Hugo de Lacy and trying desperately to promote his floundering career. It was a cruel pill for Nick to swallow after all that de Lacy had done to him.

He would miss Arminta's advice and her guiding hand but it was more than that. He would miss her company. He often wondered if perhaps he had been mildly in love with her. But she was now firmly part of the past and Nick was determined to make a fresh start. He shrugged as he walked away from the library and down the street. C'est la vie. Life goes on.

But keen as he was to start, Nick knew he had first to carry out his research. He had to join this book club and listen to the views of ordinary people. He fingered the piece of paper with the information he had taken down from the notice board. He hadn't a minute to waste. He would ring this Marion person immediately and enrol in her new club. The sooner he got started the better.

Matt Bollinger was in relaxed mood as he poured himself a glass of the fine Bordeaux he kept for special occasions. He had been given a case of the wine last year by a grateful client and every so often when he had something to celebrate he treated himself to a glass or two. And he had something to celebrate right now. He had settled into his apartment and the new job was going well although he was still working his butt off getting his marketing department off the ground. And the children were carving out new lives for themselves and seemed to be happy.

And now, without even trying, the attractive woman upstairs who he had been eyeing for the past few weeks had presented him with the perfect introduction. All in all, Matt felt he was entitled to treat himself to a nice glass of his special Bordeaux.

He took out the little notice she had given him and studied it again. Marion Hunt it said and her phone number. If he had set out to plan them, things could not have worked out better. And it had all happened without any effort on his part. Ms Hunt had actually invited him to ring her. He'd be crazy not to seize this opportunity and whatever else he might be, Matt knew he wasn't crazy. He took out his mobile phone and dialled the number.

He listened patiently as it rang for a moment and then he heard her voice announcing her name.

"Marion Hunt speaking."

Very proper, he thought. So many people these days just said hi and you didn't know whether you'd got Joe's Hamburger Joint or the City Morgue.

"It's Matt Bollinger," he announced in a strong, confident voice. "Your neighbour. We met on the stairs?"

"Hello, Matt."

"I'm calling about the book club?"

"Oh, yes," she said, her tone brightening perceptibly. "Have you decided to join?"

"Not quite," Matt said. "But I've been giving it some serious thought and I'm definitely interested."

"That's fantastic," he heard her say.

"However, I need some more information. There are one or two details I'm not clear about. I was wondering if we might sit down and have a chat some time?"

"Certainly. When would suit?"

"I'm free right now," Matt said, hopefully.

"Well then, why don't you just pop up to my apartment? I'd be delighted to answer any questions you might have."

"Give me twenty minutes."

"You know where I am? number 65."

"I'm sure I'll find it," Matt said with a light-hearted laugh as he put down the phone and finished his wine in one long gulp.

He rubbed his hands together in glee. It had been even easier than he imagined. Now he had got himself invited into her apartment. And it was only the second time they had talked. Well, he had better make the most of it, he thought as he headed for the bathroom to get ready.

First he stood under a hot shower and gave his body a thorough soaping and rinsing. When he had finished he stepped out of the tub and quickly towelled himself dry. Then he took out his razor and applied it to the stubble on his chin. He studied himself as he shaved. As usual, he was pleased with what he saw. Not a single grey hair on his fine dark head despite all the hassle he'd gone through over Anna. But that was all behind him now. His blue eyes had still retained their boyish sparkle and his skin was smooth and mercifully free of lines and wrinkles. He would easily pass for a man of thirty, he thought as he splashed some aftershave on his face. Well, if not thirty, then certainly thirty-five.

Washed and shaved, he went into the bedroom and opened the wardrobe. What was he going to wear? Something casual. This was an informal occasion. It wouldn't do to get overdressed. He selected a pair of navy blue slacks and pulled them on. Next, a dark sports shirt and over that a light sweater. He selected a pair of black casual shoes and slipped his feet into them. Dressed, he ran a comb through his hair and examined himself in the mirror on the wardrobe door.

He looked debonair. No, more than debonair, he looked dashing. He just wished he had a nice bouquet of flowers to present to her. That would really rock her on her heels. But it was much too early for that sort of thing. If he played his cards right, the time for flowers would come. Right now, he had to impress her with his interest in books and that wasn't going to be easy for Matt Bollinger hadn't read a book for ages. But he wasn't going to let a small detail like that get in his way. Matt strode confidently out of his apartment and bounded up the stairs to number 65 and pressed the buzzer.

Marion was waiting, dressed casually like himself in jeans and sweater and Matt noted favourably the way they emphasised her fine figure.

"Please come in," she smiled as she held the door open.

He slipped politely inside. The first thing that struck him was the décor. It was spectacular. The apartment was exactly the same as his but the difference was stark. Someone with good taste and stylish imagination had been at work on the decoration. Light pastel shades gave the sitting room a bright airy feel. Some well-chosen modern paintings hung from the walls and a couple of rugs gave the feeling of warmth. A huge vase of dried flowers sat before the fireplace. The Scandinavian furniture was a perfect complement.

"What a beautiful room," he said, stopping to gaze around.

"You like it?"

"I certainly do. It looks stunning."

He saw her give a modest little smile and immediately knew he had said the right thing. Complimenting a woman on her taste was a sure way of getting on her good side.

"Did you hire an interior decorator?"

"Are you joking? You know what those people charge. I did it myself."

"Really?" he said, turning to look at her.

"Yes."

"I'm amazed and extremely impressed. You have superb style."

"I had a little help," she conceded. "From my friend, Trish Moran. We did it between us."

"Well, you certainly did an excellent job," Matt said. "If you ever get tired of your day job you have another career waiting for you."

"That could happen sooner than you think," Marion replied and they both laughed.

"I was just out on the terrace getting a breath of air," she continued. "Why don't you join me?"

He followed her through the sliding doors and onto the terrace where a little wrought-iron table and chairs stood beside a large pot of geraniums. But it was the fantastic view that immediately caught his eye. It was like looking out on a giant Christmas tree. All over the city he could see the lights twinkling like stars.

They both stood looking at the view.

"This is magnificent," he said. "And it must look even better in the daytime. It's much better than mine. All I can see is the road and a little bit of the river."

Marion beamed. This Matt Bollinger was turning out to be a really nice man. He was saying the loveliest things.

"That's because I'm higher up," she said. "I chose this one specially. You see, I bought off the plans."

Matt shook his head, sadly.

"You beat me to it. By the time I got round to buying my place, all the best units were gone."

"It's always better to get in early," she replied, knowledgably. "Then you can have your pick."

"Maybe I'll take your advice the next time I'm buying," he said, with a playful smile as she turned away from the rail.

"So you want to hear more about the book club?"

"That's right. Basically, I'm quite interested."

"Good."

"But there are a few things I'd like to clear up. I'm very busy at work right now, so I don't have a lot of spare time."

"Do you mind if I ask? What do you do?"

"I'm in marketing. I work for a company called Atlanta Technologies. We make mobile phones."

She nodded approvingly.

"Yes. I can see that would keep you busy alright. Been there long?"

"A few months. We're still at the start-up stage."

"And things are frantic. I can understand."

"More than frantic. They're manic. But it will settle down eventually."

"Let's go back inside," she said, suddenly stepping off the terrace and back into the living room.

Matt followed her in and closed the door.

"It gets quite chilly out there at this time of year," she said. "Now, can I get you a glass of wine?"

A glass of wine and he was barely inside her apartment. Things were progressing very smoothly indeed, Matt thought.

"That would be nice."

She went off to the kitchen and came back with two glasses. They sat facing each other near the window.

"I may have given the wrong impression when I spoke to you earlier," she began.

"Yes?" Matt said, giving her his very best smile.

"This club is meant to be a fun thing. The way I see it, we would all sit around like this with a nice glass of something and just discuss a book we've read. We'd choose the book in advance of course. You'd have plenty of time to read it."

"That brings me to my second point. I enjoy reading but I wouldn't regard myself as a literary expert or anything like that."

"Good Lord," Marion said with a look of horror, "that's the very last thing we want. The book club isn't meant to be a heavyweight debating society. It's primarily a social thing really, a way of meeting people and passing these dreary nights. And the thing that would unite us all is our interest in books."

"And how often would we meet?"

"Well," she said, brushing a stray lock of ebony hair from her face, "I was thinking we might meet every couple of weeks. That should give everyone time to read the book we're going to discuss. And the meetings themselves shouldn't take up more than an hour or two."

"Well, that doesn't sound too onerous," Matt said. "Have you had a good response?"

"Very good," she said at once, with an enthusiastic gleam in her eye. "I've been inundated with enquiries."

"That's fantastic. So you reckon you'll get it launched, okay?"

"Absolutely!" she said with confidence. "It was a bit slow to start but that was because of the Christmas holidays. But in the last few days, it has taken off."

"I'm really pleased," Matt said, taking a sip of his wine. "What gave you the idea in the first place?"

Marion shrugged. "It was very simple really. I got a book as a Christmas present from one of my friends. And I enjoyed it so much that I wanted to talk about it. But when I started looking around for a book club, I couldn't find anything convenient. So I decided to start my own."

"That shows initiative. We could do with people like you in Atlanta Technologies."

"Oh, I don't know. I'm not sure I'd be able for all that hi-tech stuff."

"What do you do?"

"I'm a civil servant. Department of Education. I'm afraid it's all very humdrum compared with your hectic job."

"I'm sure you get plenty of excitement too," Matt said, reassuringly.

"Not really. I'm in greater danger of being bored to death, if the truth was told."

He glanced at his wine glass. It was nearly gone. He was enjoying himself and indeed could sit here all evening just listening to this attractive woman talk. But he must be careful not to overstay his welcome. Not on his very first visit.

He stood up. "Thanks for the wine and the chat."

"So will I put you down as a positive?" she asked, hopefully.

"Oh, I think so. You've done a superb job of convincing me."

Her face brightened at the news. "Well, I'm very pleased to hear that. I'm sure you're going to contribute a great deal to the book club, Matt."

"Let's hope so," he said, with a grin.

Her face broke into a warm smile. "You will. All right, then. I'll be in touch about the first meeting."

"Goodnight, Marion," he said as they parted at the door and he skipped lightly along the hall, barely able to believe his good fortune. They were getting along splendidly. Now all he had to do was sit back and wait for the first meeting of the book club.

Yes, Matt thought, all in all, it hadn't been a bad evening's work.

Chapter Eight

Marion gave the sitting room a last look-over. After weeks of planning, the night of the inaugural meeting had finally arrived and everything seemed to be in order. She had placed cushions on the settees, set out chairs, switched on the table lamps, turned up the central heating and placed little bowls of nuts for anyone who might be feeling peckish. She had a couple of nice bottles of wine chilling in the fridge and glasses at the ready on the sideboard. And for those who might prefer coffee or tea, she had a tray with cups and saucers and a plate of biscuits set aside in the kitchen.

This was the first night and it was imperative to launch the book club on a high note. The last thing she wanted was to be rushing around like a wild thing trying to find corkscrews and drip mats and getting completely tied up in knots. What sort of impression would that give at the very first meeting? People would think they'd enrolled in a lunatic asylum.

It was amazing the way everything had turned out in the end. At one stage, she had been seriously worried that she wouldn't get the club off the ground at all and would have to abandon the attempt. The initial response had been pathetic. It had been so bad that she had even contemplated going on the Joe Duffy show and appealing for members over the airwaves. The first evening she had spoken to Matt Bollinger she had been so desperate that she lied through her teeth to get him to join. He didn't know it, but Matt was only the second person she had managed to recruit after her friend Trish.

And then, it had suddenly started to snowball. Her phone hadn't stopped ringing with people responding to the notices she had stuck up around the neighbourhood. It had been a complete turnaround. By this morning, she had received more than a dozen inquiries and six firm acceptances. And everyone had sounded very enthusiastic. She now had enough people to form a solid nucleus that could be built on over time. Marion was confident that once the book club was established, word would spread and they would attract more members. But not too many. She had views on this subject. She didn't want the club to be crowded with people like a rowdy football match where everyone is shouting to be heard. That would be a recipe for disaster.

Thinking of Matt Bollinger gave her spirits a lift. She had enjoyed their little tête-à-tête over that glass of wine. There had been something present – a little touch of *je ne sais quoi* that had added a delicious frisson to their meeting. She wondered if he had noticed it too.

Her original instinct had proved correct. Matt had turned out to be a very interesting man, a man of discernment and judgment. She thought about the way he had admired the décor and the furnishings and complimented her on her good business sense in buying off-plans. He hadn't just said it to be polite. She could tell he really meant it. And that always gave her a contented feeling. Matt was one of the people who had made a firm commitment to come tonight despite his busy schedule and she appreciated that. She would go out of her way tonight to make him particularly welcome.

This afternoon, she had left work early so as to have everything prepared. She wanted no last-minute hiccoughs. This was an important meeting and it had to go smoothly. She wanted people to feel cosy and relaxed. After all, none of them had met each other before. Indeed the only people Marion had met were Matt and Trish who had emphasised once again that she was only coming as a favour and her continued presence could not be taken for granted. That would depend on who showed up and how the evening went. She was a busy woman with a heavy social schedule and she didn't want to waste her time if Marion's book club turned out to be a refuge for crushing bores.

"I don't think that's likely to be a problem," Marion had told her, emphatically. "I've managed to attract a good cross-section of people. And most of them sounded very interesting on the phone."

"Well, let's hope you're right. I've got better things to do than listen to someone regaling me with the gory details of their recent gall bladder operation."

"Don't worry. I'm sure that won't happen," Marion replied with just a little edge in her voice. Trish had been something of a disappointment. She hadn't given the book club the wholehearted support that Marion had expected. And she had been the inspiration for it in the first place with that book she had given her as a Christmas present.

Marion had given some serious thought to the club since the idea had first occurred to her and she had also engaged in a little research by ringing round existing clubs to find out how they operated. The people she had spoken to had all been very helpful with advice and tips but she quickly discovered that no two book clubs were exactly the same. Some met in people's homes while others used the local library. Some took themselves very seriously and went on for hours debating the finer points of literature which wouldn't suit Marion at all. Others were more like social gatherings for people to meet and have a friendly chat.

Her favoured option was to have the meetings in members' homes and for the venue to rotate so that the burden of organising the event would be shared equally. Not that she anticipated too much organising. She didn't want the club to become fussy and formal. What she envisaged was a glass or two of wine and a relaxed evening where people could unwind and have a civilised debate.

She had come to the conclusion that fifteen members was

probably the maximum that could be comfortably accommodated. Any more and the club would become unwieldy. Ideally, everyone should be able to talk about the chosen book and hopefully spark off a debate, a bit like a lively dinner party. If there were too many people all trying to get a word in, it would just descend into a scrum.

There would have to be some rules of course. For instance, how often should they meet? Marion felt once a fortnight would be reasonable. It encouraged continuity and gave ample time for even the slowest reader to finish a book. And there would have to be a limit on speaking time. You couldn't let people just ramble on forever otherwise someone with a strong personality might dominate the group and the evening would turn into a lecture rather than a discussion.

There was also the question of a membership fee. Some of the clubs she had investigated did this in order to defray expenses. Other clubs used the fee to buy copies of the book at a discount from one of the big booksellers so that people didn't have to go hunting all over the place to get a copy. The choice of books to discuss was another area to be decided. Should they draw up a list or would it be better if they simply picked a book at the end of each session?

These were the sort of issues that Marion felt should be decided at this, the first meeting of the club. Since it had been her idea to set it up, she had also decided to assume the role of chairperson and in preparation had drawn up a short agenda. A printed copy of this now rested on each chair.

She checked her watch. It was ten past seven. She had asked people to be here for seven thirty. That would give them sufficient time to introduce themselves before the serious business of the evening got under way around eight o'clock. Marion cast her eye over the room once more. She didn't seem to have forgotten anything. She decided to go into the kitchen and pour herself a glass of wine to help her unwind.

Apart from the nightmare at the beginning when she couldn't get any members, starting the club had been great fun. It was the first time Marion had ever undertaken anything like this but she had thoroughly enjoyed it. It had brought out organising skills she didn't know she possessed.

And in the middle of it all she had been startled to get a phone call from none other than her former acquaintance Alan McMillan. He had rung her at work one afternoon as she was using the office photocopier to print off the agenda and caught her completely off guard.

"I hear you've bought a new apartment," he said quite jauntily.

"Who is this?" Marion asked, not recognising his voice.

"It's Alan."

"Alan who?"

"McMillan, of course. Your old boyfriend."

She froze at the mention of the word. Alan McMillan! She hadn't heard from him for years. She had completely forgotten all about him. She didn't even know that he was still in Dublin. But why was he ringing and how did he get her number?

"I thought I'd touch base with you and see how you're getting on," he continued in a chirpy, confident tone as if they were still the best of friends. "I've finished my legal training and now I'm fully qualified."

"That's good," Marion said, trying to regain her composure.

"So how is the apartment working out? You didn't invite me to the housewarming party."

She caught her breath. How did he know so much about her, she thought? Who has he been talking to?

"It was restricted to my *friends*," she replied, laying great stress on the last word and hoping he would catch the obvious sarcasm in her remark. But if he did, he just let it pass over his head.

"I've been thinking about you quite a lot recently," he continued. "I thought we might have lunch some day. Just for old time's sake. I've got an awful lot to tell you. You know I've landed a very good job and I've bought a penthouse with wonderful views of the river. You should come and see it."

"I'm very happy for you but I've no desire to see your penthouse."

"Why not, Marion? You'd love it. In fact, instead of lunch, why don't I cook you a meal some evening? Just the pair of us? A nice candle-lit dinner? It would be very romantic."

Marion decided this conversation had gone on long enough. It was time to cut him short.

"I'm very busy," she replied.

"Oh c'mon," Alan coaxed. "I'm sure you could find the time. I'm working quite close to you now. I could pick you up."

"I don't eat dinner. Or lunch for that matter."

"Well, a cup of coffee, then. I miss you, Marion."

"I don't think that would be possible," she said. "I don't know where you got my number but please don't ring me again. I've got nothing to say to you."

She put down the phone so hard that she thought she had cracked the cradle.

The call had left her shaken. It was like hearing from a ghost. No! More like a vampire! And he had sounded so cocky with his talk of his good job and his fancy apartment. But she had one bad experience with Alan McMillan and there was no way she was letting him back into her life. She immediately banished him from her mind and proceeded with the work of organising the book club.

Now she poured a nice cool glass of wine and took it into the living room. From the window she could see the lights of the city, strung out like a necklace of stars. She loved standing here. It usually had a calming effect on her but tonight it didn't seem to be working. Indeed, she was beginning to feel quite jittery. She had put so much work into this meeting and she just hoped that nothing went wrong.

As she raised the wine to her lips, she heard the door buzzer sound to announce the first arrival. She immediately put down her glass and rushed to open the front door. She found the large figure of Trish Moran standing in the hall with a big smile on her face and a bunch of daffodils in her hand.

"I brought these to wish you good luck. They should help to brighten up the flat. Not that it really needs brightening up," Trish added hastily, just to be diplomatic.

"Come in," Marion said, pleased to see her friend. A bit of moral support would be very welcome just now. "The flowers are beautiful. Bit early for daffodils isn't it?"

"I think they come from Holland. They grow them in glasshouses. Are you all excited?" She held Marion by the shoulders and gazed into her eyes.

"Just a little. But I've got to remain calm. I haven't met most of these people and I don't want them getting the impression that they're dealing with a headless chicken. It might put them off."

"Rubbish!" Trish said, dismissively. "You'll carry it off brilliantly. Now tell me exactly who is coming. I hope you've got lots of nice men. You know what I keep telling you."

"Indeed I do. You're beginning to sound like a broken record."

"Well isn't that the whole object of the exercise? To find you a suitable partner?"

"It most certainly is not," Marion retorted with some vehemence. "The object is to discuss books. There's the list," she added, giving Trish a sheet of paper. "Just let me put the flowers away and get you a glass of plonk."

When she returned from the kitchen, Trish had settled herself on the settee and was studying the list of people who had promised to attend.

"Liz Broderick?"

"I'm afraid I don't know very much about her." Marion confessed. "She rang me at a bad moment and I didn't have time to talk. I was barely able to give her the address and the time. But she did promise to turn up."

"Christy and Ellie Grimes?"

"They're a retired couple," Marion explained. "Christy rang to say his wife has recently had a stroke."

"Good lord!"

"But she's making a very good recovery. And apparently she's a voracious reader. She gets through three or four books a week."

"Well, she sounds promising. Now let me see. Who else have you netted? Nick Barry? Matt Bollinger? Isn't that a brand of champagne?"

"Matt is my neighbour," Marion explained, feeling the warm

glow return. "I think you'll like him. He's extremely charming and I've a suspicion that he might be a widower. At least, he told me he didn't have a wife."

"What does he do for a living?"

"He's in marketing. A big multinational company called Atlanta Technologies."

"Is he sufficiently charming to engage your interest?" Trish playfully inquired.

Marion found herself blushing. How could that witch Trish read her mind? Did she possess a sixth sense?

"I'll let you decide for yourself," she smiled. "But I would remind you again that the primary purpose of this club is literary discussion."

Trish laughed. "That doesn't rule out a little romance. Now what about this Nick Barry person? Who is he?"

"I'm not sure. But he sounded very keen. Said he wanted to join for some research he was conducting."

"Research? He's not a serial killer looking for victims, I hope?"

Marion forced herself to smile. "If he is, he didn't confide in me about it."

Trish put down the list. "You haven't attracted an awful lot of people, have you?"

This was the last thing Marion needed to hear. After all her hard work, surely Trish wasn't going to put a damper on everything?

"It's only the first meeting. And I expect the membership will grow once we get established," she said, defensively.

"Hmphhh! It might also shrink. I'm not sure if I'm going to hang around."

"I did my best," Marion protested, beginning to feel downcast. "I've no control over who responds. I can't go out and just pull people out of their cars."

Trish immediately wrapped her arms around her. "I'm only teasing. It's going to be a roaring success. If you like I could bring Seán along to boost the numbers."

"But he works nights, doesn't he?"

"I'm sure he could get away," Trish said. "Now listen. You just relax and think positive. I've no doubt when word gets around you'll be beating people away with a big stick."

At that moment, the buzzer sounded again. Marion put down her glass and jumped up once more.

"Here's the first one," she said, straightening her dress. "Do I look okay?"

"You look smashing," Trish said. "This is a book club, remember. Not a catwalk. Now just go out there and put on your most winning smile."

A few minutes later she was back with a middle-aged couple. The woman looked like a small sparrow but she advanced determinedly into the room with the aid of a walking frame. Her husband was a thin man with silver hair and he supported her by holding her left elbow. Trish calculated that they were in their late fifties.

"Make yourself comfortable, Mrs Grimes," Marion said. "This is my friend, Trish Moran."

"Delighted to meet you," Trish said, standing up and helping the woman onto the settee.

"Call me Ellie," she said. "This is my husband, Christy."

They all shook hands.

"Would you like a cushion for your back?" Trish asked, politely.

"I think I'll be all right," Ellie said, settling down on the settee.

"Can I get you a glass of wine?" Marion inquired.

"That would be nice," Ellie replied.

"And what about you, Mr Grimes?"

"You wouldn't have a bottle of Guinness by any chance?" Christy asked.

"I don't think so," Marion said, suddenly looking perplexed. She thought she had covered everything but it hadn't occurred to her that any of the guests might be looking for beer.

Ellie gave her husband a sharp dig in the ribs with her good elbow. "He's acting the goat, as usual. A glass of wine will do him fine."

Marion went off again to the kitchen and Trish engaged the couple in conversation.

"I'm told you're a fantastic reader," she said to Ellie.

"She's read nearly every book in the library," Christy interjected before Ellie had a chance to reply.

"Don't mind him," Ellie said. "He's always exaggerating."

"No, I'm not," Christy said, proudly. "She just doesn't want people to know. But she can get through a book in a day. She's read every single one of Charles Dickens's books, including the one he was writing when he died. He never finished it, you know."

"*The Mystery of Edwin Drood*," Ellie said. "I just read it out of curiosity."

Trish raised her eyebrows. "I'm very impressed. That's certainly better than I ever managed."

"She loves reading," Christy went on. "And then she had her stroke about eighteen months ago. But she didn't let it put her off her stride. Dr Hynes says he's never seen a person recover so fast. Remarkable was the word he used."

Ellie smiled shyly. "There's no point lying down under it," she said. "And it was only a small stroke, anyway. It wasn't serious."

"It certainly was," Christy said. "Sure you were in hospital for six weeks. And everybody knows they don't keep you in hospital nowadays unless there's something really wrong with you."

"Well, I think you're very brave," Trish said. "And you've got the right spirit. Sometimes people in your situation just go to pieces."

At that moment, Marion came back with two glasses of wine and just then the buzzer sounded again. She glanced at her watch. It was twenty past seven. She was glad to see that so far the attendance had been punctual.

She returned with an attractive, blond-haired woman in a warm coat and boots. Marion took her coat as she made the introductions.

"This is Liz Broderick. Ellie and Christy Grimes and Trish Moran."

"I hope I'm not late," Liz apologised. "I drove straight from work and I wasn't quite sure where I was going."

"You're in perfect time," Marion said soothingly. "Now why don't you just take a seat while I get you a glass of wine?"

Liz sat down on a chair beside the settee.

"What kind of work do you do, Liz?" Ellie inquired, politely.

"I'm an office manager. With a printing firm."

"That sounds like an interesting job," Christy said.

"Well, it can get quite frantic at times," Liz admitted. "But I like it when it's busy."

"Have you worked there long?"

"Only a few months. I took it up after my husband died. I needed something to keep myself occupied."

"I'm sorry to hear that," Trish said, sadly. "What happened to him?"

Liz lowered her eyes. "He was killed in a traffic accident. He was out walking the dog one morning when a car mounted the pavement and hit him."

Everyone's face fell. For a moment there was an embarrassed silence.

"My God," Ellie said. "That must have been an awful shock for you."

"It was. And to tell the truth, I haven't really got over it."

"I'm sure you haven't," Ellie said. "Something like that would put the heart across you."

She looked up as Marion returned with a glass of wine for Liz.

"Anyone want a top-up?"

Marion waved the bottle and Trish held out her glass while she poured.

Christy quickly put his hands over his own glass.

"Not for me," he said.

"Me neither," Ellie said. "Are you expecting many people tonight?"

"Just two more," Marion explained. She glanced quickly at Trish. "I thought I'd keep it small to begin with. We don't want a mob of people at the first meeting."

"You're dead right," Christy said. "There wouldn't be room for them, anyway."

"But I've no doubt it will grow," Marion hastened to add. "That's one of the things I was hoping we could discuss tonight."

"You've a lovely home," Ellie said, glancing round the room. Marion smiled.

"Do you think so?"

"I do indeed. I think it's beautiful. It must have cost you a fortune."

"Well, it wasn't cheap," Marion replied. "But it's nice and cosy. And it suits me fine."

The buzzer sounded once more.

"Excuse me," she said. "There's someone else."

She came back with two men in tow. Trish let her eye travel over them as they entered the room. The older one was smartly dressed in a white linen suit and had a confident air of self-assurance. She guessed at once that this must be Matt Bollinger, Marion's neighbour. The other man was younger with broody dark eyes. Presumably, this was Nick Barry. Full marks to Marion, Trish thought with approval. Both of them looked quite dishy.

She had guessed correctly. Marion drew the newcomers into the room and made the introductions, smiling all the while at Matt Bollinger. Everyone shook hands and then the men sat down while Marion went off to get more wine.

When she returned, she glanced at her watch. It was now twenty-five to eight. Thank God, they had all arrived on time and everything was going according to plan. She left them to chat for a few more minutes before deciding it was time to begin. She walked to the window where she had a commanding view of the room. She took a deep breath, cleared her throat and commenced the little speech she had already rehearsed.

"Have you all been introduced to each other?" she began.

"Yes," Nick Barry responded.

"Good. Well, if everyone is seated comfortably, I'll like to start the ball rolling. First of all let me welcome you to the inaugural meeting of our book club. You will find an agenda on your seats and you will see that we have a lot of business to get through tonight. So if everyone is in agreement, I think we should begin."

At that moment, there was the loud sound of the buzzer going again. Marion stopped in the middle of her speech. Good Lord, she thought. Who on earth can this be? I'm not expecting anyone else. And I'm just about to open my introduction. Talk about bad timing!

She paused and looked around the room at the sea of silent, expectant faces.

"Would you excuse me for just a moment," she smiled and went off to answer the door.

She pulled it open and immediately felt her heart jump into her mouth.

Alan McMillan was standing in the hallway.

Marion gasped. Even though it was a long time since she had seen him, she recognised Alan McMillan at once. His hairline had receded slightly and his face had filled out and his eyes seemed more intense but otherwise he had barely changed at all. He was exactly as she remembered him, right down to the smug smile on his preening face. But he was the very last person she expected to find standing at her front door on the first night of her club.

"What do *you* want?" she managed to splutter.

"I've come to join the book club," he explained, shifting energetically from one foot to the other and beaming confidently at her.

"The book club?"

Marion could hardly believe her ears.

"Yes. I saw your advert and recognised the telephone number. And since I'm very interested in literature, I decided to come along. So here I am."

She felt a wild panic grip her.

"You can't join," she said, quickly.

"Why not? Your advert said you were looking for new members."

"The membership is full."

She went to close the door but he stuck his foot in the jamb.

"Don't be silly, Marion. You're behaving like a child."

"Please go away," she said, firmly. "You're not wanted here."

"That business with your flatmate, Julie. You never gave me a chance to explain."

"I don't want to hear your explanations. It was over a long time ago as far as I'm concerned. Now please go away."

"If you close that door, I'll only ring the buzzer again," he warned. "I'm prepared to stand here all night."

Marion shut her eyes. Why is this happening to me, she thought? Why tonight of all nights had Alan McMillan come back to plague her? Behind her in the sitting room, she could hear a buzz of conversation breaking out. People would be wondering what was going on. Damn Alan McMillan. I wish I'd never set eyes on him.

She quickly made up her mind. She couldn't stand here all evening arguing. She had no option but to let him in before he started a commotion. She opened the door wide.

"Come in," she said. "But the first sign of trouble and I'm calling the police to eject you."

"There'll be no trouble, Marion. Honest," he promised, smiling broadly and stepping briskly across the doorway and into the apartment.

Once back in the sitting room, all heads turned to look at the new arrival. Trish gave Marion a mystified glance. She shrugged in response and led Alan to a spare chair and grudgingly stuck an agenda into his hand. Even though everyone else in the room had a glass of wine, she pointedly refused to offer him one.

"Ladies and gentlemen, we have a late arrival. Mr Alan McMillan has decided to join us."

She made another quick round of introductions and finally resumed where she had left off before the interruption. She glanced at her watch and saw that it was now almost eight o'clock. A quarter of an hour wasted on this idiot!

"I was about to say earlier that because this is the inaugural meeting of the club, we have a number of ground rules which should be laid down. But first I think a brief explanation is required for those of you who may not be familiar with the book club concept. The idea is that we will meet at regular intervals to discuss a book that has been decided in advance. Any type of book will be acceptable so long as it meets with the agreement of the members.

And just to make it clear: this is not a university course, so you don't have to be an expert on world literature."

"Thank God for that," someone muttered.

She thought it might have been Nick Barry again. She gave the room a reassuring smile and continued.

"Now, you should all have a copy of the agenda. The first item is the frequency of meetings. Does anyone have any suggestions?"

Her announcement was followed by silence and then Nick put up his hand.

"How about holding them every week?"

Immediately, Trish intervened.

"I think once a week is too often," she said. "Some of us are very slow readers."

There was laughter around the room and then Liz Broderick put up her hand.

"Would once a month be better?"

There was some brief discussion and then someone suggested meeting once every three weeks. Marion would have preferred once a fortnight but she had to be careful not to appear to dictate the agenda.

"Is that a firm proposal?" she asked.

"Yes."

"All right. Once every three weeks. Can we have a show of hands?"

Everyone's hand went up except Nick's.

"That's clearly carried," Marion said. "Now, the next item is venue. Does anyone have a proposal?"

"We could meet in the library," Christy Grimes said. "There's a big room at the back that they use for functions. I'm sure the librarian would let us have it, if we asked."

Marion didn't want to hold the meetings in the library. It would mean ceding some control to an outside agency and besides the times didn't suit.

"That's one option," she said, "but one of the problems with it is that the library closes at eight thirty so we would have to start early and finish in a rush. Are there any other suggestions?"

Matt slowly put up his hand. "Would it be a good idea to meet like this in someone's home? I think it's much more relaxed than the library. I have an apartment in this block and I wouldn't mind holding the meetings there."

"Thank you, Matt. That's a very generous offer."

Marion gave him her best smile. He really was a lovely man and his suggestion was edging closer to what she preferred.

"We could hold the meetings at my place from time to time," Liz said. "It would take some of the pressure off Matt."

"I don't really mind," Matt conceded, gallantly. "There really wouldn't be any pressure. I live on my own."

"That's two kind offers we have," Marion said. "Would anyone object if we rotated the meetings round all the members' homes? Perhaps, that would be the fairest way to do it."

She looked at the faces but no one stirred.

"No?" she said. "Nobody thinks that's a good idea?"

"I do," a voice piped up. Marion spun her gaze to see Alan McMillan's eager face. "I think it's a wonderful idea. I'd be delighted to host a meeting in my home."

She gave him a withering look. She didn't want Alan McMillan's support, even if it was helpful.

"Shall I put it to a vote?" she asked.

This time, all the hands went up.

"Good," she said. "We're really racing through the agenda. Now the next thing we have to decide is the membership. Does anyone have any views about how big the club should be?"

Ellie spoke. "I don't think it should be too big. Otherwise people wouldn't get a chance to talk and everybody would be speaking at the same time and cutting across each other."

"Good point," Alan said.

Marion glanced at him once more. He seemed to have settled into the meeting extremely well especially since he shouldn't have been here at all.

"I disagree," a voice said. It was Nick Barry again. "The more people we have the better, as far as I'm concerned. It means a wider exchange of views and a bigger cross-section of opinion. And that is what I am hoping to hear."

Marion could see that Nick could be trouble. He had an independent streak. This was the second time he had crossed her.

"Do you have a proposal?" she asked, sweetly.

"How about fifty?"

At this suggestion, Christy gave a snort. "Fifty? Why don't you make it a hundred? Then it would be like Croke Park on a Sunday afternoon. Sure, you'd never get a word in edgeways."

"Has anyone else got anything to say?" Marion prompted.

Matt was leaning forward again. "I'm with Christy on this, although Nick does have a fair point. But we have to be realistic. If we had fifty people all trying to talk at the same time, it would be chaotic."

"Hear, hear," Liz agreed. "I think the membership should be smaller. It would also be more comfortable."

"Would you care to make a suggestion?" Marion urged.

"Fifteen?" Liz said.

"Anyone else?"

"Twenty," Nick put in.

"I think we're going to need a show of hands," Marion said. "Those in favour of Nick's proposal, please show."

Only Nick's hand went up.

"Those in favour of Liz's proposal that we limit the membership to fifteen?"

This time, all the hands but Nick's went up.

Marion smiled. "Fifteen it is. Now the question of membership fees."

From then on, the meeting proceeded at a brisk pace. By half past nine most of the items on the agenda had been covered. It had been agreed that the next meeting would be held in three weeks' time and the book to be discussed would be Daphne du Maurier's novel *Rebecca*.

"There shouldn't be any difficulty getting hold of it," Marion said. "The library will have it. And of course, if anyone wants to buy their own copy, it should be available in most good bookshops."

As the evening progressed, she was pleased to see the initial

127

stiffness go out of the meeting and people become more relaxed. She felt relieved. The guests were now chatting freely with each other, saying what a wonderful idea it was to start the club and how much they were looking forward to the discussions. Even rebellious Nick Barry had given up being contrary and was now talking animatedly to Matt. She was privately delighted that everything had gone exactly as she had planned.

"There's just one final item," she said as the meeting prepared to break up. "We're going to require a secretary. Someone who will keep in touch with the members and make sure that everything runs smoothly. It would be a sort of co-ordinating role."

This was an important job and Marion wanted it for herself. It would mean she could keep an eye on things, which was only fair since it had been her idea to start the club in the first place. And it shouldn't involve too much work.

But she had to allow the suggestion to come from the members themselves. She didn't want people thinking she was some kind of bossy dictator who imposed her will on everyone. She had already discussed the matter with Trish who had agreed to put her name forward.

She smiled serenely at the group, some of whom were now standing up and preparing to leave.

"Do we have any volunteers for the job of secretary?"

There was silence for a moment while Marion glanced frantically at Trish only to find her in conversation with Ellie. She signalled fiercely to catch her attention but before she could respond, another voice chipped in.

"I'll do it."

"I'll second you," someone said and suddenly all the hands in the room shot up.

"Elected," somebody said.

Marion felt the smile slowly vanish from her face.

Alan McMillan had just been elected secretary and was now smiling at her like a cat that has just caught a rather large mouse.

"Grrrrhhh!" Marion growled through gritted teeth after everyone had left and only herself and Trish remained. "How the hell did we allow that to happen?"

She poured herself a large glass of wine and plumped down on the settee beside her friend with a furious look on her face.

"You were supposed to propose *me!*"

"He jumped in before I had a chance," Trish tried to explain. "And the next thing they had elected him. There was nothing I could do."

"Grrrhhhh!" Marion said again.

"The mistake you made was leaving it to the last minute. By then, people just wanted to get home. They would have elected a kangaroo if someone had proposed one. You should have dealt with it earlier."

"But I wasn't expecting Alan McMillan of all people, to volunteer for the job. In fact, I wasn't expecting Alan McMillan full stop."

Trish gave her a warm hug. "There, there. Don't let it upset you," she said, soothingly.

"Upset me? I'd be delighted if I was merely *upset*. I am apoplectic. I am so angry I'm about to combust. First he turns up here uninvited and then he waltzes off with the secretary's job. After I did all the work! My God, I can't believe the nerve of that guy."

"Try to look on the bright side," Trish said. "The meeting was a huge success and despite my earlier reservations, I think you've managed to recruit some very interesting people. Matt is a great catch and Liz is very nice. And the Grimeses. Even Nick turned out okay. He helped clear away the glasses at the end. And he's quite dishy. I think you've got off to a flying start. I really do."

"But what am I going to do about Alan McMillan? The thought of him as secretary makes my blood curdle."

"There's nothing you *can* do," Trish said. "You'll just have to put up with it."

"But why did he do it? Do you think he's out to spite me?"

"Of course not. He did it to get closer to you. Surely even you can see that?"

"Closer to me? The more I see of him, the more I want to

strangle him. Did I tell you he rang me at work and asked why I didn't invite him to my housewarming party? The cheek of him! How did he even know I'd moved here?"

Trish shrugged. "He's obviously been keeping tabs on you."

"I know what I'll do. I'll propose his expulsion," Marion said, brightening up. "He's not the type of person we want in the book club. In fact, I don't think he has ever read a proper book in his entire life except possibly *The Little Red Hen* at nursery school."

"You can't do that," Trish said, quickly. "People will think you're a megalomaniac."

"I don't care what they think. The idea of having Alan McMillan running the club is more than I can endure. It's either him or me. One of us has to go."

Trish finished her glass and stood up.

"No, I'm the one has to go. It's way past my bedtime. Have a good sleep on it. Things will look much different in the morning."

Chapter Nine

As usual, Trish was right. Things did look different. They looked worse. Marion had suffered a very bad night's sleep. She had tossed and turned in bed as the injustice of what had occurred festered deeper in her brain. It had been her idea to start the club. She had put in all the work from the initial research to sticking up the notices. She had organised the inaugural meeting and then Alan McMillan had just strolled off with the key job. It wasn't just unfair. It was a rank perversion of justice that should be referred to the European Court of Human Rights.

She was tired and cranky as she drank her black coffee and gazed out the window at the early morning sky. There was a bright glow on the eastern horizon that heralded a fine day. At least that was something positive. Marion had seen so much rain recently that there were times when she thought she was living in Rangoon.

It was just coming up to nine o'clock when she got into work and flopped down at her desk. At once, she switched on her PC. As usual, there was a pile of work waiting for her. But work was one thing that she welcomed right now. Work would help to take her mind off the one issue that was threatening to obsess her. By mid-day, she had cleared all the correspondence, signed off various files and prepared a number of reports for her superior, Mr McDonald. It was time to think about lunch.

Just then, the phone rang.

"Good morning," Marion began. "How can I help you?"

"It's me."

She felt a bolt of red-hot electricity go shooting up her spine. She stared at the phone as if it had just taken a lump out of her. Alan McMillan's unmistakable Northern twang came barking out of the earpiece.

"What do *you* want?" she managed to say.

"I just thought I'd ring to compliment you on a very good meeting last night. You know, you have a natural talent for that line of business. You got through a very lengthy agenda in excellent time."

"Am I supposed to thank you?" Marion said, caustically.

"Not really. But credit where credit is due. And I think the idea of starting a book club was a brainwave. I'm going to enjoy being secretary. That's one of the reasons I'm ringing. I think you and I should meet to discuss a few things."

"I've already told you. We have nothing to discuss."

"Oh yes, we do. I may be secretary but the club is really your baby. And I'd like to share responsibility with you. I've never done anything like this before and I'm going to need some advice and guidance."

"Maybe you should have thought about that before you proposed yourself for the job," Marion said, testily.

"I was only offering to take some of the burden off your shoulders," he replied. "You had already done all the groundwork. I thought I was being helpful."

"The most helpful thing you could do right now is get into the Liffey and start walking."

"There's no need to be nasty, Marion."

"Nasty? That's positively polite compared to some of the things I could say to you."

"Now, now," he said, teasingly, "who got out of the wrong side of the bed this morning?"

"Look," she said, abruptly. "I thought you had a damned cheek turning up in the first place. You weren't invited and nobody wanted you. But I can't stop you being a member of the club. However, I draw the line at any further co-operation. From here on, you're on your own. And one final thing, please don't ring me at work again."

She put down the phone, feeling somewhat better for getting those things off her chest. Maybe this might work out quite satisfactorily after all, she thought. Maybe I'll enjoy watching Alan McMillan squirm and wriggle as he tries to do the secretary's job. In the meantime, her stomach was beginning to growl with hunger. It was time to get something to eat.

About the same time that Marion was giving Alan McMillan a piece of her mind, Christy Grimes was walking down Abbey St looking for a second-hand bookshop that someone had told him about. There had been a disagreement earlier at home, one of those rare occasions when Ellie and he had a difference of opinion. They had located one copy of *Rebecca* at the local library and Ellie had insisted that she should have it first, given that she was a much faster reader than her husband.

"Otherwise, the three weeks will be up and I won't have read it at all," she said firmly. "And then I won't be able to talk about it at the next meeting."

This was a difficulty that Christy had not foreseen. Indeed when he first took down Marion's name and telephone number from the notice board, he hadn't envisaged that he would be involved in the book club at all. He had done it for Ellie. But of course, he should have realised that his wife would never go and sit among a group of strangers on her own. She would insist that he come along with her. And that was exactly what had happened.

Christy wasn't a reader. Okay, he had once read a James Bond spy thriller that he had picked up at the church bring-and-buy sale but that was only because he'd seen the film. And it had taken him all summer to finish it. Of course he looked at the sports pages of the papers from time to time, especially when Liverpool had a big match coming up. But that didn't really count as reading. Not proper reading like Ellie went in for. But now that she had roped him into this book club he was going to have to learn. And fast, if he wasn't going to make a fool of himself in front of all these new people!

In the end, he had agreed that his wife should have the library copy and he would go out and get his own. He had done a quick calculation in his head. If he was going to buy a new book every couple of weeks, it would cost him a pretty penny. And then he remembered a fella he had met in the pub one time telling him there was a good second-hand bookshop in Abbey Street, which was what had brought him into town on the bus.

What was the name of the book again? Was it *Daphne* by Rebecca something or the other way round? These women's names had him confused. Why didn't they have titles like he remembered when he was a boy, *Captain Blood* or *Gunfight at Cactus Gulch?* You would forget a title like that in a hurry. Now it was all these fancy names that didn't give you a clue what the book was about and you could never remember anyway.

He searched in his pocket for the piece of paper where he had written it down. *Rebecca* by Daphne du Maurier! He had never heard of either of them. But Ellie said she remembered a film that was made from it ages ago, a good film too with Joan Fontaine and Laurence Olivier in it. It was scary, Ellie said, with a good love story attached. Christy didn't much care for love stories but he knew the women went for them big time. He just hoped it didn't have too many high-falutin' words in it. He didn't want to spend the next fortnight with his head stuck in a dictionary.

No, even on telly Christy preferred a good adventure story with plenty of action and a bit of human interest thrown in. Or a real-life story like the story of Larry Byrne who grew up with him in Ballybough and had a row with his father when he was fifteen and ran away and joined the French Foreign Legion. Larry had travelled all over the world until one day he got word that his old father was dying and wanted to see him again. So he came home at last and was reconciled with the old man on his deathbed. Now there was a story to bring tears to your eyes and make you think about life. There was a real story! It was a wonder nobody had ever written it down.

Mind you, he had enjoyed the meeting the other night. And Ellie had been thrilled. He could see she was going to enjoy this book club enormously. It hadn't been the least bit stuck-up or posh. Everybody had been nice and friendly and they had gone out of their way to look after Ellie, making sure she was comfortable and topping up her wine glass every so often. That Marion girl, now, she was a very good hostess and she had organised everything very well. And her apartment was beautiful. When you stood at the window, you had a view right over the city. You could even see the lights of Liberty Hall.

Apartments were what the young people were going for nowadays. They were shooting up all over the place. And the price of some of them would make your hair stand on end. To think they had bought their house in Phibsboro for less than £3,000 although that was years ago and everything was cheaper back then. When he started working for Mr Madigan in Moore Street his wages had been £2.50 a week although he always got a packet of meat on Saturday night thrown in as a bonus. Christy smiled. Two pounds fifty wouldn't even buy you a pint of stout nowadays.

No, apartments were fine but they would never suit him and Ellie. They were comfortable where they were and they knew all the neighbours, people like themselves who had been there for years. And besides, Ellie would miss her garden. She was dying to get back among her roses and chrysanthemums as soon as she was better. All in God's good time, Christy thought as he stepped lightly along the street.

He found the shop at last and walked boldly through the glass doors. They had more books than the library. They were piled everywhere, from the ceiling to the floor. They were bound to have what he was looking for.

A young man with glasses was approaching him.

"Can I help you, sir?"

"You can indeed," Christy said. "I'm looking for a book called *Rebecca* by Daphne something or other."

135

"Du Maurier," the young man said. "Do you want paperback or hardback?"

"Whichever is the cheapest," Christy said.

Alan McMillan already had his copy of *Rebecca* safely tucked in the big black briefcase that rested beside his desk in his office in Chancery Street looking out at the glistening domes of the Four Courts. The first thing he had done after the meeting was to contact a friend in the book trade and ask him to locate a copy. It had only taken fifteen minutes and Alan had despatched a courier to pick it up as soon as he got into work. After managing at last to get back inside Marion's golden circle, he was not going to allow himself to slip back out again over a simple thing like reading a book.

It had taken him a long time to get back with her. Indeed there had been occasions when he doubted if he would ever manage it at all, when his chances appeared slim and his future looked bleak. A lesser man might have simply given up and gone away, abandoning Marion as a lost cause. But not Alan! He was made of sterner stuff. And his perseverance had finally paid off. He had managed not only to make contact with her again but to insinuate himself right into the heart of her company.

He knew he had been extremely lucky. It was just by a stroke of good fortune that he had seen her notice advertising the book club in the window of a newsagent's shop and recognised her phone number. His first impulse was to ring at once and apply to join. But something made him hesitate: a memory of her reaction the last time he had spoken to her on the phone after he had bumped into one of her old flatmates and she had told him about Marion's new apartment.

On that occasion, she had been decidedly frosty. In fact, it felt like there were icicles clinging to the end of the phone when she finally cut him off. He hadn't realised that she could carry a grudge for so long. What was it? Five years? Most people would have got over it by now. And all because of some innocent hanky-panky with that randy little Julie! It wasn't the end of the world, for God's sake!

Nobody had been killed. Why did she have to make such a big deal about it? But he had come to realise that it was this very streak of determination in Marion that he found so appealing.

He had never forgotten that occasion. It stood out as a turning point in their relationship. He had gone round to Marion's flat to leave in a record album and found Julie alone. She seemed in a playful mood and offered him a drink. He had accepted. She had started flirting and one thing led to another. Before he knew what was happening, the two of them were in bed together naked. And he had certainly enjoyed it. Julie knew how to make a man happy, he would say that for her. But the whole thing was an accident. He hadn't planned it although he *had* gone willingly. Julie didn't need to twist his arm or anything.

And then Marion arrived home early. He could still see the look of horror on her face when she found them together. What a shock that must have been. But never in a hundred years could he have anticipated her reaction. She had cut him off completely. She had refused to accept his apologies. She wouldn't listen to his explanation. She wouldn't even take his phone calls. He had been reduced to writing her long grovelling letters to which she never replied. He had expected a mild rebuke and maybe a week or two in the doghouse but he wasn't prepared for such a cold, heartless response. But then, he hadn't realised that behind Marion's mild demeanour there lurked such an iron will.

And that was exactly what had forced him to look at her afresh. Until then, he had more or less taken her for granted. Alan had been lonely when they first met and it felt good to have a regular girlfriend who made his life a bit more comfortable. He enjoyed their trips to the cinema and their meals together and their expeditions out to Killiney and Dalkey on the DART. It was nice to have someone to share his time with, a woman with whom he could confide his hopes and share his ambitions. Marion was a good listener and her advice was always sound. He got a nice feeling when he walked out with her on his arm. But he had never really appreciated her. Not until she found him in bed with Julie.

Then he began to realise what a prize he had foolishly thrown away. The fact that she cut him completely out of her life, refused to see him again or even take his phone calls proved that she was a woman of strong independent will. It showed that she had depths of character he didn't know existed. And strangely, that appealed to him. She had clearly demonstrated that he needed her more than she needed him. And that made him want her even more.

He went out with other women but none of them measured up to Marion. None of them had her sense of humour or her intelligence or her handsome good looks. None of them was able to listen to his problems the way Marion did. He couldn't get her out of his mind. And the fact that she had rejected him made her all the more desirable. Gradually, his interest in her began to turn into obsession. He had to find her. He had to make contact again. He had to win her back.

And then one day, he ran into one of her old flatmates in a restaurant in town. Naturally he asked about Marion. The flatmate told him she had bought an apartment in a modern building in Smithfield in the heart of the city. She had been at the housewarming a few weeks earlier. And the flatmate also told him she was still single and didn't have a regular boyfriend.

At once, Alan's hopes were revived. Since he had last seen her, a lot of things had changed. He had finished his law degree. He had secured a well-paying job with a prominent firm of Dublin solicitors called Weatherup and Bailey and was busy expanding into the area of employment law as he had planned. He was earning a good salary and his career was on the rise. He had purchased a spanking new penthouse apartment which had shot up in value and he had recently begun to dabble successfully on the stock market.

He was no longer a struggling student with barely enough money to keep body and soul together. Now, he was a rising young man who drove a fancy Volkswagen Touareg which caused looks of admiration wherever he went. He could afford to treat her well and show her a good time. He had the money to buy her nice presents. If only he could meet her again, Alan was sure he could win her back. And then he saw the advert for the book club.

He couldn't believe his luck. This was the opportunity he had been waiting for. But he needed to be careful. He had to prepare his ground. After thinking it over, he hit on a clever plan. He got his secretary, Ms Coleman, to ring Marion's number pretending to be interested in joining. Ms Coleman was able to report back that the inaugural meeting would take place in Marion's flat on Tuesday evening at seven-thirty. And she had managed to get the address.

Alan was overjoyed. He decided to go unannounced. She had advertised for members after all, so she could hardly object when he presented himself at her door. And he would turn up a little bit late, banking on the hope that she would be too embarrassed to turn him away and too concerned that he might cause a scene.

It had worked like a charm; better even than he had expected. Not only had he gained admission to her apartment but by another stroke of fortune, he had got himself elected secretary. Now he had a perfect excuse to ring her and keep in touch. And their work on book club business was bound to bring them closer together. She had sounded tetchy this morning when he called but she would get over that. Alan knew it was only a matter of time.

In his short life, Alan McMillan had encountered many challenges right back to his humble beginnings in the back streets of Belfast. And he had overcome them all. Marion Hunt was another challenge and one he was determined to surmount. He knew he would never be happy till he had won her back. But already, he had made an excellent start. And Alan was a fighter. He had no intention of giving up.

But first, he had to read this damned book.

Chapter Ten

"You'll never guess what I've just done," Liz said excitedly into the phone.

"Don't tell me. You've met a handsome movie star who has fallen head over heels and wants to whisk you off by helicopter to his Caribbean hideaway where he'll make mad passionate love to you?" Cathy Burke replied.

"If only," Liz laughed. She was in a light-hearted mood this morning. In fact, it was more than light-hearted. She actually felt giddy. It was the first morning in a long time that she had felt so well. Miraculously, the depression that had haunted her since Tim's death appeared to have lifted. Was it possible that it was all a result of that one single meeting in Marion's apartment?

But that's what appeared to have happened. She had come home from the meeting last night feeling excited, had taken a hot bath and gone straight to bed. And she had slept right through till half seven in the morning. It was the best night's sleep she had got for months and she woke up feeling invigorated.

"I've joined a book club," she said.

"A what?"

"A book club," Liz said again. "I attended the first meeting last

140

night and it was very enjoyable. I met some lovely people there. And now I expect you to join too."

"Any of them men?"

"Is that all you ever think about?" Liz protested. "Have you got a one-track mind?"

"Possibly."

"Well, there were men there and several of them were quite handsome. But that's beside the point. You know how you've been telling me I should get out more often? Well, I saw this advert looking for members to join a book club and I decided to give it a go. And I'm really glad I did."

"You surprise me," Cathy said. "I wouldn't have thought a book club was your sort of thing."

"Why not? You know I love reading. It's one of the things that have been keeping me sane recently."

"And what exactly do you have to do?" her friend wanted to know.

"Just sit around and drink wine and talk about a book we've all read. It's a sort of discussion group."

"It sounds very snooty to me. Is it full of intellectual types?"

"Far from it. In fact, it was all very friendly and informal. We're meeting again in three weeks' time and we're still looking for members. And you did say that if I joined a club, you'd come with me. Now I'm holding you to your promise."

"Oh, no," Cathy said, quickly. "I'm not really the literary type."

"Neither am I. That's the beauty of it. All you need is the ability to read. And talk. I think you qualify on both counts."

"I've got the children to consider. I can't just waltz off and leave them."

"Max could look after them. It's only one night every three weeks."

"Let me think about it," Cathy said. "Now when are we meeting for lunch?"

They chatted for a few minutes longer while Liz got out her diary. She always enjoyed her lunches with Cathy. She had an infallible ability to cheer her up. At last they agreed a date and Liz put down the phone. Trust Cathy to mention men, she thought. As if that was the answer to all her problems when what she really needed was just something to take her mind off things. And the book club seemed to have provided the ideal solution.

She looked at the big clock above the office door. It was a quarter past twelve. Things were beginning to slow down as they approached lunchtime. If she nipped out now, she would have time to make a dash for the bookshop and be back again for one o'clock. She had already called the shop and asked the assistant to leave aside a copy of *Rebecca* for her. She would take it home this evening and settle down beside the fire as soon as she had taken a shower.

The book had been her choice after Marion had asked the meeting for suggestions.

She had read it years ago on a holiday in Italy before she met Tim and she could still remember the intense pleasure it had given her. She was really looking forward to reading it again and discussing it at the next meeting of the club.

And with a bit of luck she would persuade Cathy to come with her. Liz felt a little tingle of anticipation at the thought. This book club was turning out to be a wonderful idea.

She couldn't wait to get started.

Liz and Christy weren't the only ones looking for a copy of *Rebecca*. Matt had also been scrambling around Dublin searching for the book and had spent his entire lunchtime visiting various shops without success. The first two places he tried didn't stock the book at all and the third, which was part of a large chain, had sold the last one earlier in the day and were in the process of ordering more. Matt had an uneasy feeling that someone from the club had beaten him to the last copy.

"How long will it take to re-order?" he asked the assistant.

"About a week. Maybe ten days. It depends if they have it in the warehouse."

A week would be pushing it. Ten days was definitely too late.

"I need a copy urgently. Have you any idea where I might get one?"

"You could try Chapters in Middle Abbey St. They do a big line in second-hand books. That's your best bet."

"Thank you," Matt said and left the shop in a hurry.

Chapters bookshop was about fifteen minutes away. At this rate, he was going to be late back from lunch. He would have to make do with a salad roll at his desk and cook something more substantial when he got home tonight. But luckily, when he arrived at his destination, he found the shop had several copies of *Rebecca* in store. He took the best one and paid the assistant.

"Has it been on television?" the sales assistant inquired.

"Why do you ask?"

"You're the second person who has bought that book this morning. An elderly man was in earlier."

"I have to read it for my book club," Matt found himself saying.

"Ah, a book club," the assistant replied as he rang the money into the till. "That would explain it."

If Matt had doubted the effect the book club was going to have on his life, the fact that he would sacrifice his lunchtime to get a copy of *Rebecca* certainly convinced him. Lunchtime was usually sacrosanct, particularly now that he was living on his own.

When he had moved into The Cloisters, he had promised his daughter, Rachel, that he would always eat one good meal a day. She had been very insistent.

"I don't want you foraging out of cornflakes boxes and tins of spaghetti hoops like a boy scout," she said, firmly. "That's how you damage your immune system and then you get sick."

"I promise," he said.

"You better," Rachel said. "I'll be checking up on you. And hamburgers don't count. It's got to be proper food, okay?"

It struck him as ironic. It wasn't so long ago that he used to worry about *her* eating habits. But he had kept his promise and on those occasions like today when he didn't manage a decent lunch, he always made sure to cook something at home in the evening. He actually enjoyed messing about in the kitchen and trying out new recipes. He found it relaxing.

Of course, it was only because of Marion that he had joined the book club in the first place. Normally he would have run a mile from the idea. Matt wasn't a reader. In fact, he hadn't read a novel since a holiday in Majorca years before when it rained all week and he got so bored that he picked up a detective thriller in the hotel lobby just for something to do. He had joined to please her and because it provided the perfect excuse to get to know her better. And he was glad he did for he had discovered an important piece of information at the inaugural meeting: Marion didn't have a current boyfriend.

He had already suspected it. He had picked up certain small signals on the evening they'd had that drink together in her apartment. It was the way she had behaved – not flirting exactly but not discouraging him either. There had been a definite vibe between them. But the book club meeting had confirmed it. If Marion had a boyfriend, he would have been there. She was looking for members and if there had been a boyfriend on the scene, he would have been the number one recruit. Matt was certain that none of the other men in the room was involved with her. That knowledge had cheered him. It meant that the field was clear.

Now he wanted to impress her. He wanted to read the novel carefully and find interesting things to say. It was probably going to be a trial but it was a small price to pay if it helped advance his goal. And there was always the outside possibility that he would even enjoy it. Matt had always been a gambler and a firm believer in trying out new experiences.

He hurried back to the office through the lunchtime crowds with a copy of the book under his arm and a ham and salad roll clasped tightly in his hand. Already he was beginning to look forward to this evening when he would cook a nice dinner and settle down with a glass of Bordeaux while he investigated the mysteries of *Rebecca*.

Nick Barry stretched his long legs under the desk and let his eye travel around the crowded newspaper office. It looked like a scene from the New York stock exchange on the day of the Wall Street crash. People were scurrying around like demented ferrets, phones were ringing, televisions were booming, voices were shouting. Over in the Newsroom, a posse of reporters was hammering away at their word processors getting their copy ready for tomorrow's editions. There was a big political scandal breaking that could mean trouble for the government. Tomorrow the papers would be full of it. It promised to be a busy evening.

He watched the reporters gabbling into their phones, frantically scribbling notes, yelling instructions across the room. There was no question about it; they had much more exciting jobs than he did. He was a sub-editor and that meant he was tied to a desk. But the reporters were at the cutting edge of the news. They went to important press conferences. They mixed with interesting people. And they got to write. They got their names on their stories and sometimes also their photographs. They were the glamour boys and girls of journalism while he was one of the backroom boys.

But Nick didn't envy the reporters the way some sub-editors did. He didn't sneer at them and make jokes behind their backs. He didn't laugh in the pub about the terrible clichés some of them used. Nick was contented with his lot. He knew he could become a reporter tomorrow if he wanted. The editor had more or less told him there was a job waiting for him if he wanted it. But all that running around chasing stories would leave him with no energy for the task he had set his mind to – writing his novel.

His thoughts drifted back to last night's meeting of the book club. He had come away feeling pleased with how it had turned out. He would have been even happier if they had taken some of his suggestions on board. He would have preferred a larger membership and more frequent meetings so as to get a wider range of opinion. That was the main reason he had joined. But these weren't major issues for Nick. Meeting every three weeks was fine and the people who had turned up had been a pretty mixed bunch, which was ideal.

There had been an excellent balance of men and women, young and old and they were drawn from different social backgrounds. All in all, they represented a good cross-section of the reading public and would provide him with the broad spectrum of views he was seeking. And Marion had said she expected more people to join as time went by which would broaden it further.

And thank God there had been no smarty-pants intellectuals. That had been his biggest fear. Nick had grown to detest people like that whose heads were full of high-falutin' nonsense about books and literature. The thought of having to listen to them drone on all night filled him with horror. They were the kind of people who had hounded him in the past and brought him down. If last night's meeting had been stuffed with intellectuals, Nick knew one thing for certain – he wouldn't be going back

He was also quite pleased with the book they had selected for the next meeting. It should provide some lively discussion. He had read *Rebecca* years before when he was at college and enjoyed it immensely. He remembered a brooding Gothic melodrama that had been a worldwide bestseller and earned the author millions of pounds. And it had also managed to win the acclaim of the serious critics. That was a rare feat in publishing but Daphne du Maurier had pulled it off. She had certainly got the formula right. He was looking forward to reading the book again and seeing how exactly she had managed it.

After last night's meeting, he had gone straight home and rummaged in the boxes of books he kept in the spare room hoping to find a copy from his student days. But he had no success. He had loaned it to someone and they hadn't returned it or else it had got lost when he was moving house. He would just have to go out and buy a new copy. But that job would have to wait till tomorrow. The way things were shaping up in the office, he was in for a very busy night.

He had been thinking increasingly about his novel and already several ideas were taking shape in his head. He had decided that it would be a modern saga. It would be filled with interesting characters and wonderful events and would encompass all the grand emotions: romance, tragedy, loss, betrayal. It would grab the readers' attention and sweep them along in a great adventure that would have their blood racing and their sensations reeling. Nick knew this was going to be a massive undertaking that would consume a lot of time and energy. It would be in a different league altogether to banging out poems in fifteen minutes for Mr Partridge.

In preparation, he had taken his word processor along to a computer shop and asked the technicians to give it a complete overhaul. He'd had trouble with word processors before and didn't want anything going wrong just when the novel had reached some critical point. He had also purchased several packages of printing paper and a box of pencils. He had spoken to the Editor and asked to be put on nights so that he would have the mornings free. Mornings were when he was freshest and his imagination was at its most fertile so it would be an ideal time for him to write. On the nights when the book club was meeting, he would arrange to have the evening off.

Everything was ready. Now all he needed was the feedback he expected to get from the members of the club. He was itching to get started. But, in the meantime, he had to earn his living.

He turned his attention back to the word processor that sat on the desk before him and studied the news report that had just popped up on the screen. Nick's job was to read it carefully and check for spelling errors, grammar, libel and matters of good taste. If necessary, he also had to cut the report to fit the space available. And when he was satisfied, he had to write the headline.

He liked his job and the pay was good. But my God, some of these cub reporters were illiterate. Where did they get them from?

He looked at the very first sentence.

Detectives are searching for a gang who robbed a large sum of money from a bank in Terenure yesterday morning.

Nick gave a loud sigh as he placed his cursor over the word *robbed* and changed it to *stole*.

Chapter Eleven

"Are you nice and comfortable?" Christy asked as he placed a cushion carefully behind his wife's back and manoeuvred her chair closer to the window so that she could look out over the garden. After several dark, cloudy days, the sun had come out at last and now it cast a golden sheen across the lawn.

"Yes, thank you very much," Ellie replied.

"Would you like another cup of tea?"

"No," she said. "I've had enough. When are you coming to join me?"

"As soon as I get the dishes washed. Now you just sit there and relax. I won't be long."

He arranged the blanket tight around her legs and went back to the kitchen where he had earlier cooked the lunch; a nice dish of coddle which was one of Ellie's favourite meals and great for warming you up on a cold winter's day. Christy was proud of his coddle which was nothing like the stuff they served up to the tourists in these fancy pubs in Temple Bar. His dish was the real thing made with rashers and sausages and potatoes and onions and carrots and topped off with his special ingredient – a ham bone. The recipe had been in the Grimes' family for generations and despite repeated requests from satisfied visitors, he refused to divulge it.

But since Ellie's stroke, he'd had to go easy on the meat. Too much cholesterol, the doctors had said. And that seemed to be the cause of the problem. The way Christy understood it, the cholesterol was what clogged up the arteries, a bit like an ould chimney that hadn't been swept. So, in deference to his wife, the coddle today had been mostly vegetables.

Some men might have been a little peeved at having to care for a sick wife all day long but not Christy. Anything that made Ellie happy made him happy too. He had watched with satisfaction as she ate her lunch, finishing every piece of food on her plate. Her arm was almost back to normal now and she could manage her knife and fork without assistance although he still took care to cut up her food into small manageable portions.

All that physiotherapy was working. Even if Ellie was beginning to find the sessions boring and repetitive, she was determined to get well again. And everybody at the health centre was kind and supportive, encouraging her in her efforts and telling her what a courageous woman she was and how she'd soon be playing football for the Dublin GAA team. They could do with some new players, Christy thought, ruefully.

She was definitely getting her appetite back. This made him particularly happy for Christy automatically linked appetite with health. When the children were small he had caused tears at the dinner table by insisting that they eat everything that was placed in front of them, particularly green vegetables. And now he was threatening to do the same thing with his wife.

"Do you want me to end up looking like an elephant?" Ellie would complain as he coaxed her to finish the last spoonful of food.

"There's no danger of that," Christy would respond with a snort. "More like a greyhound."

"But that's the second helping of spuds you've just given me."

"Don't be arguing," Christy would respond. "You have to eat to get better."

"And what about my cholesterol? I'm supposed to be watching it."

"Stop your fussing. There's nothing on that plate that isn't on your diet sheet. I paid special attention."

Ellie groaned. She knew when Christy got a bee in his bonnet nothing would deflect him. "The point is I'm eating more than I did *before* I had the stroke."

"You can never get too much good nourishing food," he would say with finality. "Now finish those spuds. I don't want to hear another word about it."

When Ellie got ill, Christy hadn't hesitated to take over the household chores and nurse his sick wife. The housework didn't really amount to much since there were only the two of them now. A quick dash around the house with the vacuum cleaner usually took care of any dust that had gathered. Once a week, the laundry was despatched into the washing machine and finished off in the tumble dryer. Anything that required the attention of the iron was given a brisk run-over. The groceries were purchased on a Friday afternoon and stored in the fridge. And every day he was bent over the stove preparing an appetising meal for Ellie. But it was a labour of love.

The one thing he dreaded was the garden. He knew absolutely nothing about gardening, which had always been Ellie's special domain. He barely knew the difference between a dandelion and a daffodil except that one had a brighter flower than the other. As a result, he had a special terror of destroying some rare specimen that Ellie particularly prized.

Since her stroke, the borders and the flowerbeds had been neglected and now they were overgrown. Even Christy could see that. They would have to be tackled fairly soon but he was putting it off as long as possible. He had mowed the lawn on half a dozen occasions but that was a simple enough operation. There wasn't much he could do wrong when cutting the grass. And thankfully it was still winter and there was practically no growth. Please God when spring came, Ellie would be well enough to tackle those damned borders herself.

He washed the last plate and left it on the draining board to dry. He poured himself a cup of tea and went back into the living room to join his wife. Now the moment had arrived when he had to read that book. He hadn't been looking forward to it at all. He was sure it was going to be an ordeal. From the sideboard, he picked up the copy of *Rebecca* that he had purchased earlier in town.

He put on his reading glasses and settled into an armchair beside Ellie.

"Now," he said, "how far have you got?"

She indicated with her finger the number of pages she had read.

"My God, you're nearly halfway through," he exclaimed. "And I haven't even started."

"You know I'm a fast reader," she said.

"Are you enjoying it?"

"Very much."

"Is there any action?" Christy wanted to know.

Ellie gave him one of her strange looks that suggested that a child wouldn't ask a stupid question like that. "What do you mean by *action?*"

"You know, is it like that last one I read, *Goldfinger?*"

"James Bond?"

"That's right. The one I picked up at the bring-and-buy sale."

"No," Ellie said, firmly. "Definitely not."

"I liked that one," Christy said, wistfully. "There was plenty of action. And your man, James Bond was no slouch when it came to the ladies."

"Look," Ellie said, "who's reading this book – me or you? Why don't you just open it and find out for yourself. You've only got three weeks, you know. So you better get a move on."

Christy sniffed. He had a suspicion that he wasn't going to like this book. He could tell by his wife's reaction that it was the sort of stuff he wouldn't enjoy. Who had picked it anyway? He tried to remember if it was that Liz woman or Matt. Liz, he concluded. She was the one. Ah well, that just proved his point. It was going to be one of those soppy, romantic, lovey-dovey books that the women went in for. He could tell before he even opened the covers that there wasn't going to be any action.

He looked once more at the book. It had a lot of pages. How was he ever going to get through it on time? He wondered if he could get away with just reading the beginning and the end of each chapter. It was cheating a bit but at least he'd get a good idea of the plot. Speed-reading it was called.

Christy gave a loud sigh that caused Ellie to glance disapprovingly in his direction. Ah, well, he thought, here goes.

He flicked the book open to the first page and began to read: *Last night I dreamt I went to Manderley again.*

Manderley was somewhere in the Far East, wasn't it? He hoped this wasn't going to turn out to be another bleedin travel book.

Meanwhile, Marion was *very* busy at work. Several of her colleagues had gone down with flu and as a result she had been landed with a load of extra work. It happened every year after Christmas, regular as clockwork. She had a suspicion that some of them were malingering, pulling sickies to extend the Christmas break but of course she could prove nothing. It was another good reason to take off for the sun during the month of January. But at least she had the evenings to look forward to when she could turn on the central heating and curl up on the settee with a nice mug of drinking chocolate and get stuck into *Rebecca.*

She hadn't read it before and was thoroughly enjoying it. Daphne du Maurier had skilfully woven together elements of romance and suspense with the result that she found herself completely engrossed in the plot and rapidly turning the pages to find out what was going to happen next. That's what was missing from a lot of modern fiction – a good story line. She made a mental note to remember that point when she came to discuss the book at the next meeting. It would be sure to spark a discussion.

In fact she had been so busy with work and reading *Rebecca* and trying to restrain her anger with Alan McMillan that she hadn't yet found time to progress her friendship with the lush Matt Bollinger. She had compared notes with Trish who had declared *both* Matt and

Nick Barry to be extremely eligible men and worthy of further investigation. But it was Matt that Marion was interested in. She would like to know him better.

To that end, she had come up with the idea of inviting him to dinner in her apartment some evening. He was her neighbour after all and she could use the book club as a convenient excuse. Although she was hoping that she wouldn't need any excuse. She was hoping that he would jump at the chance to have dinner with her.

She would cook something nice and splash out on a couple of bottles of good wine and once she had him alone she would set to work finding out all about him. There was an air of mystery surrounding him that had caught her imagination. In particular, she was intrigued to find out why there was no woman in his life. It was odd, to say the least, that a man as good looking as he was and with such obvious charm and good manners, should still be single. Marion would enjoy hearing him explain.

Maybe he had a dark secret. If so, she would unravel it. Perhaps he was nursing a broken heart. Then Marion would mend it. Perhaps he was searching for his ideal woman and hadn't succeeded in finding her yet. If that was the case, she would set about convincing him that his quest was over. Whatever happened, she knew she was going to enjoy the experience.

But something was about to happen to derail her plans. Despite her best efforts, she couldn't manage to escape from Alan McMillan. The last time they had spoken she had made it clear that she didn't want to hear from him again so she was completely knocked out when he chose to ring her one evening a few days later, just as she got home from work. Marion had scarcely taken off her coat in the hall when she heard the phone trill.

"Hello," she said in her bright cheery voice, expecting the call was from Trish. The two women were planning to go out this evening to the opening of a new restaurant to which Trish had managed to wangle an invitation. It promised to be a good night with plenty of nice food and drink, and all on the house.

"How are you?" the voice asked.

Marion felt her back arch. Alan McMillan's voice had that curious effect on her, like when a cat sees a dog.

"What do *you* want?" she demanded, making no effort to conceal her hostility.

"You don't sound well," he said.

"I'm perfectly well, thank you."

"You sound tired. Did you have a hard day at work?"

"My work is of no concern to you. Now do you mind telling me why you are ringing me, after I specifically told you not to?"

"You told me not to ring you at the office. That's why I'm calling you at home."

Marion growled. Dealing with Alan McMillan was like wrestling with an octopus. No sooner had you got one tentacle nailed down than another one wrapped itself around your neck.

"Would you please include my home in that instruction, as well as the office," she snapped.

"I'm worried about you," Alan McMillan continued, not paying a blind bit of heed to what she had said. "You're very conscientious and that's to your credit but sometimes I think you take too much out of yourself."

"I'm under pressure," Marion barked. "I'm going out tonight and I have to get ready."

"Anywhere nice?"

"Yes. Somewhere very nice, somewhere even nicer because you won't be there," she growled.

"Ouch!" Alan McMillan said and she heard him laugh.

The man was infuriating. He had such brass neck that it was impossible to insult him. Maybe she should just put the phone down and then he would get the message.

But before she could do anything he had started speaking again.

"I need to ask you something," he said. "I've been thinking about the next meeting of the club and I've just realised I don't remember where it's supposed to be held."

The question left her stumped. She suddenly realised that she couldn't remember either. Both Liz and Matt had offered but she had a sinking feeling that in all the confusion of the inaugural meeting they had forgotten to agree a venue.

"I'm not sure," she heard herself say and immediately regretted it. With someone like Alan McMillan, a concession like that would immediately be taken as a sign of weakness. He would take advantage of it. "I think it's in Matt's apartment but I'd need to check."

"It's not Matt," he said. "I distinctly remember him offering and then Liz came in and offered her place. But I don't think we actually made a decision."

"I'll find out," she said quickly. "There's no rush. It's more than a week away."

"But as secretary, I need to get reminders out to everybody. We have to do this thing properly, Marion. We can't leave anything to chance."

She felt her skin bristle. There was a clearly implied criticism that she had been slipshod in not arranging a venue.

"I'll check and get back to you," she said, feeling herself beginning to get flustered which was the very last thing she wanted to do just now.

"You're busy. I can do it myself."

"Just give me your number," Marion snapped.

"That's awfully kind of you," Alan McMillan purred.

Marion wrote down his phone number on a notepad and terminated the call. Damn him, she thought, as she went into the bathroom and turned on the shower. He's like a limpet. Now that he's got attached to me, I'm going to need a hammer to prise him away.

The following morning, when she got into work, she began ringing the numbers she had reserved on her mobile phone for members of the book club. She was feeling frazzled. The restaurant opening had been a great success but she had eaten far too much food and drunk too many glasses of Sauvignon Blanc and she hadn't got back to Smithfield till almost three. What she needed now was another cup of strong black coffee.

She got Matt at the first attempt. He sounded pleased to hear from her.

"I'm really enjoying *Rebecca*," he said. "I've read almost half of it which for me is something of an achievement. It should make for a very lively discussion at the next meeting."

"Well, that's why I'm ringing," Marion said. "We can't remember where we're supposed to be having the next meeting. I've a funny feeling we didn't actually decide. Was it supposed to be your place?"

"I don't think so," Matt said. "But you're very welcome. I said I'd be happy to host it."

His voice sounded confident and soothing which was exactly what she needed to hear. Marion thought she could listen to him all morning, particularly given the nervous condition she was in right now.

"Well, that's very generous, Matt. But I need to check with the others in case someone else volunteered and I've forgotten. You see, Alan has to send out reminders."

"Can't he just ring them? It would be much quicker."

"Written reminders are better. People tend to remember them."

"You're right. But remember, if you're stuck you can always come to my place. I'd love to have you."

She thought he laid special emphasis on the last word which immediately cheered her up.

Next, she got Liz who sounded rushed and hassled but immediately calmed down when she heard Marion's voice.

"Hello, Marion," she said. "It's lovely to hear from you. I was expecting a call from one of our suppliers. It's a bit hectic here this morning, I'm afraid."

"I know the feeling," Marion sympathised. "I won't keep you long. We're trying to remember where we agreed to hold the next meeting of the book club. Was it your house?"

"You know, I can't remember either," Liz said. "I did offer but I'm not sure that any final decision was made. But of course I'd be only too glad."

"It's all right," Marion said. "We'll get to the bottom of it. It's just one of those things that seem to have been overlooked. I'm afraid that first meeting was a bit chaotic. We should have had someone taking minutes."

"No, don't blame yourself. I thought you handled it very well. There were a lot of decisions to be made and you did it all very efficiently."

"That's very kind," Marion said.

"How are you anyway?"

"I'm fine, thank you."

"I'm really whizzing through *Rebecca*. It's a wonderful novel. I read it before years ago. But this time, I'm getting much more out of it."

"So you'll have plenty to say at the next meeting?"

"You can be sure I will."

"That's what the club is all about, Liz. Good lively discussion. Nice to talk to you," Marion said and put down the phone.

It took her another twenty minutes to reach the other members and none of them could recall where the meeting was supposed to be held. Marion sat back in her chair and bit her lip. So they hadn't fixed a venue after all. She felt like a fool. And she was forced to accept that if it hadn't been for Alan McMillan they would have been left floundering. She would have to ring him and let him know. But before she did, she would have that black coffee.

She walked to the end of the office and took the lift up to the canteen. Thankfully, there were only a handful of people around. Marion was in no mood for lengthy queues or gossipy conversations this morning. It was only ten o'clock but already she was feeling drained. And she still had to ring that blasted Alan and admit that he was right and she was wrong. She *had* been slipshod. How on earth had she let that happen?

She ordered her coffee and sat at a window seat while she drank it. Outside the sun was shining. She could see the tops of the daffodils already pushing up through the black earth and the buds beginning to swell on the old sycamore trees along the drive. In no time at all it would be spring.

What was she going to do about Alan McMillan? Despite her best efforts to forget him, he had returned like a spectre from the past to haunt her. Just like Rebecca, she thought, and immediately wondered at the strange coincidence.

She had absolutely no feelings for him yet he had insisted in worming his way back into her life. Any other man would have got the message by now and left her alone but he seemed to be impervious to insult. No matter what she said or did, he just kept bouncing back like a rubber duck. It was maddening. Marion could fully understand why some women were driven to murder.

She would dearly love to expel him from the club. But Trish was right. She couldn't do it. He hadn't done anything wrong and the other members would think she was crazy. And she had to admit that he would probably make a very efficient secretary. No, there was nothing for it but to put up with him and just hope he would eventually realise that there was no future in pursuing her. She was never going to change her mind.

She finished her coffee and went back to her desk. She couldn't help but groan under her breath at how far he had actually managed to get in the space of a few short weeks. Now *she* was ringing *him*.

She reached him at the first attempt as if he had been waiting for her call.

"You were right," she said. "We forgot to organise a venue."

"I knew that," he said, smugly.

Marion bit her lip. "Both Matt and Liz have offered. So we can take our pick."

"Don't worry about it, Marion," she heard him say. "It's already decided."

"Oh."

"Yes. I've got the reminders printed and ready to go out."

"So where is it going to be?" she asked.

"My place. I'm really looking forward to welcoming everyone. Especially you, Marion. You're going to love it when you see it."

Chapter Twelve

Nick slept late and didn't get out of bed till twenty past ten by which time he had missed the radio news and the review of the morning papers. This was part of his daily routine. Every morning he made a point of listening to the news with his morning coffee and toast. It alerted him to what stories were breaking and kept him abreast of what the opposition newspapers were up to. Nick regarded it as a form of insurance policy.

As a sub-editor, his job was to keep on top of current developments which meant constantly being alert. He still recalled with horror the inferno that erupted when Harry Swift, who sat across the desk from him, had led the front page with a news report that had appeared in one of the rival papers two days earlier. The Editor had gone ballistic at the thought that old news should get into the paper and worse still, onto the front page. It gave the impression that the paper didn't know what was going on. It was all the union could do to persuade him not to fire Harry on the spot.

It wasn't Harry's first gaffe. A few months earlier he had run a picture and a news story about a prominent businessman who had been caught in the arms of a young lady with the exotic name of Miss Whiplash who specialised in something called oriental massage.

The businessman's defence was that he was attending her for a sports injury. He had subsequently turned out to be the Editor's brother-in-law and the Editor had not been pleased.

Such were the perils of working on a national newspaper. Nick had learnt that it wasn't all champagne and fancy lunches like some people believed. It was busy and exciting and often satisfying but it was also potentially lethal. But the experience had taught him a valuable lesson. If Harry had been on the ball it would never have happened. So even on his days off, Nick listened to the news. Unfortunately the episode had also shattered poor Harry's nerve and he was never the same man again.

Nick had slept late because he was exhausted. The political crisis was rumbling on which meant that the atmosphere the previous evening had been like a pressure cooker waiting to explode. And then to make matters worse, the press had broken down and they hadn't started printing the paper till well after midnight. As a result, he didn't get home till two-thirty by which time all he was able to do was fall into bed and go straight to sleep.

This was the second time in a week that something like this had happened. He was beginning to discover that switching to night shifts wasn't as simple as it first appeared.

The idea had been that he would leap out of bed each morning at eight o'clock and start work on preparing his novel feeling rested and bursting with fresh creative energy. But instead, he found that most mornings he didn't get started till well after ten o'clock and sometimes it took another half hour just to get his brain into gear. As a result, the ideas were slow to emerge and when they did, he found they were often as tired and jaded as he felt.

So far, he hadn't actually started to write anything. He was saving that till later when he had a chance to listen to the opinions of the book club members and get a feel for what they liked. He had spent his time playing around with ideas for plots. He knew broadly what he wanted – plenty of action, buckets of drama, gallons of tension and suspense. He wanted a plot that would excite the readers and hold their interest. But try as he might, the plot just wouldn't come.

His wastepaper basket was already brimming with rolled-up balls of paper from discarded ideas.

He tried to reassure himself that this was normal. It was a long time since he had written anything and he was out of practice. If he just stuck with it, the ideas would eventually start to flow. But Nick found he just had too many damned distractions to allow him to focus properly. And with these recent late nights at the office, he had no energy either.

One thing in particular weighed on his mind. He hadn't yet managed to get his hands on a copy of *Rebecca*. And he was supposed to have it read for the next meeting of the club which was drawing closer by the day. He had tried various bookshops but none of them had a copy in stock. And the library didn't have one either when he rang to enquire.

It made him feel guilty. He had briefly considered coasting along at the meeting with recollections of the first time he had read the book. But it was so long ago that he had forgotten most of it. And it felt too much like cheating. What would happen if everyone else decided to do the same thing? The book club would collapse. No, if it was going to be a success then everyone had to pull their weight.

The best he could manage was a promise from one shop to order a copy and have it for him in a few days time. It was really pushing it right up to the deadline. However, the exercise hadn't been a complete waste of time. He had come away with a manual titled: *How to Publish a Successful Novel in Ten Easy Steps.*

It was written by an American woman called Mabel R. Zuckfeld. Nick had never heard of her before, although the cover said she was the author of several bestselling novels and Hollywood film scripts which sounded impressive. There was a picture of her on the back grinning from ear to ear, as well she might if she had been as successful as the blurb claimed. He had bought the manual out of interest and not because he expected to learn anything. Nick didn't believe that books like this could actually teach people how to write.

But he was in for a surprise. When he got it home, he discovered that it contained lots of valuable information about the technical side of writing. Ms Zuckfeld was very big on the importance of grabbing the reader's attention from the very first sentence and maintaining it right to the end. *Keep them turning the pages,* she wrote. The manual maintained that this was the secret of commercial novel-writing.

Nick had spent hours poring over the contents and taking notes. There were chapters on characters, tension, pace, diction, atmosphere and plot. There was no doubt that Mabel R Zuckfeld knew her stuff and had been round the course. One whole chapter told how her first novel, *Blue Moon Over Hawaii,* had been rejected by twenty-six publishers and savaged by the critics when it finally hit the bookshelves. But her next novel, *My Tender Heart,* had become a major bestseller on five continents and a successful movie which netted her over two million dollars.

When he read this, Nick immediately recognised a fellow sufferer at the hands of the cursed critics. But Mabel's success over her detractors cheered him up no end. It was what he hoped to do himself. Reading Mabel's story gave him the encouragement to continue. The trouble was it also took up two whole mornings of his valuable time when he should have been working on his own novel. That still remained his number one priority. Mabel R Zuckfeld's advice about publishing might come in useful when he had a completed manuscript. But first he had to write it and so far he was finding it difficult even to come up with ideas.

He brought a cup of coffee from the kitchen and sat down at his word processor and while he waited for it to boot up, he gazed out the window. It looked out over a grimy backyard that contained a clothesline, a dustbin, several empty beer crates and a small patch of scraggy lawn where a sickly yellow carpet of grass struggled to survive.

It was a gloomy sight, made more dismal by the dark clouds that loured across the sky threatening yet more rain. After several days when the weather had been nice and bright, it had suddenly turned nasty again. If Nick was still writing poetry, he could fashion a verse or two from the scene that lay before him. He could feel the lines already taking shape in his brain.

Clouds like warplanes scudding across the grey vista of the earth,

Waiting to unload their grim cargo on the unsuspecting world.

Immediately, he stopped himself. There was no point in wasting valuable creative energy on poetry. He had been down that road before and all it got him in the end was ridicule and abuse. Instead, he must focus on the work in hand. As the computer screen began to brighten, he took a sip of coffee, sat up straight in his chair and prepared for work.

Three hours later, he sat back from the screen. He had finally assembled a rough cast of characters and started the outline of the plot. But he wasn't happy with it. It didn't seem to be coming right. No matter how hard he concentrated, he couldn't come up with a truly satisfying storyline. His imagination refused to deliver that essential ingredient: a plot that would grab the reader's interest and hold it to the end like Mabel R Zuckfeld had recommended.

He felt a depressing mood settle over him. He knew he could write well. He knew he could produce strong characters. But no matter how much he racked his brains, the plots he had devised all sounded dull and predictable, like something he had read a hundred times before. And without an exciting plot, he knew he was wasting his time.

By now, he was feeling tired. Maybe that was the problem. These late nights were burning up his energy. Perhaps, if he got a good sleep, his brain would be in better shape, fresh and fertile and brimming with exciting possibilities. Maybe tomorrow the plot would start to take shape.

His gaze returned once more to the window. The sky had grown darker and more threatening but it hadn't yet started to rain. The weather matched his sombre mood. With a bit of luck, he might make it to the bookshop to pick up his copy of *Rebecca* before the rain began. And he would start to read it right away.

Nick switched off the computer and pushed back his chair. From the rack in the hall, he selected a warm coat and an umbrella and opened the front door. The whole way along the street, one thought kept hammering in his brain. *I must find a plot. I must find a plot.*

The buzzing of the alarm clock dragged Liz from a drowsy sleep and into the reality of another cold, dark morning. Tim had bought the clock years before when he was working frantically to get Broderick Security Systems off the ground and needed to rise early. Its insistent clamour would waken even the most determined sleeper. Through bleary eyes, she struggled to read the time. 07.30. She had better get up if she wanted to compete with the morning traffic. Liz liked to be at her desk by eight thirty before the rest of the staff came in at nine. That half hour allowed her to get through lots of small jobs that would otherwise get swamped in the subsequent rush. She liked to think that it gave her a head start.

She drew back the curtains and gazed out at the leaden scene, little fringes of dawn beginning to brighten the eastern sky. She hated this time of year with its cold and damp and longed for the spring to arrive and the sun to come out. But at least it was dry today and that was a small blessing.

It was amazing, the change that had come over her recently. From feeling listless and depressed, she had suddenly come alive again. It was like the way it was before Tim died. She could feel her energy returning. And it could all be traced back to that decision to join the book club. If you had told her a month before that this transformation would have come about by such a simple act, she wouldn't have believed it. Yet it appeared to be true.

Joining the book club had finally forced her out of the torpor that had enveloped her since her husband's death. It had given her a new focus and a fresh purpose. She had met new people and now she had a task to complete. She had to read *Rebecca* again and come up with some interesting observations in time for the next meeting. It was the perfect complement to her daily job at Quick Print. And in the process, she could feel herself starting to live once again.

The previous weekend she had a lovely lunch with Cathy Burke in a little restaurant in Chatham St. The place had been packed but that hadn't stopped Cathy regaling her with outrageous stories. It had been just like the old days. The food had been delicious and healthy, with lots of fresh salads and juices. But the gossip had been even better. Cathy seemed to know everything that was going on and could recount all the gory details of the latest scandals as if she was a columnist for one of the glossy magazines and had the inside track.

In fact, her stories were so colourful that Liz often doubted if they were actually true and wondered if she was making them up just for her benefit. But she was enjoying herself so much that it didn't matter. Cathy was a true friend. She had stood by her through the dark days. And she was wonderful company. A lunch with her was like a tonic and the effect lingered for days.

The two women went back a long way. They had first met at college where they had studied History together. They graduated on the same day but while Liz had stayed in Dublin to try and find work, Cathy had taken herself off to Chicago only to return eighteen months later with a tall, blond dentist called Max in tow. Now she was the mother of three children and Max had one of the biggest dentistry practices in Ballsbridge.

They had hit it off right from the beginning. They attended college dances together and compared boyfriends. They shared books and clothes and the same wicked sense of humour. When Liz needed a sympathetic ear, Cathy was the person she inevitably turned to. When Cathy had a problem and required advice, she took it to Liz. The two of them were so close that they were known around the university campus as the terrible twins. And when they eventually married, they remained firm friends. Liz was godmother to Cathy's first child, Amelia. They celebrated birthdays and anniversaries together and made a point of meeting regularly for lunch when they would cast a cold eye over their little social world and have a few laughs.

It was all harmless fun and the lunch had reminded Liz once more just how carefree life could be. And she had another good reason to be happy. She had persuaded her friend to attend the next meeting of the book club. Liz had experienced a little thrill of triumph at the achievement.

"I'll go on one condition," Cathy finally agreed.

"What?"

"That nobody asks me any intelligent questions. If this club is going to be like an exam course, you can forget it."

"There'll be nothing like that," Liz rushed to reassure her. "This is meant to be fun. And you'll really like the people you meet."

"I just hope they're not a bunch of literary snobs with long hair and glasses. I couldn't stand that."

"Oh no, they're ordinary people like you and me who just happen to enjoy reading."

"And what is this book we're supposed to study?"

"Read," Liz corrected her. "It's called *Rebecca*. By Daphne du Maurier. You can borrow mine if you can't find your own copy."

Cathy looked quizzical. "Did they make a film of it?"

"They did indeed. Alfred Hitchcock."

"I think I saw it," Cathy said, brightening up. "All right. I'll go. But if I don't like it, I won't be back. You've been warned. Life's too short."

"It's a deal," Liz said cutting a piece off her poached salmon and spearing it with her fork.

On her way home from the lunch, she thought once more how completely her attitude had changed since joining the club. Maybe that was what she needed after all – something to shake her up, some impetus to put her troubles aside and get on with her life. It was what everyone had been telling her including the bereavement counsellor she had reluctantly gone to see after the funeral.

There is such a thing as grieving too long, the counsellor had told her in her kind sympathetic voice. The ancient peoples knew that. They accepted that death was inevitable but they also believed that the bereaved person had to move on and pick up the threads of their own life again.

At the time, Liz hadn't fully understood what the counsellor was trying to tell her. She was still in a state of shock at the suddenness of her husband's death. And she was getting comfort and advice from all sides so that her head was spinning with information. But now it was becoming clearer. She could see the sense of what the counsellor had said. Joining the book club was the best thing she could have done. It had lifted her out of herself and she had an uncanny feeling that it was going to change her life.

She got out of bed, took her dressing gown from the back of the bedroom door and padded out to the kitchen where she poured a glass of orange juice and put the kettle on to boil. From the window she could see the grey dawn begin to dissolve into an equally grey morning. This constant dull weather would depress a saint. She should take a break, go away somewhere bright and sunny. So far she hadn't been able to muster the energy but now that she was beginning to feel better, she might just do it. In fact, she might nip round to the travel agent's this very lunchtime and see what they had to offer.

She finished her orange juice and put a slice of bread into the toaster before setting off for the bathroom. There was a time when she used to check her weight regularly but that habit too had fallen by the wayside. She hadn't weighed herself for ages. Nevertheless, this morning she decided to step on the scales and was delighted to find that her weight had remained constant. That knowledge cheered her up as she slipped out of her dressing gown and stood under the warm jets of the shower.

She found herself humming a tune as she began to lather on the soap. There was something else that had changed. When was the last time she had hummed in the shower? Something was definitely happening to her. She ran her fingers along her shoulders and down her arms and across to her breasts, luxuriating in the warm soapy water. And then she suddenly stopped and felt her heart give a little leap.

Was she imagining it or was something there, on her left breast, something small and hard? Immediately, Liz washed away the soap and turned off the shower. She stepped out and stood under the light. Now her heart was thumping as she ran her fingers slowly along the smooth surface of her skin.

There was no mistake. There was definitely something there; a small firm lump about the size of a pea. She felt fear grip her like a vice. Liz closed her eyes and heard the blood beginning to roar in her head.

Chapter Thirteen

"You won't believe what he's done now," Marion groaned as soon as Trish had given her order and the waiter was out of earshot.

They were having a late lunch at La Taverna, a new Italian place off Clare St. The lunch was Marion's idea. Ever since this morning's conversation with Alan McMillan, she had been silently fuming and badly needed to find a sympathetic ear before she exploded with indignation.

Trish allowed her eye to travel round the room, taking in the empty Chianti bottles in their straw baskets that hung on the walls along with the bright, glossy travel posters of Naples and Venice.

"Have we been here before?" she asked, looking slightly bewildered.

"No," Marion replied. "It only opened a couple of weeks ago. Before that it was a lingerie store."

"It's the Chianti bottles," Trish decided. "Every Italian restaurant I've ever been in has Chianti bottles and travel posters. Wouldn't you think they'd get a bit of imagination?"

"Oh for God's sake," Marion said. "You haven't been listening to a word I said."

"*Excuse* me," Trish replied, in a huffy tone. "What's biting you?"

"Alan Bloody McMillan, that's what. He rang me when I got home from work before I even had time to draw breath. And you'll never guess what he has done."

"Surprise me."

"He has only gone and organised the next meeting of the book club for his apartment."

Trish gave her a confused look. "Am I missing something here? What's the big deal?"

"Oh, don't you see? This is all part of his grand plan. It's his way of getting me to go there. He even said he was specially looking forward to welcoming me."

"I still don't get it," Trish said.

"It's a plot. He knows I'd never go within a hundred miles of the place under normal circumstances. And he's taken to ringing me up for a chat as if we were all palsy-walsy again. He has even tricked *me* into ringing *him*."

For the next few minutes Marion harangued her friend about the iniquities of Alan McMillan and his cruel machinations while Trish sat patiently and listened. The way Marion spoke, she made him sound like a Mafia godfather.

But just talking like this made Marion feel better and she knew that Trish would have something interesting to say and some good advice to impart when she had finished.

"The worst part of it is that he was right. We *had* forgotten to fix a venue for the next meeting. And of course that just gave him the high moral ground. He even insinuated that I hadn't done my job properly. The arrogance of him!" Marion said and sat back at last in her chair, feeling exhausted after all the effort.

But before Trish could reply, the waiter approached and put down their drinks. Trish had ordered wine but Marion was sticking to water. She still hadn't fully recovered from last night's debauch at the restaurant opening.

Trish took a long sip from her glass and wiped her lips with her napkin. "Can I ask you something? Why are you telling me all this?"

"Because I want your advice. Don't you think he's behaving outrageously?"

"Well, you have to hold the meeting somewhere."

"But *not* in his apartment. I was thinking more of Liz or Matt. They both offered."

"He *is* the secretary," Trish said, reasonably. "I suppose he can hold the meeting wherever he likes."

"He's trying to take over the club!" Marion wailed. "In fact he has already succeeded. And this is his way of getting revenge on me because I dumped him."

"Oh, c'mon, Marion. Don't you think you're exaggerating?"

"You don't know this guy. He's unbelievable. You can't insult him no matter what you say or do. And he never gives up. I'll bet you right now he's sitting in his office somewhere scheming and plotting new ways to antagonise me."

Trish smiled. "Now, why don't we just calm down a little and try to see things rationally."

"Calm down?" Marion exploded. "Why don't you look at the facts? It was my idea to start the club. I put in all the work. I organised the first meeting. And he turns up uninvited and takes over the secretary's post. Tell me how you would feel."

"The secretary's job was a mistake," Trish conceded. "If we'd been a little smarter it would never have happened."

"Well, it *has* happened. And now what are we going to do?"

Marion felt like weeping at the injustice of it all. And contrary to expectations, she was getting no sympathy from her friend. You would even think that Trish was on Alan McMillan's side the way she was reacting.

"I haven't abandoned the idea of calling a special meeting and voting him out," she continued. "We could do it quite easily if we just put in a little preparatory work. He doesn't even need to know about it till it's all over."

"We've discussed this before," Trish said. "I don't really think you can do that. I'm sure it's illegal. And he *is* a solicitor."

"Illegal? What's illegal about it? We can do what we like if we get the members to agree."

"You'd destroy the club," Trish said. "We haven't even had a proper meeting yet and already people are getting expelled. How do you think the others would react? I know if it was me I'd think I'd joined the Moonies or something."

Marion gritted her teeth. Was Trish deliberately being awkward just to annoy her?

"But we have to do something," she wailed. "We can't let him get away with this."

"I've already told you what to do. Nothing. Just ignore him. If you have sufficient patience, he'll get tired and go away of his own accord or else he'll make such a mess of the job that the members will remove him without you having to lift a finger."

Marion looked at her like a stricken sheep. "I can't ignore him," she said. "You don't know how clever he is. He'll not allow himself to make any mistakes. Don't you see that? He'll make sure he's the best secretary the club could ever have."

Trish was studying her now from the other side of the table. A strange look had come into her eyes. "You know I'm beginning to think you're protesting a little bit too much."

"What!" Marion squawked. She couldn't believe what her friend had just said.

At that moment, the waiter returned with their meal, grilled veal cutlets and salad for Marion and spaghetti carbonara for Trish.

Marion waited till he had gone, then put her fists firmly on the tablecloth and leaned across the table. "What did you just say?"

Trish smiled nervously. "I said you were protesting too much."

"Does that mean what I think it means?"

"It means that you're giving a very good impression of someone who is secretly quite impressed by Alan McMillan. If he doesn't interest you, then why are you going on so much about him?"

Marion gasped. Was Trish really talking like this? "I'm going on about him because I detest him and it infuriates me to see the way he's manipulating us like we were all a bunch of idiots."

"Are you sure?"

"I'm absolutely positive."

"It could be that you still find him a little attractive."

Marion almost choked. She felt like taking the plate of spaghetti and pouring it over Trish's stupid head.

"*Attractive? Attractive?*" she could hardly speak for rage. "I never found him attractive. I went out with him because I felt sorry for him. He's the most obnoxious creature I've ever had the misfortune to meet. Even his own mother couldn't find him attractive!"

Trish had started to eat. "Oh c'mon now," she said, her mouth filled with pasta. "He's not so bad looking. Quite a lot of women would be flattered by his attention. And you've just said yourself that he's clever."

"Jack the Ripper was clever. Attila the Hun was clever."

Trish ignored her. "And he dresses well. And he can be quite charming. And he does have a very good job. You know, some women would think you're very fortunate to have him chasing after you."

"But you told me yourself to dump him."

"That was then. He needed to be taught a lesson. But I think he's learned it by now. I don't believe Alan McMillan would ever make that same mistake again."

Marion stared. Suddenly, her head felt light. "I don't believe I'm hearing this. From you of all people. My best friend."

"That's what best friends are for, to tell you some home truths."

"You're actually suggesting that I take him back?"

"I'm suggesting you might consider it. What have you got to lose? You've no regular boyfriend right now, have you?"

Marion took a deep breath. "Hell will freeze over before I take Alan McMillan back."

"Give me a break," Trish said. "Do you have to be such a drama queen?"

"I mean it. And it's got nothing to do with what he did. I find him utterly repulsive. If he was the last man alive and the future of the human race depended on it, I would not allow Alan McMillan within a hundred yards of me."

Trish smiled. "Eat your lunch," she said. "It's getting cold."

Marion glanced at her plate then slowly pushed it away. "I've lost my appetite," she said.

Christy looked up quickly when he heard the key being inserted in the lock and the front door open. He put down the book he was reading and stood up.

"Is that you?" he shouted in the general direction of the hall.

An impatient voice answered. "Who do you think it is? Michael Jackson?"

"You wouldn't know around here," Christy muttered. "I was only asking."

He walked out to the hall where Ellie was being assisted into the house by their daughter, Jackie, who had volunteered to pick her up from the physiotherapy session this morning.

"Hi, Dad," she said as Christy quickly bent to kiss them both. "How are you today?"

"Sound as a pound," Christy said. "And you?"

"Never felt better," Jackie said.

"And Anto? How's he keeping?"

"He's grand."

"Well, that's good," Christy said, taking hold of his wife's arm and helping her along the hallway. "Do I take it from the sound of you that you had a tough session?"

"Tough doesn't begin to describe it," Ellie grumbled, wearily. "I thought they were trying to finish me off. My back must be black and blue from all the pumping they gave me."

"Well, it's doing you good."

"Are you sure? Why is it every time they torture me, you tell me it's doing me good? I'd like to know what they would do to me if they were really trying to hurt me."

Jackie smiled behind her mother's back and raised her eyes to Heaven.

"Just come into the kitchen and sit down," Christy said. "I've got the kettle on. A nice cup of tea will soon perk you up."

"Do you need anything from the supermarket?" Jackie asked. "Now that I've got the car, I could run up there for you."

"You're very good," Ellie said. "But I think we're okay. Your father went at the weekend."

"We're fine. Just sit down and rest yourself," Christy said, spooning tea into the pot and pouring in hot water.

Jackie sat down beside her mother at the kitchen table while Christy took a cake from the cupboard and began cutting it into slices. It was a special low-calorie cake baked without butter. Recently, Ellie had been treating herself to a thin slice.

"They really worked you hard this morning, Mum," Jackie said.

"Tell me about it," Ellie sighed and rubbed her leg. "I feel like I've just been locked in a washing machine."

Jackie smiled. "But you're really coming on. It'll be no time at all till you're right as rain."

"And she'll be able to do her gardening again," Christy said, hopefully. "I'm afraid to touch it in case I pull up one of her special gazelles."

"Azaleas," Ellie corrected him. "They're flowers and they're called azaleas." A satisfied smile had now stolen across her face. "Actually, I *do* have some good news," she confided. "Dr Hynes examined me this morning after I'd finished with the physio and you know what?"

The others stopped what they were doing and turned to listen.

"He said next month, if I kept up the progress, he's going to take the walker away. He said I'd be fit enough to get around without it."

"My God," Christy said and almost dropped the teapot in his excitement. He put it down carefully, threw his arms around his wife's neck and hugged her close. "That's brilliant news. Absolutely bleedin brilliant. I'm over the moon."

"Yes," Jackie agreed, equally excited. "If anyone deserves it, you do."

"She's a fighter," Christy continued. "Always was. And she came from fighting stock. You should have seen your grandfather, Dando, in his younger days. He was the toughest man on the Dublin docks. And there were some rough diamonds down there, I can tell you."

"Well, it's not definite," Ellie cautioned. "Dr Hynes said it all depends on my progress."

"Of course you'll make it," Christy said, rummaging in the cupboard till he found a bottle of Jameson whiskey. "This calls for a celebration."

"You're not going to get me drunk?" Ellie laughed.

"Not at all. Just a tincture. We've waited a long time for this news."

He poured a shot of whiskey into the teacups and raised his own in a toast.

"To Mrs Ellie Grimes! The bravest woman in Phibsboro."

"Go easy," Ellie said. "It's only physiotherapy. I haven't climbed Mount Everest or anything."

"Not yet," Christy smiled and polished off the whiskey in his cup.

Ellie took a sip and wrinkled her face. "It's too strong. I need something in this."

"Tea," Christy said and poured from the pot.

Jackie hugged her mother again. "I'm really pleased for you, Mum. Wait till the others hear the news. They'll be delighted."

"Have a slice of cake," Christy said, pushing the plate into the centre of the table.

After a small silence, Ellie said, "Did you finish the book? The meeting's tomorrow night."

"Is this the book club?" Jackie wanted to know. "How is it coming along?"

"Slowly," Ellie said. "If your father was back at school he'd be in the remedial class. It's taken him almost three weeks to read one simple book that I read in three days."

"Well, I never wanted to join in the first place," Christy protested. "You know I was never a great man for the reading. But since you ask, I did finish it. This morning when you were out."

"Did you like it? You know you're going to be asked to talk about it?"

Christy paused and stroked his chin. "Well, if you want my honest opinion, I thought it was a bit slow."

"Slow?" Ellie said. "What do you mean slow?"

"There was too much ould talking and not enough action. And I never got one good laugh in the whole book."

Ellie appealed to her daughter. "He's looking for laughs and the book is about a murder. Did you ever hear the like?"

"And I thought the ending was very bad," Christy continued. "It left me up in the air."

A look of disgust had crept into Ellie's face. "I've heard enough. You know, I'm beginning to wonder if I should bring you to this meeting at all. You're liable to make a holy show of us."

"Well, you asked me if I liked it and I'm only telling you the truth. I prefer a good yarn with a bit of adventure and a happy ending. Like the story of Larry Byrne who grew up with me in Ballybough. Did I ever tell you that story, Jackie?"

"Many times, Dad."

"Well, that's what I call a *real* story. There's nobody writing stuff like that any more."

"Just as well." Ellie said. "Somebody might burn down the library."

Jackie finished her tea and stood up. "I think I'll leave you pair to your literary discussions. I've got to go. This meeting tomorrow night sounds like it's going to be a lively affair."

She kissed her mother goodbye and Christy walked with her to the front door.

"Thanks for all your help, love," he said. "You know how much we appreciate it."

"It's my pleasure. You know, the improvement in Mum is amazing. She'll be back to her old self before we know it. She's already getting her spirit back."

Christy glanced over his shoulder to the kitchen where he could hear his wife continuing to make growling sounds in preparation for his return.

"I think you might be right," he said, nervously.

Liz's first reaction when she found the lump on her breast was to sit down and try to control the shaking that had suddenly come over her. She felt dizzy and her head was swirling with menacing thoughts. Chief among them was one terrifying fear – this could be cancer.

Please God, she thought, please God give me a break. Her heart was now thudding and beads of perspiration were beginning to break across her brow. Her whole body was shaking uncontrollably from the shock. She willed herself to think rationally. What did she know about breast cancer? Practically nothing and it was entirely her own fault. Despite her recent interest in health, the possibility of breast cancer had never once crossed her mind.

She had regularly come across articles about it in magazines and newspapers. It seemed to be everywhere nowadays. Several prominent people had developed it and gone public including the singer Kylie Minogue. And the Department of Health had recently launched an awareness campaign. Liz had seen the posters. But it all seemed to have passed her by. She had assumed that it just didn't apply to her; other women maybe, but not her.

But now its spectre had sought her out. There was no denying that this tiny lump that she could feel quite firmly beneath her skin could be a cancerous growth. And Liz had a vague idea that treating it might involve surgery and months of chemotherapy. God forbid, it might even kill her. With pounding heart, she managed to make her way from the bathroom to the bedroom where she sat down and waited for the shaking to stop.

Why was life being so cruel? To dash her down, then lift her up and now threaten to dash her down again. It was as if some malevolent spirit was playing games with her. But she had to take a grip on herself and try to calm down. Finding the lump had given her a terrible shock but she mustn't let her imagination run away. She mustn't blow things out of proportion. This could be any number of things. Cancer was only one of them. The lump could turn out to be something entirely innocent. Thinking like this eventually helped the shaking to stop and she was able to go into the kitchen to make a cup of coffee.

She could feel the coffee revive her. The first thing she had to do was make an appointment to see Dr Brady. He would know what to do. Another thought flashed into her mind and brought a ray of hope. She had heard somewhere that early detection was vital. And the lump was still small. She put a hand on her breast and felt it again, firm and hard like a little marble. Whatever it was, she had found it in time and that could only be good.

In situations like this she would normally call Cathy and unburden herself. But something held her back. Poor Cathy had been listening to her problems for the past nine months. What if the lump turned out to be totally innocent? She would look like a hypochondriac. It would be better to wait till she had consulted with Dr Brady before she mentioned this to anyone else – even such a close friend as Cathy. They might have nothing to discuss at all she thought, as her hopes rose again.

She finished her breakfast and went back to the bedroom to get dressed. She made up her mind. She would stick with her normal schedule and go into work. She checked her watch. She was running late and would probably get caught up in the traffic. But once she got into the office, the dictates of the job would keep her mind occupied for a while. Later, she would ring Dr Brady and make an appointment to see him as soon as possible. In the meantime, she would try to carry on as normal.

Now that she had made some decisions, she felt a sort of stability return. She stood before the wardrobe mirror and quickly combed out her blonde hair then spent a few minutes applying a little mascara and a slick of lip-gloss. She chose a dark business suit from the rack of clothes in the wardrobe and slipped on her shoes. Grabbing her handbag from the dressing table, she extracted her keys and locked up the house. Ten minutes later she was in the stream of traffic heading into town.

Thankfully, it was a busy morning. It was a blessing in disguise for it kept her distracted. But by lunchtime the staff had all drifted off in search of something to eat and Liz was left alone in the office. Once she was sure there was no one around, she sat down at her computer and logged onto the internet. She was sorry now that she hadn't paid more attention to those articles on breast cancer. But the internet could help with information.

She found the search engine and typed in *lump on breast.* Just seeing those words on the screen caused a shiver to run through her. Immediately the computer threw up pages of entries and she began to read. It was a bad mistake. Although the articles she downloaded were all written in a cosy reassuring style, their message was stark. They told her things she didn't want to hear. The lump could be malignant. It could presage breast cancer. It could mean surgery.

As she trawled through the web, she began to get frightened. The pictures and diagrams she saw there really scared her. If it was cancer, she might need to have chemotherapy treatment or even have her breast removed. In the worst case, it could spread throughout her body and kill her. Liz felt a cold sweat break on her brow. In the end, she could take no more. She logged off and shut down the computer and sat trembling at her desk.

She had to see Dr Brady today. She couldn't wait. He would be finished morning surgery by now. She found his number in her address book and dialled. She listened to the soft purring as if in a trance. And then she heard the sound of the phone being picked up.

"Dr Brady's surgery," a bright, female voice announced.

"Hello," Liz said, trying to keep her voice as steady as possible. "My name is Liz Broderick. I'm a patient of Dr Brady. I'd like to make an appointment to see him, please."

"Dr Brady is at a conference this week. He won't be back till Friday."

She felt the disappointment like a stab from a knife. This was something she hadn't expected. Friday was two days away.

"I've discovered a lump on my breast," she said.

"Oh," the secretary replied. "In that case, I could arrange for his locum to see you."

Liz tried frantically to think. Dr Brady was her regular doctor. She felt comfortable with him. And maybe two days wasn't so long to wait.

"No. I'd prefer to see Dr Brady."

"Are you sure?"

"Yes."

"Would you like me to make an appointment for Friday?"

"Yes, please."

"I could fit you in on Friday evening."

She would have preferred the morning but this was outside her control. She would go immediately after work.

"Okay."

"That's fine," the secretary said. "Dr Brady will see you at seven o'clock on Friday evening, Mrs Broderick."

Liz put down the phone. She felt better now that she had made the appointment. She had set events in motion. Now she just had to wait and hope that everything would turn out all right.

But in her panic she had forgotten something and now she remembered. Tomorrow night was the meeting of the book club and she had been looking forward to it with anticipation. But now things had changed dramatically. Her earlier enthusiasm had gone. She didn't relish the prospect of sitting in a room full of people when she had this terrible worry eating at her mind.

She couldn't go and face all those people. She would have to ring and tell them she was ill. They would probably be disappointed. It was the first proper meeting and they would want a full attendance. But there was no way she could go through with it.

She would ring Marion right now and tell her. She reached for her handbag to find her number when her mobile suddenly sounded. It was Cathy.

"Are you all set for tomorrow night?" she chirped. "I've read the book. I had to skip through it pretty fast, mind you. But I *did* enjoy it."

Liz opened her mouth to speak but Cathy continued.

"I'll pick you up. There's no point bringing two cars. What's the best time?"

"It's due to start at half seven," Liz said.

"Right. I'll be outside your place at a quarter to seven. Where's the address?"

"Grand Canal Dock."

"Forty-five minutes will give us buckets of time. You know,

you've convinced me, Liz. I'd forgotten how enjoyable reading can be. I think I might actually enjoy this meeting."

Cathy was chattering away excitedly with all the zeal of a recent convert. She couldn't refuse now, could she, thought Liz, especially since she had encouraged her to come. And what about Marion and the others? She couldn't let them down.

Cathy was still talking.

"I hope the club is as good as you say. Maybe you might meet a nice man?"

"Who knows?" Liz said as she put down the phone.

Right now, meeting a nice man was as far down her agenda as it was possible to get. Her top priority was seeing Dr Brady on Friday and getting an expert opinion on this lump on her breast. In the meantime she would have to drag herself to the meeting and hope for the best.

Chapter Fourteen

Alan gazed with pride over the dark waters that lapped beneath the windows of his penthouse apartment at Grand Canal Dock. In its black expanse, the bright lights of the city were reflected back at him as if from a mirror, dancing and shimmering in the eddying current. On the other side of the river, he could see the shining glass and steel of the financial centre. He could almost hear it hum with industry and life. In daytime, his eyes could take in the green slopes of Howth Head and if the light was good and the day was clear, the far-off Mountains of Mourne.

It was a sight that gladdened his heart. But the pleasure didn't come simply from the spectacle that lay before him. It came from what it represented – a monument to his skill in financial planning. The penthouse was the best investment he had made so far. He had bought it in 2004 for € 400,000, the bulk of which he had borrowed from his bank. Today it was worth almost a million. The knowledge that he had carried out that transaction practically unaided and it had yielded such a lucrative result filled him with enormous satisfaction.

His career was definitely on the rise. The signs were all around him in the salary he earned, the clothes he wore, the car he drove, the apartment he lived in. He felt his breast swell when he thought of the distance he had travelled since the time when he was the only child of an impoverished widow in Belfast, constantly struggling to make ends meet, sneered at by the other boys at school because of his darned socks and scuffed shoes. If only his mother was alive today to see how well he had done, she would be proud of him.

Now he had all this. He could eat at the best restaurants, mix with important people, take expensive holidays. And he was only thirty-two, just at the beginning of his career. He knew that even greater things lay ahead if he worked hard and grasped the opportunities that were beginning to come his way. Already he was starting to dabble on the stock market and his financial skill was producing handsome returns. The thought made him tingle with joy.

With a small sigh of contentment, he turned away from the window and faced back into the elegant sitting room where his guests were already waiting, chatting animatedly in little groups. He had gone to some expense to prepare for this evening. He had arranged for a caterer to provide dishes of hors d'oeuvres and they rested on little tables around the room: bowls of prawn and ginger, crab cakes, platters of roast beef and horseradish, plates of pork and chilli, olives, capers, patés, cheeses. The hors d'oeuvres alone would make a satisfying meal and he was glad to see the guests were tucking in and clearly enjoying themselves.

To accompany the food, he had ordered several cases of fine French wines from an importer in Hardwick St and bottles of Emilion Cabernet and Sauvignon Blanc sat already opened beside the plates. He had told his guests that they should feel free to help themselves and he could see that most of them had happily followed his advice.

He checked his watch. Five minutes more and he would commence proceedings. He let his eye travel once more around the room. They had gained an additional member since the last meeting. Liz had brought a friend. She had been introduced as Cathy and the pair now sat together on a settee deep in conversation with Nick Barry. Alan's sharp eye had sensed that Liz was somewhat downcast tonight. He had seen it when she came in. Her face looked pale and she seemed a little subdued.

But the poor woman's husband had recently died, and quite suddenly too, by all accounts. Alan had made a few inquiries and learned that Liz's husband had been a successful businessman who had been killed while out walking his dog. It must have been a terrible shock for her. No doubt that was the reason for her melancholy. He would make a special point of drawing her out tonight and perhaps, as the evening progressed she might relax.

Alan was dressed in a pair of dark slacks, hand-made black shoes, pale blue shirt and a cravat. In addition to having his hair trimmed this morning, he had given his wardrobe some attention, spending half an hour in front of the bedroom mirror before he was satisfied with his appearance. He thought he now looked quite smart in a casual sort of way. He was determined to make a good impression. Not just on the members of the club, important as they were. But on the one member who mattered most to him, the woman for whom he had gone to all this trouble. Marion.

He had arranged this evening down to the last detail and so far he was delighted at the way it had worked out. He had actually managed to entice Marion to his apartment. It was something he never thought he would be able to achieve. But he had managed it. Luck and skill had both played their part. And when the meeting was over, he planned to detain her on the pretext of book club business. He would give her a tour of the penthouse which was bound to impress her. And then he would make his pitch.

He would outline the wonderful life they could have together, the ease and comfort and security. He would tell her he was prepared to put the past behind them and start afresh if she would too. They had been good friends once and could be again. Alan was confident when he had finished, Marion would be unable to resist. He would sweep her off her feet and into his arms. But there was only one drawback. So far, she had failed to turn up.

Her friend Trish was here, chatting amiably to Christy Grimes whose wife appeared to have pinioned him in a corner of the settee with her good arm so that he looked like a wrestler held in an arm lock. But there was no sign of Marion. He wondered if he should have a quiet word with Trish. If Marion was ill or something had happened to detain her, Trish would surely know. But if she was ill she would have called to tell him or asked Trish to pass on her apologies. There was one other explanation which Alan didn't even want to contemplate. She had decided not to come.

Surely she wouldn't be so rude. But he felt a bitter little worm of disappointment begin to gnaw at him as he glanced around the room once more. He couldn't delay much longer. But without Marion, what was the point? He glanced at his watch once more. It was now seven thirty-five. He made his decision. He had no option. He would have to press on.

He lifted an empty wine glass and tapped it gently with a spoon. Immediately, the hubbub of conversation died away and the guests turned their expectant faces towards him. Even though he was feeling slightly crestfallen, Alan mustered a winning smile.

"Good evening, ladies and gentlemen. And welcome to the second meeting of the book club. I'm expecting a lively discussion tonight for I have been reading Daphne du Maurier's classic novel *Rebecca* with great interest and I'm sure you have all enjoyed it as much as I have. Of course no novel is perfect and some of you may have criticisms to make. Feel free to do so. The whole point of the club is to express our views and exchange opinions and hopefully at the end of the evening we will all go away better informed as a result."

At the moment, the doorbell rang. Alan stopped speaking. He could barely contain his excitement at the sound. Immediately, it rang again. He felt his heart gladden and his spirits revive. He turned once more to his guests.

"If you would just excuse me for a moment, I think we may have a latecomer."

He left the room and walked quickly out to the hallway. He pulled open the door and at once, his heart flooded with relief. Marion was standing on the doorstep, looking slightly flustered, her long dark hair tossed with the wind but still looking beautiful.

"I'm sorry I'm late," she said. "My taxi got caught up in traffic."

Alan made no attempt to conceal his delight. He felt like hugging her with joy.

"You're not late," he warbled. "We haven't started yet. Please come in. I'm so glad to see you."

He waited while she took off her coat.

"You're looking lovely tonight," he whispered.

"Thank you," Marion said, coldly.

"Go right inside and pour yourself a glass of wine. We're just about to begin."

He put her coat away in the cloakroom and returned in time to see her squeezing in beside Matt Bollinger on a couch. Alan resumed his position with a triumphant feeling now swelling in his breast. Everything was back on track. Marion had turned up. At last, he had got her just where he wanted her.

He watched her glance around the room, her eyes admiring the décor and the fine furnishings and the expensive drapes that hung from the windows. Later, when the meeting was over, he would show her the magnificent view of the river. She couldn't fail to be impressed.

"Now," he said, smiling once more to the assembled guests. "Could we have a volunteer to start us off?"

By any yardstick, it was a very successful meeting and Alan directed it with skill and aplomb. Nick led off and said that *Rebecca* had been an excellent choice for their first book and congratulated Liz for having suggested it. He went on to make some general remarks about the quality of the writing and the unrelenting pace of the narrative and the brooding atmosphere of menace that pervaded the novel.

"What I found amazing about the book is that the dominating character is someone the reader never even meets – the dead Rebecca. She is the person who haunts the novel from beginning to end."

The guests listened intently to what Nick had to say. His comments were taken up by Matt who said he had thoroughly enjoyed the book. What impressed him most was the skilful way in which the author had built up the suspense and maintained it to the last page.

"Once she gets a grip on you, she never lets go," he said. "*Rebecca* is what I would describe as a classic page-turner."

People nodded their approval and then Ellie Grimes followed. She said she was in total agreement with the previous two speakers. She liked the strong characters and the touches of romance.

At this point, Christy sniffed loudly and Ellie gave him a deadly look that caused him to lower his head and look away.

"I know some people don't like romance," she said, pointedly, "but that's their hard luck. I certainly do. As for suspense, Matt is absolutely right. It's more than a page-turner. The pages were stuck to my fingers. Once I opened it, I couldn't put it down. I read it in three days flat," she finished, to general laughter.

Throughout the proceedings, Alan guided the group with the confidence of an orchestra conductor. He gently coaxed a response from Liz who made a very good contribution about how she had first read the novel years before and it had made such an impression that she had never forgotten it. She was followed by her friend Cathy.

All the while, Alan kept glancing at Marion who he was glad to see had now relaxed and was sitting comfortably with a glass of wine in her hand. When her turn came to speak, she made some interesting comments while Alan vigorously nodded his head in agreement and when she had finished he made a point of complimenting her on the shrewdness of her observations. A smile of satisfaction crossed his lips. Yes, he thought, things are coming along very nicely indeed.

By the time ten o'clock came around, everyone in the room had given their view on the novel except Christy Grimes. At last, Alan turned to him.

"Well, Christy, what do you think? Would you like to tell us what you thought of the book?"

Ellie, who had been keeping a tight grip on him throughout the meeting, hit him a poke in the ribs.

"I didn't like it," Christy said.

187

Alan raised an eyebrow. Christy was the first person who had dissented from the favourable consensus.

"Would you like to tell us why not?" he suggested.

Christy glanced at his wife and then cleared his throat. "I would have preferred more action."

Alan saw Ellie scowl and poke him again.

"Action? How do you mean?"

"Well I like a book with a good plot and exciting characters."

"Mother of God," Ellie muttered.

But now Christy was getting into his stride. "For me, the characters are the most important because if I don't like the characters, then I lose interest. But they have to be doing something. I don't like books where everybody is just sitting around talking."

"Very good," Alan prompted. "What sort of books do you like?"

"I read a James Bond book one time and that was very good."

Ellie gave a loud groan but Christy was now in full flow and nothing was going to stop him.

"I'll tell you the sort of book I'd like to read. When I was a chiseller in Ballybough, I had a friend called Larry Byrne and he had a row with his father and went off and joined the French Foreign Legion. Out there in the desert, he got involved in all kinds of exciting adventures. And then he heard word that his ould da was sick and wanted to see him before he died. So he decided to come home again and the two of them were reunited at his deathbed."

As Christy finished his story, the room had fallen silent.

"That's the sort of book I'd like to read, something with an exciting plot and plenty of action and good strong characters. But there's nobody writing that sort of stuff any more."

He turned to his wife who was shooting daggers at him.

"I knew you'd make a show of us," she hissed. "Can I not bring you anywhere?"

But across the room, Nick Barry was suddenly sitting on the edge of his seat and staring intently at Christy.

Alan was now moving swiftly to bring the meeting to a close. There was a brief discussion about the next book they should read.

Trish suggested something modern and after some discussion, it was agreed to choose *The Boy in the Striped Pyjamas* by John Boyne and to hold the next meeting in Liz's house.

The meeting began to break up. People stood chatting in little groups while they got ready to leave. Alan was beaming with delight. He could barely contain his excitement. The evening had gone even better than he had hoped. Now all he had to do was carry out the second part of his plan. He would corner Marion and persuade her to stay behind and have another glass of wine while he showed her over the apartment. But where was she?

As he started to look for her, several people approached to thank him for his hospitality and congratulate him on the way he had conducted the meeting. Alan graciously accepted their compliments. But it took him several minutes to extricate himself and when he did, Marion had disappeared.

Perhaps she's using the bathroom, he thought as he hurried frantically to the hall. But there was still no sign of her. He leaned over the banisters. A number of people were making their way down the stairs towards the lobby. Among them, he could make out Liz and Cathy and Nick Barry. And then he saw them.

His mouth fell open and he felt his heart go sinking to the floor.

Marion was leaving with Matt. That was bad enough. But what was far, far worse, she had her head on his shoulder and his arm was wrapped protectively around her waist.

"Are you all right?" Matt asked with concern as soon as they were outside in the fresh air. "Is there anything I can do for you?"

Everything had happened so fast that he still wasn't quite sure what it was all about. One minute he had been sitting beside Marion on the couch and the next minute she was grabbing his arm and telling him she wasn't feeling well and had to get out fast.

It had taken him completely by surprise. He was enjoying the experience of having her warm body pressed close to his. Every time she moved, he felt a little tingle of pleasure. And then there was that sexy perfume she was wearing. The scent of it had really got him excited. He could have sat there all evening just breathing in the heady perfume and feeling Marion's soft thigh pinioned tight to his.

"I'm fine," she replied.

"Are you sure?"

He looked at her closely. Was she coming down with something? Flu, maybe? There was a lot of it around at the moment. That might also explain why she had been late for the meeting.

"You startled me, the way you jumped up at the end and grabbed my arm. I thought you were going to be sick."

"I nearly was," she said. "But now I'm right as rain. Honestly." She smiled into his eyes and clung closer to his arm.

"Well, that's a relief," he said, eyeing her shrewdly. "So was there some other reason you were in a mad rush to get out of Alan's apartment? I didn't even get a chance to say goodbye."

"Do you want to know the truth?"

Something approaching a wicked gleam had now crept into her eyes.

"Of course."

"It was our host. I just couldn't stick him a minute longer. Did you notice the way he was preening himself all evening before his captive audience? Like he was the top dog and we were all his obedient little puppies?"

"He did hog the limelight a little," Matt conceded.

"Hog it? You'd think he was James Joyce the way he was going on. It was driving me crazy. If I'd stayed there a minute longer I would really have been sick, believe me."

Suddenly Matt found himself laughing.

"There's appears to be a devious side to you that I wasn't aware of, Ms Hunt."

She pulled a face. "Devious? Me?"

"Yes, you. But thank God you're all right."

"There's absolutely nothing the matter with me."

"I think I know exactly what you need," he said, with a grin.

"Yes?"

"A large gin and tonic."

"This is wonderful," she said, cuddling closer. "A man who can read my mind!"

They drove to a little bar in Smithfield within walking distance of The Cloisters. Inside, it was warm and snug and thankfully quiet. Matt ordered the drinks and brought them back to their table.

"You don't like Alan very much, do you?" he said.

He watched her turn up her nose in disgust.

"Is it so obvious?"

"Just little hints I've picked up."

"I have a confession to make. I can't stand him."

"Was that the reason you were late?"

She nodded. "I almost didn't come. I told him I was caught up in traffic. But it was really because I couldn't face the prospect of sitting there making polite small talk while he showed off his damned penthouse."

Matt wondered if there was some undercurrent here that he wasn't aware of. But why should he complain? It had all worked to his advantage. Now he had Marion alone and she seemed in a receptive mood. For weeks he'd been angling for this.

"You must admit it was a very good meeting," he said. "It would have been worth it for the food and drink alone. That wine he was serving must have cost at least €80 a bottle."

"Yes but who was he trying to impress? And what was his real agenda? Why did he get involved in the first place? Everyone else I can understand. But Alan McMillan?"

"So what *was* his agenda?"

"I think I know," she said cryptically, "but I don't want to bore you. Let's just say that Alan McMillan doesn't strike me as someone to get mixed up in a book club."

"I'm mixed up in it," Matt said.

A coquettish smile crossed her face. "But I recruited you personally, remember?"

"Yes and I've been wondering why you did that," he said, taking a sip of his whiskey.

She laughed. "I'll let you into a secret. When I approached you that morning on the stairs, there were only two members of the club, me and my friend Trish."

"So you only asked me because you were stuck?" Matt said, pretending to be offended.

"No, there was more to it than that."

"Tell me."

"You shouldn't be asking me questions like this."

"I'm curious," Matt said.

"I'd seen you around the building a few times and I kind of admired you. I liked the cut of your jib."

"The cut of my jib? Is that supposed to be a compliment?" he laughed.

"Yes, it is. Now you tell me something. How come a handsome man like you doesn't have a regular girlfriend?"

"How do you know that? How do you know I don't have a string of girlfriends?"

"Because I've been observing you. And I've never once seen you with a woman. It's a logical conclusion to draw, isn't it?"

Matt toyed with his glass. This conversation had suddenly taken a serious turn. Marion had revealed aspects of her character that he wasn't aware of. That morning she approached him about the club hadn't been an accident after all. It had all been part of a plan.

He wondered if he should tell her.

"I'm separated from my wife," he said.

He watched her face fall.

"Oh. What happened?"

"She left me for another man."

"Oh dear," she said. "That must have been painful."

"It was. Extremely painful."

"How long were you married?

"Seventeen years."

"That's a very long time. I'm sorry. It must have been awful for you."

"Well, it certainly wasn't a barrel of laughs, that's for sure."

She looked into his eyes and slowly ran her finger along his cheek.

"All I can say is your wife must have been a very foolish woman."

Matt finished his drink and ordered two more. For the next half hour he told her all about the break-up of the marriage. This was the first time he had spoken so fully to anyone about what had happened. And Marion was a comparative stranger. But talking to her made him feel good. She was a very sympathetic listener. He felt like he was sharing a burden.

"What about your wife?" she asked. "Do you still see her?"

"Not so much any more."

"And this man, Jack Arnold? How do you feel about him?"

"I felt bitter for a while. But I've let it go. I've built a new life now."

"I'm not sure I'd be so forgiving," Marion said.

"But what's the point of holding a grudge? It doesn't alter anything. The only person I would be hurting is me."

"Well, people do say that time is a great healer," she said and laid her head on his shoulder.

Without thinking, he found himself caressing her hair. He liked the soft, warm silky feeling.

"I shouldn't be unloading this stuff on you," he said.

"I don't mind. I asked you."

"Well, thanks for listening to me. Talking to you did a lot of good."

On the way home, Marion sat in the front seat of the car with her head cuddled against him. When they arrived at The Cloisters, he parked and they took the lift up to her apartment. Outside her door, they paused.

"I was wondering . . ." he began.

"Yes?" she prompted.

"Would you mind if I asked you to have dinner with me some evening?"

"Are you kidding?" she laughed. "I'd mind if you didn't."

His smiled. "Good. So I'll make the arrangements. What sort of food do you like?"

"I'm not fussy. You decide."

They stood looking at each other for a moment. Then, suddenly, he took her in his arms. She felt her heart race as their lips met in a passionate kiss. When they finally parted she was out of breath.

"Whooooaa!" she said. "I haven't been kissed like that in a long time."

Matt slowly released her.

"Goodnight, Marion," he said. "I'll be in touch."

Chapter Fifteen

Alan sat in his plush office in Chancery St and fumed. He was feeling extremely annoyed with Marion. In fact, he was more than annoyed – he was absolutely furious. He couldn't stop thinking about the way she had behaved last night at the book club. Her actions had been despicable. After enjoying his hospitality all evening, she had calmly walked off into the night with Matt on her arm, without so much as saying goodbye. All his well-laid plans had come to nothing. And the final insult – neither of them even had the decency to thank him for all the work he had put in.

It was inexcusable behaviour and Alan felt outraged. He would never have expected such bad manners. He had spent the best part of €1000 on the food and wine alone in the hope of impressing Marion and persuading her to give their relationship another chance. But he might as well have set fire to the money for all the good it did him. As far as he was concerned, the evening had been a disaster.

The only saving note was that the other members had enjoyed it. At least they could appreciate his efforts. Several of them had come to him afterwards and thanked him. And he knew the meeting had gone well from the enthusiastic response of the guests. He had succeeded in stimulating a lively discussion and getting the first proper meeting of the club off to an excellent start. But what did it all matter if he hadn't convinced Marion? She was the one he had set out to impress. She was the reason he had joined the club in the first place.

Alan felt anger boil up in him like a geyser about to burst. Apart from taking her coat when she arrived, he hadn't got a single opportunity to speak to her alone, never mind giving her the grand tour of the penthouse he had planned. She had ignored him all evening. And in his own sitting room! She hadn't even made the effort to get to the meeting on time. He was convinced she had been deliberately late. It was a calculated snub in front of the whole book club. And no doubt, everyone present had taken note.

He squirmed as he thought of the insults he had been forced to endure. He had been extremely patient with Marion but she was proving to be a tougher nut than he expected, revealing depths of callousness and cunning that he hadn't known she possessed. After five years, she still seemed determined to make him suffer for that single mistake with Julie – one stupid incident that most reasonable women would have long forgiven.

He had accepted that getting back into her good books would not be easy. He knew it would involve a certain amount of grovelling. He had apologised. He had tried to explain. He had gone out of his way to be nice to her. But obviously it was still not enough. What more did she want from him – his fingernails?

If only she would agree to sit down and talk, he was certain he could convince her. If only she would let him show her the wonderful future they could have together. He had money now and the prospect of much more. Recently he had bought shares in a pharmaceutical company called Vorax. They had been a tip-off from a broker he knew and they had been performing spectacularly well. Alan had bought them at €1.50 each and now they stood at €11, a mere three months later. If he cashed them in, he would make a tidy profit.

The future was bright. He could afford to treat Marion well, buy her nice clothes, take her on foreign holidays. She had already had a glimpse of his penthouse, although he was bitterly disappointed that he didn't get the opportunity to show it to her properly. That view of the water alone would have taken her breath away.

If they got together again, there was no reason why she couldn't move in with him. Nothing would delight him more. She could keep her apartment in Smithfield as an investment property and draw a rental income from it. She could give up that boring job of hers and become a lady of leisure. Between them, they could have it all, move in the best circles. Alan could imagine the life they could have. They would make an ideal couple, the type who got invited to rock concerts and first nights at the theatre and got written up in the celebrity columns – a young couple about town. The type of people others would look up to and envy.

Marion was a good-looking woman and would look even better if she had the money to spend on nice clothes. Alan had that money and would have more. It was all there, waiting for her. Why couldn't she see the glittering life that he was offering her? Why did she insist on pursuing this silly vendetta over an incident that meant nothing to him and which had long been buried with the passage of time?

There had to be a reason. He was beginning to wonder if perhaps there was a streak of cruelty in Marion. Maybe she was one of these women who enjoyed dominating men and making them suffer. But she had never shown it before. He remembered the Marion he used to know, back in the time when they first met. She had been kind and considerate, then. He remembered those long walks together over Killiney Hill when he would confide his hopes and ambitions and she would listen and give advice. That was the Marion he recalled with affection. That was the Marion he had fallen in love with. That was the Marion he wanted back.

No, it had to be something else. Something or someone had to be motivating her, encouraging her to behave like this. Some malign influence had to be at work. But who? And then it came to him like a flash. Matt Bollinger! Of course! Alan must have been blind not to see what was going on right under his nose. They had left his apartment last night arm-in-arm like a pair of lovers. They must have been carrying on together for some time. It was obvious!

Now it was all becoming clear. Matt Bollinger saw Alan as a rival and was determined to eliminate him. That's what this was all about. It wasn't Marion at all. Left to herself, she would probably come running back to him in an instant. But Bollinger was standing in the way, no doubt poisoning her mind, egging her on, encouraging her to snub and humiliate him.

This thought sent Alan into a fury. He would never have suspected Bollinger of behaviour like this. He had formed an opinion of him as a gentleman with civilized standards of behaviour. Not the type of person who would turn the woman you loved against you while spending the evening drinking your best wine and then waltzing off with her before your very eyes.

A cold anger rose up in Alan's breast. If it wasn't for Matt Bollinger, he would have been reconciled with Marion a long time ago. She would have forgiven him and they would be happily carrying on their relationship together – a beautiful relationship that held such potential and had now been so cruelly dashed.

He sadly shook his head. He had been far too trusting but that had always been his nature. He saw the best in people. And of course, that viper Bollinger had been extremely clever at concealing his real intentions. To look at him you wouldn't think butter would melt in his mouth. Well he hadn't been clever enough for Alan. And now he had rumbled him.

What did he know about Matt Bollinger? Very little apart from the fact that he lived in Marion's apartment block and appeared to be single. Alan made up his mind. He would make it his business to find out more about him. He knew the very people who could help him. And he would start today with some discreet enquiries.

Marion was feeling elated this morning. Last evening had passed off extremely well in the end. She could still recall the passion behind Matt's kiss, the strong manly arms enclosing her, that handsome, confident face looking down into hers, the thrill of excitement that coursed through her entire body when their lips met in that warm embrace. And to think she almost didn't go to the meeting because of her fears about Alan McMillan! How foolish she had been. And now she had the prospect of an intimate dinner to look forward to, just the two of them, herself and Matt. All in all, she thought with quiet satisfaction, it had been a very good night.

Matt was a very handsome man. She thought once more of those rugged good looks, the piercing blue eyes, the broad shoulders and well-developed physique, the head of dark, well-groomed hair. And he was older and more mature. She felt safe with him and confident in his company. Matt was exactly the type of man she aspired to, the type she needed in her life right now to love and protect her. He was exactly the sort of man she had been looking for.

But this cosy feeling was quickly shattered when the phone suddenly jumped and she heard Trish's shrill voice on the line.

"Well," she said, accusingly. "I hope you're feeling pleased with yourself?"

"What do you mean?" Marion asked, completely taken aback.

"Your behaviour last night was totally reprehensible."

"What behaviour? I don't know what you're talking about," Marion said, immediately going on the defensive.

"Oh, yes, I think you do."

"Then tell me."

"First you turn up late."

"My taxi was caught in traffic."

"You don't expect me to believe that for one moment, do you? Everybody else managed to get there on time."

"Okay, if you want to know the truth, I almost didn't go. You know the way I feel about Alan McMillan. I was in two minds whether to go to his damned penthouse party. But I did the right thing in the end and forced myself."

"Well, I've no doubt he saw it as a snub. But that's not the worst part. You couldn't get out of the place quick enough. You left faster than a bat out of hell. You didn't even thank him for his hospitality."

Marion gulped. It was true. She should have done it, although it would have stuck in her throat.

"Anyone could see that the poor guy had gone to a lot of trouble to make a success of the evening," Trish continued. "And by the look on his face, he was devastated by your conduct."

"I didn't mean to be rude," Marion explained, nervously. "Well, not deliberately rude. I just couldn't take any more."

"A simple 'thank you' wouldn't have gone astray. It's only good manners. I don't know what he spent on the catering. But it was like something you would get in a five-star restaurant. The wines alone must have cost him a fortune."

Marion didn't know what to say. Suddenly she could see just how bad her conduct had been and how it must have looked.

"You can't behave like this, Marion. You're setting a very bad example for the book club. People notice these things. And you don't want to destroy it after all the hard work you've put in."

She felt a twinge of remorse. Trish was right. She *had* behaved badly. But she couldn't help herself. She had felt so angry with Alan.

"You're right," she conceded. "I should have said something to him."

"Well that's not all," Trish continued. "He saw you leave with Matt. Couldn't you have been a little more discreet?"

"I can leave with whoever I please," she said, getting indignant again.

"But did you have to humiliate Alan?"

"Humiliate Alan? What are you talking about? I just wanted out of his damned apartment. I'd been forced to watch him preening himself for the whole evening."

"How do you think it looked, you waltzing off with another man after totally ignoring him like that? I think you owe him an apology."

Marion gasped. Trish was way out of line. She wasn't going to sit here and be lectured like this.

"Let's get a few things straight. Alan McMillan has no claim on me. I've already told you I have absolutely no interest in him. And I've told him too. In fact I'm sorry I ever got involved with him in the first place. I think he's a schemer who has managed to worm his way into the secretary's job and if you think I'm going to tailor my personal life to take account of his feelings, you have another think coming."

"So you admit you went home with Matt?"

"That's none of your business."

"It's a simple question. Did you or not?"

"He offered me a lift and we do happen to live in the same building. Is this suddenly a crime?"

"You're getting touchy. That's not what I meant. Where did you go when you left Alan's place?"

"This is beginning to sound like a police interrogation."

"I'm simply interested."

"We went for a drink," Marion said. "What's wrong with that?"

"Now you're getting defensive. I didn't say there was anything wrong with it."

"If you must know, I think he's a very charming man. He's very sensitive and caring."

"I'm sure he is. But it didn't happen by accident. You had it planned. I heard you ask him to get you out of Alan's apartment."

"Yes, but *he* asked *me* to go for a drink."

"You could have refused."

"Now, *that* would have been bad manners. Besides, I like him. In fact I've liked him for some time, if you must know."

"So this may be the start of something?"

"Who knows?" Marion said, tartly. "We'll have to get acquainted a bit more. But so far, I like what I see."

"Well, just be careful. And remember to keep me informed. I want to know all the gory details. And in future try to be a little more sensitive to other people's feelings."

"I'll bear that in mind," Marion said firmly and put down the phone.

She sat back in her desk. Trish had a damned cheek lecturing her like that. She had a soft spot for Alan McMillan. Marion had noticed it before. But if she continued to take that tone their friendship would be in jeopardy. The trouble was, Trish didn't know Alan the way she did. She just saw his nice side. She didn't see the devious, manipulative individual who wouldn't take no for an answer and was beginning to make her life a misery.

She should have handled things better last night but Marion was certain of one thing. Alan McMillan had to get the message loud and clear. There was no way she was going to apologise to him. If she did that, she would only encourage him and that was exactly what he wanted. She knew what he was up to but it wasn't going to work.

Nick pushed his chair back from his desk and stared at his computer screen. He was very pleased with what he had written. After weeks of stagnation, the ideas had started to flow again. It was funny the way a few simple words could cause events to turn 360 degrees on their axis.

This morning, he had jumped out of bed at eight o'clock, had a quick breakfast and by half eight he was seated at his word processor and raring to go. The doubt and uncertainty that had plagued him for the past few weeks had suddenly disappeared. Now he felt confidence flow through him like a tide.

For the next few hours he worked at a frantic pace, buoyed up by the torrent of energy that seemed to have engulfed him. By one o'clock, when he finally sat back from his desk, he had completed a rough synopsis of the novel. He was now ready to begin the serious writing. But before he did that, he had an important phone call to make.

He let his gaze drift out of his window to the grimy backyard. This morning, it didn't look half so bad. The sun was bright in the heavens and the little patch of lawn that had lain dormant all winter was now beginning to take on a tinge of green. A few stray daffodils were pushing up their heads. A flock of sparrows had appeared on the clothesline and were noisily quarrelling. Nick felt a smile play around his lips. For the first time, he felt sure of what he had to do.

Joining the book club had been an inspired decision. It had given him access to the sort of audience he was hoping to write for. And now it had provided the inspiration he was seeking to help him start his novel.

He switched off the word processor, stood up and stretched his arms. It was time to have a shower and get ready for work. If he hurried he would have time to grab a quick bite of lunch before going into the office. From what he had heard on the radio news this morning it was going to be another busy night. The political crisis that had been rumbling along had now erupted into a full-scale crisis.

But first he had some business to attend to. He glanced quickly at his watch. Now was probably the best time. He'd be sure to catch him at home. He took out his mobile and dialled the number, drumming his fingers on the desktop while he listened to the gentle purring of the phone. At last, he heard the call being answered.

"Hello," he said. "Is that Christy Grimes?"

Most mornings when Liz came into the Quick Print office, there was a pile of work already waiting for her. Mornings were always the busiest time of the day when clients rang in with orders and problems that hadn't been resolved the day before demanded her attention. And this morning was no exception. It was half eleven before the hectic pace began to slacken and she was able to get a few quiet moments to herself. This was the time she usually reserved for personal phone messages and private business.

There was a green space at the back of the building where people sat on warm days to eat their lunch and where the diehard smokers gathered regardless of the weather. It contained a small rose garden and a bench. Liz went there now. Fortunately, the place was deserted. She sat on the bench and thought of what lay ahead.

Today was Friday and this evening she had her appointment with Dr Brady. So far, she had managed to keep her anxiety at bay. But it had been a struggle and now that the time was drawing closer she could feel the fear return. She knew it was irrational. In just over seven hours she would see the doctor and he would examine her. Worrying about the appointment wasn't going to change anything. And seeing Dr Brady would begin the process of treating whatever was wrong – *if* there was anything wrong. Liz kept clinging to the possibility that the lump on her breast would turn out to be innocent and there would be nothing to worry about.

Nevertheless, the fear was real. What she needed was reassurance, a supportive shoulder to lean on. So far she had resisted the urge to tell Cathy but now she was beginning to change her mind. She needed to talk to her friend immediately. She needed to hear her voice. She wasn't going to get through this long day without support. She took out her mobile and dialled her number.

"Hi," Cathy said, all cheerful and bouncy. "How is life treating you?"

"I've got something to tell you," Liz began.

"Shoot."

"I've found a lump on my breast."

There was a momentary silence and she heard the concern in Cathy's voice.

"My God. What does it look like? Is it big?"

"It's about the size of a pea."

"That doesn't sound very big. When did you notice it?"

"A couple of days ago."

"Why didn't you tell me? What sort of friend are you? You know I'm always here for you." She paused. "That's why you were off form last night. I could sense there was something wrong. You were worried."

"I didn't want to alarm you."

"You should have told me. I'm angry with you. Where are you now?"

"At work."

"You should be at home, resting. I'm coming to get you. Just stay right were you are."

"No, I'm perfectly fine," Liz protested. "I prefer to be at work. It gives me something to do."

"You'll have to see a doctor. As soon as possible."

"I've already made an appointment to see Dr Brady this evening."

"Good. What time?"

"Seven o'clock."

"I'm coming with you. I'm not letting you face that ordeal on your own. And I won't be put off. I'll see you at Dr Brady's surgery."

"Okay."

"And afterwards, I'm buying you dinner. Just you and me. I'll leave something for Max and the kids in the oven. We're going to have a good long talk and you're going to tell me everything."

"Thanks, Cathy."

"And Liz . . ."

"Yes?"

"Try not to worry about this. Thousands of women find lumps on their breasts every day and they turn out to be nothing more serious than a carbuncle."

She missed the worst of the rush-hour traffic and was at the surgery for ten to seven. When she arrived, she found Cathy already waiting with a box of Terry's *All Gold* chocolates in her lap. As she took her seat, Cathy gave her a big warm hug and flicked open the box.

"Take some," she commanded. "Never mind your dietary concerns. This is comfort food."

Liz didn't feel like eating chocolates but rather than risk an argument, she did as she was told and selected several sweets.

"At a time like this, you have to treat yourself. Now, how do you feel?"

"A bit tense," Liz admitted. "Thanks for coming. I really appreciate it."

"Forget it," Cathy said with a dismissive flick of her wrist. "This is what friends are for. Now try to look on the bright side. You've only had this thing for a few days. It may be nothing at all. But if it is something, you've caught it in time."

It was the same logic that Liz herself had applied earlier.

"And even if it *is* the worst-case scenario, which of course it won't be, you must remember they have made tremendous medical advances in recent years. They've got all sorts of wonderful treatments now."

Liz sighed and held Cathy's hand. "I'm scared," she confessed.

"Ssshhh! There's nothing to be scared about. Everything is going to be all right."

She gave her friend another hug.

"You must think me a terrible hypochondriac," said Liz.

"Why should I think that? You're right to get these things checked. Was that why you didn't tell me?"

"Yes."

"Poor little dote. You know I wouldn't think anything of the sort. Now just try and relax. Dr Brady will soon put your fears to rest."

At five past seven, the doctor put his head out of the consulting room, looked around the surgery and called Liz.

"Good luck," Cathy whispered. "And don't worry."

Dr Brady was in his early thirties and had a warm reassuring manner which was why Liz liked him. She had seen a lot of him in the weeks since Tim had died. Tara, his female nursing assistant was also on hand. She was young and pretty and reminded Liz of Cathy's eldest girl, her godchild, Amelia. She moved immediately to put Liz at ease.

"How are you?"

"A bit nervous."

"There's absolutely nothing to be nervous about," Tara smiled. "Would you like to remove your blouse and bra?"

She took the garments from Liz and hung them from a peg on the door.

Meanwhile Dr Brady was pulling on a pair of surgical gloves.

"You've done the right thing," he said with a big broad smile. "The sooner we get this checked, the better. Now this will only take a couple of minutes. Try to relax. It will all be over before you know."

"Would you like me to assist you onto the couch?" Tara asked.

But Liz shook her head. "I think I can manage, thank you."

She got up on the couch and lay on her back. Dr Brady bent over her.

"Now," he said in his soothing manner, "just show me where the problem is."

Liz pointed to her left breast, just below her armpit. The doctor bent closer. She shivered slightly as the cold glove touched her skin and he began to probe with his fingers.

"Is that painful?"

"No."

He pressed a little harder. "How about that?"

"No."

His fingers moved around the breast, gently probing. Then he switched attention to the right breast and carried out the same procedure. At last, he stood back from the couch.

"You can get dressed now, Liz."

She got down from the couch. Dr Brady was back at his desk and was busy scribbling something on a note pad. No one spoke. Liz could feel her heart pounding like a drum. She put on her bra and buttoned up her blouse. At last, she forced herself to break the silence in the room.

"Do you know what it is?"

Dr Brady swung round in his chair. "Not from my initial examination. We're going to require further tests."

"What kind of tests?" Liz asked, feeling her mouth go dry.

"Let's put it this way, there's something there, which shouldn't be there. But whether it's dangerous, I can't say at this stage." He tore off the note and sealed it in an envelope. "This woman is a specialist in this area. I want you to ring her and make an appointment. She'll arrange for you to have a mammogram which should tell us more."

Liz took the note and noticed that her hands were trembling. "So it could be serious?"

"It could be any number of things. I can't tell from my examination. Ring the specialist and make an appointment. I've asked her to treat your case as a matter of urgency. I'll let you know as soon as I get the results." Dr Brady was suddenly smiling again. "Try to think positively, Liz."

But his confident manner didn't fool her. Something in his attitude had already warned her that the news was bad.

No sound disturbed the silence of the Grimes's living room save the steady ticking of the cuckoo clock and the gentle turning of pages. The cuckoo clock held pride of place on the wall beside a framed photograph of Christy and Ellie on their wedding day. Christy had won the clock in a pub quiz ten years before. The winning question that clinched it for him was: *Who was known as the Little Brown Saint?* Christy's opponent, who was a skinny taxi driver called Vinnie O'Toole, generally perceived to be a know-all, had immediately shouted out: "Nelson Mandela."

But Christy, whose mother had a special veneration for him and always kept a plaster statue of him on top of the wireless in their house in Ballybough, said quietly: "St Martin de Porres". And since that was the correct answer, he won the clock.

It never kept the correct time and the cuckoo turned out to be very temperamental and often decided not to appear when he was supposed to every hour, but the clock always ticked away and it never actually stopped and since it was the only thing that Christy had ever won in his entire life, it stayed on the wall beside the wedding picture.

Christy and Ellie sat now in comfortable chairs at each side of the window where they could look out at the garden. It was another sunny day. Christy had remarked earlier to his wife that the weather seemed to be picking up, thank God, and maybe they had seen the last of the rain. The garden looked tranquil. The daffodils were pushing up strongly through the damp earth and a few birds scavenged for worms along the lawn that Christy had cut only an hour before. He thought he had done a good job although he knew it wasn't as good as Ellie could do when she was in the fullness of her health. Maybe, with a bit of luck she'd be able to assume control of the garden by the time the next cut was due.

Each of them had a copy of John Boyne's novel, *The Boy in the Striped Pyjamas*. This time, Christy had managed to get both copies from the library. And whereas Ellie was halfway through, Christy was still struggling with the first chapter. But already he sensed that he was going to enjoy this book better than the last one. For one thing, it was shorter and didn't have so many big words.

He turned a page and glanced at his wife. She had a habit of moving her lips as she read as if she was speaking the lines as she went along.

"Are you enjoying it?" he asked.

"Very much. How about you?"

"I think so," Christy said.

"What do you mean you 'think so'? Either you are or you're not."

"Well, you know me," Christy said. "It takes me a while to settle into a book. I have to get the feel of it before I can make up my mind."

"Mother of God," Ellie exclaimed. "I never met anybody like you. I can tell by the very first page if I'm going to like a book."

"Ah but you're a reader, you see. That's the difference. You've had more experience than me."

Ellie gave her husband a quizzical look, not sure whether he was being smart. "Well, in that case, you'd better get your skates on or we'll be waiting for another fortnight before we hear your learned opinion."

"I'm going as fast as I can," Christy said.

"And try to think of something interesting to say. Last time you made a show of yourself with all that ould guff about Larry Byrne and the French Foreign Legion."

"It wasn't guff," Christy said, warming to the subject. "I told them the truth. That's what they wanted to hear."

"They were just being polite."

"No, they weren't. They were really interested. I could tell by the way they listened to me."

Ellie let out a loud groan. "Say something about the characters and the plot and the atmosphere. Novels are about more than action, as you call it."

"I *did* mention the characters. I said I liked exciting characters. I distinctly remember saying that."

"And for God's sake don't say there were no laughs in it. Not every book is meant to be funny, you know. Most of them are supposed to be serious."

"Yeah, well, maybe that's why people don't buy them."

"For God's sake," Ellie said, throwing her eyes to heaven, "would you stop talking and keep reading. You've another 200 pages to go."

Christy turned his attention back to the novel in his lap. Secretly, he was pleased. Ellie was rattled because she had no real answer to what he had just said. And he knew the others had found his comments interesting. He could see it in their faces. Just because he hadn't read as many books as his wife didn't mean he didn't know what he liked.

Anyway, the book club was supposed to be about getting people's honest opinions. It would be no good if everyone just agreed with each other and said what they thought the others wanted to hear. If you wanted to get a good argument going then you had to have disagreement.

He turned a page. This book was about a young boy. He wasn't sure if chisellers were exciting enough for his taste. Gangsters and crooks and spies, now they were exciting people by their very nature. But young boys didn't really have an opportunity to do anything adventurous although there was that Harry Potter fella that they were all raving about. But that was supposed to be about magicians and wizards and stuff like that. Just fairytales really, Christy decided, and turned another page.

He glanced across at his wife. She was very perky today and that was a sure sign that she was getting better. Dr Hynes had promised to remove the walking frame if she continued to improve and Christy couldn't wait. Next weekend, he planned to take her down to the supermarket. It would do her good; build up her confidence. And once she got her confidence back, he knew there'd be no stopping her.

He coughed gently to attract her attention as another thought came into his head.

"Yes?" Ellie said looking up from her book and peering at him over the top of her reading glasses.

"I was just thinking," Christy said. "We'll have to bring the book club here some night. It'll be our turn."

"So?"

"I was wondering what we could give them. We'd have to have wine, of course. They've sort of come to expect wine. But what about food?"

"I can make sandwiches," Ellie said.

"I was thinking of a nice dish of coddle."

"Coddle?" Ellie said, in astonishment. "At a meeting of the book club?"

"What's wrong with that?"

"Are you mad?" Ellie said. "You can't give people coddle at the book club meeting."

"Why not?" Christy said defiantly. "Everybody likes my coddle. It's filling. And it's very nourishing. I'll bet you anything, they'd love a nice dish of Dublin coddle. I'll put extra onions in it for flavour."

"You'll do nothing of the sort," Ellie retorted. "Do you want to have everybody talking about us?"

"Why would they talk about us? Sure they'd be happy as sand boys. They wouldn't go home hungry, anyway, that's for sure."

Ellie put down her book and removed her glasses, which Christy knew was the prelude to an ultimatum. But before she could speak there was a loud ringing from the phone in the kitchen.

"We'll continue this discussion another time," Christy said and got up out of his chair.

He was gone for several minutes. When he returned, there was a big wide grin all over his face.

"Well?" Ellie said. "Anything important?"

"You'll never guess who that was," Christy said.

"Tell me?"

"Nick Barry."

"From the book club?"

"Yes," Christy said, looking smug and self satisfied. "He wants to meet me."

"What for?"

Christy sniffed and tossed his head. "He wants to talk about Larry Byrne and the French Foreign Legion."

Chapter Sixteen

Marion quickly forgot her phone row with Trish in her eager anticipation of Matt's dinner date. She was very keen to see him again, to look into his strong, confident face, to listen to his warm voice, to watch him smile. They had parted on a high note and now she missed him. She couldn't remember feeling this way about a man before.

But the days slipped by and there was no phone call. He must be busy at work, she decided. Yet it was odd that he didn't phone her. He had seemed as eager as she was to meet again. Why then, did he not ring? Gradually, the doubts began to creep in.

She started to look out for him around the apartment block where she used to see him waiting for the lift or parking his car. But now he seemed to have disappeared. Marion wondered what was wrong. Had she imagined the whole episode after the book club meeting, that warm embrace, that passionate kiss? Had he decided in the cold light of morning that he didn't want to pursue their relationship any further? Was he avoiding her? Was that the reason for the silence?

Once or twice, she considered calling him. She had both his office and mobile numbers. She could easily ring on the pretext of checking some book club business. But pride prevented her. Matt wasn't stupid. He would quickly see through her pretext. It would appear as if she was chasing him and Marion wasn't prepared to do that. If he had dumped her, then so be it. She would take it on the chin. She was a big girl now.

She tried to tell herself it was no big deal. He was just another man and there were plenty more where he had come from. She had never had any problem attracting men in the past. She could do it again. But deep in her heart, she knew this wasn't true. Matt Bollinger wasn't just another man. He was special. In the short time she had known him, she had quickly realised that Matt possessed qualities she had never found in any other man. He was warm and affectionate. He was charming. He was confident. He was witty. He was loving. And these were the things she would miss if her worst fears were realised and she didn't hear from him again.

And then about a week later, just when she was on the verge of giving up and putting him out of her mind for good, she picked up the phone one morning and heard his voice on the line.

"Hi," he said, sounding bright and cheerful.

"Matt," she gasped.

"Look, I have to apologise for not being in touch. I had to go over to Brussels on urgent business. A problem we had to resolve. I just had to drop everything and go. So I didn't have time to call."

"That's all right," she said, feeling a flood of relief wash over her. "You don't have to apologise."

"But I said I'd be in touch."

"These things happen. Anyway, you're in touch with me now."

She heard his warm, throaty laugh.

"Well, the good news is we've got the problem under control and now I'm back in Dublin and anxious to have that dinner we talked about. When would suit you?"

"You tell me."

"Let's not waste time. Why don't we do it tonight? Besides, I can't wait to see you again. Do you like Italian food?"

"I love it."

"Then you're going to adore this place. Mama Rosa's in Blackrock. What time is best?"

"Half eight?"

"Brilliant. I'll call for you at half seven or is that too early?"

"No. Half seven is fine."

"*Perfecto! Arrividerci! Ciao!*"

"*Arrividerci,*" Marion muttered under her breath as she heard the melody of *Nessun Dorma* begin to play in her head.

How Matt discovered Mama Rosa's restaurant was one of his favourite stories. He had come upon it completely by accident one spring day several years before when he had made a lunch appointment at another, more prestigious, establishment in the same neighbourhood. On this occasion, he was dining with an important client for whom he had just designed a marketing campaign and he was hoping to impress him.

But when he arrived at the restaurant, he discovered there were no tables available. And to make matters worse, the arrogant little manager had insisted that Matt had no reservation. Indeed, he behaved as if he was doing him an enormous favour by simply allowing him across the doorstep. Matt was furious. He knew he had made a reservation just a few days before but he forced himself to bite his tongue. Rather than risk a scene and embarrass his guest, he decided to leave and drive out to Sandycove to another place he knew.

Then, just as they were leaving, he happened to see a newly painted sign hanging outside a small establishment further along the street that he hadn't noticed before. He checked the menu and it looked okay so he decided to take a chance. And he had the best lunch he could ever remember. His guest obviously thought so too, for the following day he rang to thank Matt for the meal and to approve the marketing campaign. Matt had been coming back ever since. It was one of his best-kept secrets although word was beginning to spread about the culinary excellence to be sampled in Mama Rosa's restaurant.

It was a small place that seated about thirty guests. It was family owned and family run. The husband, Mario, was the business manager, the son, Carlo, was the chef, his brother Alberto was head waiter while the matriarch, Mama Rosa herself, was the defining presence and public face of the restaurant. She designed the menus and sat behind the little cash desk each day to welcome her guests with a warm smile and a cheery *"Ciao, amici!"*

The superb cuisine was based on simple recipes learned over generations in the small Italian village of Monte Angelo in Liguria where the family originated many years before. But there was something in the care that was taken in the kitchen, the freshness of the ingredients and the skill of the chef that produced magical dishes to stun the palate and stimulate the gastric juices.

Now Matt whistled softly to himself as he emerged from the shower in his bathroom and began vigorously applying the towel to his dripping torso. He checked his watch. It was five past seven. In twenty-five minutes he would be seeing Marion again. He was in excellent form. Now that he had resolved the Brussels problem he had some time on his hands. The last few months had been bruising but it had been an exciting time, just as Jim Carville had promised.

After drying himself, he wrapped the towel round his waist and examined his chin in the bathroom mirror. Time for a quick lick of the razor! He soaped his face and stretching the skin with his left hand, he skilfully shaved away the accumulated stubble of the day. He washed off the remaining soap, applied some after-shave balm and examined himself again.

He was pleased by what he saw. His full head of dark hair glowed with vitality. There was barely a crease or a wrinkle on his face despite his age and the trials he had been through. He examined his stomach: tight and firm, the six-pack still in good repair. He was holding his age well. There was many a younger man who would have envied his youthful profile and obvious fitness. He vigorously brushed his teeth, combed his hair and went into the bedroom to get dressed.

He opened the closet and looked at the row of suits and jackets he had accumulated over the years. What would he wear? Something formal such as a nice dark suit with shirt and tie or something a bit more casual? This was an important dinner and he was determined to look his best for Marion. After reflecting for a few minutes, he opted for a blue linen jacket and dark slacks. He had been wearing a suit all day and tonight was meant to be relaxing. And the jacket would go well with the cotton sports shirt that Peter had bought him as a Christmas present.

Five minutes later he was dressed. He checked the time again on the bedside clock. Twenty five past seven. Perfect! He made sure that he had his wallet, keys and credit cards and cast a last glance at himself in the bedroom mirror. He looked good. He picked up the single long-stemmed rose he had bought earlier and the box of Belgian chocolates he had picked up at Brussels airport. He gave the apartment a final quick inspection before closing the door. A few short steps brought him to the lift that would whisk him up to Marion's apartment.

She was waiting. And Marion too had taken time to prepare although for her it had been rather more hectic. After Matt's phone call this morning she had immediately gone to Mr McDonald and asked for the afternoon off telling him that some urgent personal business had cropped up. She had a lot of leave days due so her supervisor readily agreed.

Next she had to make a hairdressing appointment and this was more difficult. But after frantically ringing around, she managed to find a salon off Grafton St which had just had a cancellation and they slotted her in for one o'clock. Here, she spent the rest of the afternoon having her hair trimmed and highlighted. For good measure, she spent another forty-five minutes in the care of the manicurist who cleaned, trimmed and buffed her nails and finally ended up with the beautician who plucked her eyebrows, waxed her legs and gave her a face massage. The whole package had cost almost €400 but Marion had no regrets. As far as she was concerned, it was money well spent.

She had finally arrived back at her apartment shortly before six o'clock feeling utterly exhausted. Immediately, she poured a chilled glass of Frascati, filled the bathtub and liberally sprinkled it with essence of violets. For the next half hour, she luxuriated in the bath and let the cares of the world evaporate with the steam.

At last, she stood up and dried herself. Now it was time to get dressed. This was a matter which had already consumed much thought. She had already made a mental selection – a little black cocktail dress with a low neckline and a higher-than-usual hemline. But she hadn't made a final decision. This was all part of the excitement. She would spend another half-hour in the bedroom trying on various outfits till she decided what suited her best.

In the end, she stuck with the cocktail dress. She decided to wear it with her black sling-back shoes and a dark jacket. The weather was still a bit chilly but she would be in a car on the journey to the restaurant and back again and the restaurant would be heated so she had nothing to worry about on that front.

Normally, Marion didn't wear much make-up but tonight was special and she went for the full treatment. After applying foundation and a faint trace of blusher, she spent a long time carefully working on her eyes – shadow, liner, mascara – then she chose a crimson lipstick which perfectly complemented the black dress and gave her a rather raffish look that she quite appreciated. Finally, she selected a pair of gold earrings and a matching chain for her neck. She sprayed a little perfume on each wrist and examined herself in the mirror. She had been transformed. She barely recognised herself. Then she heard the doorbell ring.

She marched boldly to the door and flung it open. Matt was standing in the hall with a single red rose and a box of chocolates in his hand. And one glance told her he looked absolutely dashing. She felt a warm feeling sweep over her.

"Good evening," she said. "You're bang on time. I like a man who is punctual."

Matt gave a playful smile. "I can't claim to have been held up in traffic, now can I? Since I've only come from downstairs?"

They both laughed at his little reference to her late attendance at the book club meeting.

He bent to kiss her on the cheek then held out the rose and the chocolates. "These are for you. I hope you like chocolates. They're Belgian and they are supposed to be very good."

"How thoughtful!" Marion exclaimed. "I adore roses. And chocolates. Come in. Make yourself at home."

She held open the door and Matt stepped into the apartment.

"Go right into the sitting room," she urged as she disappeared into the kitchen to find a vase for the rose. "Would you like a glass of wine?"

"I wouldn't say no."

"White okay?"

"Sounds good to me."

A minute later she returned with two glasses of Frascati from the bottle that she had opened earlier. Matt turned away from the window.

"I was just admiring your view once more. You know, every time I see this place, I could kick myself that I didn't get in earlier."

"Then you might have got my apartment. And where would that have left me?"

"I hadn't thought of that," he laughed as they clicked their glasses together in a toast.

"Good health!"

"I've booked the dinner. And I've taken the liberty of ordering a taxi. It means we can have a couple of drinks without worrying about being stopped by the gendarmes."

"That makes sense," Marion agreed. "Did you have any problem getting a reservation? It was very short notice."

"They know me," he said. "And besides, they always keep a table in reserve, just in case the President decides to turn up."

"So what's she going to do tonight if she wants to come?"

He raised his eyebrows. "She'll have to go elsewhere."

"Or we could offer to share. I wouldn't mind having a good conversation with the President. There are a few things I'd like to tell her."

They both laughed and he turned to look around.

"I love this room. You have really do have excellent taste."

"Thank you."

"It's so restful. It's just the sort of place to come home to after a busy day at the office. Maybe I could persuade you to take a professional look at my apartment sometime?"

"I'd love to," Marion said moving to the stereo player and putting on Beethoven's *Moonlight Sonata*. The soothing strains began to fill the room. She could feel the romantic temperature begin to rise.

She looked into Matt's blue eyes. He was the epitome of the strong, handsome man that she read about in books. The closer he came to her, the faster her heart began to beat.

"You look very smart tonight," she breathed.

"And you look beautiful, Marion. You look lovelier than ever."

They moved together till their lips were almost touching. He placed his hand on her neck and drew her face close to his. She closed her eyes and waited for his kiss.

At that moment a loud buzzing sound shattered the atmosphere in the room.

"Damn!" she exclaimed. "It's the intercom."

Matt glanced quickly at his watch. "Probably the taxi. But he's early. I told him eight o'clock."

She let out a little sigh of irritation. "I suppose we'd better go," she said.

She spoke into the intercom and told the driver they were about to come down.

Matt quickly finished his wine and set down the empty glass while Marion went off to get her jacket. Five minutes later they were seated together in the back of the cab, speeding across town to Mama Rosa's.

Mama Rosa was expecting them. A plump, dark, matronly figure in embroidered cotton blouse and long flowing skirt rose from her perch behind the cash desk and advanced to greet them with arms outstretched.

"*Ciao, amici!*" she said, kissing Matt on both cheeks and then turning her attention to Marion who she enveloped in a warm embrace, kissing her not twice but three times, then holding her at arms' length to examine her.

"*Che bella signorina!*" she said as she gazed adoringly into Marion's eyes. She turned again to Matt and poked him in the chest with a podgy finger while firing off a stream of rapid Italian. Then she clapped her hands. "Alberto!"

A thin, black-haired youth of about twenty-six emerged from the kitchen and more Italian was issued from Mama Rosa while Alberto nodded his head like a marionette.

"*Si, Mama,*" he said finally and following his mother's instructions he led Matt and Marion to the best table in the room, in a quiet alcove where they could have privacy and still look out over the entire restaurant floor. He straightened the starched linen tablecloth, moved the little vase of spring violets to the centre of the table, presented them each with a menu and left.

"What was that all about?" Marion asked once she had settled down and recovered her breath.

"I think she likes you," Matt said, his eyes twinkling.

"But what did she say?"

"She said: 'What a beautiful young lady!' and then she poked me in the chest and said I was a sly dog for keeping you hidden away. And did you notice you got three kisses?"

"Yes."

"Well that's usually reserved for a special friend. I only got two."

Marion smiled. So far, she was enjoying Mama Rosa's enormously and they hadn't even looked at the menu yet.

Alberto was back with a carafe of water and a basket of freshly-baked bread.

"You like to drink your usual wine, Signor Matt?"

Matt turned to Marion. "This is an excellent wine called Millefiore. It means a thousand flowers. I think you'd like it."

"What a beautiful name!" said Marion.

"It comes from a little town in Liguria near where Mama's family is from. It's a delicate red with just a hint of sweetness but nice and light and refreshing. Would you like to try it?"

"It sounds like nectar for the gods."

"Just wait till you taste it," Matt said and nodded his assent to Alberto who hurried away and returned with a bottle. He held it out for Matt's inspection then politely poured for Marion who raised the glass to her nose and savoured the delicate bouquet. Then she took a sip and closed her eyes in bliss.

"You like it?" Alberto asked.

"It's delicious," she exclaimed with a sigh of satisfaction.

Alberto smiled then skilfully poured for both of them.

"I'm glad you like it," Matt said, clearly pleased. "Now, let's hope you enjoy the rest of the meal just as much."

Marion opened the leather-bound menu and let her eyes travel down the list of handwritten dishes that met her gaze. Her experience of Italian restaurants had so far been limited to the various establishments that dealt in pastas and pizzas and had empty Chianti bottles on the walls. But this was in a different league altogether. The extensive list ran to five pages; the names of the dishes were written in Italian and a more detailed explanation followed in English.

She struggled with the menu for five minutes till at last Matt was compelled to rescue her.

"Don't worry about it," he said. "It's confusing even for someone like me and I'm a regular here. Let's try to narrow it down a bit. For starters they've got a range of salads, soups, cured meats with melon plus the regulation pasta dishes. They make their own pasta here on the premises and it's very good. What do you feel like eating?"

Marion, who was quite hungry, opted for soup.

"There's a vegetable soup here which I can strongly recommend. It's a regional dish and contains rice, smoked sausage and pasta as well as vegetables. Take it from me, it's fantastic." He smacked his lips.

Marion dutifully nodded her agreement. "Okay."

"Good, now for the main course. They have fish, meat, poultry and shellfish. There's a very good selection. They even have *coniglio*."

"What's that?"

"Rabbit. It's cooked in red wine with herbs and lentils. And it's served with string beans and baby potatoes. It's a speciality of the house."

But Marion wasn't persuaded. "I'd keep thinking of the Easter Bunny," she said, shaking her head and Matt smiled.

"Okay, how about veal?" He pointed to an item on the menu. "This one is cooked in olive oil and marsala wine and comes with spinach and sautéed potatoes."

"That sounds good," Marion said. "Why don't I have it?"

"You've chosen well," Matt complimented her and waved once more for Alberto's attention. He gave Marion's order and chose for himself a salad of tomatoes and mozzarella cheese to be followed by hake fried in light batter and served with scalloped potatoes and zucchini.

"We haven't selected a pasta dish and you said they make their own," Marion pointed out.

He gently squeezed her hand. "We'll save that for the next time we come. Now drink your wine," he said, topping up his own glass from the bottle that Alberto had left on the table. "I want this to be an experience you will never forget."

The meal surpassed even Matt's expectations. It was as if Carlo was putting on a special effort in the kitchen just for their benefit. Alberto was never far from the table, ready to swoop at the first sign that they needed something: more Parmesan, more *balsamico*, more bread, more wine, more water. When the last dishes had been cleared away, Matt leaned across the table and gazed at Marion.

"Well?" he said. "Let's have your verdict."

"That's the best meal I've ever eaten. Better even than my mother's Christmas dinner."

"You mean it was *that* good?" he laughed.

"Yes. It was absolutely superb."

He grinned. "I'm pleased. Now what about dessert?"

"Oh God, No," Marion cried, quickly covering her stomach with her hands. "Do you want me to explode all over their nice clean table-cloth?"

"It doesn't have to be anything heavy or gooey. They've got some beautiful home-made cassata, or honey cake or figs in wine."

"Nothing!" Marion said, emphatically. "I couldn't touch another thing. I'm surprised I've been able to manage so much. It's a tribute to Carlo's culinary skills."

"Are you sure?"

"Absolutely certain."

"Well, perhaps the next time. But you *will* have a *digestivo*?"

He summoned Alberto once more and spoke quickly to him.

"They have a fabulous liqueur here called *strega*. It means 'witch' but don't be put off by that. It's a delicate fusion of herbs and distilled spirit. If you think the wine was nectar wait till you sample *strega*. You'll think you've died and gone to Heaven."

"If you really insist," Marion smiled.

"You'll love it," he assured her. "And it's very good for the digestion."

He ordered two glasses of *strega* then reached out and held her hand while he looked into her face.

"I was thinking of cooking a meal for us some evening," she said. "A nice candlelit dinner. Just you and me."

"You mean you can cook as well as everything else?" he said, with obvious delight.

"I can cook basic food. I'm not likely to win any Michelin stars, mind you. But I enjoy it. Do you think you could trust me?"

"Marion, I'd be honoured."

"Then we'll do it."

She gazed lovingly into his eyes. "Thank you for a wonderful evening," she said.

"It's been my pleasure. But you are what made it special. I've eaten here dozens of times but never in the company of a beautiful woman like you."

She felt herself blushing at the praise. She lowered her eyes. "You say the nicest things, Matt."

"I tell the truth. So you will come with me again?"

"Of course. Try and stop me."

He smiled and raised his glass.

"This is only the beginning, Marion. I hope you and I will have many more nights like this."

She lifted the glass of yellow liqueur to her lips and felt it warm her tongue. More nights like this, she thought. If only it was true, I would die a happy woman.

It was after eleven when he finally paid the bill and Mama Rosa organised a cab to take them back to Smithfield. There was a last round of handshakes and hugs and kisses and promises to return again soon and then they were seated in the back of the taxi, speeding towards the river.

He clasped her hand. She laid her head on his shoulder and felt his fingers caress her hair. She closed her eyes and his warm lips brushed her mouth. She put her arms around his neck and held him tight.

When they arrived at The Cloisters, Matt paid the driver and rode the lift to her apartment. He waited while she fumbled with the key and once inside, he clasped her in his arms again. He pulled her closer, his hands caressing her breasts, her thighs. His warm lips descended once more onto hers.

She could feel her body melt as a wave of passion flamed through her. She ran her fingers wildly through his hair. She wanted this moment to last. She didn't want him to leave. She drew his face closer to hers.

"Don't stop," she whispered. "Please don't stop!"

Chapter Seventeen

Normally, Alan checked the stock-market reports first thing when he arrived for work each morning. Before he even had his obligatory cup of tea, made for him specially by Ms Coleman with his personal supply of Earl Grey tea leaves, he would spread out the pages of the *Financial Times* and scan the news columns to see how his shares in Vorax were performing. Each percentage rise represented a growth in Alan's wealth. He now owned 40,000 of the shares valued at €11 each which he had purchased at €1.50. If he was to sell them today, he would make a profit of €380,000. It was quite a handsome return.

But he had no intention of selling. He had carried out research on the company and received regular reports from his broker and everything suggested that there was plenty of growth still left in Vorax. It was an expanding pharmaceutical firm developing a range of important new drugs. Its future looked good. Alan planned to wait. If the shares continued to climb as they had been doing, there was absolutely no reason why his profits could not increase to half a million euros in the next few months.

Then he might sell and invest the proceeds in another penthouse apartment. His broker was telling him only last week that rents in the docklands were now reaching €5,000 a month for good apartments with views of the water. And meanwhile the property values continued to soar. The thought of all this potential wealth caused a frisson of excitement to course through Alan's brain.

But this morning he didn't get an opportunity to study the markets closely as he usually did. Since he was one of the few solicitors in Dublin specialising in employment law, he had recently found himself inundated with cases involving migrant workers. Every day a new one landed on his desk. Usually they involved employers underpaying their staff.

Alan had a certain degree of sympathy with the employers. As far as he was concerned, this was the capitalist market at work and if migrants were prepared to work for buttons that was their business. Most of them were only too happy to get it. Back in their home countries the buttons they earned in Ireland would seem like a fortune. But the law was the law and had to be obeyed.

This morning he had received an urgent call from a builder who employed 100 Ukrainian labourers to put up apartments on a construction site in Donnybrook. He had hired them through an agency and was paying them €3 an hour which was well below the statutory minimum wage. He might have got away with it if some bolshie trade union official hadn't started sticking his nose in. Now he was threatening to call a strike and splash the whole story over the press. The builder was in danger of losing his licence. In desperation, he had sought Alan's help.

He had spent the entire morning trying to sort out the mess. After much negotiation with the workers' spokesman, a gruff Ukrainian bricklayer called Boris, Alan had persuaded the builder to pay the men the minimum wage plus back money and to provide them with subsidised accommodation. As a result of the delay, he didn't get back into the office till after midday.

When he arrived, he found a pile of mail waiting for him but he pushed these aside while he spread the *Financial Times* on his desk and eagerly turned the pages till he arrived at the stock market report. There it was. At once, he felt his heart gladden. Vorax shares had risen again and were now standing at €11.50. Overnight, he had made a profit of €20,000. Alan couldn't resist the smile of satisfaction that played around his lips. He had been proved right yet again. His judgment had been vindicated. There was more profit to be squeezed out of Vorax yet.

He sat back in his chair and closed his eyes. If he left the shares till they climbed to €15 which was perfectly possible, he might have enough money to invest in *two* more penthouses which would bring him an income of €10,000 a month or €120,000 a year. And this was on top of the capital appreciation that would accrue. He had seen his own apartment rise in value by almost €600,000 in the space of a few years. There was no reason why it shouldn't continue. Alan felt his forehead throb with excitement at the thought that in a very short time he could be a millionaire.

Wouldn't Marion regret it then, if she persisted with her nonsense and continued to snub him? When Alan was sailing round the Mediterranean in his yacht, partying at the hotspots in Monte Carlo and Puerto Banus and getting his picture splashed all over the papers wouldn't she just eat out her heart with envy and regret? But of course that was unlikely to happen. Behind her stubbornness, Marion was a sensible woman. Alan was convinced that she would eventually realise what a golden opportunity was being presented to her. To be romantically involved with a self-made millionaire instead of writing letters to irate school principals in the Department of Education for the rest of her life— there was no contest!

He sifted through his messages while Ms Coleman hurried off to make him a refreshing cup of tea. He could see that he had a very busy day ahead. At the bottom of the pile he came across a long thin envelope marked STRICTLY PRIVATE AND CONFIDENTIAL. Immediately he knew what this was – the report he had commissioned on Matt Bollinger from a firm of private investigators called Snoop, Pry and Partners. Eagerly, he tore open the envelope and devoured the contents.

Mr Bollinger was an interesting man. Forty-one years of age. University education, married with two adult children. Separated from his wife, Anna. Holding down a good job as Marketing

Manager with a mobile phone company called Atlanta Technologies. Now living at No 23, The Cloisters, Smithfield, Dublin.

Alan had requested the agency to provide a report on Matt Bollinger's movements. He eagerly turned the pages till he found what he was looking for. Immediately he felt a pain in the pit of his stomach. The report confirmed his worst fears. Only last night, Matt Bollinger had taken a young lady identified as Ms Marion Hunt to dinner at a restaurant called Mama Rosa's in Blackrock. They had held hands. In the taxi they had embraced. With every line he read, Alan felt a dagger pierce his heart. The pair was seen to enter Ms Hunt's apartment on their return at 11.30 p.m. and Mr Bollinger did not emerge again till 6 a.m.

Alan felt his blood run cold. His hands trembled with rage as he finished reading the report. The scheming rat had not left Marion's apartment till six o'clock! They must have spent the night together. What other interpretation could there be?

His rage gave way to silent fury. Matt Bollinger was not just another of Marion's admirers. Now he had become her lover! And as far as Alan was concerned, that changed everything. He had crossed a line. He was no longer a rival. Now he was a deadly enemy.

"Now," Christy said, settling himself at a table near the window that provided a good view out onto the street. "With the missus not well, I don't get out to the pub as much as I used to. But seeing as it was yourself was asking, I decided to make an exception."

"I'm very glad you did," Nick said, putting down two creamy pints of Guinness and joining Christy at the table.

"Mind you, I used to give it a lash in me younger days. Oh, yes, there were few men left standing when Christy Grimes got into his stride. Do you know what me personal record was?"

"Tell me," Nick said.

"Twenty-two pints at the one session."

Nick's mouth fell open in astonishment. "Twenty-two pints of Guinness?"

"As God is me judge. I have witnesses to prove it. And afterwards,

I walked out of the pub straight as an arrow and home to me bed. And up for work at seven o'clock the next morning without a bother on me."

Nick shook his head to show his appreciation. "You must have had some stamina in those days."

"Cast iron," Christy said, pleased with Nick's admiring response. "Still have, as a matter of fact, but I've slowed down a bit. Do you know that I never had a day sick in me entire life?"

"That's truly remarkable," Nick said.

"It's in me genes, you see. I inherited it. Same way as some fellas go bald at eighteen I inherited a rock-solid constitution. Anyway, I had to give up that drinking caper once I got married. Fair's fair. I couldn't be out gargling all night with chisellers to rear. It wouldn't be right. It wouldn't be doing the decent thing by the missus."

"How is she anyway?" Nick inquired, spotting an opportunity to steer the conversation away from Christy's drinking exploits.

Christy took a deep draught from his glass and wiped his lip with his sleeve. "Sound as a pound. Now there's another one with the constitution of an ox. You'd think to look at her that a good breeze would blow her away. But let me tell you something, she's as tough as ould boots. And a will to match! You know, when she got that stroke, the very first thing she said was: 'Christy, I'm going to beat this thing.' And she never gave up. The doctor's going to take her walking frame away any day now."

"Well, that's good news," Nick said wondering when he could diplomatically move onto the subject he really wanted to discuss; the story of Larry Byrne.

Before he joined the book club he had spent days wrestling with the plot for his novel and had come very close to despair. Everything he came up with sounded so hackneyed and unoriginal. It was as if his brain had turned into porridge. No matter how hard he worked at it, nothing seemed to spark into life. And Nick knew one thing: if the book was going to be a success, he had to devise a plot that would grip people's imagination.

And then he heard Christy tell the story of Larry Byrne. As soon as he heard it, he knew it was exactly what he was looking for. It had all the right ingredients: suspense, drama, passion, remorse and reconciliation. It would fit perfectly with his plan to write a blockbuster saga. Nick was convinced he could mould that plot into a novel that would literally walk out of the bookshops.

The next morning he had called Marion and got Christy's phone number and then rang him at home. Christy had agreed at once to talk and suggested that they meet in his local which was how he came to be sitting with him now in the public bar of Mohan's pub in Phibsboro.

"Ellie is with the daughter right now," Christy went on. "The chisellers are very good to us. They're paying for our holiday in Italy whenever Ellie gets the all-clear. Do you have any family yourself, Nick?"

Nick shook his head. "I'm not married."

"A handsome young fella like you shouldn't have any difficulty in the mot department. I would have thought they'd be tripping over themselves to go out with someone like you," Christy said, demolishing most of the pint.

Nick smiled. "Who knows? Maybe I'll get round to it eventually. But at the moment I've got other things on my mind."

"Don't leave it too late," Christy warned. "Chisellers can be a handful but they're a blessing in disguise. Our ones keep a close eye on Ellie. She's had a rough time, you know, with that stroke. But she never complains. She's one of the rare ould stock. You should have met her father now, Dando Doyle. Toughest man on the Dublin docks, he was. He ate razor blades for his breakfast."

"Really?"

Christy smiled. "It's only an expression. But he was a hard man all right. Many's the fella thought they could cross Dando and lived to regret it."

"Well, that's the reason I wanted to talk to you," Nick said, spotting his opportunity. "I'm very interested in life in Dublin in the old days. That story you mentioned the other night at the book club . . ."

"About Larry Byrne?"

"That's right."

"Oh, Larry was a character all right," Christy said, draining the remainder of his pint. Nick, who had barely touched his so far, decided to follow suit and waved to the barman for another two.

"What do you want to know about him?" asked Christy.

"Well, the whole story, really. You mentioned that he joined the Foreign Legion."

"He did and got involved in all sorts of wonderful adventures. Fought against the Hottentots or was it the Fuzzy Wuzzies? Anyway he got a medal from the French government for outstanding bravery in the field."

"Where is he now? Would it be possible to talk to him?"

"He's dead," Christy said. "Got ate by a lion."

Nick stared in astonishment. This story was getting better by the minute. "In Africa?"

"No. In the circus. When he left the Foreign Legion, you see, he had to get a steady job. He couldn't be soldiering all his life. After a while, you get too old for that lark."

"Was he a lion tamer?"

"Ah no, you need to have qualifications for that class of work, certificates and stuff like that. No, Larry cleaned out the cages. And one day he went into the lion's cage and he must have stood on its tail or something but didn't it rear up on him and before they could rescue him, it had ate a good few lumps out of him. You know, I don't think they feed those animals properly," Christy said, sadly shaking his head.

"That sounds terrible."

"It was. There was skin and hair everywhere. The cage was covered in blood. It looked like Dr Crippen had been at work. Anyway, the doctors tried to save him but it was too late. He was too far gone. A decent ould skin was Larry, God be good to him."

"If we could just start at the beginning," Nick said, taking a notebook out of his pocket. He had considered bringing a portable tape-recorder but decided it might be too intimidating and put Christy off his stride.

"Are you writing this down?"

"If you don't mind, otherwise I might forget bits of it."

"Well, before we get started," Christy said, draining his glass again. "Maybe we should get another round in?"

Nick signalled to the barman who brought more fresh glasses.

"You mentioned a row with his father," he said then. "What was that all about?"

Christy sniffed. "Leaving school. You see, Larry's father was a great man for the education. He'd never had much of it himself but he believed the way for a young fella to get on in the world was to get a bit of learning under his belt."

"He was dead right," Nick said.

"And Larry was bright as a blade. He did very well at school and his father was hoping he'd get his name down for a trade. Maybe become a plumber or a spark or something like that. And he could have done it too if he had applied himself. But when Larry turned fifteen he began to get restless. He could see all his pals getting jobs and going around with new clothes and jingling money in their pockets and he wanted some of it too.

"Mind you, most of the jobs were dead-end. His ould father could see that and when Larry said he was leaving school, his father said he was doing no such thing but was staying on till he got his Leaving Cert. Well, there was an awful row. Larry was very stubborn. He said he was leaving and his father said he was staying, so one night when they were all asleep, Larry slipped out of the house and got the boat to Liverpool."

"Where did he get the money for the fare?" Nick put in.

"Robbed it out of his mother's purse. He'd no option, you see. Anyway, as soon as he got to Liverpool, he made his way to the recruiting office and joined the Foreign Legion. They never asked any questions about his age or anything like that. And before he knew it, he was shipped off to the training camp in Africa.

"Well, of course, when his father found out it nearly broke his heart. He was sorry that he hadn't listened to Larry. But there was nothing he could do. Not a word was heard from Larry for years.

Not a line or a phone call. Nobody knew if he was alive or dead. And then the poor ould da took sick and the doctor said it was the mahogany waistcoat for him. There was nothing could be done. And the whole time he kept asking for Larry. Where was Larry? He wanted to see Larry before he died. In the end, the mother wrote a letter addressed to Mr Laurence Byrne c/o the French Foreign Legion in Paris. Well, weeks went by and nothing happened. But they never gave up hope. And then one afternoon, what do you think happened? Didn't a taxi draw up outside the house and this smart young man got out. The neighbours all gathered round to see who it was. And lo and behold it was Larry. He must have been about thirty by this time. And his face was tanned by the sun and he was lean and fit from all that soldiering and all the women thought he looked like a film star."

"That must have been very dramatic," Nick said.

"Oh, dramatic is not the word. Sure the neighbours were taking about nothing else for months."

"What happened next?" Nick asked, eagerly.

"He went into the house and when the family saw him, they all broke out crying and wailing and kissing him and making a big fuss over him. He asked to see his father and they brought him up the stairs to the bedroom where the old man was dying and when he saw him, Larry knelt down at his bedside and threw his arms around him. 'I'm sorry, Da,' says Larry, 'for all the pain I've caused you.' And the old fella said: 'I forgive you, son, and I'm sorry too.' And the two of them sat there for hours reminiscing about the old days when Larry was just a nipper. And when he stood up at last, there were tears in his eyes. The next day, the da called for the priest to hear his last confession. 'I'm dying a happy man,' he said. 'For the prodigal son has returned.' And he just closed his eyes and passed away."

When Christy had finally finished, Nick found he had a lump in his throat.

"What an amazing story," he said.

"And it's true as I'm sitting here. Sure you couldn't make up something like that."

"Okay, if you don't mind, let's start from the beginning – I want you to tell me everything you can remember about Larry – every detail."

An hour or more later Nick folded away his notebook and stuck his pen in his pocket. "Well, thanks again for taking the time to meet me," he said sincerely.

"It was my pleasure," Christy said. "I never get tired of telling that story."

Nick smiled to himself as he said goodbye and started walking into town. He was bursting with enthusiasm. At last he had found his theme and his plot. He couldn't wait to get back to his word processor. It would be hard work but he would enjoy every minute of it and he knew in his heart that the book would be a success.

Before he knew it, he had arrived in D'Olier St. He had a few hours to kill before he went into work. Might as well grab a bite to eat somewhere, he thought. As he jostled through the crowds, he saw a familiar figure emerge from a doorway and begin to walk ahead of him along the footpath. Who was it? Then he realised. He began to run to catch up with her.

"Liz!" he cried. "Wait for me! It's Nick."

At the sound of Nick's voice, Liz stopped and turned round to look. She had been daydreaming. Her mind had been somewhere else, back in Dr Brady's surgery the day of her visit. She had been thinking about it ever since. All weekend, it had been preying on her mind, last thing at night and first thing in the morning like a bad dream that she couldn't shake off.

If she thought the visit would provide her with some kind of reassurance, she had been sadly disappointed. It had simply reinforced the uneasy feeling that had been with her ever since she found the lump in her breast. She had left the surgery feeling even more downcast. The doctor had been cheerful and told her to be positive. But Liz had seen through him. She knew it was only an act. Something about his manner had warned her. He hadn't told her the truth. She knew he had seen something in the lump that was bad news.

Cathy was in the waiting room. Immediately, she got up and put her arm around Liz and led her out to the car park.

"How did it go?" she asked, anxiously.

"I've got to have some tests done. He's given me a letter for a specialist."

"I expected that. But he didn't tell you anything bad?"

Liz shook her head. "No, nothing like that."

"Well, that's a promising start," Cathy said in her breezy, upbeat voice. "Now let's go and get something to eat and you can tell me everything."

She had booked a table at a smart restaurant called Scipio's. Normally, Liz would have been delighted to sit with her friend and catch up on the gossip over a glass or two of wine. But tonight it was probably the last place she wanted to be. She felt as if the familiar black cloud had descended on her once again. She would have much preferred to have gone straight home to a hot bath and a warm bed.

As it turned out, Scipio's had a pianist playing jazz tunes and a menu that was heavy on Mediterranean cuisine but very few diners. It wasn't an encouraging sign. Cathy had ordered a quiet table so the young man in the white shirt who greeted them at the door led them straight away to a spot at the back of the restaurant that was partly concealed by a large potted palm. He gave them two menus and departed.

"Well?" Cathy said in a loud whisper once they were seated. "Tell me exactly what happened."

"There isn't much to tell," Liz said with a shrug. "He doesn't know what it is."

"That's a good sign," Cathy said, determined to look on the bright side. "If it was something bad, don't you think he would have spotted it right away?"

"He said there was something there that shouldn't be but he couldn't tell if it was malignant. That's the woman I have to see."

She produced the envelope from her bag and handed it to Cathy who glanced at it quickly.

"Dr Patricia Forbes? I've heard of her," she said. "She's supposed to one of the best."

"Well, let's hope *she* will be able to enlighten me," Liz said, gloomily. "This uncertainty is really getting me down."

"Don't be silly. Of course she'll enlighten you."

"Dr Brady said she would send me for a mammogram."

"That's standard," Cathy said. "Now tell me. Do you have any side effects?"

"Like what?"

"Do you feel tired? Have you lost energy?"

"I was great until this happened. Now I feel depressed."

Cathy waved her hands. "That's only to be expected. Anyone in your position would feel depressed. But you're in good hands now. Believe me, if there's anything wrong, this woman will diagnose what it is."

The waiter was back. "Would you like to order now?" he asked, politely.

Liz, who had scarcely glanced at the menu, asked for a tuna salad with no dressing while Cathy ordered lamb cutlets.

"Would you care to have some wine with your meal?" the waiter inquired.

"We'll have a half carafe of house white," Cathy said. She quickly glanced at Liz who looked very down in the dumps. "And two gin and tonics right away."

"Right away," said the waiter.

"Listen," Cathy said when the waiter was gone, "you have to look at this thing calmly. There's nothing anyone can do till you have the results of this mammogram. In the meantime, worrying about it isn't going to help. Why don't you just put it right out of your mind?"

"Don't you think I want to?" She sighed and looked across the table at Cathy. "I know there's something wrong."

"Oh for God's sake, how can you know? The doctor doesn't even know."

"I just do."

"Rubbish!"

"No, listen to me. There was something in his manner. I know he saw something but he didn't want to say. He wants the specialist to confirm it."

"Nonsense," Cathy said with emphasis. "That's simply protocol. Dr Brady is only a GP. He doesn't have the training to diagnose something like that. And doctors are always non-committal. Some of them wouldn't tell you what day of the week it is. It's all part of their professional mystique."

"Please God you're right."

"Of course I'm right. Now try to cheer up. In a couple of week's time we'll probably laugh at this and wonder what all the fuss was about."

The waiter was back with the wine and the gin and tonics.

"I'm sorry to be such a mope," Liz said, taking a sip of her gin and tonic. "Every time I see you I seem to have some burden to dump in your lap."

Cathy gently touched her friend's cheek. "You're not a mope. You're just a poor unfortunate who's suddenly got all the cares of the world thrust on her shoulders."

"Promise me something," Liz said.

"Of course."

"Don't breathe a word of this to anyone."

Cathy looked aghast. "Are you kidding? Even if they pulled my teeth out with rusty pliers, I wouldn't tell."

Liz forced herself to smile. She took Cathy's hand and squeezed it. "You've always stood by me," she said. "Thanks for coming with me. Thanks for everything. I really appreciate it."

"Forget it," Cathy said, polishing off her gin and tonic. "I'm your friend. What did you think I was going to do?"

Chapter Eighteen

But, despite her best efforts, the gloomy feeling persisted right through the weekend. Liz couldn't shake it off. Cathy rang several times to check on her and invite her over for Sunday lunch. But she couldn't face the prospect of those laughing children and that happy family atmosphere. She just wanted to be alone. She busied herself around the house, cleaning, polishing, washing, doing jobs that didn't really need to be done, anything to keep busy. On Sunday afternoon, she went for a long walk along the Clontarf seafront as far as Raheny and later forced herself to begin reading *The Boy in the Striped Pyjamas* for the next meeting of the book club. It carried her through till bedtime.

Early on Monday morning, she rang the office to say she would be delayed. She wanted the privacy of her own home when she called to make her appointment with the specialist. She waited till nine forty-five, then rang the number that Dr Brady had given her. She got a pleasant young woman.

"I'd like to make an appointment to see Dr Forbes."

"Are you being referred by your GP?"

"Yes," Liz said. "He's given me a letter."

"Just let me check her appointments diary."

There was a pause and then the woman was back.

"Tuesday week at eleven o'clock. Is that suitable?"

Liz felt her heart sink. This was eight days away. How could she wait that long?

"Is it possible to see her sooner? My doctor said it was urgent."

"That's the earliest appointment available," the woman said. "Dr Forbes is booked right up."

"Are you sure?"

"Positive," the woman said, a little tersely.

"All right," Liz said, reluctantly. "Do I have to prepare for the appointment? Do I need to be fasting or anything?"

"No, nothing like that. Do you know where the consulting rooms are?"

"Yes."

"Okay," the woman said. "Just turn up at eleven. We look forward to seeing you."

Liz put down the phone feeling utterly demoralised. Now she was faced with more delay, more uncertainty. She wanted this over quickly. If the lump on her breast was malignant, she wanted to know so they could begin treating her. But this waiting was becoming unbearable.

She forced herself to go into work. At least she would be busy. She worked through her lunch break to catch up and before she knew it was half five and time to go home. A long night awaited her. How was she going to fill it? She would make some supper and continue reading. But *The Boy in the Striped Pyjamas* was a short book and she would probably finish it tonight. With a bit of luck it might last till bedtime.

She tidied her desk. By now, only her boss Mr Armstrong remained. She went into his office to say goodnight. He looked up when she came in.

"Are you all right, Liz?"

"How do you mean?" she asked, taken aback by the abruptness of his inquiry.

"I've noticed that you don't seem your usual chirpy self today."

"I'm fine," she said, forcing a smile onto her lips. "Just feeling a little bit frazzled."

"Well, I'm glad to hear it. You know you can always talk to me if there's anything wrong."

"That's very kind," Liz said and made her way out of the office and onto the street. Do I look so worried, she thought, that people are beginning to take notice? I must pull myself together. But the memory of this morning's phone call and the visit to Dr Brady kept forcing themselves into her mind as she began walking along D'Olier St. And that was when she heard someone calling her name.

She stopped and turned round and there was the tall figure of Nick Barry striding along the pavement behind her. She hadn't seen him since the night of the book club meeting when they had shared settee space together.

"I caught a glimpse of you and thought I recognised you," he said, catching up with her. "How are you?"

"I'm good," she said without much enthusiasm. "Just finishing work."

"You work near here?"

"Oh yes. Quick Print. I'm the office manager."

He smiled. "You know, I wondered what you did for a living. Office manager –I'm surprised."

"What did you think I did? Robbed banks?"

He laughed. "I don't know. Anyway, it's good to see you. Have you started the new book yet?"

"I started it yesterday. I'm about halfway through. I'm enjoying it."

Nick pulled a face. "I haven't even got my copy yet. I'd better do it tomorrow." He glanced at his watch. "I have to get into work soon. But I was going to grab something to eat in one of the pubs first. You don't feel like joining me by any chance?"

She hesitated. He was so upbeat and cheerful, so full of energy and life. Maybe this was what she needed, some lively company for an hour or so. If nothing else, it would help to shorten the evening.

"Why not?" she said.

"Now, what would you like?" Nick asked, after finding a comfortable seat for Liz and himself in the back room of a little pub off Fleet Street. It was an old-fashioned bar, one of the few still remaining in the city after the orgy of redevelopment that had taken place in recent years. It had once been the home of the Dublin literary set and a memory of that age still lingered, drawing occasional tourists to view the place where famous writers had once met.

"I'd love a nice cool glass of wine," Liz said.

"Anything to eat?"

She considered. She hadn't eaten anything since breakfast when she'd had a slice of toast and marmalade. She'd better not start neglecting her food or she'd be in real trouble. "What do they have?"

"Baguettes mainly," Nick said. "They do a mean tuna with red peppers."

"Okay," she said. "Would you ask them to go easy on the mayonnaise?"

Nick made his way to the counter. He was known here. The pub was close to the *Daily Trumpet* office and he occasionally called in for a quiet drink to soak up the faded atmosphere and dream of literary greatness. He gave his order to the barman and waited while he prepared the food and drinks. Then he ferried them back to the table where Liz was studying a photograph on the wall.

"You're not on a diet, are you?" he asked.

"No. Why do you ask?"

"Asking them to go easy on the mayonnaise."

"Oh that. I just watch what I eat, that's all."

"You don't need to diet. You look fabulous."

"Thank you," Liz said, feeling a slight blush colour her cheeks as she sliced her roll in two.

"Some women are always going on diets. Why is that?"

"Because they want to look thin, I suppose."

"And yet plump women were once considered the height of beauty. Did you ever see a Rubens painting?"

"I know. But fashions change."

"Well, I don't think you need to worry about that. You have a wonderful figure."

Liz found herself smiling. It was nice to be complimented by a handsome man. It hadn't happened to her much recently.

"This is a lovely old place," she said, looking around. "I feel like I've stepped back about fifty years."

"It's got a lot of history," Nick agreed. "The writers and artists used to drop in here for a drink in the old days. There's a drawing of them on the wall somewhere."

"And it's so peaceful. You can have a decent conversation."

"And hear yourself think."

"I rarely go into pubs anymore because they've got so noisy," Liz continued. "Everybody seems to be pushing and shoving and barking into mobile phones. It's like the bazaar in Istanbul."

"Or the *Daily Trumpet* newsroom," Nick replied with a grin.

"Is that where you work?" she asked, taking a bite of her tuna baguette.

"Yes. I'm a journalist."

"Oh," she stared at him. She had been wondering where she had seen his face before. Was he a gossip columnist or something? Maybe she'd need to be careful what she said in case it ended up splashed all over the papers. Although she wasn't a celebrity, she thought. What she had to say or do was of no interest to anyone.

"That's an interesting job. How did you find the time to join a book club?"

Nick laughed. "Before you get carried away, I'm not a reporter. I'm not out chasing big stories every day. I don't go to fabulous parties and interview famous people."

"So what do you do?"

"I'm a sub-editor."

"An editor?"

"No, a *sub*-editor."

"Is there a difference?" she asked with a look of confusion on her face.

He laughed as he reached for his drink. "A big difference," he said caustically. "My job is to sit behind a desk and clean up the mess the reporters leave behind."

She looked bewildered. "You've lost me. What sort of mess?"

"Oh, things like factual errors, bad grammar. You'd be surprised at the stuff that lands on my desk. I'll let you into a little secret. Many of them can't write very well. Some of them can't even spell."

Her eyes widened in surprise. "Really?"

"Oh yes. And I'm not just talking just about the cub reporters. Even the big-name correspondents do it as well. In fact, some of them are the worst. And you'd think they would know better."

"It still sounds interesting," Liz said. "At least you never get bored. There's always something new every day."

"Well, that's certainly true. Don't get me wrong. I'm not complaining. The work pays well and it allows me the time to concentrate on my main career."

"Oh and what *is* your main career?" Liz asked.

Nick took a sip of beer. He had been a little bit indiscreet just now and he had promised himself to keep his project secret. But he was still on a high after his earlier conversation with Christy Grimes. And he was enjoying talking to her like this. He wondered if he should confide in her.

"I'd rather not say."

"Oh c'mon," she cajoled. "Now you're teasing me."

"I don't mean to, honestly. It's just something I'd prefer not to discuss."

He took a bite out of his baguette while Liz studied him intently.

"I know," she announced at last. "You're a writer."

Nick almost choked. He put down his baguette and stared at her. "How on earth did you know that?"

She was now grinning in triumph. "Woman's intuition. You have that look about you. It *is* writing, isn't it?"

"Promise you won't go broadcasting it around the book club," Nick said, nervously. "I really don't want people to know."

"Of course I won't," she said gleefully. "What are you writing anyway?"

He lowered his eyes. "A novel."

"But that's marvellous," she exclaimed. "A novel! I'm very impressed. I don't think I've ever met a real live writer before."

Nick felt a warmth developing towards Liz. She was obviously an appreciative woman. And she had this amazing manner that encouraged him to open up and tell her things.

"Well, now that you've met one, tell me what they look like?"

She chuckled. "I'm not sure."

"Writers are just like other people, you know."

"Oh, no. You mustn't say that. Writers are different. They have heightened sensibility. They've got creative imagination. Writers see things differently. They feel emotions more intensely."

"Please," Nick said, laughing and clasping his hands to his ears. "You'll give me a swelled head."

"But it's true. And writers have to be more disciplined. Sitting at a computer day after day must take a lot of perseverance, not to mention stamina. I'd love to write a novel but I know I'd never be able to do it."

"Nonsense, of course you could. You can write English, can't you?"

"Yes."

"Well, you just start with what's around you. Ideas come from everywhere. They come from your own experience, from something you read in the paper." He paused as he thought once more of the extraordinary story he had just heard from Christy. "They even come from other people's experiences."

"You make it sound too simple. If it was that easy everybody would be doing it."

"Well, there are some drawbacks," he admitted, taking another sip of his beer.

Liz had now finished her baguette and was sitting forward, listening to him intently.

"Like what?"

"Rejection, for one thing. If you're going to become a writer, you need to develop a thick skin. A lot of people get turned down at their first attempt and that can be very demoralising. And even when you succeed in getting published, you have to face the critics." He winced as the painful memory of the indignities he had suffered at the hands of Hugo de Lacy returned. "Some of it can get quite personal. It can be very hurtful."

"I didn't realise," Liz said. "And here I was thinking it was all glittering parties and fabulous lunches."

"For some it is. But for most writers, it's just bloody hard work."

She smiled and patted him gently on the arm. "I'm quite sure that's not going to happen to you."

"It already has," Nick said, getting carried away and throwing caution to the winds.

She stared at him. "How do you mean?"

He took a deep breath. "I published a couple of books of poetry once."

A look of recognition was creeping across her face. Suddenly she put her hand to her mouth. "Now I remember. I've been trying to recall where I saw you before. You were a famous poet. You were all over the newspapers."

"The voice of the inner city," he said, bitterly.

"That's right. You won a prize, didn't you? Why did you stop writing?"

"Mainly because of the abuse I suffered. I was called a fake and an impostor. The media built me up and suddenly decided to pull me down again. It was a total nightmare. I couldn't take any more."

She placed her hand on his and gently caressed it. "You should rise above it. You shouldn't let it get you down. I'm sure many great writers of the past had to endure similar abuse. If they had allowed it to affect them, some of the classic works of literature might never have been written."

"You're right. That's why I've decided to press ahead and write my novel. It's what I always wanted to do anyway. I never set out to be a poet."

"I want to hear all about it," she said, releasing his hand and lifting her glass. "What is this novel going to be about?"

"Larry Byrne," Nick said.

She screwed up her face in confusion. "Larry Byrne? Who's he?"

"A boy from Dublin who had a dispute with his father and went off to join the French Foreign Legion. Christy Grimes told us about it at the last meeting of the book club, remember?"

"Of course, I was fascinated."

"Well, that's the story I'm going to write."

She sat back and gave a little cry. "But that would make a marvellous novel. It's got all the right ingredients: family strife, adventure, reconciliation. Oh, Nick!" She seized his hand again. "If you did that properly, it couldn't fail to be a success."

Her enthusiasm was just what he needed to hear. It bolstered the confidence he had been feeling since his earlier talk with Christy. "I'm ready to start work on it. It's going to be a big sprawling saga. I've drawn up some wonderful characters. Now that I've got my plot, I just have to sit down and start writing."

"I can't wait to read it," she said. "It sounds brilliant."

He laughed, nervously. "You might be waiting a long time. Writing a novel can be very slow."

"I've got an idea," she said, suddenly clapping her hands together. "Why don't you let me read each chapter as you write it? I might be able to advise you as you go along."

He thought for a moment. She was right. Two pairs of eyes were better than one. It sounded like a wonderful idea. "Would you?" he exclaimed. "You wouldn't mind?"

"Not at all. I'd be delighted. I'd enjoy it enormously. And I'm quite a good critic."

"I know. I've heard you at the book club."

Suddenly, he felt euphoric. This woman sitting beside him had turned out to be a godsend. He had his plot and his characters and now Liz had offered to read the chapters and offer critical advice. He was itching to sit down at his word processor and get started.

He finished his pint. "Do you believe in Fate?" he asked.

"Ummmh. Sometimes."

"I do. If I hadn't decided to walk along D'Olier St today we wouldn't have met and none of this would have happened."

He pointed to her empty glass. "Another?"

She shouldn't really. She should go home and have a nice warm bath. And besides, she had to drive. But for the first time since she discovered the lump, she was feeling something approaching enjoyment in the company of this interesting man.

"Okay," she said.

The waiter quickly brought the fresh drinks.

Nick raised his pint.

"A toast," he said.

"To what?"

"To us. The start of a beautiful friendship."

Liz felt a pleasant feeling wash over her. "I'll drink to that," she said.

Marion was high as a kite. She was so excited that she couldn't sit still. Events had moved so swiftly that they had practically taken her breath away. Only a few short weeks ago, she had been sitting alone in her apartment looking out at the rain because she couldn't find anyone to talk to and suddenly this wonderful man had walked into her life and everything had changed.

It was like one of those romantic novels she had been so fond of reading when she was younger, only this wasn't fiction. This was really happening. Matt Bollinger had taken her to this marvellous restaurant and bought her a fabulous dinner and then he had spent the night making passionate love to her. And next weekend he was taking her out to lunch to meet his children.

She felt so happy she could barely restrain herself. She could feel the giddy rush of adrenalin pumping through her system and straight into her brain. It made her feel dizzy with joy.

Her mood was so upbeat that her supervisor, Mr McDonald, who was a civil servant of the old school and had been in the Department of Education forever, had several times frowned in disapproval from his desk at the top of the room that day. Not that Marion had paid him any heed. There was no rule in the Civil Service that said you couldn't be happy. Indeed, in her opinion, the more good spirits around the office, the better.

But it was so unlike her. Normally, she was brisk and efficient but today she had been frothy as a month-old puppy. I should really get a grip on myself, she'd thought. I'm behaving like a silly schoolgirl after her first kiss. What on earth has come over me? But she just couldn't help it. Marion was so happy that she felt like grabbing people by the shoulders and shouting it in their faces.

Tedious letters and memos that would normally make her groan with boredom had brought a smile to her lips. Weighty reports that would have sent her to sleep had brought joy to her heart. Indeed, her levity was so infectious that one of her colleagues, Madge O'Leary from Dingle, had whispered to her over coffee: "Are you on them ecstasy tablets or something? You've been hopping around all morning like an ould rooster that's got into the hen house."

She had been so carried away with herself that the day had practically flown by. Matt had called at ten o'clock just to say hello. They had chatted briefly for a couple of minutes under the steely glare of her supervisor who had a strict policy about personal phone calls at work. Matt had finally rung off with a promise to call her again in the evening.

After that, time passed like the scenery from a speeding train. Lunch was a small green salad and an apple. What *was* happening to her? Was she losing her appetite as well as her sense? The afternoon drifted by in a euphoric blur and then it was time to leave for the day.

She arrived home to The Cloisters shortly before seven o'clock and immediately got undressed and stood under the hot shower. She had nothing planned for the evening. She would have a nice cup of tea, put on some relaxing music and continue reading *The Boy in the Striped Pyjamas* in preparation for the next book club meeting. Trish had suggested it because someone in work had told her it was a wonderful book. Marion had discovered that it read like a children's story but something told her this was not going to be any fairytale.

She made some scrambled eggs for supper and put on a CD but had no sooner settled down when there was a sharp buzzing sound from the intercom. When she answered, a loud voice bellowed in her ear.

"What are you doing locking yourself away like a hermit? Open up at once! I want to hear everything about this torrid love affair you're involved in!"

Marion sighed. Talk of the devil. Here was Trish at her front door. There would be no more reading tonight, she thought as she pressed the security button to admit her friend.

Trish came bounding in the door, a bottle of wine in one hand and a large box of Dairy Milk chocolates in the other.

"Now," she said, throwing her coat off and planting herself firmly on the settee. "Once you've got the cork out of that bottle and the cellophane off those chocolates, I want you to sit down beside me and tell me everything that's been going on. I want a blow-by-blow account."

"I was going to call you," Marion said when she returned from the kitchen with a corkscrew.

"Never mind all that. Just spill the beans."

"Well," Marion began, "we had a wonderful evening. We went to a lovely little Italian restaurant in Blackrock. Family run and the most delicious food. We had —"

"It's the food of love I'm interested in," Trish interrupted. "Get down and dirty."

"Can't you let me get on with my introduction?"

"Forget about the introduction. Cut to the chase. What about your date?"

"What can I say?" Marion replied, pouring two glasses of wine and enjoying this immensely. "Matt was a perfect gentleman. As I expected. He arrived at my door with a box of the most delicious Belgian chocolates and a single long-stem rose. I kept it, of course. There it is on the mantelpiece."

Trish peered at the rose in the vase where Marion had placed it. "Well, that was a romantic beginning."

"And so the evening continued. You know it does a girl's heart good to be treated like a lady once in a while. And I must say that Matt scored ten out of ten in that department. His manners are impeccable."

"Does that include his bedside manner?" Trish said with a wicked gleam in her eye as she picked a large raspberry cream chocolate from the box and popped it in her mouth.

"You know I don't believe in kiss and tell."

"Oh, come off it. You can tell me. I'm supposed to be your best friend. Did he or didn't he?"

"Let's simply say an enjoyable evening turned into a passionate night."

"You wanton hussy!" Trish said, throwing the sweet wrapper at her friend. "And on your very first date. Couldn't you have waited till you got to know him a bit better?"

"I know him well enough already," Marion smiled and took a long sip of wine. She loved these sessions with Trish. She enjoyed teasing her and keeping her in suspense.

"And I bet you know him even better after last night. What time did he go home?"

"Six o'clock."

"My God, it must have been a heavy session."

"There you go," Marion said. "Jumping to conclusions. We sat and talked and played romantic music."

"I'll bet you did."

Marion sniffed. "Not everyone is a sex maniac."

"Everyone I know is."

The two women laughed and Trish poured more wine.

"So when is your next outing?"

"Saturday. His daughter is visiting from London this weekend and Matt thought it would be a good opportunity to introduce me to the children."

"That's an extremely positive sign," Trish said, nodding her head. "It means he's running you up the flagpole."

"He's doing what?"

"Seeing if you meet with their approval. How many kids has he got anyway?"

"Two. Rachel is the daughter. She works in London. There's a son called Peter who lives in Dublin somewhere."

"And what about Mrs Bollinger?"

"She's got a partner. He doesn't talk about her much."

"Oh well," Trish said, "these things happen. So do you think this is the One? Is he Mr Right?"

Marion toyed with her wine glass for a moment before responding. "Let's put it this way. I'm walking on air. I think about him all the time. I want to be with him all the time."

"Those sound like the symptoms, all right," Trish said, reaching for another chocolate. "It sure sounds good to me."

It was after ten o'clock when Trish finally departed. Marion was still clearing up when the phone rang.

"Hello," she said in a cheery voice.

"Hello, Marion."

She felt her back stiffen as she recognised the unmistakable voice of Alan McMillan. At once, she went on the defensive.

"What do *you* want?" she asked, stiffly.

"You don't sound very friendly."

"You must be psychic."

"Tut, tut. You don't have to be like that."

"Funny, but you just seem to have that effect on me. Now what do you want?"

"I'm calling to see if you enjoyed your little dinner."

Marion froze. "What did you say?"

"I asked about your dinner in Blackrock. Mama Rosa's restaurant? Was it good? Can you recommend it?"

There was a menacing tone to his voice that caused a chill to run along her spine.

"How did you know about that?" she asked in a faltering voice.

"A little bird told me."

"Are you spying on me?"

"Good Lord, no. Whatever put that idea in your head? I was merely inquiring if you enjoyed your dinner. What's the problem with that?"

"Plenty," Marion said. "What I do is my private business and I'll thank you to keep your dirty little nose out of it. If you must know,

I had a wonderful dinner with a wonderful man. Someone whose boots you aren't fit to hold, never mind clean."

"Matt Bollinger by any chance?"

Marion gasped. For a brief moment, she felt her heart leap but before she could reply Alan McMillan was continuing.

"I know all about it. I know what time you got home. I know he stayed the night with you. Why are you doing this to me?"

"Doing what, for God's sake?"

"Humiliating me, punishing me, making me suffer for some silly indiscretion that happened years ago."

"It's got nothing to do with humiliating you. I'm just not interested in you, that's all. Why can't you get that into your head?"

"He's making you do it, isn't he?"

"This is crazy," Marion said. "Nobody's making me do anything."

"Let me tell you something, Marion. I won't give up. Matt Bollinger may romance you but I was going out with you before he ever came on the scene. I got you first and there's an old saying: Finders, Keepers."

There was a click and the line went dead. Marion sat stunned. One single phone call from Alan McMillan and the wonderful feeling she had enjoyed all day had completely vanished.

Matt settled himself in his favourite armchair near the window and opened *The Boy in the Striped Pyjamas*. Thankfully, the frantic pace at work was beginning to slow down. Most of the start-up problems had now been sorted out, although there were still a few little snags to be smoothed out. Working for Atlanta Technologies had proved to be a challenge but he would be glad when he could start to relax a little, particularly now that Marion had entered his life.

He smiled as an image of her swam into his mind. He was a lucky man to have found her. Marion had turned out to be just the kind of woman he had been looking for – beautiful, witty, warm, affectionate and loving. She was exactly what he needed – a companion, a lover, a soul mate, someone he could confide in, someone he could rely on. He hadn't believed it would happen again. But Matt was falling in love.

He glanced at his watch. He had arranged to see her at later and he had been looking forward to it all day. In the meantime, he was going to read this book. Now that he had joined the club he had discovered the pleasure of reading. That was another gift from Marion, he thought. And he was keen to be an active contributor. He felt he hadn't done justice to the last book, *Rebecca*. He had been extremely busy and had rushed it in his determination to get it finished. Thankfully, *The Boy in the Striped Pyjamas* was much shorter and with a bit of application he might finish it tonight. Then he would nip upstairs to see her, maybe have a glass of wine on her terrace if it was mild enough and spend a pleasant hour together while they gazed out at the lights of the city. And at the weekend she was meeting his children. It was important to Matt that they should like the new woman in his life. He was planning to take them to a nice restaurant and show her off. And it would also give him an opportunity to meet Rachel's new boyfriend. She had sounded quite excited when they spoke yesterday on the phone. She said his name was Gavin and he was in publishing. A commissioning editor, she had announced proudly which sounded to Matt like a very responsible position, although he knew absolutely nothing about the publishing business.

As he turned a page, he wondered where Gavin was going to sleep. Normally Rachel had the second bedroom but did she expect to share a bed with her boyfriend? And what should Matt do? Should he fix Gavin a sleeping bag on the settee or just turn a blind eye and let them bunk up together? And if he did that, would he be failing in his responsibilities as a father, particularly under his own roof? It was a knotty question. He knew what he would do. He would bounce it off Marion this evening and hear what she had to say.

He was particularly pleased with the way Rachel was turning out. The London experience had done her a power of good. Living alone and fending for herself had obviously had a stabilising effect and now she was rapidly developing into a mature young adult. The sulky, brooding adolescent who had caused him so much concern just a few short years ago was now a distant memory. Indeed, Rachel didn't even want to be reminded of it, referring to that period dismissively as her "cocoon" phase. Before she emerged as a beautiful butterfly, presumably!

He was proud of both his children. They had turned out well, which was a major achievement in these times when you heard such awful stories about young people going off the rails and getting involved with drugs and crime. He knew they had been hurt by the break-up of the marriage. It sometimes made him feel guilty. It was something they had no control over and for which they were not responsible. A thought flashed into his mind: Why do we demand such high standards from our children, when we behave so badly ourselves?

Yes, Matt thought, as he uttered a sigh of contentment, life is falling back into place. He was achieving a measure of peace at last. He had the love of his children, he had job satisfaction. He had a new home. And to cap it all, he had met a wonderful woman who had awakened in him the kind of joy that he thought he would never feel again. He had clearly been given a second chance.

Just then the phone rang. That will be Marion, he thought confirming our appointment. He lifted the phone and pressed it to his ear.

"Hi," he began. "How are you?"

But it wasn't Marion. It was a smooth cultivated voice that he recognised immediately. It was the voice of Tom Stafford, his solicitor.

"Tom!" he said, with some surprise. "I wasn't expecting to hear from you."

"I'm sorry," the solicitor said. "I wouldn't have disturbed you except something has come up. It's rather urgent. I need to talk with you as soon as possible."

"What is it?" Matt asked, feeling a knot tighten in his stomach.

"It involves Anna," his solicitor said. "I'm afraid it's not good news."

Chapter Nineteen

The Grimes household was in uproar. At half past nine, just as Christy had finished clearing away the breakfast things, Dr Hynes had rung to say he would like to see Ellie for an assessment.

"When?" Ellie asked.

"This morning."

"Mother of God!" Ellie said.

"A window of opportunity has just opened up in my schedule," Dr Hynes said. "And I thought it would be a good time to take another look at you. Can you get down here for eleven o'clock?"

"I'll try," Ellie said. She was still shaking as she put down the phone.

Christy emerged from the kitchen, drying his hands on a tea towel. "Who was that?"

"Dr Hynes. He wants to see me at eleven o'clock."

Christy took one look at her. "The walking frame!" he said.

"That's what I was thinking too," Ellie said.

The first thing Christy did was ring Ace Cabs and order a taxi for half ten. "And tell him not to be late. This is an urgent medical appointment," he told the young woman at the base who took his call.

As soon as he put down the phone, it rang again. This time it was his daughter Jackie.

"How are yiz all keeping?" she wanted to know.

"I'm keeping well," Christy said, "but your mother has to be down to the doctor for eleven o'clock. He says a window of opportunity is after opening and he wants to give her an assessment."

"I'd take her," Jackie said, "but Anto's got the car."

"Don't worry. I've just ordered a cab. How are you, anyway?"

"Not a bother. Look, I was going to call down to see you. But it can wait till Mum gets back from the doctor. Why don't I drop by around one o'clock?"

"If we're still alive," Christy said.

By now, it was twenty past nine. Ellie decided that she needed a shower, even though she'd already had one this morning when she got up.

"I have to be clean for the doctor."

"How much dirt do you think you've got on you since eight o'clock?" Christy demanded to know.

"He'll be examining me. And I have to smell fresh."

"If you smelt any fresher people would think this was a chemist's shop. Now, do you want me to help you?"

"No, thanks very much. I can look after myself."

"And how long is it going to take?"

"Fifteen minutes."

Christy sighed. He knew what Ellie's fifteen minutes meant – at least half an hour.

"Well for God's sake make it snappy or this window of opportunity might close again."

In the meantime, he decided to put on his best suit and tie. This was something of an occasion. It was the day they had been waiting for since Ellie's stroke, over eighteen months ago. With a bit of luck, Dr Hynes would take away the walking frame, which was much the same as giving her a clean bill of health.

It would mean that she would be able to resume light work, particularly in that damned garden. Christy had noticed this morning that the grass was shooting up again at an alarming rate after the recent rain. And the weeds were sprouting like beanstalks. If Ellie didn't get to work on it soon, it would look like the tropical jungle in the zoo.

From behind the frosted door of the shower, he could hear the splash of water.

"Are you okay in there?" he asked.

"Won't be long," Ellie replied.

"I've ordered the taxi for half ten. You know what these bowsies are like. If you're not ready, he won't wait."

"I can't hear you," Ellie shouted above the noise of the shower.

"I said if you're late, the taxi will leave."

Christy muttered under his breath. Ellie had got very independent recently and wouldn't let people do things for her, although he noticed that she still allowed him to make the breakfast and clean up afterwards. But it was a good sign. It was an indication that she was getting better. And she *had* made enormous progress. It wasn't so long ago that she couldn't walk at all and now she was able to take a shower on her own. It was all down to her determination. Ellie was a fighter. Please God Dr Hynes would give her the okay.

He took his one good suit from the wardrobe. He had bought it ten years ago from a tailor in Capel St and it still fitted him like a glove. It was Christy's special suit that he wore for birthdays and anniversaries and funerals. Whenever he put it on, people knew that something important was going to happen.

He selected a clean shirt and tie and then he decided to polish his shoes. No point sinking the ship for a hap'orth of tar. He went down to the kitchen where the shoe brushes were kept and gave the shoes a quick polish. When he came back up to the bedroom, Ellie was emerging from the shower in a cloud of steam.

"What are you doing?" she inquired.

"Getting dressed like yourself."

"You're only in my way," she complained and proceeded to bundle her husband out of the room.

At that moment, there was a loud honking of a car-horn from

outside the window. Christy pulled back the curtains and saw the taxi sitting outside the front door with its engine running. He checked his watch. It was a quarter past ten. The bugger was early for a change.

"Grimes?" the taxi man inquired as Christy opened the front door.

"That's me."

"Where's the patient?"

"What patient?"

"I was told this was a medical emergency."

"Medical appointment not medical emergency," Christy said. "But you'll have to wait till my wife is ready. Would you like to come in?"

"I'll wait in the cab," the taxi man said with a scowl. "But she better get her skates on. This is costing me money."

"Suit yourself. I was going to offer you a cup of tea," Christy said. He closed to door and bellowed up the stairs.

"The taxi's here and if you don't hurry up he'll be gone."

Then he hurried back up to the bedroom, fuming.

For the interview with the doctor, Ellie had insisted on getting dressed up in a nice blouse and skirt and her best coat.

"This isn't a ball you're going to," Christy said caustically, glancing out from behind the curtains to make sure the taxi was still there. But Ellie simply shot him a withering glance.

Getting dressed had added another twenty minutes to the process and caused Christy's blood pressure to soar. If this goes on much longer I'm going to end up in intensive care myself, he thought miserably.

Then they ran into traffic at the Cabra Road which had him biting his nails on the edge of his seat. By the time they arrived at the surgery, he was shaking like a leaf from nerves.

There was a queue of people waiting. There always was a queue for Dr Hynes, which Ellie said just proved what a good doctor he was.

"The day there isn't a queue is the day I'll get worried," she was fond of remarking.

But as soon as they came into the surgery, the doctor's secretary came bustling out of her little office and told them not to worry, Mrs Grimes was next because she had a prior appointment and this caused a rather satisfied grin to appear on Christy's face.

At five past eleven, the door of the consulting room opened and a woman emerged. The secretary appeared again.

"Your turn, Mrs Grimes," the secretary said and took Ellie's arm. Christy stood up to assist her but the secretary told him he wouldn't be needed and to remain behind. So Christy sat down again feeling deflated.

The secretary led Ellie into the consulting room and the door closed. Christy looked up at the ceiling. Then he looked at the walls. Then he looked at the floor and studied the pattern in the carpet. In the end, he picked up a magazine from the pile that sat on a table in the middle of the room. *True Love Confessions* it was called so he quickly put it down again, hoping no one had noticed.

Ellie was a long time in the consulting room. Christy tried to imagine what the doctor was doing. Probably taking her blood pressure and getting her to do exercises to test the strength and mobility in her arm and leg. He prayed that everything was going to be all right. If Dr Hynes didn't give Ellie the all-clear, it was going to be a terrible blow to them all but especially Ellie.

After what seemed like an age, the door opened once more and Dr Hynes called Christy into the room. He was a middle-aged man with a jovial manner and a little potbelly from eating too many good meals. Ellie was sitting on the examining couch. Christy glanced at her quickly to see if her expression would give any sign but her face was blank.

"Now, Mr Grimes," the doctor said, sticking a thumb in the pocket of his expanding waistcoat, "your wife has made an amazing recovery. I've rarely seen a stroke patient make such excellent progress."

Immediately, Christy felt his confidence rise.

"I think she's now ready to walk unaided and I've recommended thirty minutes exercise each day. I suggest a short stroll to begin with or maybe a trip to the shops. And she can undertake some light housework. We'll increase the exercise as time goes by."

Christy was practically speechless with joy. "That's brill," he whispered.

"However, she still has to take it easy and this is where you come in."

"Yes?" Christy said, standing to attention.

"Mrs Grimes tells me that you have been a significant help with the household chores."

Christy beamed. "I do me best."

"You'll have to continue with that."

"Game ball."

"She also tells me she's anxious about her garden."

"She loves the garden," Christy warbled. "She can't wait to get stuck into it again."

"Well, she'll have to hold off for a while longer, I'm afraid."

"Oh."

"What I suggest is that you should do the gardening work under Mrs Grimes' direction."

Christy felt his heart sink. He swallowed hard. "Okay," he said. "What have I got to do?"

"Whatever Mrs Grimes tells you. There's been a lot of growth in recent weeks so I'm sure there's plenty of work to be done."

Out of the corner of his eye, Christy thought he could see Ellie give a little smirk.

The doctor patted her warmly on the back.

"Congratulations, Mrs Grimes. You've been an example to us all. Come and see me again in six weeks' time and we'll monitor your progress."

He pulled the door open and Christy and Ellie were out again in the waiting room.

They arrived home at ten to one and Christy immediately put on the kettle to make some tea. What a morning it had been. He wasn't sure if all this excitement was good for him. He was over the moon that

Ellie was able to walk again without assistance but now there was the bleedin' garden to contend with.

He was coming to hate that garden. In fact it was worse than that. He was terrified of it. He could just picture the weeks of drudgery that lay ahead: pulling weeds, trimming bushes, pruning roses, cutting grass while Ellie stood over him like a slave driver. The thought of it made his stomach queasy.

Just then, they heard the doorbell ring.

"I'll get it," Ellie said brightly, glad of the opportunity to exercise her newfound freedom.

Christy continued with the tea till he heard the excited voices from the hall.

"Mum! You're walking without your frame! That's wonderful!"

It was Jackie. In all the commotion, he had forgotten that his daughter had promised to call.

He put another cup on the tray along with a plate of coconut cream biscuits. This was a celebration after all. When he went into the sitting room, Jackie was still hugging her mother.

"This is brilliant news," Jackie said. "Oh, Mum, I'm so pleased for you!"

Christy felt the pride for Ellie surge again in his breast. "Isn't she a marvel?" he said, putting down the tray and giving his daughter a peck on the cheek. "Dr Hynes said she was an example to us all. He said she was amazing."

"And so she is," Jackie said, hugging Ellie once more.

Christy poured the tea. He wished he had something stronger to mark the occasion. He wondered if there was a bottle of wine stuck away somewhere in the kitchen cupboard.

"How did you know I was seeing the doctor?" Ellie asked.

"Dad told me. But I wanted to see you anyway."

"Oh?" Ellie said.

"Yes. I've got some news of my own."

"Go on," Ellie said.

Jackie was beaming. "I'm pregnant," she said.

Christy almost dropped his cup with shock.

"I wanted you to be the first to know. After Anto, of course. I got the confirmation last night. Three months."

"Holy Moley," Christy said, "I'm going to be a grandfather!"

He closed his eyes and fell back in his seat. Ellie and Jackie in the one morning! He didn't think he could take any more good news.

Nick sat down at his word processor and opened the cover. He was bursting with energy and eager to get started. This morning he had leaped from bed when the alarm sounded at eight o'clock, had a shower and a quick breakfast and now he was ready. This was the moment he had been waiting for. He had his plot, he had his characters and now he had his motivation. Liz's words of encouragement were still ringing in his ears. She had told him the novel was bound to be a success. And he believed her. All he had to do was write it.

Ten minutes later, his fingers were flying like lightning over the keyboard as the story began to unfold onto the screen. Barely had he typed a sentence when another one sprang immediately into his head. Whole conversations, vivid descriptive passages, chunks of dramatic action flowed effortlessly from his teeming brain. It was just like the old days when he was writing poetry. Only this time, there was one important difference. Nick was achieving his life's ambition – he was writing a novel.

From time to time, he paused for breath and glanced from the window at the yard below. But the scene that once depressed him, now seemed to inspire him. The sun was out, the daffodils were shooting up and the sparrows were back, noisier and more quarrelsome than ever. But now, he found the view invigorating. Each time he looked at it, he felt renewed.

He was astonished how everything had been transformed since he heard Christy Grimes speak at the book club. It had been the catalyst he needed to get him started. Christy's story had unblocked his imagination and now the novel was flowing like a tide as if it was already fully formed in his head and just waited to be transferred onto the page. Whole scenes, new characters, snatches of dialogue all jostled for attention in his restless brain. His fingers could scarcely keep up with the tremendous energy that seemed to be surging right through him and straight onto the keyboard.

By midday, he felt he should take a break. He had been working steadily for over three hours which was the maximum period a person could write before the creativity began to dry up, according to the manual by Mabel R Zuckfeld. Yet, Nick's imagination seemed to be firing in overdrive. His mind was as fresh and active as it had been when he first sat down at eight-thirty and his energy was showing no sign of diminishing. He was almost afraid to take a break in case he broke this train of thought and some of the wonderful ideas he had stored in his head would be lost.

Nevertheless, he forced himself up from his desk and into the kitchen where he boiled the kettle and made a cup of coffee. While he chewed on a biscuit, he found his mind drifting back again to Liz. It was a tremendous piece of luck running into her like that. She was exactly the support he required right now. And what was more, she would bring a feminine perspective to his novel. He thought of Arminta O'Shea and the way she had guided his poetry career and dealt with publishers and critics – although sadly, Arminta had let him down in the end. But something told him Liz was going to be different. He trusted her and felt safe with her. Together, they would forge a winning combination.

He would have to thank her for her generous offer to read the chapters for him. Maybe he would buy her a present. He wondered what she would like. And then a thought popped into his head. He would write a little thank-you note and drop it into her office along with a good bottle of wine. He could do it on his way into work. Saying thank-you to someone never went astray.

Buoyed up with his resolution, he finished his coffee and went back to his desk. No sooner had he sat down than his brain was once more flooding with ideas. He worked non-stop for another two hours until finally he dragged himself away to get ready for work. Before he did, he tapped the counter on his word processor and was amazed to discover that he had written almost 5,500 words.

He smiled with satisfaction. That was twice what Mabel R

Zuckfeld had recommended in her manual. At this rate, he would have his novel written in record time.

About the same time that Nick was thinking about Liz, she was thinking about him and the interesting change that had come over her since their chance meeting. She couldn't get him out of her head which meant that instead of brooding about the lump on her breast, her mind was consumed with thoughts about Nick. She found to her surprise that she was fascinated by the tall, handsome young man with his charming manner and interesting life. She had never met a real writer before and Nick had completely swept her up in the excitement of this novel he was writing.

Their first real proper contact had been the night of the book club meeting in Alan McMillan's apartment. She had met him before of course at the inaugural meeting in Marion's place but it wasn't till the second time that they got chatting. He had joined Cathy and her on the settee and kept them entertained with general small talk till the proceedings got under way. It was talking to Nick that helped her get through that ordeal. She hadn't wanted to attend and if it hadn't been for the fact that she had encouraged Cathy to come along and felt guilty as a result, she probably wouldn't have turned up at all.

But Nick had generously taken them both under his wing, making sure their glasses were topped up and their plates were always stocked with interesting titbits from Alan's extensive buffet. And all the while he maintained a steady stream of interesting conversation. Cathy had commented later on the way home in her car what a handsome man he was and wondered aloud if he had a partner.

But it was the accidental meeting in town yesterday that had really opened Liz's eyes. She was amazed at the sheer animal energy Nick seemed to possess. She could feel it radiating from him like electricity. It had affected her too. It reminded her of the zeal that Tim had shown when she first met him, the absolute determination to succeed. She remembered thinking how she had never met a man before who knew so clearly what it was he wanted to do. Nick had that very same urgency and conviction.

But there was another side to him too, a vulnerable side that aroused her protective instincts and made her want to help him. She could see how affected he had been by the attacks on his poetry. It must have been terrible to have everyone turn against you like that, to be hounded and called a liar and a cheat. It must have hurt him badly, but he had come back. He had refused to be intimidated. He wanted to write this novel and he was determined to see it through. And Liz admired him for that.

She had thoroughly enjoyed those few drinks with him in the pub. There had been an easy familiarity between them that encouraged her to relax. They had talked together like old friends who had known each other all their lives. It had been a long time since she'd had that kind of conversation with a man. And was it just her imagination or was there a little spark between them, some mysterious rapport? She wondered if Nick had felt it too.

She had been thinking about him ever since. Cathy had been absolutely right, as usual – Nick was an extremely handsome man. She thought of that trim, well-built body, the tall carriage, the dark Mediterranean features. And those dreamy eyelashes were to die for. She knew a lot of women who would give anything to have lashes like those. They were wasted on Nick. He didn't need them. He was handsome enough already.

She would have to find out more about him. And then, she had an idea. She would ring the library in the morning and check if they had a copy of his poems in stock. She wanted to read them for herself and see what all the fuss was about. And the next time they met she would tell him honestly what she thought.

At that moment, she heard the doorbell ring. She rushed to open it and found Cathy Burke on the step.

"I'm not staying," she said, quickly. "Just dropping by to make sure you're all right."

"You really are an angel," Liz said. "Come in and have a glass of wine."

"I'd better not," Cathy said. "One glass might lead to another."

"Something else, then?"

"Okay. I'll have a Ballygowan," Cathy said, following her friend into the kitchen. "I hope I'm not disturbing you?"

"I've just got home," Liz confessed.

"Busy day?"

"Yes, thank God."

"Well, I must say you're looking a whole lot better," Cathy said, taking her by the shoulders and staring into her eyes. "And your attitude seems to have improved. You sound much more upbeat."

Liz smiled. So Cathy could recognise it too.

"I had an odd experience yesterday," she said as she searched in the fridge for a bottle of sparkling water.

"Oh?"

"You'll never guess who I had a drink with after work?"

"Tell me."

"Nick Barry."

Cathy raised her eyebrows. "Our Nick Barry? From the book club?"

"The very one."

She unscrewed the cap from the bottle and saw that she had now got her friend's full attention.

"You surprise me," Cathy said.

"Why?"

"I don't know. Somehow I never pictured you and Nick . . ."

Liz burst out laughing before she could finish. She realised that the excitement of the whole thing was making her giddy. "There you go jumping to conclusions. All we had was a drink and a chat."

"You make it sound so innocent," Cathy said. "But if life has taught me one thing it's that nothing is ever simple in these matters. How did all this come about?"

"I just ran into him on the street as I was about to go home. He had an hour to spare before going into work so he invited me to join him for a drink. And you know something? I'm glad I did. I really enjoyed it."

She poured the sparkling water and the two women sat down at the kitchen table.

"Well, I'm absolutely delighted," Cathy said. "I think it's good for you to have some men friends. It's what I've been saying all along. Haven't I told you that you need something like this to lift you out of yourself?" She took a sip from her glass. "What did you talk about?"

"Books, literature, writing. You know he's a journalist?"

"No, I didn't."

"He's a sub-editor on the *Daily Trumpet*."

"Really? Are you planning on seeing him again?"

Liz *would* be seeing Nick again when he brought her chapters of his new novel to read but she had promised not to tell anyone about it. "Don't you think you're making a mountain out of a molehill?" she asked, playfully. "It was only a chance meeting."

"Maybe," Cathy said. "But he didn't have to invite you for a drink. And you didn't have to go. I wonder if there isn't something deeper going on here."

Liz smiled. She was enjoying this banter with her friend.

"And he *is* quite handsome," Cathy went on. "I said that from the very beginning. Maybe he recognised a kindred spirit in you."

"Do you think so?"

"Yes, I do. And if nothing else, he appears to have cheered you up. I don't suppose you would kick him out of bed?"

Liz laughed again. "You're going too fast. First he has to get into it."

Chapter Twenty

The taxi screeched to a halt beside a bus stop, the door opened and Matt quickly jumped out, thrusting a twenty-euro note into the waiting hand of the driver.

"Keep the change," he said and immediately checked his watch as the taxi sped away amidst a barrage of horns from the oncoming traffic.

It was twenty-five minutes past two and his appointment with Tom Stafford was scheduled for half past. With a bit of luck, he would make it on time. Matt hurried along the footpath keeping a watchful eye for the shabby doorway that signalled the entrance to the offices of Stafford and Partners. He knew the solicitor's office well. He had been there on numerous occasions during his legal wrangle with Anna over the separation. But he hadn't expected to be back again so soon.

The phone call last night had startled him. He knew at once that it was something serious because Tom Stafford, while a first-class lawyer, was also a man who firmly believed in keeping work and home life in two separate compartments. Which probably accounted for his youthful appearance, Matt thought ruefully as he found the doorway he was looking for and pressed the buzzer to gain admission. At sixty-six, Stafford looked like a man half his age. So, if he thought it was necessary to ring him at home late at night, then the matter had to be important. And it was.

From the brief account he had garnered over the phone, Matt learned that his wife had instructed her lawyers to seek increased maintenance support from him. The instruction had only reached Tom Stafford late in the evening after he arrived home from a charity dinner and he had thought it best to contact Matt at once to set up an urgent meeting.

"Can she do this?" Matt asked, amazed and shocked by the news.

"That's what we have to discuss," Stafford said.

"But I thought we had settled it all at the time of the separation."

Stafford cut him off. "Look, we aren't going to solve this problem tonight, Matt. Now, I suggest we fix a meeting. And in my view, the sooner we do it, the better."

In the end, Matt had to settle for this two thirty appointment, his solicitor's last words ringing in his ears.

"Get a good night's sleep. I want you bright-eyed and bushy-tailed when we meet."

It was easier said than done. Matt had cancelled his visit to Marion on the pretext of a sudden business matter and had gone to bed feeling angry and deflated. He couldn't face her in the mood he was in. But it was several hours before he finally drifted into a troubled sleep. If Anna was looking for increased maintenance it could mean big trouble. And why had she suddenly decided to do it?

The appointment had also disrupted his work schedule. He had to rearrange a couple of interviews, cancel a lunch appointment and take a taxi into town rather than attempt to battle the Dublin traffic in his own car. As a result, he was feeling far from bushy-tailed as he climbed the rickety stairs to the old-fashioned premises of Stafford and Partners just as the hands of his watch touched half past two.

Tom Stafford was waiting. He was a tall, lean man with a mane of silver hair and a tanned, weather-beaten face. He wore a smart blazer with a golf-club crest to complement his immaculate charcoal grey slacks. Matt couldn't help thinking once again that he looked more like a middle-aged film star than a solicitor. But the two men went back a long way. Matt had first been introduced to Stafford over twenty years before and ironically Anna had been involved in that meeting too. They had just got married and were buying their home and needed a solicitor to carry out the legal work. A colleague had recommended Tom Stafford and Matt readily agreed.

Stafford had undertaken the work with speed and efficiency and hadn't overcharged. Over the years, Matt sent other work his way. The two men became good friends and on those occasions when he required legal advice, it was to Tom Stafford that Matt automatically turned. He had acted for him in the messy separation from Anna and now he was about to advise him again with this latest problem.

He rose from his desk as a secretary showed Matt into his office and immediately extended a bony hand in welcome. Matt took it and felt the firm pressure that always reassured him whenever he shook hands with Tom.

"I'm glad you could make it. Now before we begin, would you like Marjorie to get you a cup of coffee?"

"I could certainly use some caffeine," Matt admitted, feeling the need of a stimulant to see him through what promised to be a stressful encounter.

Stafford immediately lifted the phone and a few minutes later the secretary was back with a tray containing a cup and saucer, a jug of milk, a bowl of sugar, a plate of biscuits and a pot of freshly brewed coffee.

Matt waited while Stafford poured.

"How are you?" Tom inquired. "Keeping okay?"

"I was fine until I got your phone call last night."

"I'm sorry to have called you so late. But I thought it was best."

"You were right," Matt replied. "There's never a good time to break bad news."

"Let me explain what's happening," Tom said, as he finished pouring the coffee. For the next five minutes, he added flesh to the bare bones of the situation he had outlined on the phone the night before. It boiled down to one simple fact. Anna was looking for more money.

"How much?" Matt asked.

"She hasn't put a figure on it yet. But it could be €300,000, possibly more."

Matt's face went pale. "Tell me this is a practical joke."

Stafford gravely shook his head. "It's no joke, I'm afraid."

"But it's outrageous. She has more money that I have."

"She disputes that."

"She has a well-paying job. Plus the money I already gave her. And I'm still technically responsible for Rachel till she turns twenty-one."

The solicitor leaned back in his leather chair. "She says you're now earning considerably more in your new job. Is that true?"

"Yes," Matt admitted. "But I'm also working a damned sight harder."

"She says you've got valuable share options in Atlanta Technologies?"

Matt stared in open-mouthed amazement. "Where is she getting all this information?"

"I don't know. But she seems to be well informed about your financial arrangements. She also says you have extra income from the sale of the family home. She's claiming a share in that too."

"What?"

The solicitor nodded.

"But most of it went on the purchase of my apartment," Matt explained.

"Did you have any cash left over?"

"A little. I was planning to divide it between the children. Set up a trust fund for them so they will have deposits for their own homes when they're older."

Tom Stafford let out a loud sigh. "Look, Matt, I hate these cases. They distress me. And they're nearly always messy. But I'm afraid I must ask you for a statement of all your financial affairs. Bank details, salary, plus a valuation on your apartment. How much did you pay for it?"

Matt told him.

"I can arrange for an auctioneer to give us an up-to-date valuation if you like."

Matt looked bewildered. "Is all this really necessary?"

"I'm afraid it is. If we're going to fight this case, I need to know exactly where we stand."

Matt felt a sinking feeling in the pit of his stomach. "But I understood when we separated that I had discharged my financial obligations to Anna. I undertook the maintenance of the children and I gave her a sum equal to half the value of the family home. I had to borrow that money and I've only just managed to pay back the loan."

"She claims the value of the family home appreciated greatly after she left and she's entitled to a share of that increase."

"Dammit!" Matt said in exasperation. "I was more than generous to her. It's not as if I'm a millionaire. I've only just managed to get my head above water. And I'm the innocent party in all this. She left me, remember. The whole thing just seems so bloody unfair."

Tom Stafford slowly shook his majestic head. "The law isn't always fair, Matt, despite what lawyers like to say. Now if you can get me those financial details as soon as you can, I'll start to prepare a response."

Matt felt sick. Just as he was beginning to build a new life for himself and the future was starting to look bright again, this had to come along to shatter him.

"What I can't understand is why she's doing this," he said. "It's so out of character. Anna was never a greedy woman."

The solicitor leaned across the desk and spoke in a soft, confidential manner. "Between ourselves, this may not be your ex-wife's handiwork."

"How do you mean?"

"Her partner, Jack Arnold? I take it you've met him?"

"Yes," Matt agreed. "And you won't be surprised to learn that I didn't like him."

"Well, it's my information that he's the real mover behind this. I can't prove anything, of course. But that is what I'm led to believe. And it wouldn't surprise me."

Suddenly, Matt felt a great surge of anger engulf him. Not only had Arnold taken his wife, broken up his home and almost left him bankrupt but now he was bent on ruining him financially the second time over.

"And he's got a particularly nasty piece of work handling the case for him," Stafford went on.

"Who's that?"

"A gouger called Alan McMillan. He's ruthless, Matt. He allows no-one and nothing to get in his way."

Alan sat in his office at Weatherup and Bailey, sipping a cup of Earl Grey tea served in a china tea cup by Ms Coleman. In Alan's opinion Ms Coleman was an excellent secretary. She possessed all the virtues that he considered essential in a personal assistant. She was efficient, punctual and ever alert to his needs and requirements. But above all else, she was discreet. Ms Coleman knew how to maintain a confidence. And maintaining confidences was vital in the legal business where so many secrets regularly passed across his desk.

As an added bonus, Ms Coleman was fifty-two and therefore not a flighty young person who spent all day on the telephone discussing her love life with her friends. Alan considered this to be extremely important. In his view, a secretary's ability to keep her mind sharply focussed on her job increased dramatically with age.

He sipped his tea and uttered a soft sigh of satisfaction. He had just returned from an excellent lunch in the Dawson St Gentlemen's Club where, over rare roast beef and excellent Yorkshire pudding, he had managed to conclude some serious business. His guest had been his stockbroker, Jack Arnold, which Alan considered to be an interesting coincidence since it enabled him to deal with the two issues that were foremost in his mind right now – the share price of Vorax and the destruction of Mr Matt Bollinger. And he had made considerable progress with both.

Vorax had now climbed to the dizzy heights of € 14 a share which meant that Alan's holding was worth € 560,000. And to think he had bought them for a mere € 60,000. He had made a profit of half a million euros in little over six months which was amazing. The shares were like a poker machine that just kept pumping out money. And the astounding thing was they looked set to continue.

Jack Arnold had confirmed Alan's gut instinct. In his opinion, the shares were set to rise to €15 at the very least. Alan had already decided this was the point at which he would sell, take his profit and buy another penthouse apartment at Grand Canal Dock. The trick about playing the stock market was to know when to get out. Stay too long and the shares might fall. Sell too soon and you might lose some of the gains. It was a balancing act. Alan had made up his mind that when the Vorax shares reached €15 he would go.

He had held a discussion with the developer at the weekend and struck a deal whereby he would buy an excellent property with views of the water for €750,000. It was a steal. Alan was discovering that this was the beautiful thing about money. It just kept on attracting more.

He had asked Jack Arnold to keep an eye out for any more opportunities in the stock market, ideally small shares with the potential for growth. That was what the market was all about – spotting opportunities. One person's loss was always someone else's gain. In the meantime he had agreed to purchase another 20,000 shares in Vorax to add to his portfolio. In Alan's view there was no point in missing out on a sure-fire success. It was a bit like knowing the winner of the Derby in advance of the race.

However, there had been one slight drawback although Jack as usual had come up with a clever solution. Alan didn't have the cash to pay for the new shares. But over the home-baked apple pie and whipped cream in the club, Jack had outlined a plan whereby Alan could buy the shares and pay for them later when they had passed the magic price of €15. Jack had very generously agreed to arrange for the purchase of the shares for Alan on account, to be settled in thirty days' time. That way, Jack got his commission and Alan got his profit and everybody was happy.

It was a foolproof scheme and Alan felt a small glow of pride in his success. He was well on his way to becoming a wealthy man. He had penetrated the golden circle and was now mixing with important people who could do favours for him and pull strings and put opportunities in his way. He was learning fast that this was the way the world went round.

Of course, he kept reminding himself, his success had not come easily. He had worked long and hard to get where he was. He had arrived in Dublin practically penniless but with a grim determination to succeed. He had studied relentlessly to pass his law examinations and then to get to his present position in the legal firm of Weatherup and Bailey. He had pursued his objectives with single-minded determination.

Alan knew he had a reputation for being ruthless but it wasn't something he was ashamed of. Indeed, it gave him satisfaction. He took a pride in it. He liked to see the look of fear and respect in his opponents' eyes when he sat down at the negotiating table. And he had achieved superb results and earned healthy commissions for the firm. He knew old Mr Weatherup was delighted with his work. Indeed only last week, he had hinted that when the next reshuffle of senior executives took place, he had a mind to make Alan a partner in the business.

Yes, he had good reason to feel pleased. Everything he had planned was falling into place. He only had to win back Marion's affections and his pleasure would be complete. But first he had to despatch Mr Matt Bollinger to the wasteland where he belonged and he was already well on his way to achieving that.

The private investigators, Snoop and Pry had gone about their work with commendable zeal and the report they had produced had been extremely thorough. Among the wealth of information it contained about Matt were details of his financial situation. Alan was surprised to discover that for a man who was holding down a senior position with a major American multinational company, Matt Bollinger was not particularly wealthy. He owned a modest apartment at The Cloisters in Smithfield in the same building as Marion and drove a smart BMW convertible. But his life-style was far from extravagant and the company owned the car.

He had commissioned the senior investigator, Mr Snoop, to carry out further research and he had come up with an interesting discovery. The reason for Matt Bollinger's modest life-style was because he had undergone a separation from his wife Anna which had left him financially strapped. He had only recently managed to clear his debts. But what Alan had been absolutely amazed to discover was that the man Anna had left her husband to live with was none other than Jack Arnold – who just happened to be his broker.

It was an unbelievable coincidence and Alan immediately saw an opportunity to kill two birds with one stone – return a favour to Jack Arnold, who had done so many favours for him and damage Matt. A quiet drink with Arnold had enabled him, to outline his plan. He should persuade Anna to pursue Matt Bollinger for further maintenance. He was able to inform Jack Arnold that Matt had accumulated further wealth and income since the separation. He assured him that Anna had a cast-iron case. He would personally represent her. She couldn't lose.

As he expected, Arnold had jumped at the opportunity and proceedings had been commenced. Matt Bollinger's solicitor was a veteran of the legal circuit, a doughty warrior called Tom Stafford. He had been around for a long time and was well liked and highly respected but Alan had no fear of him. He was looking forward to the challenge. When he had defeated Tom Stafford, it would be another feather in his cap.

A smile crossed his lips. Paying his wife increased maintenance would completely finish off Matt Bollinger. He would probably have to sell his apartment. His modest life-style would be wiped out. Instead of wining and dining at intimate restaurants like Mama Rosa's, he'd be lucky to make it to the nearest hamburger joint. Would Marion have the same affection for him then? Alan laughed quietly to himself. He didn't think so.

But Alan had no sympathy for him. Matt Bollinger had brought this on himself. He had crossed Alan and had to be punished. If he hadn't interfered with Marion and turned her against him, Alan would have no interest in him. It just went to prove what happened when you tried to steal another man's woman – particularly when that man was Alan McMillan.

He finished his Earl Grey and rang a little bell for Ms Coleman to come and take the tea things away. He stood up from his desk and walked to the window where he gazed out across the city at the spires and chimneys and rooftops gleaming in the pale afternoon sun. This was his adopted city. Already he owned a little part of it and with luck he would own more. Ah yes, he thought with a quiet sigh of satisfaction, he was well on his way.

In the meantime, there were things to do. He still had the book club to take care of. He had to buy a copy of *The Boy in the Striped Pyjamas* and get out the reminder notices for the next meeting which was being held in Liz's house. He would have to keep up his involvement with the book club. It kept him close to Marion. And when Matt Bollinger sank without trace, as he inevitably would, Alan would be there waiting for her to come back to him.

Liz was surprised to find a bottle of wine and a beautiful handwritten note had been left into her office while she was taking a late lunch. She opened the note and was pleased to discover it was from Nick. She read it with delight. There was still something of the poet about him. In the note, he had written: *Your kind words and generous support have uplifted my heart and renewed my spirit.*

She read it again. From any other man it might sound insincere. But coming from Nick, she found it very touching. And the wine wasn't just some supermarket plonk but an expensive bottle of Merlot which must have cost him a pretty penny. Well, isn't it nice to have a handsome man pampering me again, she thought as she put the note and the wine into her bag and sat down at her desk. Maybe Cathy is right. Maybe Nick has more than just this novel on his mind. And if so, how should I respond?

But she didn't have long to wait before Nick contacted her again. A few days later as she was travelling home from work, her mobile rang. She picked it up and recognised his voice. He sounded very excited.

"I've just finished the first chapter," he said. "And I wanted you to be the first to know."

"That was quick," she replied, feeling touched and proud.

"I know. That's the amazing thing. After talking to you, I sat down at the word processor and the stuff just came pouring out. Did you get my note by the way?"

"Yes, I did. It was beautiful. Thank you very much. And thanks also for the lovely bottle of wine."

"You earned it. You were a great inspiration to me."

Liz laughed. "All I did was talk."

"No, you mustn't be modest. You did much more than that. You gave me encouragement. And I really appreciate your offer to read my stuff. That's why I'm ringing. I'd love you to look at this chapter."

"How many words are we talking about?"

"Seven thousand give or take a few."

"My God, you *are* turning it out fast."

"This chapter is very important because it sets the tone for the rest of the book," Nick went on. "So, obviously I have to get it right. I'd really appreciate what you have to say about it."

"I can't wait to read it," she said. "When can you get it to me?"

"Tonight, if you like. I'm not at work. I could drop it round to you."

Liz thought quickly. She had nothing planned for this evening. It shouldn't take her more than an hour to read the chapter. But first she would have to get showered and grab a bite to eat.

"Okay," she said. "Why don't you call at eight o'clock? Let me give you my address."

"Brilliant," Nick said. "You're a darling."

Am I? she thought as she switched off the phone. A darling? It's been quite a while since any man called me that.

She got home before seven, checked phone calls and emails, had a shower and then went off to the kitchen to prepare something to eat before Nick arrived. As she was making a quick pasta dish and a salad, the thought occurred to her that she should offer him some supper. She had watched Nick devouring that baguette in the pub the other day and had a sneaking suspicion that he might not be feeding himself properly. She decided to make enough pasta for two people so if he felt hungry she would have something for him.

She was just finishing the washing up when she heard the doorbell ring. It was three minutes to eight. He's certainly punctual she thought as she quickly dried her hands on a tea towel and went to open the front door.

He was standing on the doorstep wearing a loose cotton shirt, faded Levis and a smart little black leather jacket. In his hand, he clutched a large buff envelope and a box of chocolates.

"For you," he said, thrusting the chocolates into her hands.

"Oh Nick," she said in surprise. "You don't have to keep giving me presents."

"Yes, I do. My mother told me never to turn up at someone's house empty-handed."

"Well, it was good advice. But only up to a point."

"Anyway, it's just a box of chocolates. I hope you like them."

"I love chocolates but I'm going to have to ration myself. I told you I'm watching what I eat these days."

He made a tut-tutting sound. "You don't need to do that. You look fabulous. Why don't you eat the whole box?"

"I already told you I'm not trying to lose weight," she said leading him into the sitting room. "It's for my health. And chocolates are full of sugar which rots your teeth among other things."

"Suit yourself. It's just a small gesture in return for all you've done for me."

"Oh, sorry! I didn't mean to sound ungrateful! I do love getting them."

"That's okay," he smiled.

His gaze travelled around the room.

"This is a lovely house. How long have you lived here?"

"Not very long."

"It must have cost a fortune."

"It wasn't cheap."

She didn't want to start explaining about Tim's death, so she adroitly shifted the conversation.

"Are you hungry?"

"Peckish," he said.

"I've just made some pasta and there's loads of it left. Why don't you eat while I get stuck into your manuscript? Otherwise the food will have to be dumped."

"Okay," he smiled. "That was another of my mother's mantras – waste not, want not."

He sat down on the settee while Liz busied herself in the kitchen with the pasta and salad. She kept up a running commentary as she worked.

"Do you ever cook?" she asked.

"Not really."

"So, do you eat out?"

"I eat mainly convenience foods," he admitted.

So her instinct had been right. Nick *wasn't* feeding himself properly.

"Cooking's not difficult, you know. It saves money for one thing. And it's better for you. And it can be great fun."

"But I don't have the time."

"Nonsense," Liz said, putting his meal on the table. "I've heard of writers starving in the garret but this is ridiculous. It's very important that you eat properly. Now would you like a glass of wine with that?"

"Please, Miss!" Nick said in a little boy voice and they both laughed.

While he ate, Liz settled down in a comfortable armchair and started to read. The only sound in the room was the gentle turning of pages and the scrape of Nick's fork against the plate.

The chapter was good. It was *very* good. Liz had been expecting something that might need some rewriting and improving. But the work she read was perfect. Indeed, it was far better than most of the material she came across in her everyday reading. When she had finished she put it down and saw that Nick was anxiously watching for her response.

"Well?" he said.

"You want my honest opinion?"

"Of course. That's why I'm here."

"It's superb."

"You mean there's nothing at all that you would change?"

"Nothing. I think it's perfect."

Suddenly, he jumped up from the settee, took her in his arms and hugged her. It all happened so quickly that it took her by surprise. But she wasn't displeased. In fact, she realised that she quite liked being hugged by Nick Barry.

"That's all I need to hear. If you had said you didn't like it, I would have been devastated. I would have gone away and torn the whole thing up."

"I absolutely love it. But I'm only one critic, for Heaven's sake."

He held her by the shoulders and gazed into her face. She found herself staring into his brooding dark eyes.

"I've already told you not to be modest. You may be one critic. But you are the only one who matters to me."

Chapter Twenty-one

Despite the brave face she had shown to Trish, Marion was really feeling nervous at the prospect of meeting Matt's children. She had two nieces of her own and got on fine with them. In fact she spoiled them and they took advantage. She allowed them to do things that their parents would never approve of. But they were only small children whereas Matt's kids were young adults and they could be much more critical, particularly Rachel who had reacted badly to the marriage break-up. In their eyes, Marion could be cast as the woman who had replaced their mother in Matt's affections. There was every chance that they might be hostile. This meeting could be difficult.

But she knew that she had to go through with it. It was an important milestone in the development of their relationship. If she managed to strike up a good rapport with them everyone would be happy, particularly Matt. It would make things so much easier.

So when Saturday came and she found him slightly distracted, she felt uneasy. This was one time when she was going to need his support and, to her dismay, his mind seemed to be elsewhere. He didn't complain or gave any indication that there was anything wrong. But there was definitely something bothering him. She could feel it. Matt was not his usual confident self. She put it down to stress.

He had been working so hard lately. When she got an opportunity, she was going to persuade him to slow down.

The day had started well. When she drew back the curtains at nine o'clock, she was delighted to see that the sky was clear and the sun was shining and the morning had an unmistakable air of spring about it. Saturday was her day for doing the laundry and cleaning the apartment. So, after a quick breakfast of coffee and a toast, Marion loaded up the washing machine, got out the vacuum cleaner and gave the place a thorough going-over. By eleven o'clock, she had completed her tasks and she took herself into the bathroom to soak in the tub for half an hour.

She couldn't believe the speed with which her life had changed in a few short weeks. The book club was now up and running and through it she had made a raft of new friends. There was no longer any question of sitting in a lonely apartment gazing out at the rain while she tried to find someone to talk to. But the most important friend of all was Matt.

As she lay in the tub, she found her mind drifting to the future. What did it hold for her? A relationship with a man who had already been married could cause obvious complications. He was sure to be marked by his previous experience. Despite the pain of the separation, he was bound to have some lingering feelings for his wife. They had been married for seventeen years, after all. How would this experience affect him? Would it colour his view about getting more deeply involved with her? And what about the children? How would they react? Would they resent her and see her as an interloper?

Some women would have called it off at this stage, not wanting the difficulties that might lie ahead. But for Marion that was not an option. She was too deeply involved with Matt. She cared for him too much. And one other thing was certain – she couldn't put this meeting off forever. At some stage she had to meet his children. As for the relationship, she realised she had no control over how it would turn out. She would simply have to let matters to take their course. If it developed into something more, that would be good. She hoped it did. But if not, she would just have to accept that too.

She finally rose from her bath and began to get ready for the lunch. Matt had promised to call for her at half twelve. He had phoned last night to say he had booked a table for one o'clock at *Trastevere,* a new restaurant in Baggot Street. It was an open-plan brasserie that served a wide variety of food from pizzas to steaks and he had chosen it in the belief that it might appeal to the young people. Let's hope he's right, Marion thought as she quickly dried herself and began to get dressed. For her part, she would do everything she could to make the day a success.

She had just finished dressing when she heard the door buzzer sound. She pressed the intercom and heard his voice.

"Are you decent?"

"I've got clothes on if that's what you mean," she replied, pressing the button to let him in.

He was dressed in a casual jacket, slacks and a pair of comfortable loafers. In his hand, he held a bouquet of flowers.

"My God," she said with surprise. "I wasn't expecting these."

"They're just a small token of my appreciation," he smiled while he planted a warm kiss on her cheek.

Marion glanced at the clock on the mantelpiece. It was exactly twelve thirty.

"Give me a moment while I put the flowers in the sink. I'll arrange them later. "

She hurried off to the kitchen and returned in a few moments.

"Okay, I'm ready. Let's go."

They drove in Matt's car.

"What's the plan? Are we picking up the children?"

"No, we're meeting them there. I think they're old enough to make their own way, don't you?"

He smiled, but Marion thought she detected a slight tension underneath his cheerful grin. However, when they arrived at the restaurant, they found only Peter and his girlfriend Zoe had arrived. There was no sign of Rachel and Gavin. Matt made the introductions and they all settled down to wait.

"They've been delayed," he said, lightly. "If I know Rachel, she's found a clothes shop somewhere and is searching for bargains. Let's order something to drink."

While they waited, Marion slipped into conversation with Peter and Zoe. She was a petite blond with shoulder-length hair and an elfin face, while he resembled his father - tall, dark and broad-shouldered. When they were out together he would tower over her. The incongruous nature of some couples never ceased to surprise her.

As they talked, Marion learnt that they both worked for the same charity organisation which looked after the homeless. It quickly became apparent that they were very committed young people who cared deeply about what they were doing. Soon they were all chatting amicably. But as the time ticked away towards half past one with no sign of Rachel and Gavin, Matt began to get increasingly nervous. He kept glancing at his watch and scanning the door each time someone entered. Marion wished he would relax. His unease was only fuelling her own growing tension.

Finally, he could wait no longer.

"I think we'd better start without them," he said and turned to Zoe. "Would you like to order?"

Peter glanced at his girlfriend, who hastily consulted the menu and ordered a pizza and salad. Peter asked for chicken fajitas. Marion was about to give her order when there was a loud shout from the general direction of the entrance and a thin young woman with a shaven head came bouncing across the room with a rather serious-looking young man in tow.

Marion took one look at her. She looked like a punk rocker with her leather jacket and nose ring. This was not what she had been expecting at all.

"Sorry, we're late," Rachel said, out of breath and collapsing into a seat beside Peter. "We went to the wrong place."

"You'd lose your head if it wasn't stuck on," Matt said with obvious relief. "We were just about to start without you."

The young man waited expectantly till Rachel suddenly remembered her manners.

"This is Gavin, incidentally." She jerked her thumb in his direction and grabbed a menu.

Gavin solemnly nodded his head and Matt quickly introduced the others. Everyone shook hands and Marion thought she saw Rachel scowl at her. My God, she thought, she doesn't like me. This is all I need. She took a quick sip of her drink to cover her confusion while Matt patiently took the order again.

"What do you work at?" Gavin said, turning to Marion.

"I'm a civil servant. Department of Education."

At the announcement of her career, she thought she saw Rachel's lip curl in a sneer. Why didn't I choose something cool like being a rock star, she thought? Then they'd be sure to like me.

Rachel continued to glare at her while Matt tried to engage Gavin in conversation. Marion felt miserable. This meal was not starting well. Despite her best intentions, she was already beginning to take a dislike to Matt's daughter. First she turns up late, then she shows a total lack of manners and now she was sending waves of hostility across the table at her like surface to air missiles.

She looked around for someone to talk to, anything to get away from that relentless stare that Rachel was directing at her. She pretended to study the menu again but when she looked up, she found Rachel was still watching her, her eyes screwed up into a look of sarcastic disapproval.

Suddenly, she leaned across the table and stared directly into Marion's face.

"Where did you meet my dad?" she demanded.

Marion swallowed hard. It sounded like an accusation, as if she had somehow stolen her father away. "At a book club."

"A book club?"

At the mention of the word, Gavin's ears immediately picked up.

"That's right."

"How did you come to join?"

Marion took another sip of her drink. She was sorry she hadn't ordered a large vodka and tonic. This conversation was turning into an interrogation. Any minute now, they would demand to see her passport.

Rachel was still staring. Marion was convinced she was shooting daggers at her. And that shaven head gave her the frightening look of a neo-Nazi boot-girl.

"I, er, started it myself."

"You started it yourself?"

"Yes."

"Why did you do that?"

She struggled hard to restrain herself. She so wanted this meeting to go well. But it was becoming very uncomfortable. Why should she have to defend herself to people she had never met before even if one of them happened to be Matt's daughter?

"Because I like books and I wanted a forum to discuss them with like-minded people."

Gavin's face suddenly broke into a wide grin. "I think that's amazing."

"It is?" Marion managed to splutter.

"Yes. Rachel and I are also members of a book club in London. I'm in publishing, you see, and I wanted to gauge consumer reaction. But then we sort of got hooked, didn't we, Rach?"

Rachel was now nodding her head vigorously and it seemed like the menacing frown had turned into a smile. "And to think you and Dad met at a book club of all places." She turned to her father. "You didn't tell me you met Marion at a book club." she said.

Matt shrugged. "You didn't ask me."

Marion downed the rest of her drink in one gulp. They had found something in common at last. She felt relief wash over her like a wave.

From that moment, the ice was broken. The food arrived and was followed by another round of drinks and soon the whole table was chatting and munching happily together. Rachel kept up a steady conversation with Marion about what books she liked and what authors she preferred.

"I'm going into publishing myself," she announced, proudly.

"Gavin's hiring me as his assistant. He's the commissioning editor."

"What does that mean?" Zoe inquired politely, in between bites of pizza.

"I'm a sort of talent scout," Gavin replied. "I look out for new writers who have potential."

"I'd kill for a job like that," Marion said. "It must be really exciting."

It was the perfect thing to say. Rachel glanced up and positively beamed at her.

"It's an interesting job," Gavin conceded. "But it's not entirely a bed of roses. Some writers can be very difficult to deal with. Some of them are notoriously precious. They won't allow an editor to change even a single comma."

"You're not serious?"

"Oh, yes I am. Some of them believe they are Charles Dickens or Jane Austen reincarnated. They think they're doing us a favour just allowing us to publish their work. You wouldn't believe the way they try to boss everyone around. I'll tell you something, opera singers would be easier to handle."

Everyone laughed.

"I never realised," Marion said. "It sounds absolutely fascinating."

Rachel was now smiling adoringly at her.

"Then you might discover a writer who has written a brilliant book," Gavin went on. "And after you publish it, you discover it's going to take them twenty years to write another one by which time everyone has forgotten who they are."

"But it does have its exciting side," Rachel added. "He gets to meet all sorts of interesting people."

"Some of them are pompous bores," Gavin said, dismissively.

"But you love it. And there's a great buzz about being involved in creative work. You've admitted that."

"Well, of course. I wouldn't stick it otherwise."

The conversation continued around the table till eventually the party began to break up. First, Peter and Zoe left and then Rachel and Gavin said they had some more shopping to do and would see Matt later.

Before she left, Rachel flung her arms round Marion and gave her a big kiss. "I loved meeting you," she said. "We've got so much in common. I'm really looking forward to having more conversations with you."

"Thank you," Marion said. "I enjoyed meeting you too."

By the time they had all gone, it was almost four o'clock.

Marion sat back in her seat and let out a loud groan. "Thank God that's over."

Matt smiled. "Was it that bad?"

"It was like sitting my Leaving Cert all over again. Or my driving test. I was nervous as a kitten."

"Well, you seemed to have passed with flying colours. The kids liked you, Marion. Rachel in particular seemed to take a shine to you."

"Not at the start, she didn't. At one stage I thought she was going to drive a stake through my heart."

"It's just her attitude. Her bark is worse than her bite. But she's maturing quickly. And Gavin seems to be having a good effect on her, thank God."

Marion took his hand and entwined her fingers in his. "More to the point, did *you* enjoy it?"

"Of course. I always enjoy seeing my children. Why do you ask?"

"I thought you seemed a little tense."

"No," he protested. "I'm absolutely fine."

Marion held his gaze. "Are you absolutely sure?"

He tried to look away. "There *is* something on your mind, isn't there? I noticed. Why don't you tell me?"

But he just waved his hand. "It's just some personal business. I don't want to bother you with it."

"That's what I'm here for, Matt."

He shifted uneasily in his seat. "You're not going to like this."

"Tell me," she demanded, a determined look on her face.

"My solicitor called me a few days ago with bad news."

She felt her heart jump. "Yes?"

"Anna is demanding increased maintenance from me. But that's not all. Do you know who is advising her?"

"Who?"

"Alan McMillan."

On Saturday morning, Nick called Liz at a quarter past nine. She had just stepped out of the shower and was drying herself when she heard her mobile go off. She wrapped the towel around her and made her way into the bedroom where she dug the phone out of her handbag,

"Hi," she said.

"It's me, Nick. I hope I didn't wake you?"

She felt her heart lift at the sound of his voice. "No, it's okay. I've been awake since eight o'clock."

"Good, I've finished another chapter and was wondering if I could bring it round?"

Liz was planning to do some household chores but she also wanted to see him. She made a quick calculation. The chores could wait till later.

"Are you talking about this morning?"

"If that's okay with you. I was thinking you could read the chapter, give me your opinion and then maybe we could go into town and grab a bit of lunch. What do you say?"

"Okay. When are you coming?"

"Right away. I'll be with you in half an hour."

After Nick's call she gazed dreamily from the window. What was happening to her? Nick just had to call and she dropped all her plans. She hadn't felt this way for a very long time. If he had said he wanted to meet her at the top of the Sugarloaf Mountain, she would probably have jumped into her car and driven there straight away.

But she did so much want to see him again. Since his last visit, she hadn't been able to get him out of her mind. She found herself thinking about him all the time. She had got his book of poetry *View from Matt Talbot Bridge* from the library and read it in one sitting. And she had loved it. Those people who had praised the book had been absolutely right. It was brilliantly original. It was a pity that he had stopped writing poetry because of the way he had been hounded by the press.

She suddenly pulled herself together. Why am I dithering like a lovesick teenager? He's going to be here in half an hour. I'd better get dressed. She finished drying herself and sat down at the dressing table and brushed her long blonde hair till it shone. She applied a little skin lotion to her face and massaged it in, then wiped off the residue with a tissue. Now her skin glowed with vitality. She picked up her mascara and turned her attention to her eyes. By the time she was finished, twenty minutes had passed.

Please God he doesn't arrive early, she thought as she started to rummage in her wardrobe for something to wear. She wanted to look good for Nick but at the same time, she didn't want him to know she'd gone to the trouble. What would she normally wear at home on a Saturday morning? Jeans? Jogpants? A T-shirt? She wanted to appear casual but still look good. In the end she opted for a pale pink V-necked cashmere sweater and a dark-brown skirt. She had just finished dressing and putting on the coffee percolator when she heard the doorbell ring.

She gave herself a last fleeting glance in the mirror, took a deep breath and marched down the hall. She pulled open the door and there he was on the doorstep looking sexily handsome in denims and a fleece. And was she imagining things or had he got his hair trimmed since the last time she saw him? Whatever it was, he looked good enough to eat.

"You're on time," she said in her most relaxed voice.

"Well, I don't want to keep a beautiful woman waiting. Especially when she's doing me a big favour," he said with a smile.

"Aren't you a real smarmer?" she said, giving him a playful frown. "Come in out of the cold. The coffee will be ready in a minute."

She led him into the sitting room where he plumped down on the settee and stretched his long legs. Out of the fold of his jacket he produced an envelope.

"Chapter Two," he said. "And please tell me you like it. I'll have a nervous breakdown if you don't."

"I'll tell you exactly what I think," she replied. "That's what you want, isn't it?"

"Yes. But I also want you to like it. I think it's good but that's only me and I can easily fool myself."

She took the envelope and put it down on the coffee table.

"I've been reading your poetry."

"Oh God," he moaned. "Where did you get it?"

"The local library."

"You mean they still have it in stock?"

"Not only that but it's been taken out quite a lot recently. You obviously still have fans out there. And I'm not surprised. I thought it was brilliant."

His face lit up at the praise. "Really?"

"Yes, really! It was everything your supporters said about it. You have a tremendous gift for imagery and language. I think it's a pity that you gave it up."

"I told you what happened."

"I know, but you shouldn't let it stop you."

He shook his head. "That's all in the past. Now I've got a new project. I'm going to be a novelist, remember."

"No reason why you can't do both," she said as the smell of freshly-brewed coffee began to drift into the room. "I'd better pour the brew," she said, standing up. "How do you like it?"

"Milk. No sugar."

"So you're taking my advice about the sugar?" she asked, playfully.

He grinned. "Do I have any choice?"

She came back with the coffee and settled down to read the new manuscript while Nick browsed through a magazine. For the next half hour, there was total silence. At last she put down the pages and turned to him.

"I love this novel," she said. "It's already got a grip on me. I can't wait for the next instalment."

"Did you find anything wrong with it?" he asked, cautiously. "Anything that needs changing?"

"Nothing major. Just a few small things. I've marked them in pencil."

"Nothing else?"

"No, I think it's marvellous. The story is so powerful and you write so well that you just sweep the reader along. It's brilliant."

"Oh, Liz, I love you when you say that."

"Would you love me if I didn't like it?"

"I'd have to think about that," he said and they both laughed.

Afterwards, Liz tried to figure out what happened next. They stared at each other for a moment in silence. Then Nick stood up and Liz followed. Next moment they were in each other's arms. She felt her heart race as his warm lips sought hers. She felt his breath hot on her skin and his hands slide down her waist and clasp her buttocks to pull her closer. Frantically, her fingers tugged at his belt and her hand was inside his pants. She felt herself melt with desire. It was so long since she'd had sex.

"Not so fast," she heard him say. "Let's do this properly."

He lifted her in his arms and carried her to the bedroom. With his shoulder he nudged the door closed. Liz closed her eyes as he laid her on the bed and began to undress her.

Afterwards, they lay in the tangled sheets and she traced a finger through the matted hairs on his chest.

"Where did you learn to make love like that?" she asked.

"I'm thirty-two years old," he said. "Where do you think I've been all my life? In a monastery?"

She straddled him and nibbled his ear.

"You were quite good yourself," he said.

"But I've had lots of practice."

"Oh?"

Liz had been debating when to tell him and this seemed to be the moment. "I was married until quite recently."

He was staring at her. "And then what happened?"

"My husband died suddenly. He was killed in a traffic accident."

"Oh my God," Nick said, his face filling with concern. "That sounds awful. I'm so sorry for you."

"It *was* a terrible shock," she went on. "But I'm slowly getting over it. It's the reason why I joined the book club."

"You must have loved him very much?"

"Yes, I did. You see I had never loved another man before. When he died, I wished that I had died too."

Nick rolled over and lay beside her. Gently, he caressed her cheek. And then his lips descended once more onto hers.

"You poor little rabbit," he whispered. "You've been so brave."

It was after midday when they finally emerged from the bedroom. Liz went into the en-suite bathroom to shower while Nick used the guest shower beside the kitchen.

"Where do you want to eat?" he said when he emerged fifteen minutes later to find Liz pulling on a pair of jeans and knee-length boots.

"I don't mind. Why don't we just drive into town and walk around till we find somewhere we like."

"Suits me," Nick said, brushing his hair in her wardrobe mirror.

Liz completed her ensemble with a chunky sweater and a smart little green woollen jacket and scarf.

"You look stunning," he said, staring at her in admiration.

"Thank you."

He took her in his arms once more and kissed her. She felt a warm satisfying glow suffuse her. This beautiful man had just made passionate love to her and now he was complimenting her and making her feel good about herself. She really was one lucky girl.

When they got into Dublin they found the city pleasantly uncluttered. And the weather had turned mild so it was perfect for walking. They strolled along by the river and then cut through the maze of little streets round Temple Bar till at last they came to Christ Church Cathedral just as a party of tourists and their guide were departing.

"Let's sit down," Nick said and deposited himself on a bench. "Have you any idea what you'd like to eat?"

Liz shrugged. "I'm easy."

"Well, I'm beginning to get hungry. That walk has given me an appetite. And I only had a slice of toast for breakfast."

"You shouldn't skip breakfast," she chastised. "It's the most important meal of the day."

Nick smiled. "Sorry, nurse. But I was in a hurry to print out Chapter Two for you."

She took his hand and pulled him to his feet. "Okay, let's get you fed. I don't want you collapsing on me in the street. Then what would I do?"

They found a place off Parliament Street that was emptying out after lunch and got a window table where they could watch the world stroll by. By now, Nick was ravenous. He ordered a steak with salad and sautéed potatoes while Liz opted for fish. Between them they drank a bottle of Sauvignon Blanc.

"When do you expect to finish the novel?" she inquired.

Nick chewed on a piece of meat. "At the rate I'm working, I could have the first draft completed in four or five months' time. Then it will probably need revision before it's ready for a publisher."

"Mmmm," Liz said.

"What does mmmm mean?"

"Something has just occurred to me," she said, holding up her fork.

"Tell me."

"You want this book to be as good as possible, right?"

"Of course I do."

"How would you like to have several more people read it? All of them people who are interested in creative writing?"

"I don't follow you," Nick said, looking confused.

"Why don't you give it to the book club?"

He put down his knife and fork and stared at her, open-mouthed. The suggestion had caught him completely by surprise. "That's a marvellous idea."

"You would be getting the views of a wide cross-section of readers," she went on, excitedly. "Which is what you want. And the more people who read it, the better. What do you think?"

"I think it's brilliant."

"You could give them chapters to read in advance and then we could discuss them at the next session."

Suddenly a cloud drifted across his face. "There *is* one problem," he said. "Nobody knows about this novel except you. I was hoping to keep it a secret."

"But you can't keep it a secret forever. Anyway who are they going to tell?"

"And what if they don't agree? It's supposed to be a book club after all, not a reading service for aspiring authors."

"Of course they'll agree. They'll love it. They'll be reading the work of a real live writer and co-operating in the production of the novel. My guess is they'll jump at the chance."

"I don't know," Nick said, doubtfully. "If the book's a failure, I'll be disgraced."

"But it won't be a failure," she said, taking his hand. "It's going to be a runaway success. How many times do I have to tell you?"

A smile broke on his face. To the surprise of the surrounding diners, he suddenly leaned across the table and planted a warm kiss on her mouth.

"You're a genius," he said. "What are you?"

Liz laughed and lowered her voice. "A genius?"

"That's right. An absolute bloody genius! Let's do it."

They finished the meal and he called for the bill.

"How would you like to round off the afternoon with a movie?" he asked.

Liz thought of the laundry and the household chores that were piled up at home. But they could wait till tomorrow. "Sure. Why not?"

She was feeling so happy that if Nick had suggested they go swimming naked in the Liffey, she would probably have agreed. Already today, they had made love, had a nice relaxing walk, a very pleasant meal and now she had just come up with an inspired idea to further his novel. And it was still only three o'clock!

As they left the restaurant, they passed two men deep in conversation at a table in the corner. One of them looked up and Liz immediately recognised Alan McMillan. But he was so engrossed in his conversation that he didn't appear to notice her.

"That was Alan," she said once they were out on the street.

"Alan McMillan?"

"Yes."

"Maybe I should go back and put your idea to him? He's the club secretary after all."

Nick looked in the window but Alan seemed so occupied with his conversation that he immediately changed his mind.

"I'll ring him on Monday," he said. "There's no rush."

The reason Alan hadn't recognised Liz and Nick was because his mind was totally focussed on the business he was discussing with Jack Arnold – the progress of the maintenance claim against Matt. But while the object of both men was the same, their motives were entirely different. Arnold simply wanted to extract more money from Matt. Alan wanted to destroy him.

That was what had brought them to this little restaurant in Temple Bar. Alan had insisted that they meet in some discreet place well away from the offices of Weatherup and Bailey. Recently, he had been growing concerned about security. Although he totally trusted his secretary, Ms Coleman, he wasn't so sure about some of the other colleagues in the firm. He knew that several people harboured resentments against him and were jealous of his success. Alan was well aware that this was an occupational hazard. There was always some bastard who was so eaten up by envy that they wanted to bring you down. And at this crucial stage in his career, he didn't see any point in taking unnecessary risks.

What worried him most was that Jack Arnold was not only a client but was also his stockbroker and was involved with him in the purchase of Vorax shares. There was always a danger that someone might accuse him of conflict of interest. And Alan was also uneasy about some of the methods he had employed to gain information about Matt Bollinger – particularly his use of the private investigators, Snoop and Pry. Although they had been worth every penny he had paid them. They had carried out their task with skill and efficiency and had unearthed nuggets of information that had been extremely useful. Mr Snoop had contacted him on Friday with further news that would come in very handy in processing their case and Alan produced it now as he tucked into his lunch of braised Wicklow lamb and roast potatoes.

"Bollinger paid almost €400,000 for the apartment at the Cloisters," he said, wiping some gravy from his chin with his napkin.

Jack Arnold's eyes opened wide. "Did he now?"

"Yes."

"Any mortgage?"

"Just a small one. Fifty thousand euros."

"So he has the guts of €350,000 in equity tied up in it?"

"That's right," Alan nodded. "Plus he has a further €150,000 left over from the sale of the family home. He has that invested with a bank at an interest rate of 4.0%."

Arnold whistled. "I'm extremely impressed," he said. "How did you manage to get your hands on this information?"

Alan smiled, enigmatically. "All part of the service."

He knew exactly where the information had come from. Mr Snoop had bribed an employee of Matt's bank to provide the details of his mortgage and other financial affairs.

"Have you had any luck with his salary and share options?"

"Not yet. But I'm working on it."

"So altogether, how much do you think we can extract from him?" Arnold asked.

Alan took a sip of the fine Beaune he had ordered to accompany the meal. "I'm going to claim for €500,000."

He smiled to himself as he spoke. A sum of that magnitude would ruin Matt Bollinger. It would finish him off. He would probably have to sell the apartment and move into a one-room bedsit somewhere. He wondered how Marion would deal with that. Matt wouldn't cut such a romantic figure when he was practically penniless and struggling to survive.

Arnold pushed a stray lock of hair back into place. He was almost drooling at the thought of all that cash.

"Of course, Anna *is* entitled to it. She's the mother of his children, after all."

"Of course," Alan agreed.

"And she was his wife for seventeen years. She contributed to his success. All that has to be taken into account."

"Indeed."

Arnold glanced around to make sure there was no one within earshot. Another thought had just occurred to him. "Is there any possibility that the court might take a dim view of the fact that Bollinger tried to conceal his assets?"

"How do you mean?"

"Well, he had that money hidden away in the bank and didn't tell her. Could they punish him in some way?"

This was something Alan hadn't considered. The thought of Matt going to prison sent a frisson of pleasure running down his spine. That would certainly put an end to him. He couldn't see Marion wanting to consort with a jailbird. But saner consideration prevailed. There was no point making a martyr out of him. Some busybody reporter might take up his case and start asking unhelpful questions.

"It's entirely possible," he agreed. "But we don't want to be too hard on him. It's in our interest that he continues to earn money. We might be able to take another bite out of him some time in the future."

"You're right," Arnold said. "I hadn't thought of that."

"I think it's best to keep all our options open."

Alan pushed his plate away and considered whether to have a dessert. He was growing increasingly fond of good food but he wasn't sure that it entirely agreed with him. Lately, he'd been having trouble getting some of his clothes to fit. He changed his mind and decided to have a brandy instead. It would be partly a celebration.

Everything was coming along nicely. Once he had got Matt Bollinger out of the way, he would resume his offensive against Marion. It would only be a matter of time till she caved in and came back to him. Especially when he sold his Vorax shares and bought the extra penthouse he was contemplating. In fact he might contact the developer on Monday and put down a deposit if he could persuade his bank manager to lend him the money.

"So what's the next move?" Arnold inquired, pursuing a piece of meat around his plate with his fork.

"We set out our claim and send it across to his legal people. I'll do it right away."

"Don't you want to wait till you find out more about his salary?"

"It doesn't matter," Alan said. "We can always update it when we get the information."

Arnold let out a satisfied sigh and sat back in his seat. He drained his glass and smacked his lips. "I must say you've done a superb job, Alan. I'm very pleased with the way you've handled this matter."

Alan allowed a slight smile to play around his lips. "Let's agree that the feeling is mutual, Jack. You've been extremely helpful to me too. What is the latest information on Vorax?"

"The analysts are convinced they'll continue to rise."

"Fifteen?" Alan asked eagerly.

"Maybe even seventeen. The word on the inside is that they're still good for another few points."

"Seventeen euros a share?" He tried to do a quick calculation in his head. If Vorax shares rose to €17, his profit would be an amazing €680,000. "Are you sure?"

"As sure as one can ever be in this game. That's what the smart operators are saying. Apparently the company is about to announce a new wonder drug next week which should give the market a further boost."

"So I should hang on?"

"Hell, of course you should. If I was you, I would buy more."

"On account?"

"Why not? You've got thirty days to pay. In that time, you'll have made your money."

Alan made a quick calculation. "Can you get me another 50,000?"

"I'll certainly try."

Alan scrambled the figures in his head. He wished he had brought his pocket calculator. He reckoned a further 50,000 Vorax shares would net him €150,000 if the price went to €17. Altogether, he would have enough money to buy the new penthouse outright. Maybe even shave a few thousand off the price because he was paying cash.

"Buy them," he said.

"I'll do it first thing." Arnold said.

Alan sat back in his chair. He felt a warm contented glow spread slowly along every nerve in his body. Everything was coming along perfectly. He would have that brandy now. And he would make it a double.

Chapter Twenty-two

"Alan McMillan?" Marion let out a loud gasp. "I don't believe it."

"I know," Matt said. "It sounds incredible. But it's true."

She closed her eyes and squeezed his hand. "Oh Matt, I'm afraid this is all my fault."

"How could it be your fault? Don't be ridiculous."

"No. Listen to me. I didn't tell you this. Alan McMillan and I have a history."

He looked at her closely. "How do you mean – a history?"

"We used to go out together. Not that it was ever serious. We broke up years ago. But he refuses to let go. That's why he joined the book club – to make contact with me again."

He was staring at her now. "So that explains why you've never liked him?"

"Exactly. I've known from the beginning that he was scheming. But there's more. A couple of nights ago, I got this weird phone call from him. He knew about us. He even knew we had been to dinner at Mama Rosa's."

Suddenly, Matt looked startled. "Why didn't you tell me?"

"I didn't want you getting upset."

"He must have been spying on us."

"That's what I thought too. He also said something spooky. He said you may romance me but he wouldn't let go. He said he found me first and finders are keepers."

"The guy must be nuts," Matt said. "He sounds like he's obsessive."

"He *is* obsessive. I'll bet this is his idea to sue you for more maintenance. How much is she looking for?"

"Three hundred thousand euros. Maybe more. She's looking for a share in the proceeds of the family home and my salary."

"That much? Oh, Matt, how will you pay it?"

He shrugged and spread his hands. "I can't."

"Is she stuck for money?"

He gave a snort. "Not in the least. She's probably better off than I am."

"So what are you going to do?"

A grim look had now entered his face. "The first thing I'm going to do is to tell my solicitor."

Marion spent most of Sunday in a deep, all-consuming rage about Alan McMillan. She had expected trouble all along – but nothing on this scale. She had never in her wildest thoughts believed he would take out his resentment on Matt.

Alan McMillan reminded her of the Glenn Close character in the film *Fatal Attraction* – scheming, manipulative and evil. He was bent on hurting Matt in his crazed attempt to win back her affection. As if destroying the one man she cared about would somehow make her change her mind! It was the thinking of someone deranged. But Marion knew that if Alan McMillan was mad he was also cunning. And that made him much more dangerous.

She wished she had never set eyes on him. But now that she had, she vowed to have nothing more to do with him. She would refuse his phone calls and if he insisted on calling to her apartment, she would threaten him with the police. Indeed she was still in two minds about whether she should report him in any case for spying on her. Even if it meant abandoning the book club, which she had gone to so much trouble to set up, she would do it. As far as she was concerned, she never wanted to see Alan McMillan's miserable face again.

Shortly after noon, her thoughts were diverted when Trish rang for a chat. She was going out for lunch with her boyfriend Seán and wondered if Marion wanted to join them.

"We're only going down to the Hippo. It won't be anything fancy."

The Hippo was an upmarket hamburger restaurant that did fantastic salads. Marion wondered if she should go. But she wasn't in the mood for lunch. She was still far too enraged with Alan McMillan to think about food. "I think I'll pass," she said. "I'm going out with Matt later."

"How did it go yesterday? Meeting the children?"

"It went very well, thank God. They're a couple of nice kids. And they brought their partners."

"So it was all nice and cosy?"

"More or less," Marion admitted. "After a shaky start."

She told her friend about Rachel and how at one stage she thought she was going to tear her eyes out. Trish's hearty laugh came echoing down the line.

"She probably thought you were going to turn into the wicked stepmother and make her wear sackcloth and do all the household chores. But you seem to have passed the first hurdle. Getting the children on side is a major achievement. From now on it should be all plain sailing."

"I wouldn't bet on it. It's turning out to be more complicated than I imagined."

She wondered if she should tell Trish about Alan McMillan. She was always a rock of common sense. She would know exactly what to do. But it was really Matt's business and he might get embarrassed if she started talking about it to other people. So she decided to say nothing.

"Enjoy your lunch. Give Seán my best."

"Will do. I'll call you again tomorrow."

"Bye," Marion said and put down the phone.

Matt was spending Sunday with the children so she decided not to disturb him even though he could probably do with some moral support. Later, he was planning to drive Rachel and Gavin to the airport and had asked her to come with him. She would wait till then and afterwards she might persuade him to go for a quiet drink and talk.

She tried to read but couldn't concentrate so she spent the rest of the afternoon moping around the apartment in a foul mood. Her anger at Alan McMillan was now extending to Anna. How could she do this? Surely she knew it was wrong? From what she knew, Matt had been a good father and husband. He had shouldered more than his share of the financial burden of the separation even though his wife was the one who left the marriage. And now, just when he was starting to make a new life, they were determined to drag him down again. She shuddered to think what might happen if they got their way. Matt could be left with nothing. How would he cope? Would he even survive? It was all so terribly unfair.

She flicked through the Sunday papers but they were filled with gossip and opinion pieces. She switched on the television but it was wall-to-wall sport and Marion hated sports programmes, so she switched it off again. In the end, she selected a couple of nice classical pieces, put on the CD player and lay down on the settee. There were some things that were outside her control and this seemed to be one of them. She closed her eyes and let the soothing melodies ease away her rage.

The telephone wakened her with a jolt. She glanced at her watch. It was half past four. The CD player had stopped and her mobile phone was clanging like a fire engine. She picked it up and pressed it to her ear.

"Hello?"

"Matt here."

"Oh, darling. How are you?"

"Bearing up. I'm just reminding you that we're off to the airport in half an hour if you still want to come."

"Of course I do. Where will I meet you?"

"In the car park?"

"Okay. I'll see you. And Matt?"

"Yes?"

"Keep your chin up."

She switched off the phone. He had sounded utterly dejected. She would have to think of some way to lift his spirits. Marion plodded off to the bathroom and turned on the shower.

By five minutes to five she was ready. She had pulled on slacks, shirt and chunky sweater and over it she had wrapped a warm, sleeveless parka jacket. A few minutes later, the buzzer sounded which was Matt's signal to meet him at the car park. She knocked off the lights, double locked the apartment door and walked along the corridor to the lift.

They were waiting for her at the car. In the lift, Marion had practised her cheery grin and now she plastered it on. No point looking as if she was going to a funeral. Rachel and Gavin were loading their cases into the boot when she arrived and greeted her with exuberant hugs. She gave Matt a quick peck on the cheek and squeezed his hand as she slipped into the passenger seat.

The drive to the airport was taken up with busy chatter from the two young people. Matt tried to join in but Marion could tell that his heart wasn't in it. He was keeping up appearances for their sake but inside she knew he was probably knotted up with tension and worry.

At last they arrived. Matt parked the car and helped them carry their cases to the departure lounge. Their flight was on time. Thank God for that, Marion thought. The prospect of keeping up this light-hearted banter for another couple of hours while they hung around the airport was more than she could contemplate.

"You must give me your email address," Rachel exclaimed as they arrived at the check-in desk and Marion fished in her bag for one of the little cards she'd had printed up at work. "We'll keep in touch. I'll let you know all the latest developments in the Big Smoke."

"Did you enjoy your visit?" Marion asked.

"Enormously. And so did Gavin. Didn't you, Gav?"

"I had a brilliant time," Gavin replied politely. "Even managed to check out some bookshops to see what's selling."

"It was his first time in Dublin," Rachel explained.

"Next time, come in the summer," Marion said. "At least the weather should be warmer."

Now it was time to head for the security gates where Matt and Marion would have to leave them. Rachel put her arms around her father and held him close then turned to Marion and flung her arms round her too.

"You mail me, you hear?" she said.

"Definitely."

She lowered her voice to a whisper. "And take good care of Dad. I'm relying on you."

Despite her mood, Marion found herself smiling. Rachel really was a lovely kid. She was glad she had met her. "You can bank on it," she promised.

They waited till the young couple had finally disappeared through the security gates before they left.

"Do you feel like a drink?" Marion asked on the way back to the car.

"Is the Pope a Catholic?"

They went to Gibneys in Malahide and Marion found a quiet corner table while Matt busied himself organising the drinks.

"I've been thinking about you all day," she said, squeezing close to him. "How have you coped?"

"Okay. Keeping Rachel and Gavin entertained helped to distract me. I rang Tom Stafford at home and arranged to meet him tomorrow afternoon in his office."

"Did you tell him about McMillan's phone call to me?"

"I mentioned it. He said we'd have a full discussion tomorrow."

He took a deep drink from his glass and put it down firmly on the table. There was a determined look in his eyes. He resembled the old, confident Matt she had known before this trouble erupted.

"I've been considering my options," he said. "I don't think I have any choice but to fight this."

She gripped his hand. "But if you lose, you could be faced with a massive legal bill on top of everything else."

"And if I let them get away with it, they'll take everything anyway. I think it's time I made a stand. No more Mr Nice Guy."

She felt her spirits rise. She pulled him closer and kissed him. "Whatever you decide to do, you won't be alone. I'll be in your corner."

"Are you sure you want to get involved? This isn't your fight?"

"Who says it isn't? I can't stand by and watch that bastard Alan McMillan do this to you. Besides, I made a promise to your daughter."

"Rachel?"

"Yes. She asked me to take care of you and I always keep my promises. We're in this together now."

His face broke into a smile. "What did I do to deserve you, Marion?"

"That question cuts both ways. Now finish your drink. I've got a surprise waiting for you at home."

Twenty minutes later, she turned the key in the door of her apartment. Once inside, she kicked off her shoes and dragged Matt to the settee where she began to pull off his shirt.

"Hey," he said, as he started to laugh. "Is this the surprise you promised?"

"Yes," she said, unbuckling the belt of his trousers.

"Well then, you'll have to surprise me more often."

308

Chapter Twenty-three

Christy Grimes was down on his knees weeding the garden when Nick called to the house unexpectedly at eleven o'clock on Monday morning. It was a bright day and already it was beginning to feel warm and balmy. The cold and the damp of the winter seemed to be receding at last. Not that this was any consolation to Christy for the change in the weather simply meant that the weeds were growing faster and thicker till they threatened to overwhelm both the garden and him.

As he worked, Ellie stood over him, giving directions. Since Dr Hynes had taken away her walking frame, she had become much more energetic. She had attacked the house with a vengeance, muttering darkly that Christy had allowed the place to fall into a shocking state while she was ill. The fact that she was now more mobile meant that she was able to poke into places that had remained hidden, like behind the dresser and under the sink. And everywhere she looked, she found work for her husband to do. Ellie was sticking rigidly to the doctor's instructions. He had said she might resume *light* household duties. As far as she was concerned, that meant Christy would continue to carry out the heavy jobs.

He felt a bead of sweat trickle down his forehead and sting his eye.

In addition, a couple of large bluebottles had emerged from somewhere and were determined to torment him, settling on his head and his arms and his nose and resisting all attempts to disperse them. Every time, he took a swipe at them, the flies just swooped away and then alighted again as soon he wasn't looking. Christy's back ached and his knees felt sore and he was convinced that all this bending and stretching was simply bringing on his arthritis. If he continued with this weeding much longer, he'd be the one using the walking frame instead of Ellie.

He dreamed of the cool sanctuary of Mohan's pub and a nice creamy pint of Guinness while he watched the football on television. At his age, he shouldn't be killing himself with gardening work. There were young fellas you could pay to do this sort of thing; fine strapping young lads who would gallop through this whole garden in a single afternoon. Although they were getting thinner on the ground, Christy had noticed, ever since that Celtic tiger had arrived to provide good jobs for everybody that wanted them.

Anyway, he knew that Ellie would never entertain strangers in her garden. She didn't trust anybody but Christy. In fact, she didn't even trust him, which was why she was now standing over him like a slave driver as he painfully made his way along the border, filling a big black refuse sack with bindweed and daisies and clumps of grass that he pulled up by the roots.

"Mind those nasturtiums," she warned. "And be careful with the chrysanthemums. You nearly pulled one up just now instead of that dandelion. If I wasn't here to tell you what to do, you'd have every plant in me garden destroyed."

"They all look the same to me," Christy groaned. "I can't tell the difference."

"Don't be making an eejit of yourself. Sure one's a flower and the other's a weed."

"They're all green and have leaves," Christy pointed out, logically. "How am I supposed to know?"

"Mother of God," Ellie sighed. "Where did I get you from?"

Christy looked along the border. It stretched as far as the fence that separated their house from Mrs O'Malley's next door. At the rate he was going, he would be at this chore all week. And then Ellie had told him she wanted the roses pruned and the creepers sprayed for greenfly by which time the lawn would need mowing again. He could see a kind of gardening Hell opening up before him and stretching away till the autumn.

At that moment, their discussion was interrupted by the sound of the doorbell ringing. They looked quizzically at each other.

"Are you expecting anybody?" Ellie asked.

Christy shook his head.

"I'd better go and see who it is," said Ellie.

She went off towards the house and Christy bent once more to his work. He was beginning to understand how those poor slaves must have felt working in the cotton fields all day in the baking sun. No wonder the Yanks had fought a civil war over that. When he looked up again, it was to see Ellie and Nick Barry approaching up the lawn.

"I hope I'm not disturbing you," Nick said in a cheerful voice.

"Not at all," Christy said, brightening up at the prospect of a break.

Nick turned to Ellie. "You're looking very well, Mrs G. So you're able to walk again?"

"A little bit," Ellie said, modestly. "But the doctor says I still have to take it easy."

"Which is why I'm doing the gardening," Christy groaned.

"I must say you're an example to us all, Mrs G," Nick said. "You're a fighter. You never gave up, did you?"

Ellie beamed with pride. "Well, there's no point lying down under these things. You have to keep going."

"That's my own view precisely, Mrs G."

"I suppose you'd take a cup of tea?"

"I wouldn't say no," Nick replied. "If it doesn't put you to too much trouble."

"No trouble at all. I'll just go and put the kettle on."

Christy got painfully to his feet.

"You seem to be doing an excellent job," Nick said, pointing to the border that Christy had methodically cleared.

"I've had very good instruction," Christy muttered as they walked back up the lawn towards the house. "But to tell you the truth, gardening wouldn't be my first choice of occupation. But herself is very fond of it and the doctor said I was to help her."

When they arrived, Ellie was already fussing about the kitchen, laying out cups and saucers and a plate of scones. It was always a big occasion when a visitor called at the Grimes household and Ellie took special pride in her baking.

"How do you like your tea?" she asked Nick, who suddenly remembered Liz's advice.

"Just a little milk and no sugar."

Ellie poured three cups and they all sat down at the table.

"Have a scone," she said, pushing the plate across. "I baked them myself."

Nick took one, buttered it and smeared on jam. Then he took a bite. He rolled his eyes with delight. "Absolutely superb, Mrs G," he said, chewing with pleasure. "I haven't tasted scones like these in a long time."

Ellie smiled. That was the second compliment she'd received from Nick. It was nice to get a little bit of appreciation now and again. "Sure it's just something I threw together."

"Well, you certainly have the magic touch. Do you mind if I have another one?"

"Not at all," she said, delighted, and pushed the plate across.

"You're probably wondering why I'm here," he then said in between chews.

That was exactly what they had been wondering.

He turned to Christy. "Remember that chat you and me had in Mohan's pub last week? About Larry Byrne?"

"I do," Christy replied.

"Well, I didn't tell you at the time but that was in the way of research."

"Research?"

"Yes. For a book I'm writing."

Ellie and Christy stared at each other.

"I didn't tell you this before. In fact only a handful of people know about it. But I'm a writer."

"A writer?" Ellie said in amazement.

"Yes. I'm writing a novel."

He looked across the table again at Christy. "I'm going to base this book on the story of Larry Byrne. And I want to ask your permission."

For a moment there was silence. Then Christy's face took on a look of triumph.

"What did I tell you?" he said to his wife. "Didn't I always say the story of Larry Byrne would make a great book?"

"So you don't mind?" Nick said, eyeing the scones again.

"Not at all. I'm delighted."

"I've just started writing but it's coming along very nicely. In fact, you can help me with something else. You see, I'm thinking of asking the book club to read the chapters as I write them and give me their feedback. That way I'll know if I'm on the right track. What do you think about that?"

"I think it's brilliant," Christy said, excitedly. "I'll give you all the feedback you want. Sure wasn't I born and reared with poor ould Larry. I could tell you what he had for his breakfast."

"Well, you already have!" said Nick with a laugh. "What about you, Mrs G?"

"Will there be any romance in it?"

Christy shot his wife a dirty look.

"There'll be loads of romance," said Nick. "And plenty of good strong characters. And a bit of humour and lashings of action the way Christy likes."

"Well, if that's the case, I don't mind."

"Excellent," Nick said. "I've already got Liz to agree. And Marion. I called her this morning to ask her. That's how I got your address."

"Then you can include us too," Ellie said. "I'll be only too happy to give you my opinion. When's your book going to be published?"

"Oh it's early days, Mrs G. I've just started. It will be a while yet."
He finished his tea and stood up. "I'd better be on my way. I've another chapter to finish before I go into work. Thanks again for everything."

He gave the scones a last lingering look.

Suddenly, Ellie swooped and gathered them into a bag.

"Here," she said. "Take them with you. I can always bake more."

"Are you sure, Mrs G?"

"I'm positive," she said.

They showed him to the door and watched him stride confidently up the street. He was a handsome young fella and well mannered with it. At the top, he turned and waved before disappearing from view.

"A book about Larry," Christy said as he closed the front door. "My, oh my, what do you think about that?"

"I think you've another few hours of sunlight left before you finish that border," Ellie said, firmly. "And I suggest you get to it right away."

Chapter Twenty-four

At three o'clock precisely, Matt once more climbed the rickety stairs to Tom Stafford's office. He had spent a busy morning at work but had managed to put together the statement of his financial affairs that the solicitor had requested. He had it now in his briefcase. The statement contained details of all the money he possessed, including the equity tied up in the apartment, the cash on deposit with the bank that he planned to use to set up a small trust fund for the children and his salary and share options with Atlanta Technologies.

He felt relaxed after his decision to fight the claim from Anna and Jack Arnold. And the knowledge that he had the support of Marion was reassuring. Yet, at the end of the day it was down to the skill of Tom Stafford to see him through this crisis that had arrived out of nowhere. And he knew this battle was only beginning. His experience with lawyers had taught him that many more weeks of meetings and legal wrangling lay ahead. It was like getting into a cage with Bengal tigers. Given half a chance they would tear him to pieces. And by all accounts, the most vicious and ruthless of them all was Alan McMillan.

Matt couldn't help wondering about McMillan. What made him tick? How come a seemingly intelligent, successful man could become totally obsessed to the point of destruction? On the surface, he appeared charming, if a little pompous and self-important. Matt's mind went back to the book club meeting at his apartment. He had been a perfect host, making sure that everyone was comfortable, topping up their glasses with wine. And good wine too. Matt knew he must have spent a small fortune on the catering. Yet, behind the façade, he had turned out to be a total bastard, the prime mover in this action against him, a man who was bent on ruining him.

And it was all because Matt had become involved with Marion. It was incredible that someone could feel such hatred for another human being, even a love rival. Despite all the resentment he had towards Jack Arnold for taking his wife and breaking up his home, he had never ended up hating him. He had never wanted to destroy Arnold the way Alan McMillan seemed determined to destroy him.

It was beyond his comprehension. It made him wonder if Alan McMillan was sane or if he was so crazed by jealousy that his thinking had become deranged. He certainly wasn't behaving like a sane person. His phone call to Marion suggested he was no longer thinking rationally. And it looked like he had been spying on their movements or possibly hiring someone else to do it for him.

Matt's new-found determination found him bounding up the rickety stairs to meet Tom Stafford. He was waiting for him in his office, his grey hair immaculately groomed, a silk handkerchief dangling foppishly from the breast pocket of his exquisitely tailored suit.

"If you're determined to stay in this dump why don't you install a lift?" Matt said, gruffly as he came through the door. "One of these days, those damned stairs are going to collapse."

Stafford grinned. "You shouldn't complain, Matt. The exercise is good for you. That's why you're looking so fit."

He immediately rang for coffee. While they waited, he engaged in small talk.

"How did your weekend go?"

"Pretty hectic. My daughter and her boyfriend were visiting from London so there wasn't much spare time to think about anything else."

"Did you get me the statement I requested?"

"Yes," Matt said, opening his briefcase and handing the document over.

The door opened and the secretary came in with a tray containing coffee, cups and biscuits.

"Thank you, Marjorie," Tom Stafford said as the secretary smiled and withdrew.

While Matt poured the coffee, the solicitor studied his financial statement and seemed to compare it with another document that lay before him on his desk.

"It's uncanny," he said. "Your statement corresponds almost exactly with the claim from McMillan. It's as if he is already aware of what your assets are."

"Maybe he is," Matt said, cryptically.

Tom Stafford raised an eyebrow. "How do you mean?"

Matt sipped his coffee. "I told you about his phone call to Marion."

"That's right."

"Well, I think he might be spying on us. Or more likely, he's hired someone else to do it for him. Maybe one of these firms of private investigators."

"What you say makes a lot of sense. The problem is you've got absolutely no evidence."

"How else could he have got this information about me? And the fact that he is besotted with Marion would give him a motive. I'm convinced he's out to destroy me, Tom."

"But you have no proof. It could be just coincidence."

Matt shook his head. "It's more than coincidence. He knew we went to Mama Rosa's together. He knew I stayed overnight in her flat. And now he has exact details of my financial affairs. Do you really believe that's just coincidence?"

Stafford puffed out his cheeks. "I would have to agree that your suspicions are plausible."

"So what are we going to do about it? Should Marion report that phone call to the police?"

Stafford raised his hands. "Let's slow down a moment. From what you've told me, he didn't actually threaten her. However, if she believes he's following her or if these phone calls continue, she might have grounds for claiming harassment."

"So what should we do?"

"Let's wait and see if the phone calls continue. Let's try and build some evidence against him before we do anything."

He sat back in his chair and fiddled with a pencil. A grave look had come across his face.

"I have to tell you Matt, that things are not looking good for you. I will counter their claim, of course. But the best that will do is to buy more time. And it will also increase your legal costs. In the end, I think we're going to have no option but to negotiate with your wife."

"Give in?" Matt asked.

"I prefer to use the word compromise. McMillan is claiming €500,000."

"*What?* I don't believe it," Matt said, looking astounded.

"It's simply his opening gambit. Just to frighten us."

"The man is crazy. I haven't got anything remotely approaching that sort of money."

"You have €150,000 on deposit and another €350,000 of equity tied up in your apartment. Plus your share options."

"The €150,000 is for the children. And to release the equity I would have to sell the apartment. Where am I supposed to live?"

Stafford sighed. "I told you before that I hate these cases. If you weren't my friend, I don't even think I would get involved. But as your solicitor, I am obliged to give you the best legal advice I can. If we negotiate, there's a good chance we can get them to reduce their claim substantially."

"We're dealing with Alan McMillan," Matt said, bitterly. "If I know him, he'll extract every penny he can. This has become personal with him."

For a long while, the two men stared at each other across the desk.

"I've come to a decision," Matt said. "I want to fight this."

"Your mind is made up?"

"Yes," Matt said. "I'll be damned if I'm going to give in to this blackmail without a struggle."

Tom Stafford lowered his eyes and brooded.

"There is one final thing you could try," he said at last.

"What?" Matt asked.

"You said that your ex-wife was not a greedy woman."

"That's true. I'm sure she's been put up to this."

"Then why don't you go and talk to her? See if you can persuade her to change her mind."

Chapter Twenty-five

Tuesday arrived and with it Liz's appointment with the specialist Dr Forbes. Suddenly, the blissful period she had been enjoying with Nick came to an abrupt end and cold reality came rushing in. In the past few days, she had succeeded in pushing her fears to the edge of her mind but now they were back again centre-stage. Even though she had been eager for this appointment and the expert knowledge that Dr Forbes would bring, now that the time had arrived, she felt threatened with doubt.

She had thought about confiding in Nick. It would be great to have another shoulder to lean on, someone to lend sympathy and support. And she knew that Nick would happily wrap her in a warm comfort blanket to help her through this ordeal. But something held her back, some barely understood reluctance to take him into her confidence and tell him how her body was threatening to let her down. If the outcome was bad, that might be the time to turn to him for strength. In the meantime, this was something she would have to face without him.

Apart from the medical people, the only person who shared her secret was Cathy and it was Cathy who accompanied her to see Dr Forbes at the clinic in Glasnevin. The sound of the car horn at a quarter past ten told her that her friend had arrived to drive her the short distance to the hospital. Liz had been up since seven o'clock, had showered and dressed and even packed a small overnight bag with a nightdress and toothbrush in case they wanted to keep her over. She was determined to be brave even though inside she was shaking like a leaf.

She locked up the house and settled into the passenger seat, pulling on her seatbelt as she did. Her friend immediately launched into a barrage of enquiries about Nick.

"Have you gone to bed with him yet?"

"What a question to ask!" Liz said, pretending to be shocked.

"It's a perfectly natural question. You're both adults and I'm assuming he *has* been to bed with a woman before."

"I refuse to answer on the grounds that I might incriminate myself."

"I take it that means yes?"

"You can take it how you like. What goes on between Nick and me is strictly personal."

"*I* would tell you."

"But I wouldn't ask. That's the difference between us."

"Was he any good?"

"At what?" Liz found herself laughing despite her inward fears.

"Did he leave you feeling that the earth had moved?"

"This is ridiculous," Liz said as the car turned onto Griffith Avenue. "Do I interrogate you about your sex life?"

"But I'm just a boring old married lady. All me and Max ever do is copulate three times a week in the missionary position. You, on the other hand, are a dashing young thing who has just embarked on a passionate romantic affair."

"Thanks for the compliment," Liz said. "But my lips are sealed."

"Unlike your thighs?"

Liz burst out laughing again. She understood perfectly why Cathy was talking like this. It was to keep her mind occupied so that she wouldn't dwell on the trial that lay ahead.

"Let's just say I like him enormously. He's very sweet. He's not selfish like a lot of men I know. And he's enormously talented. He's writing a novel."

Cathy turned to stare at her. "A novel? Really?"

"Uh, huh. I've read several chapters and they're absolutely brilliant. I think it's going to be a huge success. In fact, we're going to ask the book club to discuss it. What do you think?"

"You mean instead of reading a book we'd read chapters of Nick's novel?"

"That's right. And give feedback and criticism."

"I think that's a marvellous idea."

"So you agree?"

"Of course. I'd really enjoy that."

"We have to get everybody on board," Liz said. "But so far, the reaction has been very positive."

"And do we all get a mention in the acknowledgements?"

"Certainly."

"What about royalties from the sales?" Cathy asked, only partly in jest. "If it turns out to be a bestseller that could mean a tidy little sum."

Liz pulled a face. "You're way ahead of yourself. First he has to get it written. Then, he has to find a publisher."

The small talk had caused the time to fly and suddenly they saw the hospital looming up through a belt of trees. Cathy drove through the gates and parked outside the main building. They got out and walked the short distance to Dr Forbes' clinic.

The moment she came through the door, Liz felt the fear come over her like a back cloud. She was no longer having a girly chat in Cathy's car. Now she was back in the real world of life and death. The receptionist asked her to take a seat and she nervously picked up a magazine, glad to have something to distract her. Cathy sat beside her and gently patted her arm. After a few minutes, a door opened and a young woman in a white medical coat came out.

"Mrs Broderick?" she asked.

"That's me," Liz said and quickly stood up.

"Would you come this way, please?"

"Good luck," Cathy whispered as Liz followed the woman into another room.

"Please take a seat," the woman said and sat down at a desk which had a little plastic nameplate saying: *Dr Patricia Forbes.*

Liz felt confused. If this was the doctor, she seemed very young. She had been expecting someone older.

Dr Forbes smiled. "Now Mrs Broderick, just relax and tell me exactly what's bothering you."

"I have a letter from my GP which explains it all."

She took the envelope from her bag and gave it over. Dr Forbes quickly read it and put it down on her desk.

"You've discovered a lump on your left breast?"

"Yes."

"When did you notice it?"

"About ten days ago."

"Is it getting bigger?"

"I don't think so," Liz said.

"How about the other breast?"

"No. There's nothing there."

"Are you feeling any side-effects? Are you listless? Tired? Lacking in energy?"

"Yes and No," Liz said. "I do sometimes feel tired but that's because I take on so much work to keep my mind from worrying about the lump."

Dr Forbes smiled. "That's perfectly natural, but hopefully we'll be able to put your mind at ease. Now, I have to ask you this. It's just a routine question so don't read too much into it. Is there any history of breast cancer in your family?"

Liz felt her heart jump. There it was at last out in the open, the dreaded C word. They had finally got to the nub of the issue.

"No," she said. "Not as far as I know."

"Good."

As they spoke, Dr Forbes was busily writing notes on a pad. She continued with her questions for a while, then put down her pen and smiled again.

"We'd better take a look at it, Liz. Would you mind taking off your blouse and hopping up there where I can examine you."

She pointed to a couch in the corner of the room. Liz's fingers trembled as she undid the buttons of her blouse. Dr Forbes seemed to sense her unease. She spoke in a soothing voice.

"Just take it easy. I won't hurt you."

Liz smiled awkwardly as she unhooked her bra and climbed onto the couch. At the touch of Dr Forbes's hand, she felt her heart beat faster. The doctor began probing and squeezing.

"Does that hurt?"

"No," Liz said.

The examination only took a few minutes but it seemed to last an eternity.

Finally, Dr Forbes said: "Okay, you can get dressed again."

She was back at her desk and writing once more on her pad. Liz still couldn't get over how young she was. She didn't seem old enough to be a senior consultant. When she looked up again, she was still smiling. A flicker of hope sprang up in Liz. Was this a good sign? Did it mean the lump was benign?

"I'm going to send you for some tests," Dr Forbes announced.

"What sort of tests?"

"We're going to take a mammogram. That's an x-ray of your breast. And a biopsy."

"A biopsy?" Liz asked in a faltering voice. This was something Dr Brady hadn't mentioned.

"There's no need to be concerned. It's a small procedure to remove some tissue from the lump. Then we can examine it. That should tell us whether or not it's malignant."

"I see," Liz said.

"Once we have carried out the biopsy, we'll know very quickly. I suggest we do it as soon as possible."

"Okay," Liz said.

Dr Forbes stood up. "Good. I'll get my secretary to ring you once we have arranged an appointment." She extended her hand. "Try not to worry, Liz. Even if the lump is malignant, it's not the end of the road. There are lots of things we can do."

"Like what?" Liz said. "Remove my breast?"

"Let's not get ahead of ourselves," Dr Forbes said in her pleasant voice. "Let's just wait and see what the tests reveal."

She opened the door and Liz was once more in the waiting room. Why is everyone so reticent, she thought? Why can't they just tell me what they think it is? She saw Cathy look up, her face expectant. Liz slowly shook her head. The visit to Dr Forbes had changed nothing. The ordeal of uncertainty would have to continue for some time more.

Chapter Twenty-six

Matt walked quickly through the vestibule of the hotel and paused when he came to the reception desk. He was surprised that Anna had agreed to this. They hadn't had a face-to-face meeting for a very long time, not since that period when Rachel was acting up and they had got together to figure out what to do. And on those occasions, Jack Arnold had always insisted on accompanying her. Tonight, he had asked her to come alone. And, amazingly, she had agreed.

He didn't have Anna's mobile number so he had called her yesterday at the busy advertising agency where she worked. He didn't want to ring her at her home and find himself speaking to that rat, Arnold, if he chanced to pick up the phone. When he finally managed to get through to her he caught the note of surprise in her voice as if he was the last person in the world she expected to hear from. But she quickly recovered her poise.

"Hello Matt," she said. "How are you keeping?"

"As well as can be expected," he replied. He didn't see any point in pretending that everything was fine when they both knew Jack Arnold was trying to destroy him.

"What can I do for you?" she asked.

"I'd like to see you."

There was an awkward pause.

"What about?"

"I think you know that, Anna. There are things we have to discuss."

"I'm not sure this is proper," she said, quickly.

"What do you mean?"

"I don't think my solicitor would agree."

"Oh, damn that," he said, angrily. "You're an adult. You can talk to your ex-husband without having to seek that slimeball's permission."

He knew at once it was the wrong thing to say. Nothing would be gained by getting her back up. He needed to approach this calmly and rationally. But he felt so angry with McMillan and Arnold and even Anna that he couldn't help himself.

She seemed to hesitate for a moment as if trying to decide.

"All right," she said, at last. "I'll see you. What's a good time for you?"

They had agreed on seven o'clock. Here at the Imperial Hotel. It was only after he had switched off the phone that Matt remembered this was where they had held those meetings about Rachel. He hoped it wouldn't bring back too many bad memories.

He checked his watch. It was now ten to seven. He felt like a drink to steady his nerves but decided against it. It might give her the wrong impression. He would wait till she arrived and then offer to buy her a drink. So, instead of going into the bar, he took a seat in the lobby and waited.

He wasn't happy with this meeting and neither was Marion when he told her. Why should he come crawling to his wife for favours when his gut instinct was to take them on and fight? He had only agreed because Tom Stafford had insisted and he trusted Stafford. But this was the last appeal. If Anna turned him down he was determined to go the legal route regardless of the cost.

He wondered if she would come. If Arnold or McMillan found out, they would try to prevent it. They wouldn't want the two of them talking like this. But at five minutes past seven, he saw the revolving doors swing open and Anna's diminutive figure enter the hotel. She was dressed in a smart coat, silk scarf and black knee-length boots. His first thought was that she looked much older than the last time he had seen her.

He stood up. She looked tired or maybe it was guilt that weighed her down like that. Deep in her heart she must surely know what she was doing was wrong. She saw him at once and came towards him. As she approached he extended his arm and they formally shook hands like two people who had just been introduced for the first time instead of a couple who had been married for seventeen years.

"I'm glad you could come," he said.

"I haven't got long. Half an hour. We've got some people arriving for supper at half eight."

"I'll be brief," he said. "Would you like something to drink?"

"Gin and tonic, please."

The lounge was almost deserted so he led her to a quiet table and went off to the bar for the drinks.

"How is the new job working out?" Anna asked when he came back.

"It's been pretty hectic," Matt confessed. "You know what it's like at a start-up. Everything is a crazy rush. But thank God, the worst of it is nearly over. In another few weeks, I might even be able to take a few days' leave."

"Why did you leave your old job?" she asked, taking a sip of her gin.

"I decided I needed a change. I'd been with them a long time." He looked at her. "Since shortly after we were married."

"A change can be good," she said. "It provides fresh challenges. You discover aspects of your personality you didn't know existed."

He wondered if she was thinking about her own situation and the fact that she had left him to live with Jack Arnold. He looked at her again. Age had not been kind to Anna. She was approaching her mid-forties and the beauty he had once seen in her face was beginning to fade. There were dark lines beneath her eyes that the makeup couldn't disguise and her skin had lost the brightness he had once admired.

"How are the children?" she inquired.

"They're fine. Rachel was over from London last weekend."

She looked surprised. "Oh? I didn't know. She didn't bother to call me."

"I'm sorry," he said. "She was busy. You know what she's like."

Anna shrugged. "That wasn't why. She blames me for everything."

"She's growing up. Maybe that will change."

"I wonder," Anna said and took another sip of her drink. Then suddenly she became brisk and businesslike. "So here I am. What did you want to talk about?"

"I want to ask you a favour," he said. "This claim you've begun."

She tensed. "I told you on the phone, Matt. I don't think we can discuss this."

"But we *have* to discuss it. You don't need to do this, Anna. I know it's not how you really feel."

She glanced away, refusing to meet his gaze. "I've been advised that I'm entitled to increased maintenance."

"For God's sake! You can't say I haven't been fair to you. I've abided by all the terms of our agreement. I've looked after the children. It's only in the last few years that I've managed to get my head above water."

Immediately she went on the defensive. "I'm told you have money left over from the sale of the house."

"That money's not for me. It's in a bank account for the children to provide them with deposits when they want to settle down. You don't want to take that from them, do you?"

She lowered her eyes.

"I'm asking you to drop it," he said, quietly. "It would be better for everybody. We don't need this bitterness."

"I can't drop it."

"Please. I'm begging you. If you go ahead with this, you're going to ruin me. You're going to take the children's inheritance. Is that what you want?"

She didn't answer.

"I can't believe you would do this to us. Don't all the years of our marriage mean anything to you?"

"I have my rights," she said, defiantly.

"Of course you have. And I've always respected them. The truth is, I have an opportunity to build a new life. I've met another woman, a wonderful woman. If you pursue this case I could end up having to sell my apartment. I'd be reduced to living in a rented bed-sit. Do you really want to do that to me?"

She shifted uncomfortably in her seat. "I can't drop it," she said. "It's not my idea but I have to go through with it."

"Why, for God's sake?"

She looked away but he saw the tears that were welling up in her eyes. "Because Jack is insisting."

"Can't you just tell him no?"

He tried to catch her eye but she avoided his face. "You don't understand. Jack is not a man you say no to."

"You mean . . .?

She pulled herself together. "I think I've said enough."

"You're afraid of him." Another thought came hurtling into his brain. "My God, is he abusing you? Is that it?"

Anna wiped her eyes.

"You don't have to stay with him if you don't want to," Matt said.

"Really?" she said, trying to regain her poise. "And what would I do if I left him? Where would I go? Maybe you could tell me that?"

She drained her glass and stood up.

"I have to go now. I knew this meeting was a bad idea. I can't help you, Matt. I have to go through with the case."

She didn't say goodbye. She just turned and walked quickly across the floor and out of the bar. Matt watched her go. He had wasted his time. This was the last throw of the dice and it had failed. She had left him with no option but to see this through to the bitter end.

Chapter Twenty-seven

Alan McMillan first heard the news on the radio at eight o'clock as he was coming out of the shower but he wasn't really listening so it passed over his head. Today was going to be another busy day. His mind was focussed on a meeting he had to attend at nine o'clock in the Westland Hotel. It concerned an unfair dismissal case that had landed on his desk and was consuming a lot of his time. It was an important case and the outcome would have far-reaching implications for similar disputes.

Of course, he had been delighted to get the case. He regarded it as further evidence that he was rapidly coming to be recognised as *the* expert in this tricky area. And his boss, old Mr Weatherup, was delighted at the attention it brought to the firm. Alan knew that a successful outcome would advance his career and bring closer the day when he was made a partner.

But the issue was complicated and meant hours of tedious work. He had driven to the meeting and spent most of the morning locked in a stuffy hotel room with both parties to the dispute while he tried to negotiate a settlement. But after four hours of talks, they were no closer to a resolution and would have to go through the whole damned thing again tomorrow.

So, he was in a foul mood as he drove back to his office just before one o'clock. To cheer himself up, he thought about the excellent progress he had made with Anna Bollinger's maintenance claim. Late the previous evening, he had received a response from Tom Stafford by fax and he could tell immediately that he was preparing to cave in. It was exactly as he had predicted. Stafford was a wily old fox but he had been around long enough to know when he was beaten and it was time to run up the white flag.

No doubt they would try to cut some deal to minimise the costs for Bollinger but they were in for a disappointment. They were going to find that Alan would not relent. There would be no deal and no compromise. This was no time for sentimental nonsense. The law was the law and he would insist on the total amount of the claim. When he was finished with Matt Bollinger, he'd be lucky to have a shirt left on his back.

As always, the thought of Matt's distress brought a smile to Alan's lips and cheered him up. He had made a big mistake by interfering in his romantic life and turning Marion against him. By doing that, he had sealed his fate. And Alan was going to make sure he paid a heavy price for that mistake.

He checked his watch. It was almost one o'clock. He decided to turn on the car radio and catch the lunchtime news. It began with some political developments. A report on the economy predicted five per cent growth for the coming year. The housing market continued to surge ahead. The news was music to Alan's ears. It meant the value of his penthouse was continuing to climb. And it looked very good for his plans to invest in another one.

And then came an item that almost caused him to choke. His ears immediately pricked up. A new wonder drug that was being developed by the pharmaceutical company Vorax had failed its tests. Shares in the company had suffered as a result. He quickly turned up the volume on the radio to hear the grim news.

"Shares in the company plummeted on the stock market this morning as reports of the setback reached investors. At lunchtime, they were standing at €10 a share, down from a high of €14.50," a chirpy commentator announced blithely, as if he was discussing a celebrity wedding.

Alan felt a shiver run along his spine. For an awful moment, he thought he was going to crash the car. He pulled into a lay-by and opened the window for air while he tried to come to terms with the news he had just heard. If the stock had fallen to €10, it meant he had lost money on the shares he had just bought. And worse, he didn't have the cash to pay for them. If they continued to fall, he could be in serious trouble. It didn't bear thinking about.

He summoned the energy to restart the car and drove quickly back to his office, cursing the traffic that got in his way. A clammy sweat was now trickling down his neck and his hands trembled as he grasped the steering wheel. Once inside his office he locked the door and set about getting hold of Jack Arnold. It took him twenty minutes of frantic phone calls before a harassed voice came on the line.

"I've just heard the news," Alan announced, breathlessly. "Tell me the worst."

"They're down to nine," Arnold replied, gloomily.

"Nine?"

"Yes. And still falling."

Alan felt his heart pounding like a drum. This was terrible news. He steadied himself as the room began to spin.

"Should I sell?" he demanded.

"I don't think that's an option."

"So what the hell should I do? You're my broker, advise me."

"Sit tight," Arnold said, his own voice unsteady. "This is only a temporary setback. The shares will rally again."

"How can you be sure?"

"They always do. This is a solid company. The market will pause for breath and then the shares will rise again. Trust me."

Right now, Alan felt like trusting the Devil sooner than Jack Arnold. But what could he do?

"Keep me informed. I want to hear everything that happens," he said in a shaky voice and put down the phone.

He sat back in his chair and felt the perspiration cascading down his brow. In a few weeks' time, he would be called on to pay for the shares he had bought on account. And he didn't have the money. If Arnold was wrong and the stock didn't recover, he would be staring disaster in the face. All his plans would turn to dust. He would be ruined. And Arnold had been wrong before. Only a few days ago, he had encouraged him to buy more Vorax shares.

He was shaken from his reverie by a gentle knock on the door. Ms Coleman appeared with a bundle of correspondence.

"Would you like your tea now, Mr McMillan?" she inquired.

Alan took the correspondence and impatiently waved her away. He was in no mood for drinking tea. What he needed now was a stiff brandy.

He leafed lethargically through the papers that his secretary had just given him; letters, faxes, statements, affidavits. He stopped when he came to a letter from a client. Attached to the letter was a cheque. It was for €250,000, the balance of the payment for a house purchase. But when he looked closely he saw that the cheque had been mistakenly made out to him and not to the company.

A tempting thought flashed immediately through his mind. This could offer a way out. But it was high-risk. If he was caught, it would mean instant dismissal and the end of his career. On the other hand, it was only for a few days. Only till the Vorax shares recovered and then he could pay it back. Alan checked that Ms Coleman had closed the door. Then he took the cheque, folded it in two and slipped it into his wallet.

Marion sat at her desk, determined to keep busy. She cleared every file that was put in front of her, wrote endless letters, read numerous reports, initialled them and sent them on to the next link in the chain of command that stretched the whole way up to the Minister. She worked so hard that her supervisor, Mr McDonald, was clearly impressed. He was overheard inquiring at tea break in the canteen if there was a promotions board coming up because Ms Hunt seemed to have suddenly developed an amazing appetite for work.

But despite her best efforts, she found her mind drifting back to the horrible developments that had come out of nowhere to threaten her new-found happiness. Matt had called her last night to say that his wife had turned down his appeal to drop the claim. Now it meant he would have to fight. But what would happen if the case went against him and he had all these legal bills to pay?

The result was too terrible to think about. Matt's life-style would change dramatically. Gone would be the fancy lunches, the nice wines that he enjoyed, the holidays they were planning together once his busy workload eased off. He would be reduced to counting the pennies and stretching to make ends meet. He would probably have to continue working longer than he intended. It was all so unfair just when he was beginning to make a new life.

She admired the way Matt had handled this crisis. She had promised to stand by him and she would keep her word. If things came to the worst, he could move in with her. Her apartment was big enough for the two of them. They could pool their resources and at least they'd have each other. Marion was certain about one thing. No matter what happened, they would survive together.

That thought cheered her up. She decided to ring Trish and see if she was free for lunch. She hadn't seen her friend for several days. A good chat would be just the ticket.

They arranged to meet at *The Boulangerie*, a delicatessen in Harcourt St that Trish said did excellent salads and sandwiches. Marion left her office at half twelve and strolled in the bright sunshine through Stephen's Green. The weather had been transformed in the past few days and now the flowerbeds were bursting with colour. When she arrived at the restaurant, she found her friend had got there before her. She slid a menu across the table.

"Been here before?"

Marion shook her head.

"You'll like it," Trish said. "The service is fast, the food is fresh and they have a very wide selection of wraps and baguettes and stuff."

But Marion didn't have much appetite and confined herself to a tuna salad. Trish opted for a roast chicken and ham baguette with plain salad.

"Will we risk a bottle of plonk?" Trish inquired.

"Why not?"

"Okay," Trish said when they had got their meal. "Tell me what's been happening on the home front."

Marion poured a glass of wine. "We saw Rachel and Gavin off on Sunday night. And she's been bombarding me with emails ever since. She really is a prodigious mailer. She sent me five yesterday. I barely had time to respond to them all."

"This is all good," Trish said with the voice of authority. "She has clearly taken a liking to you."

"Oh, and Nick Barry rang a few days ago with a strange request. Did you know he was writing a novel?"

Trish's eyes widened in surprise. "No, I didn't."

"He's a writer apparently, as well as a journalist. He had a big success a few years ago with books of poetry and now he's trying his hand at a novel."

"I think I remember that," Trish said. "And he does have a sort of chic bohemian look, now that you mention it. Have you noticed his eyes? I'd kill for eyes like those."

"Anyway, he wanted to know if he could circulate chapters of his novel to the book club as he writes them. You know, get our feedback? He thinks it will help him."

"That's an original idea," Trish said, "and it might be exciting. What did you say?"

"I told him I didn't see why not, provided everyone else agreed. However, my opinion is not particularly important. I may not be attending any more meetings of the book club."

Trish put down her glass and stared across the table in shock. "No more meetings? Why ever not? You set up the damned thing, for God's sake!"

"Because that bastard Alan McMillan will be there. I don't think I could trust myself to be in the same room with him without ripping his throat out."

"My God," Trish exclaimed. "This sounds serious. I think you need more wine."

336

Marion had promised not to speak about Matt's problems but she couldn't contain herself any longer. She had to talk to somebody before she went crazy and Trish was her best friend.

"I don't want you to breathe a word of this to anyone."

"No, of course not," Trish agreed, paying close attention now that the prospect of some juicy information had suddenly materialised.

"He's trying to destroy Matt."

"He's what?"

"It's true. He's gone completely off his rocker. He's got Matt's wife to pursue him for increased maintenance. And if he succeeds, Matt will be left without a cent."

Over the course of the next few minutes, Marion told her friend all the horrendous details. When she had finished, Trish blew out her cheeks and whistled softly.

"This is truly amazing. Alan McMillan sounds like he's totally deranged. And this Jack Arnold person is a total rat."

"I just told you he's gone off his rocker. He's obsessed with getting me to go back to him. So you can see my predicament. How can I sit at a meeting of the book club with him when all this is going on?"

"We could expel him," Trish said firmly. "That's what you wanted to do."

"It wouldn't work. He's a lawyer. He'd find some way round it. And it would mean explaining this messy business to all the others. I don't think Matt would want that."

"Then we'll just freeze him out. Give him the silent treatment. He'll soon realise that he's not wanted."

Marion sighed. "That won't work either. And it would probably destroy the club. He only joined because of me. If I'm not there, he'll most likely leave."

Trish reached out and stroked Marion's arm. "And he's doing all this because he thinks he'll win you back? Is this guy living in the real world?"

Marion shrugged. "It's crazy but that's exactly what he does believe. He seems to think that relationships are based on status rather than affection. He's got it into his head that if Matt is penniless, I'll lose interest in him."

Trish slowly shook his head. "I think he's dangerous. Maybe you should go to the police?"

"It might come to that. But in the meantime, Matt is in a very vulnerable position. He's determined to fight it. But if he loses, he'll be ruined."

"My God," Trish said. "Poor Matt. And poor you." She wrapped her large arms round Marion in a bear hug. "What are you going to do?"

"I don't know what to do, except give Matt support. It's between him and his ex-wife."

She tried to smile bravely.

"I know this sounds trite," Trish said, "but try not to worry. Something's bound to turn up. And remember, I'm always here for you. All you've got to do is pick up the phone."

Chapter Twenty-eight

Liz got her appointment for the tests much sooner than she expected. She had been busying herself with preparations for the next meeting of the book club which was to take place at her house so she was caught off balance when Dr Forbes's secretary rang her at work two days after the visit to say they had secured a slot for the following day.

"Sorry about the short notice," the secretary said, "but someone has just dropped out and Dr Forbes did say this was urgent."

"That's fine," Liz said. She had got to the stage now where she just wanted the waiting to end. As far as she was concerned, the sooner Dr Forbes could diagnose the lump, the better. At least the awful uncertainty would be over.

"Good," the secretary said. "The appointment is for ten o'clock. The tests should be completed by lunchtime."

"Anything else?" Liz asked.

"Yes. You'll need someone to pick you up when you've been discharged. It's only a minor procedure but we'd prefer if you didn't attempt to drive."

"Okay."

"And afterwards we advise that you rest for a few hours."

"Thank you," Liz said and put down the phone.

Now she would have to tell her boss. As luck would have it, Friday was probably the best day to be away. It was usually slow since a lot of the work had already been taken care of earlier in the week. She decided to tell him at once.

Mr Armstrong's office was at the rear of the building. She rang to see if he was free, then walked down the corridor and knocked on his door. He was poring over some invoices when she entered.

"I need to take tomorrow off," she said. "Something has come up."

"Oh?"

"A hospital appointment."

"Nothing serious, I hope?"

"No," she laughed nervously. "It's just some tests. It's only for one day."

"Well, that shouldn't be a problem."

"I'll make sure that everything is in order before I leave."

"Fine, fine."

Mr Armstrong took off his glasses and studied her. "Are you sure everything is all right, Liz?"

"Oh yes," she said cheerfully. "It's just routine."

"Okay."

"Thank you."

"And Liz. Good luck with the tests."

She left the office feeling relieved. That hadn't been so bad. She wondered if this was the right time to tell Nick. She had been seeing him almost every day. He had even stayed over one night when they had gone out for a late supper. His novel was powering ahead and it seemed that every few days he had another chapter for her to read. Not that she had very much to do. The writing was so good that the only things she could fault were small matters of style.

Nick had even begun to joke that the book was writing itself. But she knew that nothing could be further from the truth. A lot of hard work was going into this novel. By now he had settled into a steady routine. No matter how late he worked at the newspaper the night before, he was out of bed, showered and sitting at his word processor for eight o'clock, a mug of coffee to hand. And he stayed there till midday, or later, writing, rewriting, revising.

The discipline was paying dividends. Each chapter seemed better than the one before. The writing was bold and confident. It told the reader immediately that the author was in command of the story and knew exactly where it was going. Nick was determined, he had researched his subject and he was fired with enthusiasm.

She knew he was onto a winner. If he could keep up this pace and this quality, she was convinced the book would quickly find a publisher and go on to be a great success. And her suggestion of having the book club read the chapters had been taken up enthusiastically by all the members she had contacted. Everyone had agreed except Alan McMillan and that was simply because she hadn't been able to reach him. Phone calls and messages had gone unanswered. As far as she could gather, Alan seemed to have disappeared.

Without her realising it, Nick had suddenly become a big part of her life. Liz was no longer a moonstruck teenager intoxicated by her first romance. She was an adult, she had been married. She knew better than most what vagaries life could throw in her way. Yet she was becoming infatuated with this handsome writer with his tousled hair and dreamy eyes. Why shouldn't she share her anxieties with him?

She checked her watch. It was almost twelve o'clock. He should still be at home glued to his word processor. She listened as the phone buzzed his number.

"Nick Barry," he said, in a brisk businesslike voice that suggested he didn't welcome any interruptions.

"It's me, Liz."

Immediately, his voice changed. Now it became warm and excited. "Liz, darling, how are you?"

"I'm fine, thanks. And you?"

"Chained to my computer but firing on all cylinders. I'm just putting the finishing touches to Chapter Seven. You'll like it. Plenty of action as Christy Grimes would say."

"Are you dropping round this evening?"

"Not tonight, I've got to go into work. I have to sprinkle my stardust on the illiterate scribblings of the *Daily Trumpet* hacks and turn them into sparkling prose."

She heard him laughing.

"I've got a favour to ask."

"Shoot."

"Can you drive me to the hospital tomorrow morning? I have to be there before ten o'clock."

"Of course. I'd be delighted." A note of concern crept into his voice. "What's wrong with you? Are you unwell?"

"I'm having some tests carried out. I'll tell you all about it in the morning."

There was a silence at his end.

Then he said cautiously, "Okay. I'll see you at a quarter past nine. And Liz?"

"Yes?"

"Missing you already!"

He arrived on time, wearing a shirt and tie and a stylish jacket. She knew he had got dressed up just for her and it pleased her.

"What's this all about?" he asked anxiously, after he had taken her in his arms and kissed her good morning.

"I'll explain it to you later. Now, do you think you can manage to drive my car?"

"I don't see why not. It's the same as every other car, I presume."

"More or less."

She gave him the keys and settled into the passenger seat. Strangely, she wasn't feeling the least bit nervous. She didn't know if it was the presence of Nick or the fact that this was the third occasion she had visited a doctor about her breast. By now she had reached a stage where she just wanted to know if this lump was malignant and what Dr Forbes was going to do about it.

"You don't have to wait around," she explained, "but they said I'd need someone to drive me home. You can go off and come back again if you want."

"Liz! What's going on? Please tell me!"

"Later. When I come out."

"Okay. I'll wait." he pulled a well-thumbed paperback novel from his pocket. "I still have to finish *The Boy in the Striped Pyjamas*."

"There's a restaurant if you want to get coffee. They told me the tests will be finished by lunchtime."

They were at the hospital for five minutes to ten.

"Liz, won't you tell me what this is all about?" he said, as he pulled the car into the parking bay.

"No. I'll tell you later, when we have a chance to talk properly."

Nick looked perplexed as he kissed her and left her at the admissions desk where a nurse had appeared to lead her away. She looked back to wave and saw him standing at the desk, gazing after her, a worried look on his handsome face.

First call was the mammogram. Liz was given a gown to wear and led to a little bathroom where she was asked to wash off any deodorant or cream she might be wearing. Then she was taken into a room where a large x-ray machine rested. The nurse brought her close to the machine and helped her place her left breast on a tray. Meanwhile, another woman lowered the top part of the machine onto her breast till it squeezed tightly.

"How does that feel?" she asked.

"Uncomfortable."

"It won't take long."

The woman proceeded to take several x-rays and then repeated the procedure with the right breast.

"That's it," she said with a smile. "All done. You can put the gown back on. You're going to need it for the biopsy."

She had to wait for half an hour till it was time for the biopsy. At last we're getting somewhere, Liz kept telling herself. These tests would tell definitively whether the lump in her breast was innocent or not. The biopsy was simpler than she had feared. She was given a local anaesthetic to numb the breast and then a small incision was made to extract some tissue. By half twelve, it was all finished. The examinations were complete. Now they would be studied and analysed. She would know the results in a couple of days.

But she still felt weary as the nurse led her back to the main reception area. Nick was waiting. He took her in his arms.

"How do you feel?"

"Drained," she said.

"Okay, let's get you home."

They got into the car. The worried look was still in his eyes.

"Would you please tell me, Liz? What exactly is wrong with you?"

She looked from the window at the cherry trees along the avenue, beginning to burst into bloom. Everything seemed so fresh and alive this morning, yet she felt so tired and grey.

"I might have cancer," she said.

Chapter Twenty-nine

Jack Arnold was wrong. The Vorax shares did *not* rally. They didn't even stabilise. Instead, they continued to fall. By the end of the first day's trading they had broken through the €8 barrier and were plummeting like a stone. Finally, Alan could stand the tension no longer. He left the office and told Ms Coleman he was not to be contacted. Anyone looking for him should be informed that he was not available. He went straight home to his penthouse and barricaded himself in.

Now he cursed Jack Arnold. Why had he listened to him? Why had he not sold the shares when they stood at €14.50? It was just below the level where he had always planned to get out. But instead, he had allowed himself to be seduced into buying more with money he didn't have. If Vorax didn't stop falling soon, he was facing disaster.

Eventually, he managed to get Arnold on the phone. He sounded depressed.

"What am I going to do?" Alan pleaded. "I'm going to be wiped out."

"Hold your nerve. They'll come back again."

But Jack Arnold didn't sound very convincing.

"You said that earlier and they still kept falling."

"That's the nature of the market. It goes up and down. Take my word. They'll be back."

Arnold quickly put down the phone before Alan could respond.

He went to the drinks cabinet and poured himself a large brandy while he turned on the television. The Vorax story was headline news. All the commentators said the failure of the company to win approval for their new wonder drug had dealt a serious blow to investor confidence. The smart operators who had gone along for the ride had already taken their profits and got out. The commentators said the shares were on a knife-edge and could fall further.

Alan felt his stomach heave. In a few weeks' time, he would be called on to pay for the shares he had bought on account and he didn't have the money. Even if he ignored Jack Arnold and sold now, he would still face massive losses. No matter which way he turned, he was trapped. He felt like a man on a lift when the cable has snapped. He was crashing to the bottom. He gave a moan like a wounded animal and turned off the television.

He slept badly that night, his slumber disturbed by crazy nightmares of burning buildings and crashing trains. He woke around seven, the bedclothes twisted and his body bathed in stale sweat. Outside the window, he could see the dawn struggling to come alive. But Alan did not want sunlight. He preferred the dark. He drew the curtains and made himself a cup of coffee. The phone was already off the hook. He didn't want to be disturbed. He settled down in front of the television once more and prayed that this second day would bring some better news. If the shares just edged up a few points, he would sell, cut his losses and get out. His dreams of becoming rich would be gone but at least he would survive.

By ten o'clock, the market was in full swing once more. But instead of a respite, Alan was faced with brutal reality. The shares continued their relentless slide. By noon, they had dropped to €6. It seemed that nobody wanted to own Vorax shares. He frantically scrambled some data with the aid of his pocket calculator and discovered that since the opening of business this morning, he had lost almost €200,000.

He felt like weeping. Why hadn't he been one of the smart operators the commentators kept mentioning with approval? Why hadn't he sold when the price was at €14.50? Why was he stuck here with over 100,000 shares that were losing their value by the minute? He sat in front of the television screen like a zombie, unable to move, afraid even to go to the bathroom in case some development occurred when he was gone. And then, shortly after one o'clock, the tide began to turn.

The movement was slow at first but gradually it gained momentum. From a low of €5.50, the shares quickly rose to €7 and then eight and nine. The recovery was under way. Alan felt like screaming for joy. The relief he felt almost drained him of emotion. Now was the time to sell. Get out now. He would have lost money, but not too much. And he would be able to cover his account when it became due.

He rang Arnold but found the line engaged. He tried his mobile and kept getting put through to his message minder. He tried the switchboard and left an urgent message for Arnold to ring him back. He wanted out. He wanted to give instructions to sell. As he watched the screen, he saw the price rise again to €10. The analysts were now saying that the smart operators were back in the market buying up the shares at bargain prices.

Another thought came to Alan. Maybe he should hold on a bit longer. The shares were recovering. Perhaps they might climb back to €15? Maybe even the €17 that Jack Arnold had predicted? Why sell now when they were rising? Perhaps he should wait? He decided to make another cup of coffee. When he came back from the kitchen, he couldn't believe what was happening. Vorax shares were back down to €8.

From then on, the collapse was inexorable. As he sat in front of the television screen, the shares folded like a punctured parachute. It was like watching a car crash. Frantically, he tried again to get hold of Jack Arnold. He needed to get out. He needed to talk to someone who could rescue him, tell him what to do. But he had no success. The bland voice on the recorded message kept telling him the person he was trying to reach was not available. Alan was forced to watch in horror as his shares slid relentlessly to the bottom.

At close of trading, they stood at €1 – lower even than when he had originally bought his first batch all those months ago. He couldn't believe the evidence of his eyes. He sat like a paralysed rabbit, staring at the television screen as the analysts pored through the details and gave their suave explanations. Suddenly, he realised it was just a game to them, like discussing a football result. Tomorrow, they would be discussing some other share. But for him it was his life and his career. The collapse of Vorax meant ruin and the destruction of his dreams.

What about his plans to buy another penthouse, to build a property empire, to mix with the rich and famous, to get his photograph in the social columns? All gone, vanished like snow off a ditch. What about his plans to win back Marion? She would never return to him now, particularly when she learnt what he had been planning with Jack Arnold.

A wave of self-pity swept over him. As he set in the darkened room, staring at the flickering television set, he felt the tears begin to roll down his cheeks. He thought how hard he had worked and struggled to raise himself from the back streets of Belfast. Now it was all gone. All his dreams disintegrated into dust! He would never pay off his debts. He owed €700,000 alone for the shares he had recently bought at Jack Arnold's suggestion. And Arnold would probably have the brass neck to charge him commission on the purchase.

He felt a bitter resentment surge in his heart towards Arnold. He was the cause of his misfortunes. He had been a fool to listen to him. And of course, *he* would escape from the fiasco totally unscathed. Where had he been this afternoon when Alan tried to get hold of him to sell? He couldn't be found. He hadn't returned his calls. Alan felt his anger build up like steam inside a furnace.

He made up his mind. Jack Arnold had got him into this mess. If Alan was to go down, he wouldn't go alone. He walked across the room to the drinks cabinet and returned with the brandy bottle. He poured himself a stiff drink and polished it off. There was one small chink of light. It would get him into trouble but by now, he didn't care. He was in enough trouble already. And when they discovered that he couldn't pay his account, all hell would break loose.

He opened his wallet and took out the cheque he had stored there yesterday. Two hundred and fifty thousand euros! And it was made out to him. He'd be crazy not to take hold of this life-raft that had been thrown to him. Alan folded the cheque away and slipped the wallet back into his jacket pocket.

He lifted the bottle and poured himself another brandy as outside the window, the cold, dark shades of night began to fall.

Chapter Thirty

Marion glanced nervously towards Mr McDonald's desk but thankfully her supervisor had his head buried in a large file and was paying her no attention. She had got practically no work done this morning because she had spent so much time on the phone, most of it taken up with personal business. First, her mother had called from Offaly with her usual list of concerns.

"I'm just ringing to say hello," she said. "Are you sure you're eating properly?"

"Of course, Mum," Marion cooed.

This was a perennial question and no matter how many times Marion assured her mother, she still kept asking.

"And you're keeping well wrapped up? This weather is very treacherous. And there are a lot of bugs about. I was just reading about it in the paper."

After all these years, Marion's mother was still worried that her daughter would either starve or freeze to death in the big city.

"I'm fine, Mum. Honest. The apartment has central heating and it's nice and cosy. And I have enough food in the fridge to withstand a siege."

"Let me give you some recipes," Mrs Hunt said and insisted on reading her instructions on how to make a nourishing soup that she swore would build her up and keep these nasty infections at bay.

When she finally managed to get her mother off the line, Matt had called as he did every morning. He had just spoken to Tom Stafford about the maintenance claim and Stafford had told him he had heard nothing back from Alan McMillan since the last communication, which was five days ago. According to the solicitor, the claim was now in limbo.

"That's odd," Marion said. "I thought he was gung-ho about this business."

"So did I."

"Maybe he's up to something?"

"Well, Tom Stafford's advice is to do nothing. The ball is now back in their court. We've just got to wait."

"Try to be patient," Marion said, tenderly. "I know it isn't easy."

She made a few more calls and discovered that nobody else had heard from Alan. And the date for the next book club meeting was the following night. As secretary, he was supposed to send out reminder notices and this hadn't been done. Marion wondered what was happening. It was all very strange.

Much as she hated to do it, she had finally decided not to attend the meeting, which was scheduled for Liz's house at eight. As she had explained to Trish, it would be impossible for her to sit in the same room with Alan McMillan knowing what he had been up to. Better to excuse herself rather than have a scene that would leave everyone wondering what the hell was going on. However, there was something important that Marion needed to talk to Liz about. She glanced at her supervisor and saw that his head was still buried in the file. She lifted the phone and rang.

Marion had been pleasantly surprised to learn that a romance had been blossoming between Nick and Liz. It had been happening right under her nose and she hadn't even noticed. She thought it was amazing the way things had turned out. She had started the book club as a forum for discussing literature and it had turned into a dating agency; first, herself and Matt and now Liz and Nick.

351

But she was delighted that Liz had found a new man after her husband had died. She deserved another chance at happiness and Nick was a superb choice. He was charming and handsome and *very* dishy. And if his novel took off, he would certainly find himself in great demand.

In fact, it was the novel that she wanted to discuss with Liz. She had been given a couple of chapters to read and been totally bowled over by how good it was. The writing was so assured and the plot so gripping that she could hardly but it down.

And it was while reading the chapters that Marion suddenly had a brainwave.

Liz was having a busy morning when Marion's call came through. In fact, she had been so busy that it was now almost lunchtime and so far she hadn't even managed a cup of coffee.

It seemed as if her whole life had suddenly been turned upside down. She thought back to a few short months ago when she had been bored and restless, unable to sleep, unable to eat, slowly going out of her mind with grief and sorrow. Now it seemed that every moment of every day was taken up with some activity. She had lunch with her sister Anne yesterday and with Cathy Burke the day before. And Cathy had organised a little supper at her house for this evening. She knew this was all part of Cathy's grand strategy: keep her busy, keep her distracted and then she won't have time to brood about her breast. And so far, Liz had to admit, it appeared to be working.

But it was also very tiring and it was beginning to take its toll. Recently, she had been feeling exhausted. And then tomorrow night she was hosting the book club and she still hadn't decided what she was going to give them to eat and drink. Certainly, it wouldn't be anything on the lavish scale of Alan McMillan's evening. Was it only three weeks since they had all sat in his sumptuous penthouse beside the river and ate crab and pate and drank expensive wines? So much had happened in the meantime that it seemed like ages ago. Well, she certainly wasn't going to compete with that magnificent spread. She wasn't even going to try. Liz's guests would be lucky to get some warm pizza slices from the convenience store and a couple of bottles of cheap vino.

But her thoughts were disrupted by the sound of the phone.

"Hello," she said, picking it up.

"Hi, Liz. It's me. Marion."

She smiled at the sound of Marion's voice.

"All set for tomorrow night?" asked Marion.

"Are you kidding? I've barely been able to think about it. Make sure to eat well before you come. You won't get much at my place."

"I won't be coming," Marion said. "That's partly why I'm ringing."

"Oh, Marion, why not?"

"Some personal business has come up. I'll explain it to you some time."

"But it won't be the same without you. Won't you change your mind?"

"I can't," Marion said, suddenly feeling guilty.

"Everyone is going to miss you."

"I'm sorry," Marion said, "but it really isn't possible. Incidentally, have you heard from Alan McMillan recently?"

"No," Liz confessed.

"Neither has anyone else. And he's the secretary and is supposed to send out the reminder notices."

"I did ring him several times and left messages but he never replied."

"It's very strange," Marion continued. "He's usually so well organised. Anyway, there's something else I wanted to talk about."

"Yes?"

"I've read Nick's chapters and I have to say they're fantastic. I couldn't stop turning the pages."

"Really?"

"Yes. If the rest of the book is like this, I think he's got a winner on his hands."

"Oh, Marion, he'll be delighted to hear that!"

"Has he thought about a publisher yet?"

"Not really," Liz said. "I think he's planning to finish the book first and then start looking for someone."

"Well, I've just had an idea. Did you know that Matt's daughter is involved in publishing?"

"No, I didn't."

"Her boyfriend is a commissioning editor with a big London publishing house. His job is to scout out new talent. I was wondering if you'd like me to introduce them."

Liz could barely conceal her excitement. "Would you really? That would be brilliant. I'm sure he'll jump at the offer."

"I'll be talking to them this evening. If he wants me to make the introduction, I'd be happy to do it."

"Oh, Marion, you're a star! I'll ring him right away. He's going to be over the moon. And Marion, is there really no chance you might change your mind?"

"I don't think so. You don't know how much it hurts me. But I don't really think I can come."

Marion put down the phone with a mixture of emotions. She felt good that she might be able to help Nick with his novel. She had a gut feeling that it was going to be a huge success. But she also felt sad that she wouldn't be attending tomorrow's meeting. She had put so much work into getting the club started and now it had been effectively hijacked by that rat, Alan McMillan. But there was no way she was going back again while he was still involved.

She looked towards her supervisor. He was till engrossed in that file he was reading. Must be something important, she thought. Perhaps they've finally captured the werewolf that has been terrorising that school in Leitrim. She reached for a report that had been sitting unopened on her desk for the past two hours and immediately the phone rang again.

"Yes?" she said.

"It's me. Trish. I've got to talk to you at once. You won't believe this. The most amazing thing is after happening."

Fifteen minutes later, Trish came bustling into the Peking Garden restaurant which was the closest place Marion could think of that would ensure them some privacy. Trish had said this news was so big it would burn a hole in the tablecloth.

"Okay, spill the beans," Marion said once they were seated comfortably and the waiter had taken their order.

"Are you ready for this?" Trish asked.

"Of course I'm bloody ready! Why do you think I dropped everything I was doing and took a cab up here to see you? I had to tell my boss that my old aunt had come down with a severe attack of bubonic plague."

"I didn't know you had an old aunt."

"I don't but I had to have a very good excuse to leave work so early. This better be good."

"Oh, it's good all right," Trish said. "But you didn't hear it from me, right? In fact we never even met."

"All right, just tell me."

Marion was all ears. Ever since the phone call, her mind had been reeling with possibilities. Trish had said the news she had to relate was going to blow her mind.

"You know I work in the bank? In the Human Resources department?"

"Of course I know that."

"Well, this morning," Trish continued, straightening the tablecloth and rearranging the knives and forks.

"Yes?"

"This morning when I came into work, there was an almighty fuss. My boss, Mr Brennan, was on the phone for over half an hour, whispering in a low voice. And then he was called away to an urgent meeting with the bank executives."

My God, Marion thought, she's beginning to sound like Agatha Christie. Why doesn't she get to the bloody point?

"What happened?" she demanded

"The meeting took up most of the morning."

"And?"

"You have to understand this is rather unusual. They're normally so busy that they try to keep their meetings extremely short."

355

Marion couldn't restrain herself any longer. She hadn't dropped everything and come running round here just to listen to Trish discuss the internal workings of the bloody bank.

"What *happened,* for God's sake?"

Trish shot her a disapproving look. "Be patient. I'm getting to that."

"Well, I wish you'd hurry up. I'll be dead of old age before you come to the point."

"When Mr Brennan eventually came back I asked him what was going on and he told me. Apparently there was a big scandal. Someone had cashed a cheque that didn't belong to them."

Immediately, Marion's face collapsed in disappointment. Was this the sum total of the vital news that Trish had to tell? Was this why she had allowed herself to be hauled into a Chinese restaurant when she didn't even like Chinese food?

"Is that all?" she said. "Is that why you've dragged me here?"

"That's not the important bit. You'll never guess who did it?"

"Tell me?"

"Alan McMillan."

Marion gasped and rocked back in her chair as the breath left her lungs. Was she hearing things properly? Alan McMillan, the pillar of the legal profession, had cashed a cheque that didn't belong to him?

"You're not making this up to make me feel better?" she said when she had recovered from the shock.

"No, of course not."

"And you're quite sure it's the same Alan McMillan?"

"I'm absolutely certain. And do you know who the cheque belonged to?"

"Tell me."

"One of his clients. It was part of a house purchase. It was mistakenly made out to McMillan and he cashed it."

"How much are we talking about?"

"Two hundred and fifty thousand euros."

Marion gasped again. This was incredible. If Trish had hit her over the head of with a bottle of soy sauce she wouldn't have been more shocked. She needed a drink. She looked around for the waiter and waved him over.

"A large gin and tonic, please."

"Make that two," Trish added. She turned back to Marion. "It gets better."

Marion blinked. This story couldn't possibly get any better.

"He's gone missing."

"What?"

Trish was vigorously nodding her head. "The bank was onto his law firm, Weatherup and Bailey, to try and sort this thing out. And they said they hadn't seen him for several days. He's not at home and he hasn't been answering his phone."

Marion blinked. So that was why no one had heard from Alan McMillan. He'd gone AWOL.

The waiter came just then with the drinks and Marion swallowed half the glass in one go and then ordered another.

"This is amazing!" she said. "Why would Alan McMillan want to cash someone else's cheque?"

Trish was smiling again. "I said this story gets better."

"You mean there's even *more?*"

"There sure is. It turns out he was gambling on the stock market. You remember the big story about that drugs firm, Vorax, and how all these wealthy people lost their shirts when the shares collapsed? Well, he was one of them."

Marion's eyes opened wide in astonishment. This was like watching a horror movie. She didn't know what calamity was going to happen next.

"Not only was he gambling. But he was buying shares without having the money to pay for them. It seems you can do that if you're in the know. And you'll never guess who his broker was."

Marion wasn't sure if her system could withstand any more revelations. "Do I need to have a nurse on hand in case I faint?"

"You might."

"Go ahead and tell me."

"Jack Arnold."

Marion felt her heart go roller-skating inside her rib cage.

"Jack . . . Arnold?" she managed to croak.

"That's right. Apparently before Alan McMillan disappeared, he wrote a letter to Arnold's employers blaming him for everything and saying that Arnold couldn't be contacted when he wanted to sell his shares. He accused him of dereliction of duty."

Marion gulped down the remainder of the gin. This was like being told that your grandmother had been found in bed with the parish priest. All these respectable people involved in such a scandal; stealing cheques, buying shares with no money, accusing each other of monkey business.

"What's going to happen?" she managed to ask at last.

"Mr Brennan is sure that McMillan will be fired. And he'll probably be disbarred which means he won't be able to practise law any more. Apparently, the legal people take a very dim view of this sort of thing."

"I should certainly hope so. And what's going to happen to Arnold?"

"He's in trouble with the Stock Exchange. He may have to resign."

Marion sat back in her chair. This was all too much. The waiter appeared with her second gin and tonic. She polished it off and put the empty glass back on the tray.

She managed to struggle to her feet. It felt like six months had passed in the last five minutes. She had to find Matt at once. She wanted to see the look on his face when she told him this news.

"Will you excuse me?" she said to Trish. "I have to go. And would you mind eating my prawns in chilli sauce when they come? I hate to waste good food."

Liz got home from work shortly after seven. The evening traffic had been dreadful and she felt utterly exhausted. It had been another roller-coaster day. She had put Marion's suggestion about the London publisher to Nick and as she expected, he had leaped at the offer. It was a tremendous opportunity. And if the publishers liked the work as much as everyone else who had read it, then the future looked very promising indeed.

Things were beginning to come right for him and that pleased her. He deserved a break. He had worked hard on this novel even if there were times when he joked that it was writing itself. Liz knew different. It took long, lonely hours of application which had to be snatched from his busy job on the *Daily Trumpet*. And it also required talent. Her relationship with Nick had taught her one thing. Anyone who thought that writing was easy was a fool.

She paused to put her bag down on the kitchen worktop and pull off her jacket. She had a number of tasks to complete this evening. First, she had to tidy up the house in preparation for tomorrow's meeting of the book club. And she still hadn't decided what she was going to give them to eat. Maybe she would just ring the local deli and ask them to prepare a couple of dozen sandwiches. After all, the guests were coming to discuss *The Boy In The Striped Pyjamas* and not her cuisine.

But first she was going to pour herself a cool glass of wine, kick off her shoes and unwind. Later, she would treat herself to a long languorous bath to ease away all the tension of the day. She went into the kitchen and took a bottle of chilled Chardonnay from the fridge. She poured a glass, returned to the sitting room and stretched back on the settee.

She was wiped out. There was just too much happening in her life and it seemed to be taking its toll. Recently, it seemed that she was always exhausted, particularly in the evenings when she got home. She thought of the energy she used to have when she was younger and they were struggling to get Broderick Security off the ground. Then, she had punched twelve and fourteen hours a day and hadn't felt a thing. She had thought nothing of working from eight in the morning till late at night. The excitement seemed to give her strength and stamina. She had never felt tired the way she did now.

A thought came into her head. It had been lurking there for several days but she had managed to keep it at bay. She hadn't told Dr Forbes the whole story. She hadn't told her just how tired she really was. What if this fatigue was related to the lump on her breast? What if it meant that her worst fears were about to be confirmed and the tests were going to show she had cancer? What would she do?

Liz shook her head to make the thought go away. It all seemed so scary. She was gradually getting over Tim's death. She had made new friends. She was getting her life together again. And she had just met a wonderful man who made her happy. Why did this have to happen to her now?

She gave a loud sigh and laid her head back on the couch. She had no strength. Her eyelids seemed heavy. She could feel the tiredness creep up on her like a tide. A few seconds later, her eyes closed and she was asleep.

She dreamed she was walking in the country. She was in a field with long grass and bluebells dancing in the breeze. In the distance she could see mountains, their purple peaks brushing the sky. She looked up and saw that Nick was with her. He was holding her hand and they were walking slowly along the field towards the trees. She looked into his face and he was smiling at her and she felt a wonderful contented feeling go surging through her breast.

At the bottom of the field they came to the trees. There was a man sitting on a log with his back to them. As they got closer, he turned and she saw it was Tim. He looked strong and handsome just the way she remembered him when they first met, all those years before.

"Hello," he said. "Where are you going?"

"Just for a walk."

"And who is your friend?"

"This is Nick. He's a journalist. He's writing a book."

"Hello, Nick," Tim said and the two men shook hands.

"I'm Liz's husband," Tim said.

"She told me about you," Nick replied. "I'm pleased to meet you."

"Do you love her?" Tim asked.

"Yes. Very much. Do you mind?"

Tim gazed into Nick's eyes. "No. I'm pleased. I'm glad she's found someone who loves her. You see, I was called away unexpectedly and had to leave her. And that made me sad."

"So we have your blessing?" Nick asked.

"Certainly," Tim said. "It makes me very happy."

At that moment, a bell began to toll from a nearby church.

"I have to leave now," Tim said.

Liz reached out to touch him. "Don't go," she said.

"I have to. I've got work to do."

"You always liked working, Tim."

He smiled. "Yes. Nothing has changed."

"Can I kiss you goodbye?"

"But you already did, the morning I left you."

He began to walk away and then he stopped and turned again.

"Don't worry Liz. I am always watching, making sure you are safe."

They watched him walk off into the trees. The bell continued to toll. It seemed to be getting louder.

Liz woke with a start and saw that the phone beside her was ringing. She shook herself awake and picked it up.

"Hello," she said.

"Liz?"

"Yes?"

The voice sounded vaguely familiar but she was still drowsy.

"It's Dr Brady. Is this a good time to talk to you?"

Suddenly, she felt a sinking feeling in the pit of her stomach.

"Yes," she said. "This is a good time."

"The tests have come back and Dr Forbes has now had an opportunity to study them."

She felt her body go weak. This was it. All the waiting was over. The moment of truth had arrived at last.

"Yes?" she said, trying to keep her voice as steady as she could even though she was trembling with fear.

"It's good news, Liz. The lump is benign."

All at once, she felt a wave of relief wash over her. She felt like jumping up and shouting for joy.

"You mean . . .?

"It means you're clear, Liz." Dr Brady sounded as if he was smiling. "It means you're perfectly healthy."

Chapter Thirty-one

Christy Grimes carefully balanced the baby on his knee, supported its tiny back with one hand and fed the bottle into its mouth with the other. The baby gurgled with pleasure. There was no doubt about it – Christy was getting the hang of it again. The skills that had stood him in good stead while he raised four chisellers were coming back into play. As his old pal Ducksy Delaney was fond of saying: he'd never lost it.

The recipient of Christy's attention was a little blue bundle also called Christy. His first grandson: Christopher Aloysius Benedict McGlue. Christy was proud that Jackie had named her first-born after him, although he had already made up his mind that he would call the boy Benny. That was the name of the new Pope. There were now three Christophers in the Grimes family and it was more than enough. If he called the boy Benny it would avoid confusion.

He sat now on the settee in the sitting room of the house in Phibsboro and while he fed the baby his gaze drifted out over the garden. It was past its peak with the approach of winter, all the bright colours fading into decay and the leaves turning brown and yellow in the pale evening light. But it still carried the fingerprints of a master gardener. Someone had obviously lavished tender loving care. Despite the ravages of the weather, it retained its well-kept appearance. The lawn was carefully trimmed, the borders were neat and tidy, the hedges and bushes were clipped and the flowerbeds were plucked free of weeds.

It was wonderful the way the garden had been transformed since Ellie gave him the sack. Christy smiled to himself. Although he had pretended to be upset by his wife's decision, secretly he was delighted. In fact, he had engineered the whole thing himself by the simple expedient of pulling up every plant in the border on the pretext that he thought they were weeds. In the end, after he had destroyed half of her best specimens, including a prize lupin, Ellie had lost her temper with him and took over the gardening herself. And now look how it had benefited.

Yes, things were definitely looking up. Ellie was now rattling around the place like a thoroughbred racehorse and you would never guess that there had ever been anything wrong with her. It was as if the stroke had never happened. Earlier in the summer, the children had kept their promise and sent the pair of them off to Sorrento for their first holiday abroad. Christy had got such a great suntan that the regulars in Mohan's pub pretended they didn't recognise him. Ellie and Christy had enjoyed themselves so much that they had booked to go back again next year.

And then, barely three weeks ago, Jackie had given birth to a beautiful baby boy. The first of many grandchildren, Christy hoped. And in five minutes time, as soon as the women had finished beautifying themselves in the bathroom, they were all off to the launch of Nick Barry's book.

Christy felt his breast swell with pride. He felt vindicated. The story of Larry Byrne that Ellie had so often scoffed at, was going to be told at last. It had been turned into a novel and by all accounts it was going to be a runaway bestseller. He had been sent an advance copy and it had done his heart proud just to see it; a fine big thick book with a striking cover in red and green: *The Prodigal Son, by Nick Barry*. And in smaller writing: *From an original story by Christopher Grimes*.

He was a decent skin, the same Nick. There were plenty of lousers who would have taken the tale and passed it off as their own without even a nod of the head to the man who had come up with the idea in the first place. But Nick had not only put Christy's name on the front cover for all the world to see, he had also sent him a cheque for €10,000 from the publisher's advance along with a note to say the payment was a fee for consultation and advice, whatever that meant. Anyway, it was going to come in handy for this holiday next year.

And to cap it all, tonight he was going to be the guest of honour at the book launch. Nick had asked him if he would like to make a little speech but Christy had graciously declined. Speechifying wasn't one of his strong points. He could hold his own in a pub discussion all right but standing up in front of a room full of hobnobs wasn't something he would enjoy. He would just stay in the background and have a quiet drink. He hoped they had Guinness on tap but he wouldn't be holding his breath. He had noticed at these literary occasions they tended to go in more for the wine.

There was a sound of footsteps from the hall. The door opened and Ellie and Jackie appeared. Jackie had put on a little black dress that fitted her perfectly now that she had got her figure back after the birth. But Ellie was in a class of her own. She was resplendent. Christy stared in amazement. She was wearing a powder-blue cocktail dress with imitation pearls and a silver brooch at her breast.

"How do I look?" she asked, executing a pirouette in front of the fireplace.

Christy blinked.

"Like a million dollars. You look even better than the first time I saw you in the Gardiner St Hall."

"Get away out of that," Ellie said. "You're after something."

But Christy knew from the twinkle in her eye that she was delighted.

"We'd better be going," Jackie said. "We don't want to be late. I told the others we'd meet them there at half seven."

Christy looked at the cuckoo clock. "Holy Moley! Is it that time already? Well, we better get our skates on. We don't want to keep Nick waiting."

He went to hand the baby over to Ellie but she immediately put up her hands to ward him off.

"Oh, no, you don't! What's going to happen if he gets sick all over me finery?"

Christy looked from one woman to the other, with a mounting sense of unease.

"So who's going to hold him?"

"You are," they said in unison.

At about the same time, Matt was putting the finishing touches to his attire. He straightened his tie in the mirror and took a red carnation from a vase on the dressing table and fastened it into his lapel. Earlier, he had been to the hairdresser and got his hair trimmed and because it was a special occasion, he had asked the barber to shave him. Now as he smiled at himself in the mirror, he admired the results. The barber had certainly done a good job. Matt thought he looked quite dashing.

He could feel a warm sense of well-being rise within him. Tonight was going to be a big celebration. Nick was launching his novel and the entire book club would be there. Earlier in the day, Rachel and Gavin had flown in from London with their chief publicist and one of the senior executives in tow. They were all billeted at the Four Seasons hotel in Ballsbridge ahead of the launch. Rachel had rung to say that the publishers were very excited about the novel and had already sold the rights to a raft of foreign publishers including a big house in the United States. There was even talk of a film. On the strength of this book alone, Nick was going to be a very wealthy man.

Matt was delighted at the news. He liked to see people doing well. And Nick deserved his success more than most. By all accounts he had worked hard on the novel and battled his way back from an earlier reverse. He had been damned by the critics, savagely ridiculed and dismissed as an impostor. Now he had returned in triumph and they would have to eat their words.

It caused him to think once more about his own situation. He too had come through a bruising time and thankfully had survived. For a while, it had looked as if he might have to sell his apartment to pay Anna's maintenance claim. And then the whole conspiracy against him had collapsed like a pack of cards. First Alan McMillan had been charged and sent to prison for misappropriating clients' funds. The last Matt heard, he was due to be released in a couple of months' time but he would never practice law again.

Then Jack Arnold had been fired from his stock-broking firm in disgrace and took Anna with him to live in London. When he spoke to Tom Stafford about it, Stafford had assured him he would never hear from them again. Matt had heaved a mighty sigh of relief. He had been just as amazed as everyone else by the turn of events. Marion had said it was Fate but Matt wasn't so sure. Sometimes people chose their own Fate. Naked greed and sheer ruthlessness had played a big part in their downfall. But whichever it was, it left the way clear for Marion and him to have a life together once his divorce came through.

And to celebrate their good fortune, Marion had persuaded him to take some time off work and come away with her to Tenerife for the entire month of January. She said it had been a long-time ambition and they would be able to sit in the sun while all their friends in Dublin shivered in the cold. Atlanta Technologies was now fully established and performing well and Matt was owed a lot of leave so he readily agreed. He was looking forward to sitting under a palm tree with Nick's book to read and a nice cool glass of wine close to hand as the warm sea lapped around his toes.

He heard the buzzer sound. That would be Marion now. He was driving her to the book launch tonight. He glanced once more in the mirror to make sure that everything was in order then went off to open the door. He found her on the threshold looking radiant in a white silk dress and satin stole.

He stared for a moment, lost in admiration.

"You look . . . beautiful," he managed to say at last.

She smiled. "Does that mean you approve?"

"You know I would approve if you turned up in an old sweatshirt and jeans. But tonight you are absolutely dazzling."

"Oh, Matt, you're such a smoothie!"

"I don't hear you complaining," he said as he wrapped her in his arms and planted a warm kiss on her eager lips.

Liz reached over to flick a stray piece of lint from the shoulder of Nick's white linen suit and stood back to admire her handiwork. Under her skilful direction, his appearance had been transformed. He wore a pale shirt open at the neck and tan casual shoes. His hair had been trimmed and the stubble that had recently become a regular feature of his chin had now been shaved clean. He looked breath-takingly handsome. She had no doubt he would have every eye trained on him tonight – particularly the female eyes.

"You've rehearsed your speech?" she asked.

"Yes," he said. "Not that there's much to rehearse. I'm going to keep it short, mainly to thank people. Audiences don't want to hear long speeches."

"You're right. They'll be in a celebratory mood tonight. Have you got a new pen for signing books?"

He flicked open his jacket to show her the row of pens he had just bought this morning.

"Rachel tells me they're expecting a couple of hundred guests," said Liz. "You won't find it intimidating?"

Nick smiled confidently. "I've been down this road before, remember? So I think I've got the hang of it by now."

"Well, let's hope the reaction is more positive this time." She kissed his cheek. "The taxi is waiting. Let's go."

Once inside the cab, Liz leaned back and closed her eyes. The events of the last year had been like a tornado tearing through her life. She thought back to that January day when she had seen the ad in the convenience store for the book club. Then, she had been in mourning for her husband, Tim. She had been suffering from the shock of his sudden death, restless and unsure of what course her life was going to take. Today, she had found new meaning and new direction. She was no longer morose and brooding; she felt fulfilled and at one with herself. Today she had found peace and serenity.

Last week, she had given up her job with Quick Print. Mr Armstrong had been sorry to let her go and tried to persuade her to stay. But the job had outlived its purpose. She no longer needed distraction. And besides, Nick required a manager and an agent. It was an exciting new challenge and Liz was looking forward to the thrill of dealing with publishers and negotiating with television companies and journalists.

The lump in her breast was still there but it hadn't got any bigger and she was now relaxed in the knowledge that it was benign and posed no threat. Dr Forbes had given her the option of a small surgical procedure to have it removed and Liz was still considering this. But she would never forget the tide of relief that had washed over her when Dr Brady rang to tell her the results had come back negative and she did not have cancer.

Yes, her life had changed dramatically for the better. Beside her in the taxi, she could feel Nick's reassuring presence. She had grown used to him in the months since they had first met but he still managed to astound and delight her. When they were apart, she missed him. When they were together it felt like the most natural thing in the world. He had become the centre of her life, her compass and her guide. And she knew that she too provided the same comfort for him. They were truly blessed to have found each other.

She opened her eyes as the cab pulled up outside the Four Seasons hotel where the reception was being held. Waiting for them were Rachel and Gavin along with the chief publicist of the publishing company and the marketing manager. They had all met before but still everyone shook hands.

"You're bang on time," Gavin said. "Everyone's waiting inside."

They went through the lobby of the hotel where a posse of photographers was waiting to pounce. Nick posed for pictures and then made his way into the ballroom with Liz on his arm. It was crowded with people drinking champagne and clutching copies of his novel. Suddenly, out of the crowd, a squat, blond-haired woman pushed her way forward till she was standing in front of him.

"Hi, Nick," she said. "I thought I'd come along and wish you well."

Nick stared for a moment before he recognised her. She had got much older and plumper since the last time he'd seen her.

"Arminta!" he said.

"I'm really delighted for you. I just wanted you to know that I'm still available for advice with your career if you're interested. You're going to need someone now that you're writing again."

Nick stared at Arminta O'Shea. She really had a brass neck. She had deserted him when the heat came on the last time and now here she was back again when things were looking up. But strangely, he felt no animosity or sense of triumph.

"That's very kind of you to offer. But I have someone else now."

He pointed to Liz who was deep in conversation with her friend Cathy Burke and her husband Max.

At that moment, Gavin appeared at his side and took his arm.

"Curtain's up," he said and pointed to a small podium at the top of the room where Nick was to make his speech.

He pushed through the throng, past colleagues from work, critics and book reviewers and a television crew busily filming the event. This was something Liz had arranged. The publicity would do no harm for sales of the book. The whole book club had turned out. He could see Marion and Trish and Matt and the Grimes family, including Christy who was clutching a new baby in his arms while trying to drink a glass of Guinness at the same time.

As he moved through the room, Nick stopped to shake hands with well-wishers and sign copies of the book but at last he reached the podium. A hush descended over the crowd as Gavin gently tapped the microphone to make sure it was working before making a short speech of introduction.

Then he announced: "Ladies and gentlemen, I give you the publishing sensation of the year, the author of the stunning new novel, *The Prodigal Son*, Mr Nick Barry."

There was a burst of applause and Nick confidently bounded up to the microphone.

"I hope you don't live to regret those words," he said to a burst of laughter.

He paused and looked around the room at the shining faces smiling up at him. He had finally achieved what he set out to do. It was just like standing in front of the senior school to read his prize-winning essay all those years before.

He cleared his throat and began to speak.

"Writing this novel has been a labour of love for me but I could not have done it without the help of some very important people. First, I would like to thank Mr Christy Grimes and his wife Ellie. Christy provided me with the basic story for the book and I am eternally grateful."

There was warm applause and loud cheers. Christy looked like he wanted the floor to open up and swallow him.

"Secondly, I would like to thank the members of the Smithfield book club who read the manuscript and offered valuable suggestions and advice. In particular, I want to thank Marion Hunt who was the moving spirit in setting up the club in the first place."

There was another loud round of applause as Marion waved and blew kisses to the crowd.

"And finally, I want to acknowledge the support of Liz Broderick."

There were whoops and cheers.

Nick reached out and invited Liz to join him at the rostrum. As she stepped up, he turned and looked into her eyes.

"I want to tell you that without Liz this book would never have been written. She has been my soul mate, my rock and my inspiration."

His hand casually slipped into the pocket of his jacket.

"And tonight, in front of all you people, I have a very important question to ask her."

An expectant hush had now fallen over the crowd.

Liz looked stunned as Nick took out a small velvet box. He turned and stared into her eyes.

"Will you marry me?"

There were gasps and then Liz flung her arms around his neck and hugged him tight.

"Are you crazy? Of course I will."

The room went wild with cheering. Somebody popped a champagne cork, then another. Flashbulbs exploded as photographers struggled to get pictures. The place was in uproar.

Behind him, Christy could hear the sound of someone sobbing.

He turned to see Ellie with tears streaming down her cheeks.

"What's the matter?" he asked with concern. "Are you not feeling well?"

"I can't help it," Ellie sniffed. "It's so romantic." She wiped her eyes with the sleeve of her dress. "It's just like something you'd read in a good book."

THE END

If you enjoyed *The Book Club*, don't miss out on
The Beach Bar, also published by Poolbeg.

Here is a sneak preview of Chapter one . . .

THE
Beach
BAR

KATE McCABE

1

When she was still at school, Emma Dunne had dreamed of a glamorous career as a model or an actress. With her cloud of blonde curls and angelic face, she pictured herself floating around Dublin surrounded by a posse of admirers. Men would queue up to date her. Club owners would fight over her and doormen would roll out the red carpet. Her photograph would appear in all the glossy magazines. She would be written up in the gossip columns. She would wear the best clothes and eat in the finest restaurants, always with a handsome man on her arm. It seemed the perfect life and she was the perfect girl to fill it.

But as she got older Emma came up against reality. Even though she was very attractive, with soft blue eyes and a slim figure, it soon became obvious that, at five feet five inches, she was too small to be a model. The agencies seemed to want girls six feet tall whose legs went up to their armpits. As for acting, Emma quickly discovered that she would have a quieter time training Bengal tigers than she would competing with the aspiring young things who wanted to get into the movies.

In any case, an accident intervened and she ended up running the family business.

Her father, Joe, had built up the Hi-Speed Printing Company from scratch, starting in 1970 with a small office in the inner city. He ran off handbills and posters and invitation cards on an old press that regularly threatened to break down just at a crucial moment when a large rush order had to be delivered.

He had combed the city for business, a virtual one-man band, knocking on doors, phoning concert promoters, calling at bingo halls – anywhere there was the prospect that someone might want a printing job done. He left for work at seven o'clock each morning and often didn't return till after midnight. Joe Dunne was a determined man but he wasn't proud. He would never turn down an order, no matter how small. It was all money and it paid the bills.

And the business prospered. Joe slowly gained a reputation for fine quality work and reliability. And his prices were always keen. In time, he was able to afford a new state-of-the-art press that could produce glossy colour brochures and catalogues by the thousand at the touch of a button. His orders grew and he hired more staff – master printers whose work was the best in town. The business expanded and he moved from his cramped little premises in Talbot Street to a spanking new facility in an industrial estate in Baldoyle.

Joe drove a BMW, took the family on holidays to Florida for three weeks every June and bought a new detached house with gardens by the sea in Sutton, where they had views of the Dublin mountains. He didn't go around boasting but he liked to think that all the hard work had finally paid off and now he had arrived.

But while those were his glory years and Joe liked to look back on them with a nostalgic smile, Emma and her mother were convinced that was when the damage was done. It was the pressure of those early years – the long working days, the rushed fast-food meals, the threatening deadlines, the near disasters, the nerve-racking crises when the old printing press threatened to collapse – that caused the heart condition that eventually forced Joe to retire from the business at fifty-eight and hand it over to Emma.

She was preparing for her Leaving Cert. when the news broke about her father's heart. He had been complaining about breathlessness for some time but he was one of those men who paid little attention to his health. Even though his wife, Nancy, had badgered him for months to go and see Dr Fagan, Joe kept putting it off. He was just a bit overweight, he would say. Why take up the doctor's valuable time when there were more deserving poor devils with real problems to complain about? Besides, Dr Fagan would think he was a hypochondriac if he went running to see him every time he was a little bit out of breath.

Matters came to a head one bright Sunday afternoon on the seventh hole at Deerpark golf course, where Joe liked to play a round of golf with his pals. He had just teed off when he felt a sharp pain shoot along his left arm and into his chest. Next minute he was lying on the ground and someone was beating on his breast while someone else attempted to give him mouth-to-mouth resuscitation. Joe didn't remember any more till he woke up several hours later in the cardiology department of Beaumont hospital.

It turned out that the main artery to his heart was almost blocked with atherosclerotic plaque. He remained in hospital for two weeks while the surgeons performed a triple-bypass operation to allow the passage of blood to his heart. After the operation, a consultant sat down with Joe and had a long talk with him. He told him he was lucky to be alive. He would have to change his busy lifestyle. He would have to slow down and take things easy.

After he was discharged, the family held a council. They sat around the big dining table while they tried to decide what to do. Joe was reluctant to take the doctor's advice. He felt he could still continue to run the company if he just cut back a little and delegated more responsibility. But this time Nancy was determined to put her foot down. Joe had worked hard for long enough. The time had come to retire completely from the business and hand it over to someone else.

While he had been in hospital, the day-to-day running of the company had been taken over by George Casey, who was Joe's deputy. But while George was a competent manager, he didn't have the drive and vision that Joe possessed. It was obvious that he could only be an emergency stopgap. Someone else would have to be found to run the firm in place of Joe. And it would have to be someone from the family.

The oldest boy, Peter, was in his second year as a junior doctor in St Vincent's hospital. He had never shown the slightest interest in the business and was horrified at the suggestion that he might give up medicine to run the family printing firm. His brother Alan was two years younger and was a sports reporter in RTÉ. And while Alan was certainly willing to help out in this sudden emergency that had arisen, it was clear to everyone around the table that he didn't have a clue about business. Nancy could see situations where Alan would be negotiating a printing contract with a client while his mind was on Liverpool's chances of winning their next game against Arsenal in the Premiership. It would never work.

Which left Emma. She knew before anyone said a word that the job was going to fall to her. She was eighteen and planning to go to college once she had completed her exams. The lingering dreams of a life in modelling or acting had evaporated by now but she still had hopes of an exciting career in publishing or marketing. Now all that would have to be set aside while she mastered the technicalities of offset printing and discounts and margins and VAT and delivery dates. It was hardly the glamorous future she had hoped for.

"You're the obvious person," her brother Peter said, aware of her reluctance and eager to make sure that the responsibility was shifted onto someone else. "Can't you at least give it a shot?"

Emma thought of what would be involved. She would have to learn the business from scratch. She would have to work long hours. She would spend much of her time in an office instead of enjoying the busy social whirl with her friends. She was only eighteen and would be entering a trade that was still dominated by men. Would she be able for it?

Her father smiled softly and gently pressed her hand. "I'll teach you everything I know," he said. "You can do it."

Emma looked at the expectant faces around the big mahogany table where they had all gathered for Sunday dinner since she was a child. The business had provided them with a good life. It would be a tragedy if it had to pass out of their hands. In a strange way, she believed she owed it to the rest of them.

She took a deep breath and bit her lip. "All right," she said. "I'll give it a go."

It was agreed that Emma would take over as managing director and George Casey would continue as her deputy while her father taught her the intricacies of the printing trade. In addition, she decided to enrol in a part-time evening course at the Dublin Institute of

Technology so that she could learn the management skills she knew she would need in the years ahead.

Some of her friends felt sorry for her. Instead of enjoying the excitement of college life, she had gone straight from school into the pressurised world of business. While they were out pubbing and clubbing, Emma was dealing with accountants and suppliers and negotiating with clients. In the evening while her friends were heading out on the town, she was trooping off to the lecture hall with her notebooks and folders.

And all the time, hanging over her was the dreadful possibility that she might fail and drive the company into bankruptcy. She knew that some so-called friends would be delighted if this was to happen. But Emma didn't allow herself to brood about this. No matter how hard she had to work, no matter what setbacks she might encounter, she was absolutely determined. Now that she had taken the helm at the Hi-Speed Printing Company, she would work her fingers to the bone to make it a success.

Of course, there were many people who were impressed by her pluck.

One of the first friends she made at evening college was an ambitious young man called Tim Mulhall. Tim had a degree in Computer Studies but he had decided to switch to management. Now he was working by day for an information technology company while he tried to get his qualification by studying at night.

One evening after the lecture had ended, he invited Emma for a drink. Over a couple of beers, he outlined his plans to her.

"The way I see it, everybody wants to get into computers," he said, "but because the industry is so young, there is a shortage of people with management skills. In a few years' time they'll be crying out for managers."

"What are you planning to do?" Emma asked.

"Start my own company. I want to work for myself. How about you?"

"I already do," she said.

Tim was amazed. "You work for yourself?"

"Well, my father started the company. But now I'm running it. Or, to be more precise, I'm learning to run it."

Tim's jaw dropped. "I think that's fantastic. You're so young. I mean . . ." He flushed with embarrassment.

"I know what you mean. I've just turned nineteen and I know I have a lot to learn but I'm very determined."

"And how do the others react to you? Don't they think you're maybe a little wet behind the ears?"

Emma thought for a moment. "Not really. I think they accept me."

He sat back and whistled softly. "That's brilliant. Running your own company at nineteen years of age. I'd give my right arm for an opportunity like that."

Tim's reaction was like sweet music to Emma's ears. Maybe taking on the company wasn't such a burden after all. Maybe it was a glorious opportunity. Maybe she should consider herself fortunate to be the managing director of the Hi-Speed Printing Company, even if she was barely nineteen.

But she hadn't been entirely truthful with Tim. Several of the older workers *did* have problems with someone so young being in charge and some of them adopted a surly resentment towards her. They regarded her as an amateur who didn't know what she was doing. But Emma taught herself to be patient and, above all, to listen to advice. These people knew the printing trade and she had a lot to learn from them. Until such time as she had mastered the complexities of the business, she was determined to take a softly-softly approach and not to antagonise anyone.

It paid off. Her father stayed by her side for about nine months, gradually easing himself out of the company while Emma assumed more and more control. At last he let go completely and gave himself over to a life of golf and healthy eating and frequent holiday breaks. After a career spent slaving to build up Hi-Speed Printing, Joe Dunne seemed content to enjoy himself. Emma took it as a vote of confidence. And she knew if a difficult problem did arise, he would always be there to turn to for guidance.

There were to be many problems in the years that lay ahead. Because she was a young woman, there were plenty of clients who thought she would be a pushover when it came to business. Blonde curls and big blue eyes didn't help and she often cursed the fact she didn't look more severe. They threatened and cajoled and attempted to bully her. They were late with payments. They complained about the standard of the work and demanded discounts and rebates. Emma knew she was on probation. She knew if she showed the least hint of uncertainty, it would be taken as a sign of weakness and the demands would escalate while word went around that Joe Dunne's daughter was a soft touch.

So she held her ground. She dealt with each client personally so that she could get to know them. She listened to their complaints and if there was merit in their arguments she was prepared to negotiate. She knew that rigidity could be seen as just as much a sign of weakness as simply caving in at the first sign of resistance.

Gradually she earned the respect of clients and staff alike. She was particularly pleased when word filtered back to her that one of her most awkward customers had been heard to say in company that Emma Dunne was a chip off the old block – firm but fair, an iron fist in a velvet glove. Emma had smiled with satisfaction when she heard that remark.

But running the Hi-Speed Printing Company took its toll, particularly on her social life. By now, she had moved out of the family home and bought a smart apartment in Howth with a large terrace overlooking the marina. It meant she was close both to her parents and to work and she liked the freedom that Howth gave her: the mountain walks, the sea, the intimate village life, the yacht club and the friendly pubs.

After she graduated from the Dublin Institute of Technology, she continued to see Tim Mulhall, who was still pursuing his dream of starting his own computer business. They would regularly meet for a drink or go for a meal in one of the fish restaurants in Howth. Emma enjoyed the relaxed nature of their relationship and she particularly liked their long walks across Howth Head, during which Tim would outline his plans for future glory when he eventually succeeded in persuading some bank to lend him the cash to start his own business. She tried to give him advice, for she really wanted him to succeed, but it gradually became obvious that unless he came up with a good idea and a clear business plan, no financial institution was likely to risk its capital with him. And while his studies had earned him promotion and a junior management position, as the years passed it became clear that the job he was doing was really a dead-end.

One evening, in frustration, Tim told her he was throwing it all over.

"Have you got something else lined up?" Emma asked anxiously.

"I've got an offer of a job in California," he said proudly.

"Wow!" she said, slightly shocked.

"The Yanks appreciate initiative. They like people with a bit of get-up-and-go. I reckon I'll be running my own company within six months."

"What is this job you've got?"

"It's something similar to what I'm doing now. I'll be responsible for a small team of programmers. It's a great opportunity, Emma."

"But sometimes far-off fields seem green," she said with a note of caution.

"I've got to go," Tim said. "I'm thirty-two. If I don't do it now, I'll wake up some morning to discover that I'm a middle-aged man looking back on broken dreams."

Emma felt a sadness take hold of her. She looked at Tim as he sat beside her, his handsome eyes flashing defiantly. Something told her that nothing was going to change for him. The job he had been offered would turn out to be just another cul-de-sac. But the weather would be better and the experience might stand to him in future years. He was right to pursue his dream, even if nothing ever came of it. At least he would have tried.

She took his face in her hands and stared into his brooding eyes.

"I wish you luck, Tim. You're doing the right thing."

He shrugged and smiled. "I'll miss you," he said.

"And I'll miss you."

"I'll keep in touch. I'll mail you and let you know what's going on."

Emma gently squeezed his hand. "I'd like that." But she doubted he would.

Emma had a succession of men friends but none of the relationships lasted for very long. Some of the men were clearly fortune hunters, attracted by her position and hoping to get a slice of her money. But they were easy to spot and she quickly gave them short shrift.

Occasionally, she met someone who interested her but her hectic working schedule played havoc with her social life. Usually the men she met were older than her, as she typically met them in the course of work – from the start the demands of her job had cancelled out the possibility of clubbing or nights out on the town with the girls.

Often, the men she met were at an age when they were interested in a steady relationship and the idea of marriage was at last making inroads on their consciousness. But cancelled dinner appointments, late arrivals, irritating phone calls at a romantic moment, these would try the patience of the keenest admirer. One by one, the romances petered out. Emma found herself in a cleft stick. She was forced to concede that, while her lifestyle ruled out relationships with free and easy younger men, finding an older man who would put up with playing second fiddle to Hi-Speed Printing was not going to be easy.

She did develop a steady friendship with one man. At forty-two, Conor Delaney was the owner of the Clear Skies Holiday Shop and one of her main clients. Twice a year, in spring and winter, Emma printed his brochures for him. It was a big order: 100,000 glossy magazines packed with enticing photos of beautiful people lounging on sun-kissed beaches or splashing in pools or having a drink at some quaint little bar. Every time the job came around, Emma found those photos tugging at her heartstrings and she would wish she was off with those beautiful people instead of stuck here in noisy, grey, depressing Dublin on yet one more rainy day.

The brochures were vitally important to Conor Delaney. They were his shop window and his big hope was that the pictures would have the same effect on thousands of potential holidaymakers as they had on Emma. He took infinite care with them, choosing the photos carefully, spending days writing the text with catchy headlines like *Let Clear Skies Banish All Your Cares* and *Relax in the Magical Surroundings of Sunny Lanzarote*.

When Conor was finally satisfied, he would throw a launch party and bring all the travel writers and representatives of the trade and Emma was always invited. Conor usually had his brochure launch in some nice restaurant and there would be lovely food and gallons of wine and the travel writers would get sloshed and promise to give him a big write-up in their next article.

Emma thought Conor had a wonderful job, much more exciting than her mundane existence at Hi-Speed Printing. He was always flying off to check out some new destination to see if it was suitable to add to his list. From time to time, he would invite Emma to come along too.

"You deserve a break," he'd say. "The company can get along without you for a few days. Why don't you come along and just chill out?"

Although Emma was often tempted, she always said no. She was attracted to Conor. She wasn't in love with him but, then, she was beginning to think that would never happen for her. For one thing, there just wouldn't be time. In that light, Conor wouldn't be such a bad deal – he was tall and handsome and affectionate and wonderful company.

But there were things about Conor that set off alarm bells. For a start, he was reputed to have a wife and three children somewhere in Killiney, from whom he was separated and whom he never mentioned.

And there was a boyish irresponsibility about him that worried her. For all his forty-two years, it was as if he had never grown up. When he was out with the travel writers, he would stay up half the night drinking and the following day his mobile phone would be switched off till after lunch. It really wasn't the best way to run a business.

But while Emma resisted any romantic entanglement, she was still very fond of him. She used him as a sounding board when she had small problems that she didn't want to bring to her father and he was always available to accompany her to a dinner party or a social occasion that required a male escort. If only he was a bit more reliable, she would sigh, if only he would lose his wild streak, he would be an ideal partner. But Emma had learnt enough about life to know that the leopard seldom changed its spots.

By the time her thirtieth birthday passed her by, she had not only mastered the intricate mysteries of the business but had also expanded it. She had installed another new press and, along with the general run of printing work, she had won an important contract to print a string of freesheet newspapers. This contract alone earned the company nearly as much as all its other work put together. Hi-Speed Printing was beginning to excite envy and admiration in equal measure from her competitors so she wasn't surprised when, from time to time, she was approached by intermediaries with offers to invest in the company or buy her out completely.

The most attractive offer was made one day in June 2005, over a delightful lunch at Patrick Guilbaud's restaurant in Merrion Street. The man who made it was called Herr Gunther Braun and he was the representative of a large German printing firm wishing to expand into Ireland.

Herr Braun spoke perfect English and he had perfect manners. He resolutely avoided all talk of business till the meal was finished and they were drinking coffee. Then he laid his cards on the table.

"We are prepared to offer you €3 million for the company and to retain your services as a consultant for five years at a salary of €150,000 per annum," he announced.

Emma almost choked. She had no intention of selling and had agreed to meet Herr Braun largely out of curiosity. But the generosity of his offer took her breath away. She struggled hard to retain her composure and not reveal her surprise.

"Who would run the company if you took it over?" she inquired.

"We would."

"You would put in your own management team?"

"Of course."

"So what would be my role?"

"You would act as an advisor and you would also recruit new business. You know the local scene. People here trust and respect you."

"And when my contract expires in five years' time? What would happen then?"

"We would review the situation. If we still required your services, naturally we would renew the contract for a further period."

Emma nodded gravely. Her head was spinning. She wished she had ordered a brandy instead of coffee.

"I'm very gratified by your interest," she said, "but I need some time to consider your offer."

"Of course. I will be in Dublin for one more week. I'm staying at the Westbury Hotel. Contact me at any time if you wish further clarification."

"Thank you," Emma said.

She rang the office and told her secretary to say that she had an urgent business appointment and to log all phone calls. Then she drove straight home to Howth, ran a hot bath, poured a glass of chilled white wine and luxuriated in the tub while she tried to digest the information that Herr Braun had just given her.

She had no idea that the company was worth so much. And she also knew that it was only the Germans' initial offer. She had no doubt that if she got into serious negotiation, she could persuade them to increase it further. And a salary of €150,000 as a consultant was tempting to say the least! Even if they decided to dispense with her services after five years, she would still have earned a handsome sum.

She was now thirty-one. She had worked for the company for the past thirteen years. It had practically taken over her life. If she accepted Herr Braun's offer she need never work again. Her parents would naturally get a portion of the purchase price and they already had a comfortable personal pension fund.

Her brother Peter was now a senior consultant in the Mater hospital and rarely ever mentioned the company, while Alan was the sports editor on a national newspaper and seemed to be in his element reporting rugby and soccer and horseracing events. They all had lives. They all had happy careers. Why should she be the one to tie herself forever to the Hi-Speed Printing Company, especially now that she had a very profitable way out?

But it was a big move to make. What would the staff think, all those hardworking people, including George Casey, who had given years of loyal service? And what about her father? He had founded the company and spent his entire career building it up. Would he think she was deserting the ship? And would she miss it? Despite her gripes and grievances, the company was the only job she knew. Even though there were times when it wore her out, there were plenty of other occasions when she got a great buzz of satisfaction from winning a contract or seeing a job well done.

Emma lay in the bath till the water began to grow cold. This was not a decision she could take lightly. She needed to think long and hard. She needed to consult. She needed to get advice. And there was one person she could turn to who would give her that advice and also be discreet. Conor Delaney. She would ring him at once and see if he was free.

She stepped out of the bath and was beginning to dry herself when she heard her mobile go off.

"Hello," she said, the bathwater dripping onto the floor.

"It's Conor." He sounded out of breath.

"Hey! That's a coincidence. I was just going to call you," she said.

"I need to talk to you. Urgently. I'm in trouble."

She arranged to meet him in the lounge of a nearby hotel and quickly got dressed. What kind of trouble could he be in? Had he crashed his car? Had he lost his credit cards? Was someone suing him? When she got to the hotel, she found him nursing a large glass of whiskey and by the look of him it wasn't the first. His tie was askew, there was sweat glistening on his forehead and stubble darkened his unshaved chin.

"You look like you've been sleeping under a haystack," she said. "What's the matter with you?"

He took a large gulp of whiskey. "I've got terrible news. My company's going bust."

For a moment, it felt like Emma's heart had skipped a beat. Was he serious? But Conor never joked about things like this and, while he had been drinking, he certainly wasn't drunk. She quickly forgot about her own good news. She sat down beside him and gently stroked his arm.

"Tell me what happened."

"Where do I begin?" he said, spreading his hands wide. "I'm being undercut by these Internet firms and then you've got all these people who own their own apartments and aren't interested in package holidays any more. Plus the competition has become fierce. I've booked a thousand hotel rooms that I can't fill. The bottom line is, I can't pay my way. I'm putting the company into liquidation." He turned his sad eyes to Emma. "I wanted you to be the first to know."

"Is there anything I can do?" she said, trying frantically to think of some way out. She hated the thought of Conor going bust after all the hard work he had put into his business.

He smiled grimly. "No. There's nothing. It's kind of you to offer. But I'm afraid I'm beyond salvation. Tomorrow when the word gets out, the vultures will swoop and pick my carcass clean."

"Oh, Conor," she said, "don't talk like that."

"It's the truth. You know what they're like."

He took another drink of whiskey. "I haven't paid you for the last two sets of brochures. €40,000, I think it is."

"Forget it," she said. "That's the least of your worries."

"No, I won't forget," he said stubbornly. "You've always been very decent to me, Emma. I can't pay you, of course, but I have another suggestion to make." He reached into his pocket and took out a couple of official-looking documents. "These are the deeds of a beach bar I own on the Costa del Sol. It's a little investment I made when things were going well. It's not worth a lot but it's something. I want you to take them in payment for the brochures."

She quickly pushed the documents away. "For God's sake, Conor! What do you think I am? I couldn't possibly take your bar from you."

"Please, you'll be doing me a favour. You'll allow me to retain some dignity. And if you don't take it, the liquidator certainly will. At least I'll know that you got something out of the wreckage." He lifted the deeds and pressed them into her hands. "Tomorrow morning I'll meet you in my solicitor's office and I'll give him power of attorney to complete the transfer. Now I don't want to hear another word. I'm going to sit here and get gloriously ossified. Will you allow me to buy you a drink?"

"I'll have a glass of white wine," Emma said and felt her heart flood with sadness for him.

The following morning, she woke early. She had been thinking about the developments overnight and now she knew exactly what she was going to do.

As arranged, she met Conor Delaney at his solicitor's office and they both signed the documents that would give her legal possession of the bar.

"Where is it anyway?" she asked.

"Fuengirola. Right now, I have a Spanish lady running it for me. It's ticking over but I've no doubt with a bit of effort it could do much better." He looked sad and hung-over.

"What are you going to do?" she asked.

He shrugged. "Don't worry about me. I'll survive."

She flung her arms around his neck and kissed his cheek. "Good luck," she whispered. "And stay in touch."

Next, she drove out to her parents' house in Sutton. Her father was sitting in the conservatory reading a newspaper while her mother pottered about in the garden.

"I've got something I want to discuss with you," she said to her father.

He pointed to a chair beside him. "Sit down."

Joe Dunne listened carefully while she outlined the offer Herr Braun had made to buy the company. When she had finished, he said: "Do you think we should accept it?"

"What do you think?"

"It's a very good offer. You should consider it seriously."

"How would you feel?"

"My feelings are irrelevant," Joe said. "You stepped in to run the firm when I got ill but I didn't think you'd be doing it forever. The others have satisfying careers. It's time you thought about yourself for a change. You're still a young woman. Maybe you might want to settle down and get married."

Emma smiled at the assumption she would give up work if she married and patted her father's cheek. "You think a good man would straighten me out?"

"He might," Joe said with a twinkle in his eye.

She stood up. "I'm not going to do anything for a while. And before I make my decision, I'll come and talk to you."

She made an appointment to see Herr Braun at midday. They met in the coffee bar of the Westbury Hotel.

"I need more time to consider your offer," she said.

"How much?"

"A month."

Herr Braun looked surprised but his good manners didn't falter. "It's a long time."

"It's a big decision. I have to think deeply. There are people I must consult."

"All right," Herr Braun said at last. "One month. But if you haven't decided by then, we will look elsewhere."

"I will have decided," Emma said.

She took George Casey out for an early lunch and outlined her plans to him. She said nothing about the German offer.

"I'm taking a break and I'd like you to run the place while I'm away. You'll be paid, of course, for the extra responsibility. How do you feel about that?"

"How long will you be gone?"

"A month," Emma said.

George Casey thought for a moment. "I can do it. In fact, I'd be glad to do it."

"You won't be entirely on your own. I'll keep in regular touch with you. You'll be able to reach me if you need to."

"There's no problem," George smiled. "Everything will be fine."

Emma went home to pick up her luggage. She had already booked a flight to Malaga and a hotel in Fuengirola. The flight left at four. She would be in Fuengirola by seven o'clock.

She felt the blood racing along her veins. It was as if she was being released from all her problems and cares, all the pressures of her busy life. It was as if she was starting out on a glorious adventure. A month in Spain would give her ample time to decide where her future lay.

She rang for a cab and finished packing her carry-on holdall. Half an hour later, she was speeding along the motorway towards Dublin airport.

before